running lean

Blessings,
Diana Sharples

running lean
Diana L. Sharples

BLINK

BLINK

Running Lean
Copyright © 2013 by Diana Sharples

This title is also available as a Blink ebook. Visit www.zondervan.com/ebooks.

Requests for information should be addressed to:

Blink, 5300 Patterson Ave SE, Grand Rapids, Michigan 49530

ISBN 978-0-310-73497-0

All Scripture quotations, unless otherwise indicated, are taken from The Holy Bible, *New International Version®, NIV®*. Copyright © 1973, 1978, 1984, 2011 by Biblica, Inc.™ Used by permission. All rights reserved worldwide.

This is a work of fiction. Any resemblance to real persons living or dead is purely coincidental. The locale of Stiles Country is also fictitious, but elements of the setting are inspired by Nash County, North Carolina, including the real-world locales of Badin Lake and Rocky Mount, as well as I-95 and Highway 301.

Any Internet addresses (websites, blogs, etc.) and telephone numbers in this book are offered as a resource. They are not intended in any way to be or imply an endorsement by the publisher, nor does the publisher vouch for the content of these sites and numbers for the life of this book.

BLINK™ is a trademark of The Zondervan Corporation

Cover design: Gayle Raymer
Cover photography: © Bryan Alldredge. All rights reserved.
Interior design: David Conn

Printed in the United States of America

13 14 15 16 17 18 19 20 /DCI/ 20 19 18 17 16 15 14 13 12 11 10 9 8 7 6 5 4 3 2 1

Running Lean [run·ning leen]

1. A term referring to a deficiency of fuel in the fuel-to-air ratio of an internal combustion engine.

2. A physical condition where not enough caloric fuel is present for optimal performance of the body.

3. A spiritual condition in which a believer relies on his human abilities only.

Chapter 1

That flag—folded in a triangle, framed in a box, and displayed on the mantle—drew Calvin's eyes like an intruder in the room. He stalled halfway down the steps to the living room.

Michael's flag.

Calvin stared. Not out of reverence for a fallen American hero. It just freakin' hurt. Six months after they'd brought his brother's body home in a casket, that star-spangled fabric could still smack Calvin in the chest like a fall off his motorcycle.

"Hey, move it. Some of us have to catch the bus, you know." His younger sister, Lizzie, wedged herself between him and the wall. She bumped the helmet in his hand and broke the flag's spell. Calvin thundered the rest of the way downstairs behind her.

"Get it together," he muttered to himself. He could find a way to walk past that stupid flag without choking on a gob of grief.

While Lizzie escaped out the front door, Calvin followed the worn path in the shag carpet toward the kitchen. In a corner of the dining room, a computer sat on a desk barely big enough to hold it. Family photos faded in and out on the monitor. Calvin's feet scuffed, shifted that way. No time to check his Facebook page again. He'd have to deal with a day without one of his girlfriend's quirky poetic messages or funny good-morning images. He could do this thing.

Calvin grabbed his fleece-lined jacket off a hook by the door and headed out. The three-bay workshop in the back housed some farm equipment, a half-restored 1978 Ford Mustang covered in a dusty blue tarp, and Calvin's Yamaha Enduro motorcycle, which was even older.

At least the tarp meant he didn't have to look at Michael's car.

The Yamaha started on the second kick. Not bad for a cold start! Calvin revved through the open workshop door and into the thin sunlight of a North Carolina morning. A little too cool to ride, perhaps, but he tasted spring and couldn't wait. He charged down the gravel driveway and whipped past the departing school bus, showing off for the freshman girly girls who'd be clustered around his sister. He could imagine Lizzie's scorn without seeing her face through the bus window.

Calvin pressed right, leaned deep, and hugged a curve, breezing over the tall, prickly grasses crowding the shoulder of Victory Church Road. The Yamaha's *ring-ding* song echoed off the asphalt, and the wind battered the heat from Calvin's face. Motion without a cage. And for the two miles between home and school, Calvin could feel free. At the stop sign at Old Bentley Road, he tickled the throttle in anticipation of the turn. A sleek red Camaro sped past, horn beeping a challenge.

Calvin hissed between his teeth. "Uh-uh. No way, dude."

He angled around the corner and tailgated his friend Tyler's car along the two-lane road. Stiles County's version of rush hour meant there was just enough traffic to keep him from passing. At the entrance of South Stiles High School, car and bike waited to turn left. In his rearview mirror, Tyler flashed a big-toothed grin beneath a swoop of pampered blond hair.

Calvin revved his engine in answer.

A warning crackled in the back of his mind: detention, loss of parking privileges, Dad taking the bike away for reckless driving.

But every other impulse pushed against all that was sensible, safe, and dull. His conscience didn't stand a chance.

He followed the Camaro into the parking lot. A wide speed bump spanned the width of both lanes ahead.

"Prepare to fail," Calvin said inside his helmet.

As expected, Tyler slowed down. No way he'd bottom out his precious car on the hump. Calvin swerved left and cranked the throttle. He lifted from his seat and bounced down to load the rear shocks as his front tire hit the rise in the pavement. The bike's engine raced as both wheels went airborne, sending a thrill through Calvin's veins.

He nailed the jump, landed clean, and cut ahead of Tyler.

Calvin glided to an area of the parking lot claimed by the school's few bikers. He pulled into a space beside a metallic black Kawasaki Ninja and stared at the 650 cc's of pure adrenaline-packed ride. *Ooh, man. Someday, dude. Someday.*

He set his kickstand and swung his leg over the cracked Enduro seat then removed his helmet. No more time to fly.

"Cal!" Tyler called from two lanes away.

Calvin shrugged off one strap of his backpack as Tyler jogged between the parked cars to join him. Standing at the other side of the Yamaha, Tyler huffed, "Are you *trying* to get yourself killed? I almost hit you."

"I knew what I was doing." Calvin scrubbed a hand through his curly hair to get rid of any helmet head.

Tyler looked away and laughed. "Yeah, well, save the stunts for the motocross track. Besides, this old thing'll be dropping bolts all over the asphalt if you keep beating it like that."

"Hey, it's not old, it's *vintage*. And it's the best dirt bike you'll ever see."

"I can hardly see it at all under the duct tape." He flashed his perfect teeth. "You goin' in? Or hanging out here with Stacey?"

"Uh ..." Calvin scanned the parking lot for his girlfriend's car.

No Facebook message. No little blue Honda Civic yet. Not right. "I dunno. She's usually here before me."

"Want to use my phone to call her?" Tyler reached for his back pocket.

Calvin pulled his lips into a crooked smirk. With seven—six—kids in the family, living on eighty acres that couldn't produce enough to cover the bills, and Dad's automotive business barely making it in the bad economy, a cell phone was another "someday" dream.

"Nah," he answered. "She won't answer if she's driving. Detective Daddy's orders. She drives safe."

"What would she say about that stunt you just pulled?" Grinning, Tyler tipped his head toward the speed bump.

Calvin straightened his shoulders. "She'd applaud its perfect execution and my superior skill on two wheels."

"Ha! Yeah, right. I'll see ya later, bro." Tyler backhanded Calvin's arm and headed for the sidewalk, so cool, so happy with his smartphone and his new car, waving to a girl who called his name. A year ago he'd been a skinny geek with braces. This year, thanks to hours spent in a dentist's chair and sweating in a weightlifting class, he was a budding rock star who barely knew what to do with his new groupies' attentions.

Calvin drummed his fingers on his helmet and scanned the parking lot again. Stacey's bright blue Civic would be easy to spot, but it wasn't in the line of sports cars, beaters, and pickup trucks streaming up the driveway. Maybe she was sick and her mother made her stay in bed. Again. It happened way too often.

Helmet secured beneath his arm, Calvin trudged into the building. The never-changing scent of chicken nuggets and pine cleaner led him toward the cafeteria. He pumped six quarters into a vending machine for an energy drink. When he bent to retrieve the bottle from the dispensing tray, his helmet slipped. He juggled both bottle and helmet up to his chest.

"Stuffing your face again, farm boy?" a familiar, and despised, female voice crooned.

Calvin shut his eyes as he straightened. "Hey, Zoe."

Skinny Zoe Bernetti stood five-foot-nothin' and had a bite like a rabid fox. With her hair stick-straight and purple-streaked, and her handmade clothes cut at weird angles, she seemed to consider herself a fashion revolutionary, but one without a clear battle plan. Artsy, manic, and snarky, Zoe had somehow earned best friend status with Stacey, leaving Calvin to figure out ways to put up with her.

Another girl circled around Zoe, her pale hair glowing like a halo in the hallway lights. "She's just teasing." Stacey poked Zoe's arm with a meticulously clean fingernail. "Be nice."

Mystery solved. Stacey was late because Zoe was involved.

"I waited for y—" Calvin blinked. "Your hair!"

Not blonde anymore. Not soft and framing her face in those gentle waves he loved to touch. Stacey ran her fingers through stark white, thin hair with neon pink streaks in the front. "Zoe did it for me. Do you like it?"

Calvin choked out an answer. "Yeah. It's ... cool."

Zoe sent him a warning frown. "You better like it. We worked on it for hours last night. No Kool-Aid. We used the professional stuff."

"It's awesome. Really." He stepped between the two girls, keeping his back to Zoe. "Walk with me to my locker?"

"Of course." Stacey bounced a fingertip against the divot in his chin. Her glittery lips spread in a smile, replacing the nagging questions with a tickling desire.

"I was thinking we could go to Oliver's Burgers after school—"

"Oliver's? Eww!" Zoe's voice squeaked like rusty truck hinges.

Calvin scowled over his shoulder. Why couldn't the pretender to the throne of punk take a hint and go away?

Stacey nudged pink hair away from her face. "Ooh, does it have to be that place? Mega-fat and carb central."

"They have salads."

"Their salads are gross."

"Ice cream?" He leaned toward her until only inches, centimeters, separated their foreheads.

"Y'all aren't gonna kiss, are you? Nasty. Someone should tell the principal."

Calvin grunted and turned his eyes toward the ceiling. *Lord have mercy!*

Pulling away, Stacey laughed at her friend. "Jealous?"

"Of you and Cherub-cheeks? Pah-leeze."

Stacey's mouth formed an *O* before she slapped a hand over it.

Calvin pivoted toward Zoe. "What? What did you call me?"

"Hey, that's what she called you last night." Zoe pointed at Stacey. "Said you remind her of a Renaissance painting. But I stuck up for you. I said, 'Calvin Greenlee may have his faults, but cracked and faded? No way.'"

Ha, ha. Sadly clever.

"Wow. Thanks for that. Really." How long before the first period bell? Time to move.

Stacey sped up to keep up with Calvin's elongated strides. "Don't be mad. Please? She's just joking around."

Calvin sighed and slowed down. "Yeah, sure. Like always." He tucked his drink bottle inside his helmet and slid a hand behind Stacey's back, started to twist his fingers into her thick, fuzzy sweater.

She flinched.

What now? She didn't want him to touch her? Because that gnat Zoe would poke fun?

Anger thrummed at the base of Calvin's skull, but another pain tightened his chest. Eight months. The longest relationship he'd ever had with a girl. And now her new best friend would mess it all up? The whole thing was just stupid.

Stacey entwined cool fingers with his. "I'm sorry we were late. Zoe called me this morning, crying. Her mother's boyfriend—"

"Guy's a total scumbag," Zoe grumbled behind them. "Yeah, Stace picked me up. Sorry for intruding on your make-out time."

Calvin blinked. So he was supposed to switch off his anger and feel sorry for Zoe now? Would he be a jerk if he didn't?

Stacey stroked his palm with her thumbnail, whiplashing his emotions to something far more pleasant.

They wove through the masses of students and entered the new wing of the building. The same mustard-yellow—aka gold—paint coated the cinderblock walls as in the older parts of the school, the same speckled tiles covered the floor, and the same beige metal lockers lined the walls. The red and black stripes along the ceiling—school colors—did little to keep the halls from inspiring naptime for the six hundred students.

Zoe strutted at Stacey's other side, practically preening when another girl stopped them to gush over Stacey's hair. The pink part was cute, but the white hair, next to Stacey's already pale skin, made her look like a ghost. Make that a zombie, thanks to the greenish cast of the fluorescent lights.

He shouldn't be surprised; Stacey applied her artistic flare to everything she touched. It was one of his favorite things about her. Calvin glanced down at Stacey's shoes as he veered toward his locker. Yep, neon-pink laces in her spotless white Vans to match the new hair color. Maybe Stacey just wanted to look like the manga characters she sketched, all skinny and intense.

Calvin spun to the first digit of his locker combination, but zipped past the second as Zoe appeared in his peripheral vision. Making sure his body blocked her view, he twirled the dial and started over. Stacey joined them, leaning on a locker to his left. Calvin yanked the door open and imagined it swinging into Zoe's pointy nose.

He angled his helmet to fit inside the locker. The drink bottle fell out and smacked the floor.

"I'll get it." Stacey bent forward. She wobbled. Her flailing hand snagged the loop of Calvin's cargo denims, and he staggered to keep from losing his pants. Stacey sprawled onto the floor, her books fanning out across the tiles.

"Stace!" He dropped to his knees beside her.

Blurting a cuss word, Zoe hovered over them. Her knee banged into Calvin's ribs, pushing him off balance. He elbowed Zoe aside and helped Stacey to her feet. She swayed in his grip and blinked rapidly, her face even whiter than before.

Calvin held her shoulder steady and smoothed her now messy hair. "What happened?"

"I ... got dizzy." She touched her fingertips to her glistening forehead.

"Are you okay? You hit the floor pretty hard."

"Yeah." She leaned against the lockers, her eyes downcast. "Probably, you know, a, um, female problem."

Calvin winced. *A female problem?* He squatted to retrieve her books, and his fingers grazed one that had been kicked out of his reach. "Did you eat this morning? I get lightheaded if—"

"I'm fine!"

Her outburst rocked him back on his heels. "O ... kay."

Another student handed the last book to him. Calvin made a stack against his hip and moved toward Stacey, but Zoe was so close she could suck up the air between him and his girlfriend. She rubbed Stacey's back and murmured over and over, "It's all right. You're okay."

Calvin read *go away* in Zoe's glance as clearly as if she'd posted an instant message in all caps. No way. He wasn't the intruder here.

Color returned to Stacey's cheeks then deepened into a blush. She laughed, looking around at people who'd stopped to gawk. "I'm fine. I ... lost a contact lens here last week and thought I'd look for it again."

"But you don't wear cont—" Then Zoe's eyes lit up, and a slight blush colored her cheeks.

The two girls giggled while Calvin rubbed a hand across his face. He passed Stacey's books to her, and she arranged them in size order in her arms. So proper. Calvin pulled out the books he'd need for physics and political science from his backpack, shoved everything else into his locker, then retrieved his bottle from the floor. He pressed the energy drink into Stacey's hand. "Drink this. It'll help you get through until lunch."

Stacey's fingers lingered against his. Eyes moist, she mouthed the word, "Sorry."

Sorry? For feeling sick?

A look passed between Stacey and Zoe. Girl secrets they weren't going to share with him. "Bell's fixing to ring," Zoe said. "We gotta go, girl."

They weren't going to shut him out that easily. Calvin pushed the fury down again and reached up to trace the curve of Stacey's cheek. She blinked. Tears matted her eyelashes.

"Don't worry about it," he said. "Come with me to Oliver's after school. Please? Just so we can spend some time together."

She nodded but turned her eyes toward the floor. He pressed his lips quickly to her forehead. Stacey tugged on his T-shirt front and gave him a half-lidded, sultry glance, the way she always did when they parted for their classes. "I'll be right here," she said predictably, patting the fabric over his heart.

"Always," he whispered.

Thick, cheap perfume swirled around them—Zoe too close again. Calvin's face and neck burned.

He had come to enjoy Stacey's daily, OCD-like routines—her morning messages with bizarre little love poems, her obsessive punctuality, and touchy-feely good-byes. Like these rituals with him were the most important things in her life. Though his home life had been wrecked by Michael's death, Calvin could count on the inventive consistency of Stacey. She could change her clothes or hairstyle or paint her car paisley swirls for all he cared. What mattered most, she was always *there*.

Zoe's sarcastic comments and plastic elf face had no place in Calvin's world. Why did she always need to be plastered to Stacey's side?

Yet Stacey's sick days, the dizziness, and her über-strict diet that drove him nuts ... Could he really blame that stuff on Zoe?

Calvin looked over his shoulder and saw the two girls heading into a science lab.

Not Zoe. That social parasite couldn't cause Stacey to do a faceplant in the school hallway. And neither could female problems. Calvin had sisters; they complained and got cranky, but they didn't turn sickly pale and pass out once a month. Something else was up.

And both girls knew what it was. He'd bet his motorcycle on it.

Chapter 2

Stacey eased onto her assigned stool in the science lab and arranged her books on the counter in front of her. The chemical tang in the air melded with the roiling acids in her stomach, intensifying the pain behind her eyes. She covered her face with her hands and inhaled scented hand sanitizer. The room tilted around her, or maybe she swayed on her metal perch.

Spicy perfume, which Zoe used by the bucketful, seeped into the bubble of air between Stacey's hands. She parted her fingers to peer at her friend.

Zoe folded her forearms on the table and leaned close. "I have Midol."

"Huh?"

"Didn't you tell Calvin you're having cramps?"

Stacey winced. Had half the people in school seen her fall in the hallway? Anyone in this room? Humiliating! And now Calvin would be ... *watching*. "No, I'm okay. I just got dizzy."

"Take your vitamins this morning?"

She stared at the counter in front of her. Vitamins. She had bottles and bottles of them, but she hated pills. Hated them since she was a child, when they pumped drugs into her after two heart surgeries. No pills. No matter how much Zoe insisted. Besides, she'd yet to figure out how many calories those things had.

Stacey leaned toward Zoe's ear. "Fasting," she whispered.

Zoe hummed acknowledgment. "Drink water. Not this stuff." Her fingers closed around Calvin's energy drink bottle.

Stacey snatched the bottle back. It was Calvin's gift to her, though it was poison to her system, a red flag against all her plans.

Zoe threw up her hands. "Whatever. You wanted accountability."

Stacey turned the bottle around to study the nutritional information. Might as well be a gazillion calories and carbs.

"Ugh! This is so hard." She collapsed onto the counter.

"Do you have any sugar-free gum? It'll help get rid of the cravings."

She dug into her purse for some sugar-free peppermint that was somewhere at the bottom. It'd keep her breath from smelling like the acid in her stomach, but it also had artificial sweeteners and other rancid chemicals. "I can't chew it now. Mr. Emerson will have a fit."

"He's always having fits," a male voice said. The counter quaked as Stacey's lab partner dumped his monster backpack onto it. "What's the matter?" Kenny asked. "You sick?"

Zoe whirled, placed herself between Kenny and the table. She struck a swimsuit-model pose, letting her hair drape over part of her face. "Hey, Kenny."

The redheaded senior peered down from his six-foot-two height. Tiny muscles beneath his eyes twitched. "Excuse me. This is my seat."

"What'll you give me for moving?"

The guy just stared.

Zoe groaned and rolled out of the way. "You break my heart, Kenny." She grazed her fingers across Stacey's shoulder. "Feel better, girl. Talk after class."

Stacey set the drink bottle on the counter again and hugged her arms. Honestly, they had to be running the air conditioner already. None of her sweaters were heavy enough.

"Maybe you shouldn't handle chemicals in class if you're sick," Kenny said.

Be strong. Can't become the center of anyone's attention. Stacey sat tall, envisioning a graceful line from her chin to her chest. "I'm fine."

Kenny nodded, his face stony. She'd never seen those flat cheeks crease with a smile's dimple. "Good. 'Cause puking on the table would be *bad.*"

Thanks, Kenny. I so needed that image in my brain.

The bell rang. Shoes and stool legs screeched against the tile floor, while thumping noises and conversations ricocheted between Stacey's ears. The classroom door slammed, sending a hammer strike to the back of her skull. She closed her eyes and drew a breath of air glutted with the stench of hydrochloric acid. As Mr. Emerson launched into his lecture, Stacey tucked the energy drink bottle into her purse. She could slip out to the bathroom during lab time to pour it out.

○ ○ ◯ ○ ○

Art was not a precise thing. It never obeyed timetables. Stacey glanced up from her secret creation toward the ticking second hand of the clock in her history class. Twenty-seven seconds left. Twenty-six. Would the third-period bell ring right when that tiny strip of plastic reached the twelve?

Mrs. Bartow droned on, talking about political strife in some distant past. Stacey's hand moved over a sheet of notebook paper. Anyone watching would assume she was taking notes.

Nearly done.

She grabbed another line from the poem scribbled in the margin of her actual class notes. She envisioned the letters, measured them, and inscribed them, perfectly positioned, on the fresh page.

Fifteen seconds.

Hand and heart raced with the clock as she laid out the last letters: *f-a-c-e*.

The bell jolted through her. Banging and scuffling surrounded her, but Stacey remained still, bent protectively over her poem as she read.

> forever
> tumultuous
> my heart
> gushing spilling over
> a violent wave of need
> crashing inside me
> yet never quenching
> the warmth that lingers
> where your fingertips
> tenderly   lovingly
> caressedy   my face

The word *tumultuous* had been her muse, despite having been spoken through Mrs. Bartow's wrinkly lips. Stacey had sculpted the letters to form the shape of a bloated female body.

Would Calvin notice? Would he get it? Did she really want him to? Warring desires. *Help. Stay away. Notice me. Be invisible.*

She touched her cheek, where she could still imagine the pressure of his fingers. Sweet Calvin. She couldn't confess anything to him outright, couldn't add to the burdens he already carried. He needed her to be strong. Raised on his mama's country cooking, he probably wouldn't understand the poem's symbolism, anyway. He wouldn't support her choices the way Zoe did.

His political science classroom was just down the hall, but she'd have to hurry to catch him before he headed to lunch. She laid the poem between her notebook and textbook then hurried out the door.

Three doors down, Stacey poked her head inside the classroom to confirm Calvin wasn't there. She rushed down the hallway, whirled at an intersection to avoid slamming into someone, then lifted on her toes to peer over heads and past shoulders of clamoring students.

Ahead—dusty-blond curls and a gray sweatshirt topping baggy jeans. She'd carefully inscribed the Yamaha logo across the back of his shirt with fabric paint, and on the front she'd drawn his motorcycle. Stacey lifted her hand and opened her mouth to call Calvin, but stopped. A girl walked beside him. Stacey nearly missed that detail, because Flannery Moore kept her hair cut boy-short and hid her narrow hips beneath baggy athletic pants. But when the girl turned her head to reveal a classic film-star profile, there was no denying who clasped Calvin's elbow and leaned close to say something in his ear.

A clammy chill flooded Stacey's face. Her balance failed her, and she stepped back.

Flannery and Calvin?

Clutching her forehead with her free hand, Stacey bulldozed a path through the other students. At last Calvin and Flannery were only a few steps in front of her, close together and laughing.

Not happening. Not possible. They'd known each other since kindergarten or some ridiculously long time like that. Flannery's father owned the local motorcycle shop, and she and Calvin were riding buddies. Her hair was short because she didn't like yanking out the tangles after a ride. She was—or at least was supposed to be—one of the guys.

The world blurred into a haze around the oblivious pair. Stacey's shoes felt like pink-laced bricks. Calvin's name tore through her throat.

He turned. His eyebrows shot up and a wide smile spread across his face. Too wide? "Hey, Stace. How're you feeling?"

"Calvin? Wh—what's going on?"

The girl, Flannery, turned her green-tinged doe eyes toward Stacey. Long, trendy bangs framed her oval face—liquid eyes, pouty lips, smooth skin. An Irish tomboy version of Audrey Hepburn. Definitely *not* one of the guys.

"Just going to lunch. Are you okay?" Calvin's voice trembled in Stacey's head where rational thought once lived. She'd come looking for him for a reason. *The poem.* Stacey slipped her fingers beneath her notebook and found the loose sheet of paper.

"Stacey, say something. What's wrong?"

Flannery stared, unmoving and haughty. She toyed with a boyish beaded necklace at the base of her long, graceful throat.

"O-okay ..." Stacey's fingers moved, flexing and unflexing. A crackling noise filled her ears, nearly drowning out the sound of Calvin's voice.

"I don't know," he said. "You look—"

"Why should you worry about me? Just go eat lunch with your girlfriend."

He winced. "Say what?"

"Your *girlfriend.*" She flung the wadded chunk of paper at his feet and ducked her head to spin around. She maneuvered around a hundred shifting shoes, dizzying splashes of color against the speckled tiles. Calvin called her, his voice bouncing off cinderblock walls until it was swallowed by the crowd. The hallway and all the students tilted and swayed like a carnival ride. Stacey lurched into a girls' bathroom and careened around the privacy wall, dropping her bag as she slid her books onto the countertop. Her pulse galloped in her temples as she clung to a sink with both hands.

Stop. They're just friends. You're freaking out over nothing.

But ... that touch ...

"Stacey?" Calvin wouldn't come into the girls' bathroom. Or maybe he would if she didn't answer.

"Th-there's someone else in here."

A toilet flushed, converting her lie to truth. Stacey peered past her curtain of white hair at her reflection in the mirror. Tears soaked up her eyeliner. Red splotches dotted her porcelain-pale cheeks and neck. Ugly. She pressed two fingers into the soft flesh beneath her cheekbones. Still too puffy. And that loose flesh under her chin ... She pinched it. Practically a turkey gullet.

Calvin deserved someone pretty. Thin. Happy. Strong. Like Flannery.

Black tears dribbled down Stacey's face. Her body insisted on breathing uneven, trembling gasps. "Get a grip. He's not cheating."

Sure, Flannery was gorgeous, but God had put the wrong brain behind those stunning eyes, that of a volleyball jock instead of a supermodel.

A girl exited the stalls and took her place at the next sink. "Boyfriend trouble?"

Not your business. Stacey channeled all her energy into standing still, forcing away the dizziness, while the other girl in the mirror fluffed her hair, adjusted her top, and walked away without scrubbing her hands.

Dis-gusting.

"Stacey!" Calvin called.

"Just a second." She blinked hard. Her face was a mess, and reapplying her makeup would make her late for class. She'd have to wash up and go simple-faced, like she did before Zoe initiated her "totally sassy, smokin' makeover." Yeah, right. Who was she kidding?

She grabbed paper towels from the dispenser, soaked them in cold water and liquid soap, and washed her face. The cool water calmed the red blotches.

Now I look like a botched marble statue. No way I can go out there now. No way!

Her purse, with her makeup in it, sat in a lump on the filthy floor. How stupid to just drop it there!

More soapy towels wiped away germs from the soft leather. Stacey cleaned the countertop and the bottom of her books as well.

After she scrubbed her hands in the hottest water, she wadded up all the towels and pitched them into the trash so she wouldn't have to touch the other gross stuff in the bin.

"Stacey, if you don't come out, I'm coming in."

"I'm fixing my makeup. I'll be right out."

The bell rang as she applied her mascara.

"Stacey. What. Are. You. Doing? You're late for class now."

"Coming."

Lipstick and blush, so she wouldn't look dead when she begged the secretary in the administrative office for a pass.

Stacey found Calvin pacing in the empty hallway outside the bathroom. He whirled and charged up to her. "What's the deal? You just freaked out back there. What did I do wrong?"

She couldn't face his intensely innocent eyes. Instead, she focused on her hazy reflection in a display case across the hall. "I saw Flannery touch you."

"She *touched* me? When? Like, she just ... *touched* me? That doesn't mean anything."

"I know. You're right. I overreacted." One hand fluttered, grasping for a reason he would understand. "It's just that she's so pretty and ... I don't think she likes me much."

"*You're* pretty. *You're* my girlfriend. Flannery is just my friend. And she does like you." A blink, his eyes flicking to one side. He wasn't very good at lying.

She let it go for now.

"I'm really sorry." Stacey touched her tongue to her lips and inched closer to him. "I'm sorry about this morning too, about falling. I didn't get enough sleep. I probably need vitamins or something."

"Good idea. 'Cause you've been sick a lot and it ain't normal."

The edge in his voice pricked her. She had to fix it. She needed him; he needed her. Stacey cupped Calvin's rounded shoulder and ran her hand down his arm. His bicep was firm, his forearm broad and muscular beneath the sleeve of his sweatshirt. Strong. Hefty. Farm boy.

She tilted her head to peer into his hazel eyes. "Forgive me?"

He sighed. "I just want to know what's going on."

"It's probably something simple." Stacey moved closer and curled her fingers around the back of Calvin's neck.

He stiffened and scanned the hallway. "Uh, you're late for class."

"And you're missing lunch. A few more seconds won't matter."

She pulled him toward her for a kiss, a lingering, *tumultuous* reminder that they belonged to one another.

His clumsy hands clasped her waist. Stacey flinched. What could he feel there, beneath her soft sweater and camisole? *Not yet.* She broke away and giggled. "That's enough. Can't let any teachers catch us engaging in *inappropriate public displays of affection.*" She inscribed quotation marks in the air.

Calvin dug his fingers into his forelocks and tugged as if trying to straighten the curls. "Girl, you are driving me crazy."

She wriggled her nose at him. "You love me for it."

A breathy laugh escaped him. "Yeah, I do. You'd better hurry, though."

Stacey pursed her lips to kiss the air between them, then half-jogged toward the administrative office to prove she still had a healthy spring in her step. But when she rounded a corner, she dragged herself along the wall. Calvin would go to the cafeteria, pile food onto his plate, and sit at his usual table with his riding buddies, Tyler and F-l-a-n-n-e-r-y. And while Stacey was lying to the school secretary so she could get a pass, Calvin might tell his friends that his girlfriend was acting weird, doing things that "ain't normal."

And that girl would give him advice.

A vent blew icy air over Stacey, sending a chill down her spine. She shuddered and hugged herself.

"Hey. Aren't you supposed to be somewhere?"

Stacey gasped and turned toward a big man wearing shorts. Hairy shins, football-player hands, soft gut beneath a barrel chest. Coach Miller.

"Oh! Yes. Sorry. Just on my way for a pass."

"Well, get a move on. Now."

"Yes, sir. Sorry."

"Why are you crying?"

"I'm not crying. I'm ... I have allergies." Stacey blinked away stupid tears. She moved, and Coach Miller's athletic shoes squeaked on the tiles just behind her.

Stop weeping like a feeble wretch. Still the tumult. Be strong, pure.

Stacey tried to recapture the meter and words of her lost poem, but they were usurped by the echoes of a wicked child singing on a distant playground.

Crazy Stacey bubble butt.
Never keeps her big mouth shut.
Chubbikins, Chubbikins.
How much does she weigh?

Chapter 3

Tyler revved the engine of his motocross bike while Calvin wiped his hands on a rag and leaned against the wall of the workshop. Getting ready for some spring break riding. Late afternoon sunlight slanted through the open bay, glinting off the signature-green tank and fenders of the Kawasaki KX 250F.

"Sounds good," Calvin shouted. He glanced at his Yamaha sitting nearby. Enough time for a ride before supper? Mom would have it on the table at six sharp.

Tyler eased off the throttle and let his engine idle. "It sounds great. Thanks. Dude, you should totally see if you can get a job at Bentley Cycles for the summer."

"Already asked. Dave's not hiring. Bad economy and all." Calvin ran one fingernail under another to dig out the grime wedged deep down.

"Grab the stand for me?" Tyler said. "I'm going to ride around, make sure the engine's running good at top end."

Calvin pulled the bike stand out of the way then held the Kawasaki upright while Tyler strapped on his matching green motocross helmet. The throttle vibrated sweetly in Calvin's grip. Nice, tight action. In a minute, he'd stand back and sniff gravel dust as Tyler roared down the driveway.

When Tyler had straddled the bike, Calvin tapped the back of his helmet. "Hang on. I'm coming with you. Just let me tell Mom."

Tyler nodded, the long visor of his helmet tipping down and back up.

Outside the workshop, two little brothers threw a basketball at a bare hoop, mostly missing it. Scamp, their Border Collie mix, jumped and yapped at the boys. Calvin smiled to himself and jogged across the weeds toward the back stoop. He let the screen door slap the frame behind him.

His mother stood by the stove in the kitchen, blonde, plump, and busy, turning fried chicken with a fork. Calvin's twenty two-year-old sister, Peyton, carried a big pot of something from the stove to the sink.

"Is Tyler staying for supper?" Mom asked without looking up.

Starchy steam billowed from the sink as Peyton drained what smelled like potatoes. Mom's sizzling chicken tugged at Calvin as if he were connected by a bungee cord. "Um, I'll ask him. We're taking the bikes out for a bit."

"Now?" Mom banged her fork on the edge of the pan then waved it at him. "Supper's nearly on the table. I won't have you riding all over creation while the rest of the family is sitting down to a meal."

What would it hurt if he was late for supper one time? Really. He'd only be taking a short ride through the woods.

"Hey, Mom, where's the parsley for these potatoes?" Peyton called, her face stuck in the refrigerator.

Mom turned her head. "Used the last of it a week ago. Get the dried stuff out of the pantry."

Calvin grabbed the moment of distraction and whirled toward the door.

"Calvin, I said—"

He pretended not to hear and made it outside.

Calvin rushed to the workshop and grabbed his helmet off a

shelf. He rammed it onto his head as he swung his leg over the seat of the Yamaha. "Let's go! Once around the field. That's all the time I got."

The Yamaha started on the first kick. Grinning at this small triumph, Calvin shot out of the garage. A check in his rearview mirror revealed Tyler took it a little slower on the loose gravel of the driveway. Calvin laughed and swerved onto Victory Church Road.

They traveled two hundred feet along the street then veered off onto a dirt access road at the north end of the cotton field. Packed soil in the ruts from Dad's truck provided good traction, and the golden sunlight gilded the newly leafed trees beyond the field. The temperature would drop quickly with the sunset, but for now it was perfect for riding. Calvin popped the clutch, and his front wheel lifted for one awesome moment.

He sped through the left turn at the back of the field. His rear tire skidded in the sandy soil between the truck ruts. Calvin muscled the bike upright and accelerated.

The deep-throated buzz of the Kawasaki engine undercut the Yamaha's two-stroke whine. Its green fender flashed in Calvin's peripheral vision.

Not happening, dude!

Calvin shifted his weight back and cranked the throttle. The Yamaha surged ahead.

He flew past acres of sandy, trenched soil, giving Tyler something to chase. Staying ahead took half finesse and half insanity, especially on this path. Tyler challenged him every few seconds.

A trail ahead led into forest. There, he and his old Yamaha would outshine the newer bike. Gritting his teeth, Calvin cut right to climb off the access road. Too much throttle; his front wheel lifted at the top of the ridge, and the rear skidded in the loose dirt. Calvin stuck out his left foot, and a lightning bolt of pain shot up his leg. Upright but moving too fast, the Yamaha plunged into the underbrush, where vines snagged the front end and flopped the bike over, tossing Calvin onto his hands and knees. The engine choked and died. Calvin lurched to his feet. The pain in his ankle sent a metallic taste to the back of his mouth.

"Ah-ohh … moron!"

Tyler sat puttering on the trail. "You okay?"

"Yeah, I'm fine."

All concern left Tyler's eyes, and he snickered. "Why didn't you slow down, man?"

The question didn't need an answer. Calvin, Tyler, and Flannery had all done idiotic stunts to stay ahead in a race. Limping, Calvin went to pick up his bike. He grabbed the handlebars and pulled back, but weeds had snarled under the fender. He yanked hard and stumbled backward when the bike came free. Hobbling on his twisted ankle, Calvin hissed a curse.

And then the Yamaha wouldn't start.

He slammed the kick-start lever over and over while Tyler sat on his Kawasaki and stared. Calvin didn't need this. Not at the very start of spring break. Not with all the other junk he had on his mind. He dropped the bike on its side and kicked weeds and dirt for several strides along the hillside.

Things got quiet. Calvin looked over his shoulder.

Tyler had cut his engine. He set the Kawasaki on its kickstand, climbed the ridge, and strolled past the Yamaha, his thumbs hooked in his jeans pockets. "Okay, what's going on?"

"Huh? Th-the bike. Won't start."

"Don't mess with me, man. I can see the bike won't start. Something else is going on, or you wouldn't treat it that way."

Calvin turned to face the woods, blowing out each breath.

"Michael?" Tyler asked. "Or your dad again?"

"Yeah, like I'm going to dump all that on you," Calvin muttered without thinking. He glanced over his shoulder, hoping his friend hadn't heard.

In the shadow of Tyler's visor, hurt flickered through his eyes. Then he shrugged and looked away. "Just trying to help."

Tyler couldn't help. He'd tried before, but their conversations always ended up with Calvin talking and Tyler not knowing what to say. With Tyler looking uncomfortable and Calvin feeling just as lost. Maybe even more. Because it seemed like something had changed between him and his best friend as well. They couldn't go through the grief together. Tyler just couldn't understand. Calvin's world had changed; Tyler's hadn't.

Calvin made a lame gesture toward the Yamaha.

Tyler slapped a hand against his thigh. "Probably something simple. Come on."

Together, they lifted the bike. Calvin straddled the seat and put his foot on the kick-starter, but Tyler thumped his arm and stopped him.

"Dude." Tyler reached in front of the handlebars and lifted the throttle cable.

Broken. The black casing had ripped apart, laying bare a section of stretched-out metal coils. A branch had probably snagged it, and the old, dried-out casing gave up. A sick feeling grabbed Calvin by the throat again.

"Bentley Cycles ought to be able to get you one of these right quick," Tyler said.

Calvin shook his head. "Dave can only get parts for my bike if he finds them on eBay or in a junkyard." Calvin ran his hand under the mutilated coils. No way could he repair this.

"But it's just a cable. There should be one for another bike that'll fit."

"Doesn't work that way." Calvin sighed and dropped the cable. "Great. Just great. My spring break is toast."

"Nah, come on—"

"Forget it." Calvin took hold of his handlebars and rolled the bike back onto the access road. "Finish your ride. See you at the house."

"It's okay," Tyler said. "I'll walk my bike with you."

The Yamaha wasn't a burden to push, but Calvin's feet slipped in the sandy dirt and his sprained ankle throbbed. In spite of the cooling evening air, he and Tyler were soon puffing.

"You're limping," Tyler said.

"Twisted my ankle. It's not bad."

"Want to ride my bike home?"

He was already late for supper. Didn't matter if the bike was broken, Mom would have Dad lock it up for a week as punishment anyway. Might as well delay the lecture a little longer.

Calvin forced a grin. "It's okay. I'll make it."

Tyler leaned into the Kawasaki's handlebars and grunted as he pushed up a slope. Still at the bottom, Calvin stopped, watching his friend. The guy could be riding, having fun, or on his way home to a happier family and his beloved electric guitar, instead of slogging through the truck ruts with Calvin.

Desperation clamped down Calvin's chest. He had to let something out, or choke. Calvin took a deep breath to steel himself then pushed the Yamaha up the slope. At the top, he swung his leg over the seat and sat to take a break.

"Ty, have you noticed anything ... different about Stacey?"

Tyler huffed a laugh. "Yeah! Her hair. It's neon."

"Well, yeah. But, I mean, at Oliver's yesterday she acted like she didn't want to be there. I mean *really* didn't want to be there."

Letting his bike lean against his hip, Tyler took off his helmet. Sweaty blond hair clung to his head. "Looked to me like she was ticked off at Flannery."

"Yeah, that was stupid. But what I mean is, she wouldn't eat anything, and she acted like she'd get an infection if she touched anything. And yesterday morning, she almost passed out in the hallway before class."

"I heard about that! But I didn't know it was Stacey."

The Yamaha's hard rubber handgrips gave Calvin something solid to hang on to, something real and simpler than the rest of his life. He stared at the pits and scratches in the orange gas tank. "She hardly eats anything anymore. She's always on a diet. Always. I thought it was a girl thing, because Peyton is always, like—" He went into a falsetto voice to quote his sister's frequent whine. "'I need to lose weight to fit into my wedding dress!' But Stacey's different. I think . . . I think it's starting to affect her." He squinted at the sun, now a ball of fiery red peeking over the treetops beyond the neighbor's fields.

"I don't get why girls do that," Tyler said. "Stacey's already thin. She doesn't need to lose any more weight."

Calvin recalled Stacey telling him she was chubby as a child. She'd been sick as a baby, had a couple of surgeries, and her mother never let her exercise, afraid she'd damage something. But she wasn't heavy when Calvin met her. And she'd gone from dieting to . . . some kind of extreme.

"Something's wrong, dude," Calvin said. "Something major."

Flexing one hand against the handlebar of his Kawasaki, Tyler sucked in his lips and looked at the ground.

"What?" Calvin asked.

"Maybe she's, like, anorexic. Or what's that deal where they stick their fingers down their throats?"

Calvin couldn't breathe. *Anorexia.* That word had seeped into his thoughts before, but he'd shoved it away. It couldn't be. Why would anyone starve themselves when they were already skinny?

Calvin shook his head and got off his bike. He pressed against his handlebars and dug his toes into the loose soil to get the Yamaha rolling again. "Tell you one thing though," he said as Tyler caught up with him. "Zoe knows what's going on. The two of them are hiding something."

Saying it out loud to Tyler brought a rush of heat to Calvin's brain. Secrets. When had there ever been secrets between him and Stacey? He could tell her anything. Why did she feel she had to hide anything from him?

"That Zoe chick is scary," Tyler said.

Calvin grunted in agreement. With the road ahead, he pushed harder and kicked his heels higher, and reached the pavement before Tyler. Back and arm muscles already burning, he puffed out his breath and struggled up the gentle grade toward home. The Kawasaki engine revved to life, and Tyler roared past him, his helmet looped over the handlebars.

Calvin squinted and watched Tyler make a tight turn on the road to line his bike up with the carrier behind his father's SUV.

Victory Church Road leveled out, giving Calvin's arms a break, and he pushed the Yamaha to the grassy shoulder in front of his house. Tyler eased up to the bike carrier until his front tire nudged the narrow ramp.

Calvin set his Yamaha on its kickstand. "I was supposed to ask if you're going to stay for supper, but everyone's probably finished eating by now."

Tyler dismounted and, with a grunt, rolled his bike up the ramp. "Thanks anyway, but I should get home. You wanna come over to my place tonight?"

"Mom's going to shoot me for being late. I'll call you later if I'm still alive."

Tyler chuckled. "Hey, can you grab the strap for me?"

Calvin fetched a cargo strap that had fallen to the ground under the SUV bumper. He snaked it over the Kawasaki's triple clamp then hung onto the bike while Tyler secured the strap on the other side. The motorcycle's front forks compressed as Tyler winched the strap tight. Another strap secured the rear wheel of the bike.

Tyler flopped his arms over the seat of his motorcycle. "Cal, I don't know about the not-eating stuff, but the way Stacey's acting lately ... it's like she doesn't even want you to talk to other people. And the thing is ..." Tyler's voice softened. "When Stacey gets all needy and uncomfortable, it's like you fold. I don't want to say this, dude, but it's like she rules you when you two are together."

"She does not!"

"Sorry, bro. That's how I see it. Flannery thinks so too."

Calvin's mouth hung open and his brain fogged. The hour they'd spent at Oliver's Burgers yesterday afternoon seared through the haze. Stacey had hung on to him the whole time, saying little and eating nothing, even when he playfully touched a fry to her lips. Dirty looks hovered between her and Flannery. And she talked about leaving long before he'd finished his food. Calvin had to remind her that he couldn't carry a drink cup on the motorcycle.

Had she always been that insecure?

"Tell you what," Tyler said, shrugging his shoulders. "Call her and invite her to hang out with us tonight. You, me, and Flannery. See what happens."

Calvin swung away, paced in a circle, then came back. "It's just, I mean, she doesn't ride a bike, man. We ride and talk about bike stuff, and she feels left out. That's gotta be it. And maybe she's jealous of Flannery because Flan can do stuff she can't. You know?"

"Ask her. I bet she won't come. Even if all we're doing is watching television."

Calvin looked toward the house, avoiding a response. A light clicked on by the living room window. Dinner was over and Dad was probably settling in to watch his shows. Outside, the colors were fading, the golden light turning gray fast.

"I gotta go in," Calvin said.

Tyler took an audible breath and pivoted toward the SUV. He lifted his helmet off the Kawasaki's handlebars and fidgeted with the vent holes on top. "I hope I'm wrong. Maybe something at home's got her messed up right now. I hope all this turns out to be no big deal. I'm going to pray for that."

"Yeah, you do that," Calvin mumbled, turning his gaze toward his boots. Tyler's answer to everything: he'd pray about it. Maybe it wasn't very Christian of him, but Calvin wanted answers, not more of Tyler's prayers. Prayers hadn't helped him feel better about Michael—

"I gotta get home," Tyler said. "Thanks for your help. The bike's running great." He edged backward along the side of the SUV. "Really, I hope Stacey's okay and that y'all can work this out. Call if you want to go do something tonight. I'll pick you up."

"Yeah. Sure."

Standing next to his busted motorcycle, Calvin watched Tyler drive off. When the SUV and its small trailer disappeared around a curve, Calvin sighed and turned to push the Yamaha up the driveway. He parked it next to Dad's big tool chest in the workshop, set his helmet on the shelf, and closed the workshop door. Finally he slumped against the rough wood siding of the building.

His first real girlfriend. What did they have in common, really? They'd seen each other in the hallway by their morning science classes, chatted online, and he'd invited her to a youth event at his church. Her family didn't go to church much, so Stacey started coming with him on some Sundays. She was funny and sweet, and so talented and pretty that at first Calvin felt she was out of his league. When he asked her to Homecoming and she said yes, he walked around grinning for a week. Then Michael got killed in Afghanistan. Stacey became like an appendage, always at his side, always willing to listen and cry with him. Flannery and Tyler tried, but most of the time they didn't know what to say or do.

I'll pray for you. I'll pray for your family. May the peace that passes all understanding . . .

Stacey never promised anything. She was just there. Always. She loved him whether he was angry or moody or doing crazy stuff on his bike to run away from the pain.

But she didn't rule him. No way. And this super strict dieting stuff was too weird. It was making her sick, and it had to stop.

Mom poked her head out the back door. "Where have you been? You were supposed to be right back. Is Tyler still here?"

"No, he had to go," Calvin grumbled. He banged his fist against the siding then walked toward his house, ignoring the ache in his ankle so his mother wouldn't notice.

Mom held the door as he went in. "Your supper is in the microwave. You'll have to heat it up if you want it hot."

"Fine. I'll heat it up."

"Calvin, what's the matter with you?"

He plodded toward the microwave in the kitchen. "My bike's busted, okay?"

She followed him, her hands on her hips. "You'll keep a civil tongue in your mouth or you won't have that bike at all."

"Sorry. How long should I heat this for?"

"Two minutes should be plenty."

He punched in the numbers. "I'm sorry I was late. We had to push the bikes back."

Mom hummed. "Tell your father what happened. I'm sure he'll help you fix it."

Calvin nodded. He watched the digits on the microwave tick down. Sure, maybe Dad could help him rig up a throttle cable, if Flannery's father at the bike shop couldn't find one. Provided Calvin could get his father to focus on anything but work and the television for ten minutes. Maybe working on something mechanical would get his attention, but if Calvin tried to talk to him about Stacey,

Dad would probably grunt and move his lips like he was chewing something while his eyes glazed over. He'd been like that since the funeral.

Michael would've given up sleep to get the Yamaha running again. And Michael would have listened to anything Calvin needed to talk about.

Calvin squeezed his eyes shut. He had to focus on what was important now.

Tyler was probably right, that Stacey would make some excuse or come up with some reason she needed to spend time alone with him rather than hang out again with Calvin's friends. And if he pressed her about passing out, not eating, losing weight, freaking out about Flannery, even changing her hair, they'd argue about all that too. But she didn't rule him. No way was Tyler right about that.

The microwave dinged and Calvin pulled out his dinner. The plate burned his fingers. He hissed and practically threw it onto the dining room table. Mom shot a glare at him from the kitchen sink. Holding back a groan, Calvin plopped down in a chair and tugged at his hair while he stabbed at not-so-fluffy-anymore mashed potatoes.

He'd get to the bottom of this mess, even if it meant getting into an argument with Stacey. He had to have some answers. Tonight.

Chapter 4

The smaller Stacey cut her food, the easier it was to spread the bits around and make it appear as if she were actually eating. Like a magician directing the audience's eyes away from the trick, as long as Stacey moved her utensils and raised her fork to her mouth, no one noticed what was on her plate, pushed to the sides, or hidden under a slice of bread.

Sirloin steak, pan-fried—*seriously, Mom?*—with sautéed mushrooms and onions. Corn on the cob dripping with butter before it hit Stacey's plate, and a salad with every kind of topping including bacon bits and egg crumbles. Daddy's favorite meal. The steak, with the mushrooms and onions scraped off, would be around three hundred calories for three ounces. Mom had given her twice that. The corn, with the butter, she estimated to be around one hundred calories. Stacey carefully trimmed the fat off the meat and cut it into miniscule pieces, and did surgery on the corn to extract half the kernels. She nudged acceptable portions to the good side of her plate. One hundred fifty calories. She pushed a little bit more to the bad side.

If Daddy were paying attention, he'd analyze her plate like a crime scene. But her sister's one-woman revolt conveniently distracted her father's eye.

"What am I supposed to do, sit around here and stare at the stupid television every night?" Renee said. "Excuse me, but I'm not into numbing my brain."

Still in his khaki-colored uniform, Daddy shoveled a huge chunk of steak into his mouth. "You were out last night. You're staying home tonight."

Renee slapped her hand on the table, rattling her multitude of bracelets. "It's Friday! And Preston promised his best friend we would be there for his band's debut."

Preston Stiles, the current boyfriend. His pretentious name befitted his family's old-money status. But money obviously didn't lift the guy above loser status in Daddy's opinion.

Stacey raised her empty fork to her mouth, tasted a bit of saltiness on the tines, and pretended to chew. She glanced at her mother, who dabbed at her mouth with her perfectly pressed cloth napkin. Mom's eyes were downcast. She wasn't crying yet in an attempt to quell her oldest daughter's rebellion, but she soon might be. And it wouldn't work. Renee had hardened to Mom's manipulation.

"What band?" Daddy glared suspiciously as his jowls worked at the wad of steak.

"Invite Preston over here, sweetheart," Mom said.

Renee's eyes widened at Mom, like she'd rather die than subject her boyfriend to the family, then she turned to glare back at Daddy. "Arbitrary Crush. They're playing a club in Raleigh."

Daddy jerked forward as if he'd choked on his food. He swallowed audibly. "Forget it. You're not going to any club two hours away from home. Or even ten minutes from home. I'm not having a repeat of last week when you came home drunk."

Mom's fork clattered on her plate. "Stan, please! Do we have to bring that up again?"

"I'm nineteen years old. I can do what I want." Renee crossed her arms over her chest, pushing cleavage up through the deep neckline of her top.

Daddy's face turned redder than his rare steak. "As long as you're living in this house—"

Renee popped out of her seat, arms and flat-ironed hair flying. "I never asked to live in this house. *You're* the one who decided we should move to this disgusting place. I *hate* it here!"

"We are here for *your* benefit." Daddy pointed at her with his steak knife.

Tears brimming, Mom reached up and tried to catch Renee's hand. "Renee, dear, can't we just have a nice meal together? I made strawberry pie …"

Pie? On top of all this? Strawberries had only forty-six calories a cup, but they'd be smothered in sugary gel, and the pie crust … She'd have to check her book to be sure, but it had to be at least two hundred for a single slice.

Time to escape, Renee. Me too.

Stacey arranged her napkin neatly on the table. No sudden movements. Nothing to attract anyone's attention.

"Sit down, Renee. You're not going," Daddy said. "I won't have you out with that older guy—"

"He's twenty-two."

"That's old enough to buy booze, and that means he's too old for you."

"I'm full." Stacey rose and leaned toward her mother to kiss her flushed cheek. "Good dinner, Mom. The steak was really tender."

Mom glanced up at her with liquid blue eyes. Her utensils rested neatly beside her plate and her half-eaten meal. Mom's fingers worked, pushing against her cuticles, ruining her manicure. She wouldn't eat if she was upset, but she'd "nibble" later, after she calmed down, and that pie would be half gone before bedtime. And she'd repair the damage done to her fingernails while watching television. Mom couldn't leave any kind of mess alone.

The argument continued while Stacey rinsed her plate at the kitchen sink then fitted it in the dishwasher. The remains of her meal churned in the garbage disposal while Stacey washed her hands. Deception complete, execution flawless. Now if she could find a way to avoid the pie . . .

Strawberries! Her stomach grumbled in a pathetic protest. Weakness tugged at Stacey's mind. *Be strong. Go upstairs and do something. Think about something else.*

The doorbell rang as Stacey crossed the living room.

"That's Preston. I'm going," Renee announced.

Her parents' complaints blended together as Renee rushed to the door. Stacey glided to the stairway, up and out of the line of fire.

"Stacey! Zoe's here!"

Oh no. Daddy's volatile mood would ricochet onto Zoe in a heartbeat. She should know better than to come here. Stacey pirouetted at the top of the stairs and galloped back down. Renee stormed past her going the other direction.

Zoe stood in the foyer, her shoulders nearly touching her ears, gray tear stains on her cheeks. A purple duffle bag hung from her two clenched fists.

"What happened?" Stacey hugged her friend before she could answer.

"Big fight with Mom," Zoe said against Stacey's shoulder. "Okay if I spend the night?"

Stacey peeked toward the dining room. Her mother collected the dishes while her father pronounced his judgment of errant daughters and delinquent boyfriends as if Renee could still hear him.

"Not a good time to ask." Stacey clasped Zoe's hand. "Come to my room. If anyone says anything, we're doing homework."

She pulled Zoe upstairs. Behind her closed door, she handed the girl a wet wipe. "So, how did you get here?"

Zoe removed her tears with two aggressive swipes. "The sleazeball drove me. Can you believe it? It was either that or steal Mom's van."

"Oh no. Was he drunk?"

"Not yet." Zoe tossed her head as if shaking off rainwater. "Never mind. I don't want to talk about it." She pitched her stained duffle bag onto the floral panels of Grandma Jenny's handmade quilt.

Stacey gasped. She reached toward the bag, then jerked her hand back and clasped her arms instead. She edged closer to the bed while Zoe looked around the room.

"Girl, we *have* to do something about this room."

"What's wrong with it?" With her friend's attention diverted, Stacey lifted the dirty bag off the bed and placed it on the floor.

She knew what was wrong with her room — at least what Zoe would say was wrong. Country craft with a touch of fantasy. Frilly and feminine, sweetness and light. The same style she'd had since third grade, which Mom had meticulously transferred to the new house when the family moved from Rocky Mount. A few pieces of Stacey's artwork, professionally framed, were all Mom would allow. It wasn't a bad room, overall. It just wasn't ... relevant.

"White furniture, pink roses, and *dolls*?" Zoe pointed an accusing finger at the collection of heirloom porcelain dolls that lived on lace-lined shelves in a white hutch. "If I wake up and see visions of kittens with wings, I will *not* be responsible for what happens."

Stacey smiled. "Aw! You don't like angel kitties?"

"Oh, I like 'em just fine. Roasted on a stick."

This brought a giggle. "You're so nasty."

"That's why you love me."

Probably true. Being with Zoe was like watching a circus act, delighting in the stunts while keeping one's own feet safely on solid ground. Zoe's manic emotions swung like a trapeze artist. Stacey understood the reasons for the shift. Turn off the tears, don't fixate on the pain, and don't let people get close enough to see ... Not that Stacey had performed the act so well herself the last few days.

She brushed germs off her quilt, at the same time brushing away the memories of her humiliating reactions to Calvin and Flannery. In her bedside table drawer she found a bottle of scented hand sanitizer.

"I brought you something." Zoe unzipped her duffle and sorted through clothes and art supplies. Her rummaging stirred up the scent of cigarettes and mildew. She always doused that stench with perfume, but it was ripe in the things she'd brought from home.

Zoe pulled out something white. "This ... is my mother's latest peace offering. I don't know where she got it. Probably some trashy online store. But she really doesn't get me. I don't do lace."

Stacey huffed. "You think I'd wear something trashy?"

"I'm ex-*a*-ggerating!" Zoe held up a lace blouse with a choker collar, cap sleeves, and a heart-shaped cutout in the button-up front. Shabby-chic Victorian, kind of pretty.

Stacey ran the fabric through her hands, surprised by the silkiness of the lining. Not cheap. Pretending to check out the buttons, she eased the blouse close enough to her face that she could take a whiff. The cigarette stench hadn't ruined it yet.

Zoe took the blouse back and held it over Stacey's torso. "Should fit. Put it on."

Would it be too tight? Too revealing? Should she even try?

Zoe stood there as if she intended to watch Stacey change right there. Nothing timid about that girl. Stacey hated taking her clothes off in front of anybody. Freshman PE class had made for the worst year of her life in so many ways.

Chubbikins, Chubbikins...

"I'll be right back." She hurried across the hall to the bathroom.

The tag on the blouse read *S* for small. It would probably fit like a corset, pushing stuff up and out. Holding the blouse against herself, she studied her reflection in the mirror. Pretty. Maybe it'd fit if the manufacturer had cut it large.

Stacey hung her sweater on a hanger on the back of the bathroom door. A dozen tiny buttons secured the lace top over her body. Although the front didn't gape open anywhere, the material didn't give and squeezed her torso when she took a deep breath. The sleeves cinched her arms. The collar cut into her throat, and the heart cutout showed some cleavage. And the bottom hem stopped short, leaving a line of bare flesh above her belted jeans. Bloated, pasty flesh. Stacey pinched it between her fingers.

Not done yet.

Such a romantic top, though. Calvin would like it. He'd blink too fast and laugh, the way he did whenever he got "flustered." Then he might stroke her face and say —

A tap sounded at the door. "What are you doing in there? Come on, let me see."

Stacey blinked. *What am I thinking? I can't wear this thing.* She flung the door open and faced Zoe. "I can't wear it."

Zoe gaped at her. "What are you talking about? It's perfect. But those baggy jeans have got to go." She grabbed Stacey's arm, turned her around, and tugged at her waistband. "Look at all this bunchy fabric under your belt. How much weight have you lost?"

"Not enough."

"How much?"

"I don't want to say."

"Why not?"

Stacey jerked her arm out of Zoe's grip. "Because! Because ... I don't want you to know what a fat cow I was before. It's embarrassing, okay?"

Zoe held her hands up defensively. "Okay, relax."

Stacey threw her head back and groaned. "I'm sorry. I love the shirt. Maybe it'll be okay when I've lost a few more pounds. Are you sure you want to give it up?"

"Yeah. It's not my style, and it's gorgeous on you. Know what? Let's go shopping tomorrow and find something that goes with it."

"I can't. I already have plans to see Calvin." Stacey nudged Zoe out of the bathroom before the girl could respond with something sarcastic. Safely alone, she changed back into her sweater then tucked the lace top into her laundry basket. It'd probably shrink when she washed it anyway.

Zoe's heels thumped the side boards of the bed as she turned the pages of Stacey's sketchbook. Stacey sat next to her. When was Zoe going to tell her what had happened at home? Probably more of the same: drunken rages and arguments over stuff that didn't matter much or some snarky comment made at the wrong moment. It wouldn't be long before Daddy and his fellow officers hauled somebody in handcuffs out of that rundown house. What would happen to Zoe and her little brother if both her mother and the sleazeball boyfriend were busted?

"You're so talented, Stace," Zoe said. "I wish I was this good."

Stacey looked at the page and saw her drawing, a sleek heroine climbing a rocky stairway in a ruined landscape. Across each step, Stacey had inscribed lines of a poem, using her eraser rather than the lead.

Nightly Vision
Anxious Devotion
Hopeless Obsession
Desperate Mission

Art therapy. She'd done the drawing last September, when Calvin was just a face in the hallway of a new school. For the good-girl daughter of a cop, now living in the vast and strange countryside, friendless and holed up in her bedroom with impossible dreams, love had seemed unattainable. Everyone knew everyone else in this place ... except her. She was the interloper, the awkward city girl.

Calvin's Facebook friend request had changed everything.

"You should make this," Zoe said.

"Huh? Make what?"

"The outfit. It's awesome."

The willowy figure in the drawing was clothed in pure fantasy, flowing sleeves and a tight-laced bodice only an elf from Tolkien's Rivendell could wear.

"In fact—" Zoe closed the sketchbook and hitched one knee onto the mattress so she faced Stacey. "We should do that. This summer. We'll make our own clothes and no one—guaranteed, no one—will be wearing anything like our stuff next fall."

"*That* outfit? Pretty extreme for school. Maybe for a Renaissance fair or a play." Still, the pattern began to form in Stacey's mind along with calculations of how much fabric she'd need and what material would produce the flowing effect. Three yards of chiffon at least for the sleeves alone.

Zoe tossed the sketchbook onto the bed and got to her feet. "This'll be great. What if we come up with designs together and make our own patterns, and then sell the clothes?"

"Then we wouldn't be unique." Stacey retrieved the sketchbook and slid it into the cubby of her nightstand.

"No, no, listen. Everyone will be copying us. We'll be the trendsetters. We'll rule that school. *And* we'll have a nice fat portfolio that will get us into design school. I love this idea!"

It was easy to get caught up in Zoe's excitement. The girl couldn't wait to get out of Stiles County. A pleasant moan escaped Stacey at the thought of driving away, being in control of her life, chasing a dream. She had dozens of ideas laid out in her sketchbook, combining sweeping lines of mythic fantasy with futuristic elements like Manga art.

"We should go on a research trip." A humungous grin spread across Zoe's face. "Not around here, though. In Raleigh. Check out the high-end malls. Hit the trendy shops. Get inspired."

"Uh, Calvin's house? Tomorrow?"

"Sunday, then."

"Sunday is Easter. Mom's probably going to make us go to church."

"All right then! During the week while we're off school."

"I'll have to check. I'm not sure Daddy will let me drive all the way to Raleigh."

Zoe stomped her foot and turned her face toward the ceiling. "What is it with your dad? He's so strict about *everything*."

No arguing that; Daddy ran the family like a division of the police station. He was all about rules. In fact, he'd been so angry about her impulse decision to bleach her hair and put in pink streaks that he'd threatened to chop it all off. Maybe God was angry too, because in the shower this morning, dozens of hairs came loose in Stacey's fingers.

Her cell rang on the bedside table. She gasped at the photo on the screen. "It's Calvin."

Zoe rolled her eyes, snatched a fashion magazine from the stack on Stacey's bedside table, and collapsed cross-legged to the floor. Stacey grimaced and took the call.

"Hi-eee!"

"Hey, Stace. How are you feeling?" His deep, mellow voice was enough to make a girl sigh. It was the most attractive thing about him. That and his sparkling hazel eyes, Cupid's-bow mouth, cherub cheeks …

"I'm fine. Much better."

"That's great. Want to go to the movies tonight with me, Tyler, and Flannery?"

"Ooh, I'd love to, but I can't. Sorry. Zoe's here."

"Oh." His voice dropped, turned the single syllable into three.

"But I'll see you tomorrow."

"Okay. So what are y'all doing?"

"Talking about designing clothes." She glanced at Zoe on the floor and wondered if the girl processed every word of her half of the conversation. Stacey eased toward her bedroom door. "So, um, what are *you* doing?"

He sighed. "My bike broke down today. Throttle cable. I don't know how I'm going to get it fixed so I can ride at all this week."

With a final glance at Zoe—who stared at a boring ad in the magazine as if it actually interested her—Stacey stepped out to the hallway. "I'm so sorry, babe. We can do something else outdoors if you want." She ran her finger along the bottom edge of a picture frame in the hallway outside her room, straightening it.

"Yeah, but ... not the same," he muttered. "Maybe I can go over to Flannery's house and borrow a bike. I don't know, though. Her dad usually fixes the other bikes up in order to sell them in his shop."

Flannery's house?

He wasn't asking her permission to go over there and ride around with that girl. It didn't sound like he even wanted her opinion. He was just making his plans. Without her.

"M-maybe you can fix your bike," Stacey said. "You're good at that stuff. I'm sure you can fix it."

"I need a new cable. I'm hoping Flannery's dad can find one."

He went on talking about cables and bike models and eBay and blah, blah, blah, as if he hadn't just dumped the news he was going to spend time with another girl instead of Stacey during spring break. And he expected her to be okay with that? Stacey pressed her forehead against the wall and squeezed her eyes shut. Tears trembled in their ducts. She couldn't turn them on and off as easily as Zoe.

When Calvin stopped rattling about his motorcycle for a second, she said, "So, I'm just supposed to find something else to do this week?"

"What? No, of course not. I'm just thinking I'll go over there one or two days. Although she doesn't have trails like at my house—But you can come too! If you want."

"I don't ride a motorcycle, remember? What am I going to do while you're having fun with—" With pretty, thin, exciting, everything-in-common Flannery.

"Stace, come on. I really want to ride this week. Just ride. I've hardly been able to get out on the bike all winter, and I've been looking forward to this week."

That's right. He'd been talking about it since before Christmas. He felt better whenever he could get out and feel the wind in his face, become one with nature or something like that. He could forget about Michael being gone for a while. How could she deny him that outlet?

Stuff the emotions. Get back in control. "Never mind. It's okay." *Maybe it'll rain.*

"We'll get together plenty this week. You're coming over tomorrow, right?"

She tried to put a smile in her voice to end the conversation. "Yes, I'll be there. Two o'clock. And I hope you get the cable fixed. I know how much you love riding. But I should get back to Zoe before she repaints my bedroom walls."

"Wait. There was, um, something else I wanted to talk to you about."

Did he have another bombshell to drop on her? She pictured Calvin sitting on the front steps at his house, the phone drooping away from his jaw while he tugged at his hair.

"But I guess, since you've got Zoe there ..."

"What is it?"

"Okay, I'm just going to say it. I'm worried about you, Stacey. I need to know what's going on. This diet you've been on since, like, forever—I don't think it's healthy. You don't need to lose any more weight."

Ka-boom. She *so* did not want to have this conversation with him.

"Really, Calvin? You know that for a fact, huh?" Did she really just talk that way to him? The words kept coming, though her heart jumped like crazy in her chest. "I'll make you a deal. I won't worry about you while you're off riding around with Flannery if you don't worry about me and what I eat."

"Huh? That's not—"

"I have to go, Calvin."

"Stacey, I'm worried about your health."

"I'm fine. I told you, I just got dizzy yesterday. It's a female thing. It happens sometimes. Why can't you believe me?"

He sighed. "I want to believe you. But—"

"I'm fine. I'll see you tomorrow." If she didn't make an excuse not to show up. Stacey pinched the bridge of her nose.

"Okay." Resignation softened Calvin's voice.

Silence stretched to an uncomfortable length, and Stacey imagined Calvin pouting. It tore at her heart. She couldn't be cruel to him. She made a kissing sound against the phone. "I love you, Calvin."

"Yeah, love you too. Bye."

He hung up. Too abruptly. He was unconvinced, angry, maybe thinking she was suddenly too much drama. Her cell phone pressed to her lips to stifle a sob, Stacey rolled her shoulder against the wall then slid down to the floor. Zoe waited in her room, her parents were downstairs, and Renee was ... somewhere. At this moment when she wanted to weep for everything that was going wrong with her boyfriend, someone was sure to ask questions. Calvin would never understand. Never. And what right did he have to judge her for anything when he was planning to hang out with another girl? So what if Flannery was a total tomboy. So what if Tyler was going to be there too? He'd probably say Flannery was a better fit for Calvin because they both rode those stupid, scary, dirty motorcycles.

"Stace? You okay?" Zoe stood at the bedroom door, looking down at her.

She sniffed, dragged her voice out of the hollow cavity of her wretchedness. "Not really. Calvin's in a bad mood."

"What'd he say?"

"Nothing much. His bike isn't running and ... we need to talk about some other stuff tomorrow." Like how she could keep him in her life and out of her business at the same time.

Zoe knelt down and stroked her arm. "He doesn't get it, does he?"

Stacey puffed out air, as close to a laugh as she could manage. One person did understand what she was going through. Zoe shared her secret, felt her desperation, and helped her through the wickedest temptations. Barely a word had to be said. Zoe *knew*.

"I don't know what to say to him." Stacey hugged herself and rocked away from the wall.

"Know what? If he can't accept you for who you are, then—"

"I don't want to lose him. I love him." Fear and pain bashed through the well holding her tears.

But Zoe smiled. "Eww." She draped her arms over Stacey's shoulders. "But if that's the way you really feel, we'll work on it. I'm here for you, girl."

Stacey pressed her face into Zoe's tiny shoulder and cried.

Chapter 5

A breeze channeled through the front porch, ruffling Calvin's shower-damp hair. The crisp air that was so welcome that morning as he worked with his father in the cotton field now made him shudder. Still limping from his riding mishap yesterday, he paced the porch from one rocking chair to the other, trying to get his emotions in check before Stacey's arrival.

He couldn't bring the exact words of their phone conversation back to his mind; they'd been lost as heat flared in his head. He remembered her voice, sharp, offended, both defensive and accusing. But he'd done nothing wrong! Why should she be so ticked because he was concerned about her? It wasn't like he'd been hounding her with the questions. He was asking for the first time. And what right did she have to tell him who he could or couldn't spend his free time with during spring break?

He remembered going up to his room and punching the air and growling at Tyler — though the guy would never know it — for being right about Stacey. Suddenly, after seven months of dating, Stacey decided to be jealous of Flannery. It didn't make sense. And there *was* something going on besides female problems. She hadn't gotten dizzy and passed out before. Not in seven months. So why now?

Five paces between one rocking chair and the other, passing the front door again. Did anyone inside notice? And how was he supposed to act now? Pretend the conversation never happened or confront her with it? Calvin pivoted again and smacked the side of his fist into a post.

Michael hadn't been around long enough to tell Calvin how to deal with this weird girl stuff. The Army took him to Afghanistan last summer, and God saw fit to take him to heaven. Calvin's already anxious heart constricted at that thought.

He squatted down on the porch steps and clenched his head between both hands. So not ready. Not ready to face Stacey after their almost-fight last night, not ready to figure out what to do next. *Clueless* floated through his mind.

Maybe ... maybe Peyton could help? Calvin twisted around to glance at the closed front door. Inside, his oldest sister was helping Mom get ready for Easter brunch tomorrow. Peyton always moaned that she wanted to lose weight, but when it came to the roast lamb and piles of desserts Mom would lay out tomorrow, Peyton would jump on the food like a hungry linebacker. Would she have any understanding at all of what Stacey was doing?

Tires crunched on the gravel driveway. Calvin turned back and got to his feet in one movement, watching as Stacey pulled her blue Honda up even with the grassless path that led to the porch steps. She smiled and gave a giddy wave before opening the car door.

Act normal. Nothing wrong. Just a little tension we'll forget about tomorrow. Calvin thumped slowly down the steps. He could play this game for a while. It'd give him time to watch her and see if her symptoms went away in the next few days, like a "female problem" would.

Stacey launched herself out of the car and bull's-eyed his lips with hers. She wrapped her arms around his neck, and they swayed awkwardly on the dirt path. "I'm sorry, I'm sorry. I was horrible to you last night." She pressed her forehead against his. "It's just that

Renee was fighting with everyone and Zoe was there ... I shouldn't have taken it out on you."

Oh. "It's okay." *Not really, but—*

"I feel really bad about what I said, and I want to make it up to you." She slipped her arms down and grabbed one of his hands. "Come here."

"Are we going somewhere?" Calvin asked as she pulled him toward the car. "I need to tell Mom if—"

"No. I have something for you. Sorry I didn't have time to wrap it or frame it or anything."

Which meant it was another of her poems or drawings. As Stacey bent inside her car to retrieve whatever it was, Calvin's gaze traveled over her form. She was wearing another of her bulky sweaters, but the bagginess of her jeans raised a warning in his brain. He didn't really pay attention to her clothes unless she pointed out something new she'd made, but hadn't her jeans fit tighter before?

Calvin tugged his hair and took a step back.

She emerged from the car with a blue folder in her hand. Calvin held his breath as he opened it. An inked drawing inside depicted a male figure in heroic pose, wearing motocross gear and holding a helmet under his arms. His round face and curly hair were the only things that resembled Calvin at all, but she'd sketched those features with as much precision as any caricature artist would have. And the motorcycle behind him looked exactly, detail for detail, like his Yamaha. Yet he knew she hadn't traced it. She could take a picture of something and copy it perfectly. At least he thought so. Beneath the drawing, Stacey had drawn comic-book-style letters spelling "Motocross Star."

Calvin wanted to hug her until she couldn't breathe. "Stace, wow. Just ... wow. This is awesome. You're so talented."

She slipped her arm around him and hugged him sideways, her

hand pressed against his stomach. "Calvin, I know I shouldn't be jealous of Flannery. I know you're just friends. Forgive me?"

He closed the folder and squeezed her. Stacey's perfume filled his nose and lungs, dizzying him. Closing his eyes, he wished he could draw Stacey into himself and live in the place where she loved him and he loved her and nothing else mattered. Where they were both normal and happy. Stacey was amazing. He didn't deserve her. He was just a regular guy with a beat-up old motorcycle and no clue about where he was going in life. She was beautiful and talented, and maybe she'd even be famous someday for her art. She was a blessing to him, definitely.

How could he doubt her?

Calvin broke the embrace reluctantly. "When did you draw this?" he asked, moving toward the steps.

"This morning, after I took Zoe home."

"This morning? Just this morning? Unbelievable! I was out riding in a tractor this morning getting the field ready for planting."

Stacey giggled. "I thought I smelled something. L'air du turf, maybe?"

"Hey! I took a shower."

She squeezed his arm as they mounted the first step. "Not you, silly. The air is rich with the aroma of the earth and bovine manure."

He snorted. "Nice try. But we don't fertilize cotton with manure."

They went inside, where the smell of turned, sandy soil was replaced by the aroma of something wonderful in the oven. The air was warm to the point of feeling thick, yet for some reason Calvin's two younger brothers were still inside, bashing Transformer figures together in an epic — and loud — battle for galactic domination. Eight-year-old Zachary climbed on top of the coffee table and launched an attack from above, voicing dive bomb and explosion noises. Jacob, two years younger, protested that Zach was cheating and shimmied under the table to escape. Peyton, holding Baby

Emily's wrists to keep her from getting in the way, yelled at Zachary for getting on the table. Zach responded by scrambling onto the couch instead.

Typical day in the Greenlee house.

Mom shuttled around the corner from the kitchen, all smiles and arms open wide to greet Stacey. "How you doing, baby girl? It's so good to see you!"

Calvin stood back while Mom smothered his girlfriend. Mom loved Stacey. In fact, she loved just about anyone who entered her house. "Loving on people" was her solution to all the world's problems. It was also her form of escape from her own problems, Calvin thought. Since Michael's passing, and after a period where all she did was cry at the slightest prompting, Mom poured herself into caring for everyone, to the point where she was almost manic about it. She was happy when she kept herself busy being the perfect wife, mother, and host. Miserable when she wasn't able to do that. Still, Mom had told Calvin that Stacey was just the kind of girl he needed.

So why, as he watched Mom compliment Stacey's new hair color, did Calvin's warm, fuzzy feelings give way to a sense that he was being manipulated? He looked at the blue folder in his hand. She'd done the drawing to say she was sorry ... so he wouldn't ask her again about her diet.

As Mom turned away from Stacey and glanced at him, Calvin saw a flash of some darker emotion cross her features. Concern? Disapproval? She turned it off too quickly for him to decipher it. "Calvin, honey, would you and Stacey be good enough to watch the baby for a little bit? I need Peyton to run to the store for me. I forgot to pick up currants when I went shopping."

"Mom," Peyton whined, sitting in a chair by the front window while trying to hold on to Emily and a bridal magazine at the same time. "His girlfriend just got here. I don't know why you do this all the time. Whenever Ryan comes over, that's the time you figure out something you need me to do."

"Stacey is practically family. She doesn't mind. Do you, sweetie? Just while Peyton goes to the store?"

Calvin shook his head while Stacey agreed. It wasn't that Mom wanted to interrupt the time he spent with Stacey, or the time Peyton spent with her fiancé, Ryan. It was just that Mom was always busy, and she extended that busyness out to everyone else.

Zach jumped off the couch, chasing Jacob upstairs, and Calvin slumped down in his place. He rotated his sore ankle while Stacey sat beside him. She took eighteen-month-old Emily into her lap.

"Are you hungry, Stacey?" Mom asked, pausing at the wide arched entryway to the dining room. "We had lunch just a bit ago, but I can fix y'all some snacks, if you want."

"Oh, no thank you, Mrs. Greenlee. I ate lunch right before I came. Besides, it smells like you've got enough things cooking in there. Don't bother fixing anything for me, please."

Of course she'd say that.

Mom disappeared, and Calvin watched Stacey bounce the baby on her knees. Bounce, bounce, bounce. Over and over. Emily giggled and squealed, but if Stacey didn't stop soon, she'd find herself with a lapful of barf.

That'll give her a reason not to eat.

Calvin looked at the drawing again, trying to recapture the joy it had given him, then slid the folder carefully onto the coffee table.

"Ah b-b-b-brr!" Stacey rubbed noses with Emily, the baby's chubby wrists held secure in her slim fingers. Finally she stopped moving, her quickened breath whispering through her smile. Her green eyes sparkled in the sunlight streaming through the front windows, tiny rectangles dancing in them as Emily jiggled on her lap.

Healthy eyes. Bright, honest smile.

He really needed to get over it. He'd misjudged her and was

causing trouble between them when she was only having some kind of monthly trouble, like she'd said.

Calvin grinned back. "I can't believe you did that drawing in one day."

She lifted her shoulders in a cute, exaggerated shrug. "You like it?"

"It's awesome. I'm going to ask Mom to pick out a frame for it."

She nibbled her lower lip in delight as her knees bounced again.

Calvin moved closer to Stacey and lifted the baby off her lap. "Down you go, Emmy. My turn to play with Stacey." He set his little sister on her feet, gave Stacey a quick kiss, then rescued the drawing as Emily palmed her way around the coffee table.

Mom came back into the living room carrying a peach-colored stoneware plate in one hand, and a lime green one in the other. "Thought y'all might like a snack," she said, setting the plates on the coffee table.

Chocolate chip cookies covered the peach plate, while on the green plate Mom had arranged apple slices in a neat star pattern around a little cup of caramel sauce. Mom gave an apple slice to Baby Emily, then shot an imploring smile at Stacey.

"Apples, honey. Fresh from the store yesterday. Good for you. And those cookies? Baked them myself from scratch last night."

Stacey seemed to shrink into the sofa a little. She fingered her hair, pulled a hunk of it in front of her mouth as if to make a protective screen against the food. Her trembling embarrassment overflowed onto Calvin. His mother wouldn't come out and say that Stacey was too thin. She'd just provide the solution coated in sweetness.

Stacey brightened. "Wow, Mrs. Greenlee. You made those last night and you're cooking again today? Do people around here ever let you sleep?"

Mom grinned. "Feeding a family this size takes a lot of doin'. I get my reward when people enjoy what I make. So you enjoy those cookies!"

She hustled away, and Calvin felt like giving a low whistle. Mom had put Stacey in a tight spot. Eat, or insult. Calvin reached for a cookie and bit into it. He wiggled his eyebrows in appreciation.

Stacey stared at him. The trembling sensation Calvin had picked up on a moment ago increased, like a low current of electricity vibrated between them. He mostly felt his own nervousness, but a flicker of movement in her eyes, and an unsteady whisper of a breath passing between her lips, showed the tension wasn't his alone. They were locked in an unspoken standoff. *I'm watching you. Eat the cookies.*

He'd happily be wrong about her, if only she would eat.

Stacey pulled herself up from the corner of the couch at last, and reached out to take a cookie from the plate. She nibbled at it, confessed softly that it was indeed good, and actually finished it. She followed it with an apple slice, while Calvin held her hand on the cushion between them and privately rejoiced.

He was just about to sneak a little closer to Stacey, maybe steal a kiss, when Peyton let the front door slam as she left for the store. With that, chaos broke loose inside. The boys upstairs yelled, sounding as if the pretend galactic battle had become a little too real. Mom called Lizzie's name three times before the girl snapped, "What?" Somehow Scamp slept through the noise, curled into a tight ball in his bed beside the television. And standing in front of Stacey with one hand on her knee for balance, Emily munched another apple slice, juice and baby saliva dribbling down her chin and glistening on her pudgy fingers.

"Did you polish that silver platter like I told you to?" Mom asked Lizzie from the kitchen.

"Mo-om, I'm ... on the computer with—"

"You can get off the computer."

"Calvin's got his girlfriend over. Why can't I spend time with my friends?"

"Calvin did his chores this morning. You haven't started yours."

"I'll do it later."

"You'll do it now. I'm going to yank the plug out of the wall in a moment."

"Mom—"

"Now, Lizzie!"

Plastic clattered against wood veneer as Lizzie threw the headphones down. Calvin sank into the couch cushion, avoiding Stacey's gaze. Lizzie had closed herself off from the family since the funeral. Calvin tried to be patient with her, even understanding, but the prima donna act was wearing thin, and he had enough drama to deal with already.

He looked at the food on the coffee table. Stacey had eaten another apple slice with a thin coating of caramel sauce. Maybe they should go outside with the food and sit in the gazebo at the back of the yard, where it would definitely be quieter. Stacey might complain that it was a little chilly, though.

Something large—maybe the size of an eight-year-old child—thudded on the floor upstairs. Of the two voices Calvin could hear, muffled by the beams and plaster of their almost historical farmhouse, one of them sounded a bit whinier than the other. Jacob would come downstairs crying soon. The kid cried a lot.

Calvin took another cookie and shoved it whole into his mouth. He and Stacey hadn't made specific plans for the day, although she had suggested they go one place or another. Stacey liked to plan things, which was cool with Calvin most of the time. Today he'd just wanted to spend time alone with her. Maybe when Peyton got back home and relieved them of the baby watching duties, they could get in Stacey's car and just drive around. Maybe end up at the mall in Dawson, or a pavilion at the park in Clarksville, or parked somewhere along the Tar River at a spot that would look great in another month. The last one sounded perfect; they could sit on the hood of her car and cuddle the chill away from each other.

Stacey's snacking had turned to excruciatingly slow nibbling. Tired of being ignored, Emily toddled up to Calvin's knee. He picked her up and put her on the couch beside him. A smell reached his nose, more powerful than the baking aromas. His baby sister needed a diaper change.

And then another more pungent, chemical smell cut through all the others.

"Ugh. What is that?" Stacey murmured, covering her nose with her sleeve.

Calvin leaned forward to peer into the dining room. Lizzie sat at the table, making angry little circles with a rag against a lightly tarnished silver platter big enough to hold a Thanksgiving turkey.

"Silver polish," Calvin answered. "She should open the back door, let fresh air in here."

They hadn't used that platter last November. At that time, Mom had barely enough energy to heat chicken and noodle soup. Dad recruited Peyton and Calvin to put together a meal, although no one in the house felt much thankfulness that day. Yet it was a turning point for Mom. She became Super Mom from that point on, like her inability to serve her family was a huge personal failure. But when things didn't go right, she'd revert to a sobbing lump. Easter brunch was going to be a challenge.

Stacey stood up. "Excuse me," she said, squeezing between Calvin's knees and the coffee table. She walked to the steps, probably heading for the bathroom upstairs. Her delicate hand gripped the wooden banister until she disappeared behind the slope of what was once the roofline of the old house.

Calvin played with his baby sister, launching tickle attacks then sitting as still as a statue until her giggling subsided. Light flowed through the dining room, along with a draft of cool air. Someone had opened the back door at last.

A high-pitched wail upstairs made Calvin jump. He breathed out as he realized it was just Jacob having another fit. His brother came flying downstairs, his pale, angelic features twisted in agony. "Mom! Mom!"

"What happened now," Mom said, coming around the wall from the dining room.

Jacob grabbed Mom's shirt hem and pointed upstairs. "Somebody's throwing up in the bathroom!"

Chapter 6

"**W**hat's *that deal where they stick their fingers down their throats?*" Tyler's question stuck in Calvin's head as he stood outside the bathroom, listening to water running in the sink on the other side of the door. Mom hovered behind him, her breath coming in quick gasps from her dash up the stairs. Jacob peered around her hips, clearly grossed out and terrified. Zachary, all wide-eyed curiosity, stood across the hall in the doorway of the bedroom he shared with his younger brother. Calvin thought he heard Lizzie's voice from the stairwell. Great. Almost the whole family was there for the unveiling.

The door opened, and Stacey came out, her head lowered. She nearly collided with Calvin and let out a yip of surprise as she jumped back.

"Are you okay?" he asked.

"What? Oh. Um." Her eyes darted around to all the staring faces. Then she turned toward the wall, pressing her fingertips to her forehead. "I'm sorry, but I don't feel well. I think I might have caught something."

Even in the dim light of the hallway, her skin glistened. Like at school the other day. Calvin sighed. "Why didn't you say anything?"

"I thought it would go away. I didn't want to ruin our plans."

Calvin's suspicions wavered. Passing out at school and now this
… What if she was really sick?

Mom came around Calvin and put her hands on Stacey. "Oh,
sweetheart. Poor thing. Lizzie, go down and get a glass of water for
her to sip. Then I need you to watch the baby for a moment. Boys,
don't just stare at her. Go into your room for a bit."

Calvin's shoulders slumped. "Are you feeling any better now?"

"Uh …" Stacey leaned toward Calvin. He remained immobile,
unable to push aside the nagging questions in his head. But she
looked miserable. What kind of jerk would he be to hold himself
back from her? He pulled her into his arms, and she in return pressed
her forehead against his shoulder.

"I'm so sorry," she whispered.

"It's okay." He tangled his fingers in her hair. "I don't want you
to be sick."

She stiffened. He tightened his grip on her, to hold on until he
got the answers he wanted. "Talk to me, Stace. Please tell me what's
going on."

Mom came out of the bathroom with a wet cloth in her hand
and dabbed it against Stacey's forehead and cheek. "Has she been
sick before this?"

Stacey's eyes widened and she gave her head a little shake. Calvin
understood. *Don't tell.* Okay, not yet. Which was fine — he wanted
to talk to Stacey alone before he said anything to Mom or anyone
else.

"It was that smell," Stacey muttered. "The polish. I thought I'd
be okay today, but then that smell just made me feel sick again."

Plausible. Still …

A glass with tinkling ice appeared next to Calvin. Mom took it
and pressed it into Stacey's hand. Taking command, fixing the sick
child. "Drink slowly, hon. Little sips."

Stacey muttered thanks and took a swallow. Holding the glass in one hand, Stacey reached over to stroke his forearm down to his wrist. Calvin jerked away and tugged the hair at the front of his head toward the bridge of his nose. Was she actually sick? And if she had the flu or something, why not admit it? This was also a girl who was so phobic about dirty silverware, who carried hand sanitizer in her purse along with a little package of disinfecting wipes just in case she had to use a public restroom. Wouldn't she lock herself away in her room if she was infected with something?

Calvin hated that this rush of reasoning only fed his doubts. He forced himself to look back into Stacey's eyes. She held his gaze while Mom went on dabbing. Though pale, she didn't look weak. There was stiffness in her stance, like she was warning him through her body language not to push her for answers.

"Maybe Calvin should drive you home," Mom said. "Use your father's truck, hon."

Brilliant idea. He'd get Stacey alone in the pickup truck, talk to her—beg her if he had to—until she revealed the truth. Calvin took a step toward the stairway. Dad's keys should be hanging on a hook by the back door.

"How will I get my car home?"

Calvin stopped, his balance teetering on his sore ankle. *Think fast.* "I'll drive your car, then your mom or dad can bring me home later. We'll sit at your place and watch TV or something." *Or talk. A lot.*

She blinked, black lashes fluttering up and down, like she was trying to think fast herself. "M-my parents aren't home."

"You can't be hanging out at her house without one of her parents there," Mom reminded him.

Thanks, Mom. Not helping.

"I'm okay," Stacey said, moving away from the wall. "I can drive home. Maybe I just need more sleep. Zoe and I were up really late last night."

Calvin followed her out to the front porch then grabbed her wrist to stop her. "Stace, I can't let you go until we talk about this."

"Please don't ruin our spring break by arguing."

"Me? I'm ruining spring break?"

She whimpered softly. Her eyes glistened, and she started to sway. "Don't you trust me anymore?"

His hand tightened around pronounced bones. What could he say? There was no truthful answer he could give that wouldn't devastate her. Then a sliver of anger stabbed him. *Why should I worry about her feelings? She's the one not telling the truth.* By turning on the tears, she was manipulating him, making him feel guilty.

Yet if he'd read all this wrong, if she was actually sick—

Calvin let go of her wrist so he wouldn't accidentally break it. "People don't pass out or throw up for no reason. I just want to know what's going on."

Stacey blinked again, her lashes now clumped with tears. "Me too," she whispered.

The tears demolished his suspicions again. Maybe she had some kind of terrible, undiagnosed disease.

Calvin caved. He squeezed his eyes tight and closed the gap between them. Stacey clung to him as he hugged her and pressed his lips to her cheek. Her hands tugged the fabric of his shirt, while her body trembled.

Scared. She was scared of something.

Maybe he should be too.

He could hold her all day, if that's what she needed. But she broke free from him and fled down the porch stairs.

"Stace!" He leapt down five steps, landed hard on the ground. Pain jolted through his ankle and he staggered into the weedy grass.

"I'm fine! Just leave me alone for a while," she called over her shoulder.

Leave her alone? A net of confusion snared Calvin's mind and his body went numb. He stopped moving and stood with his arms limp as Stacey made it to her Honda. She fumbled her keys, fell into the driver's seat, and cranked the ignition until her starter motor screeched in protest.

Calvin swallowed, pulled air back into his lungs, and watched her roll down the driveway and speed away.

o O O O o

The glaring white computer screen made Calvin's eyes water. No other lights were on around him. After a late night coloring eggs for Easter baskets, Mom, Peyton, and Lizzie had finally gone to bed, and Calvin had been able to sneak downstairs for private time on the computer.

He wiped his eyes, stretched his legs under the desk, and reopened the email from Stacey. No poetry or pretty pictures in this message. And no answers. Only more questions.

I'm sorry I ran away from you today. I wish I could tell you everything, so maybe you'd understand. Things happened before I met you, before we moved here from Rocky Mount. Moving here was a fresh start. And when I met you, I thought I'd never be sad again. I can't go back to what I was! I can't even talk about it. Please don't ask me to. It took me so long to get where I am now. Please believe me. I'm ok. I love you so much and hate it when we argue. I need you to trust me. You've been through so much since the funeral and I don't want to put you through anything more. Please just trust me. I'm fine.

I love you.

Stacey

What happened to her in Rocky Mount? What did it have to do with her getting sick months later? He didn't have enough information, and Stacey sure wasn't going to give it to him. But whatever had happened affected her now and was messing with their relationship. Didn't he have a right to know?

Calvin closed his tired eyes and tried to remember anything Stacey might have mentioned in the past. His body relaxed in the chair, ready for sleep, but he inhaled deeply and forced himself to sit up. He had research to do, and he couldn't do it during the day with his family hovering around. Maybe he had a right to know what was going on, but no one else did.

First, something to help him stay awake. Calvin got up from the desk in the corner of the dining room and carefully maneuvered around the long dining table and chairs on the way to the kitchen. If he even made one tiny yelp from a stubbed toe, his mom would be out of bed in a flash, wondering if Zachary was walking in his sleep again, or Jacob was crying from a nightmare. Calvin found a large plastic tumbler in a cabinet and pushed it against the refrigerator ice dispenser, hissing at the racket of the grinding icemaker and falling cubes. He filled the glass with Mountain Dew from a half-empty two-liter bottle, swigged the drink until he needed to come up for air, then topped up the glass and returned to the computer.

He scanned Stacey's Facebook page. She hadn't posted anything new today, but Zoe tagged her with a cryptic message, which made Calvin think the two girls had been discussing things privately.

> fb wont ever get it cuz u no wat u got to do hes so out of it Im here 4 U {3

They couldn't be any more different. Stacey never used abbreviations and apparently Zoe couldn't even bother with punctuation. Or words longer than four letters.

FB. Facebook? No, farm boy. Zoe was referring to him.

"Oh, I'm fixing to *get it*, girl," Calvin muttered to the screen.

He scanned down Stacey's page, clicking farther and farther down her history of statuses and photos and likes until he realized he was stiff from not moving in his seat. All the eye strain wasn't getting him anywhere. She'd told him once that she was careful about what she put on her social network pages because her father kept a close watch on those things.

She had a page on an artists' website where she posted her drawings. He'd looked at those images before, but scanned through them again to see if anything strange jumped out at him. Fantasy art, realistic drawings of people she knew and singers she liked, and some school projects. If Stacey used her art to reveal something deep about herself, the symbolism eluded Calvin.

Calvin blew all the air out of his lungs and slid the cursor back to the search bar. His knee jiggled under the desk. His eyes burned and his head hurt. He took another long drink then typed in the only word he knew would give him solid information.

Anorecsia.

Did you mean: **anorexia** the search engine asked.

"Shhh-oot. Yes . . ." Calvin clicked to continue.

The search engine found millions of links. Millions! Websites for medical information and recovery programs. YouTube videos. Blogs and Wikipedia. Where could he begin? Which one of these sites would tell him whether or not his girlfriend actually *had* it?

He clicked on the most official-looking link on the first page. Calvin shifted in his seat and leaned close to the computer screen to read the web page, a column of small text with ads on both sides. The small black type on the white background soon had him seeing double, and his mind stumbled and skimmed over the medical terms.

"Ugh, this isn't working."

Videos on YouTube would be easier. Calvin blinked back the

sleepiness searing his eyes and reached for headphones toward the back corner of the desk. His knuckles bumped something, which clattered to the floor. Papers fluttered after it.

"Crud." He leaned sideways and gathered what papers he could see then slipped the untidy pile back onto the desk. He found the headphones on the floor and put them on.

He searched "anorexia" on YouTube, spelling it right this time. Three hundred thousand results came back. Wow. Rubbing his jaw, Calvin clicked on the first one.

Bones. With pale, sagging skin draped over them.

Accompanied by moody piano music, the pictures shifted, one to the next. Models with knobby knees and rail-thin arms. Women in bikinis with ribs rippling down their torsos. A naked woman with her back to the camera, her shoulder blades and each bone in her spine casting deep shadows. Not Stacey. She didn't look anything like that. She—

"Calvin Thomas!"

He jumped and the headphones jerked halfway off his head. He spun in the chair to face his sister.

"What are you doing?" Peyton cried. In the dim light from the computer screen, her face looked like a specter. "Ca—Are you looking at pornography?"

"No! I'm—" He spun around and click-click-clicked until everything was gone. "I couldn't sleep. I'm just looking at videos of— for—um ..."

"Uh-uh. I saw what you were looking at. How could you? Oh, this is gonna kill Mom."

He threw the headphones on the desk and stood. "Don't say anything to her. It wasn't porn."

"Really? You had your face practically plastered to the screen, and I know I saw a naked woman."

Calvin grabbed his hair with both hands. "Be quiet! Look, I promise I wasn't doing anything wrong."

Peyton crossed her arms in front of her baggy pajamas. "Calvin, I know you've had a hard time since Michael died—"

"It has nothing to do with Michael!" Calvin caught his breath, realizing he'd almost shouted. *Way to go, moron.* "I was ... researching something."

"What?"

He stared at his sister. The one person in the house he might have talked to about his problems with Stacey, and here she stood judging him, convinced he'd been looking at pornography. She wouldn't believe him now even if he told her the truth.

Probably because it wasn't true. Stacey didn't look anything like those emaciated women.

He stood firm. "Psychology project. Eating disorders."

Peyton tilted her head. "Calvin, don't lie to me. Just yesterday you said you didn't have any homework over spring break. Besides, I saw your last progress report. You're not even taking psychology."

His panic turned like a shifting whirlwind, getting darker and more violent. Worst grades of his life last semester, and Peyton was poking her nose into his private stuff. "What were you doing looking at my progress report?"

"Mom left it on the desk."

"It's none of your business."

"It is my business. You're my brother—"

"You've got no right to judge me about anything like you're so perfect."

"Don't make this about me. You're the one looking at porn."

"And what were you doing that time you were out all night with Ryan, Miss Abstinence-Until-Marriage."

Her eyes widened. He'd got her.

"You just ... worry about yourself," she stammered.

"Good advice. Why don't you take it?"

A door opened. Someone walked through the living room—Calvin could guess who by the heavy thud of his footsteps.

"What's going on in here?" Dad asked.

Calvin glared at Peyton and shook his head. "Don't," he whispered.

Peyton sighed. She turned her head to speak over her shoulder. "I heard noises. Calvin was messing around on the computer."

"It's almost two thirty. Both o' y'all get to bed. We got church in the morning."

Calvin followed Peyton upstairs. At the door of the room she shared with Lizzie, Peyton whirled to face him. "Don't think you can get away with it again."

"Oh, right. Yeah. I'll remember that. Thanks, *Mom*."

"Calvin—"

"Whatever. I didn't do anything wrong." He angled past her and headed up another flight of narrow, steep stairs to the partially finished attic room he'd shared with Michael. The plywood floor creaked beneath his feet and the bed thumped and rattled as he fell into it.

Calvin stared at the roof joists, his eyeballs throbbing and his limbs trembling. As the minutes passed, marked by the chirruping of frogs outside, his anger faded but was replaced by fear. He was afraid to sleep, afraid to dream, afraid of nightmare visions of bones with Stacey's face.

Chapter 7

Calvin leaned toward the bathroom mirror as if a closer view would help him figure out what he was doing wrong. His tie never looked right when he knotted it himself. The cone-shaped part always ended up lopsided.

He straightened and sighed at his reflection. Clean, presentable. Exhausted.

Ghosts of his nightmares flitted before his eyes. Skinny girls with smiling mouths and hollow stomachs. Nothing even remotely pornographic about them. The images were scary, like staring at death with the flesh still on.

Calvin swallowed a taste like sour milk.

If Peyton had looked on for a half second longer, she would have known the truth. And she might be helping him, instead of holding an accusation like blackmail over his head.

Sounds of his family getting ready for church filtered through the bathroom door. Lizzie's whine could cut through a concrete wall.

Calvin ran a comb under the faucet and slicked his curly hair back from his face. It wouldn't stay that way, but at least Mom wouldn't fuss at him for a while.

Someone slapped the other side of the door. "Hurry up in there! I gotta go," Zachary yelled.

"Go in Mom and Dad's bathroom."

"Cal-vi-i-in!"

Envisioning the boy dancing from one foot to another and holding himself, Calvin groaned and gave up. His brother pushed past him before he had the door all the way open.

Looking the best he could manage for the formal Easter Sunday service, Calvin carried his suit jacket and dress shoes downstairs. He plopped onto the sagging cushions of the living room couch, and then his eyes were drawn to the flag. Again. Strangely, though, the flag didn't punch him in the gut this time. It felt ... normal. It belonged. He understood it. Unlike the new burden on his heart that was flashing horror movie images into his brain. Could one problem make the other one fade?

No, not right. Nothing would make him stop missing his brother.

Calvin focused his mind on stringing new laces into his shoes, replacing the ones Scamp had chewed.

Mom came out of her bedroom, the floral smell of her perfume advancing before her. She swung to the foot of the stairs. "Y'all hurry up. We are *not* going to be late for Easter service."

Peyton came downstairs with Lizzie two steps behind. "Ryan is on his way. I'm riding with him."

One problem solved. Ryan would distract Peyton during church.

Lizzie dropped to the floor in front of Calvin and stuck her face under the coffee table. "Mo-om! Where are my sandals?"

"Wherever you left them," Mom said, rattling around in her purse for something. "Where in the world are my keys?"

"Wherever you left them," Lizzie muttered.

Calvin grunted. *Good one, Lizzie.*

His sister slapped the coffee table and stood. "I left them right here by the couch. Calvin, did you do something with my sandals?"

He scrunched up his face. "I didn't touch your stinky sandals."

"Shut up. They are not stinky."

Dad's heavy tread thumped the floor behind the couch. "Y'all stop arguing. You'll upset your mama." He followed Mom into the kitchen. "Babe, help me with this tie, will you?"

Upstairs, a little-boy voice bellowed, *"Cowabunga!"*

The distinct hollow sound of a bouncing ball struck the steps three times. Calvin turned his head in time to see a soccer ball rebound off the last step then come down on top of Mom's antique curio cabinet. Everything inside the curio tinkled and rattled. A bronze horse figurine tipped off the top and thudded to the floor. A stack of mail fluttered down after it.

"What was that?" Mom shouted. She rounded the corner from the kitchen.

"Nothing broke," Jacob called.

"Jacob! How many times have I told you not to throw footballs, basketballs, baseballs, volleyballs, soccer balls, hockey pucks, Frisbees, or foosballs in the house?"

"A hundred and eleven?" Jacob's voice faded as he dashed into some hiding place upstairs.

An involuntary grin came to Calvin's tight lips. Laughing would guarantee a smack on the back of his head.

Michael would have loved it.

Calvin missed laughter.

Mom muttered to herself as she checked the curio contents and bent to retrieve the figurine. "Lizzie, did you get your baby sister dressed?"

"Yes, Mom. She's in her playpen. I still can't find my sandals."

Zachary, smartly dressed in a pale yellow shirt and a purple-and-gold–striped clip-on tie, came into the room and threw himself onto the couch beside Calvin. Grinning, he raised a finger to his lips to signal Calvin's silence.

Having restored everything to its proper place on the curio,

Mom turned. She sighed and rolled her eyes toward the ceiling. "Elizabeth, your sandals are on top of the drapery rod."

Lizzie whirled toward the windows and gasped. "Zachary!"

"Ha, ha!" Zachary rolled off the couch and crawled under an end table to escape his enraged sister.

Lizzie climbed on Dad's recliner to retrieve her sandals while Zachary ran outside. Yapping, Scamp dashed out behind Zachary before the screen door smacked the frame. Jacob appeared at the foot of the stairs. Still in his underwear. Silence fell for a single breath.

"Oh, dear Lord, have mercy on this family," Mom said in a tone that sounded nothing like a prayer. "Calvin, would you *please* get the rest of the kids into the van while I dress this child?"

Calvin bounded up. He grabbed Mom's keys off the end table — where she had left them after her third trip to the grocery store yesterday. "Everyone, in the van. Lizzie, get Emily."

"Ooh, thinks he's the boss now," Lizzie cooed, "like he's just so perfect."

"Not," Peyton muttered as she beat him to the front door.

"Wow. We're all just *so* holy, aren't we?" Calvin thudded across the porch behind her.

Inside the house, Jacob wailed, Mom complained, and Dad barked short commands. Calvin searched for Zachary under the front porch. He could guess what Mom would say about the kid's soiled church clothes. He didn't want to think about what she'd say if Peyton ratted on him about what she thought she'd seen last night. *Happy Easter.*

○ ○ ○ ○ ○

Piano notes echoed sweetly through the sanctuary and a hundred voices lifted to the ceiling. *Alleluia, He is risen, Alleluia.* Calvin sang half-heartedly. He glanced at Peyton, who was standing at the other end of their pew, and caught her staring. Probably thinking he was a hypocrite for singing at all.

The hymn ended and a woman stood to sing a solo. Calvin sat down while attempting to arrange his khaki slacks. The hand-me-downs from Michael were already too small. When the hymn moved into an instrumental part, Calvin leaned toward his father to whisper, "Can I borrow the truck this afternoon?"

Dad kept his eyes forward. "Where you going?"

"To see Stacey."

"Easter. We spend it as a family. And she should be with hers."

Calvin huffed and settled back against the wooden pew. Stacey had said her parents went to church twice a year — Easter and Christmas. Maybe. Would they be bothered if their daughter went out this afternoon?

Dad coughed, his fist against his mouth. "You can see her tomorrow. Think we need to talk later this afternoon, you and me."

A warning stiffened Calvin's spine. Had Peyton said something to Dad? Calvin stared at the singer, tried to look like he was listening.

He barely heard the words.

After the service and the holiday greetings with other church members — the pastor and his wife, other elders of the church, and Mom's friends in the women's group along with a few regular customers from Dad's automotive shop — Calvin's family tumbled out to the parking lot and loaded into Mom's nine-passenger van. Calvin sat in the back seat with Lizzie. All the way home, the boys in the middle row played some distorted version of rock-paper-scissors, which always seemed to favor Zachary and brought Jacob to whining tears again.

Sitting next to Calvin, Lizzie dug in her purse for something then gave up with a sigh. "I heard Dad say he wanted to talk to you. You in trouble?"

Calvin guessed she couldn't find her iPod to shut out the noise and decided to talk to him instead. Nice. He answered with a shrug.

"Want to hide in my room? He'll never look for you there."

Calvin grunted. "Tempting. If I can stand an overdose of boy band singers. Pro'bly get a rash."

Lizzie's chin jutted upward with her snort. "You could learn a few things from those guys."

"Like what? How to make tweenie girls sigh? I could get arrested for that. Child endangerment."

"You wish. You're the least dangerous guy I know."

He resisted a smile. "Think so? We'll see."

"Don't even think about it."

Calvin looked out the side window like he was too cool for the conversation. "It's on now, sister."

She groaned. "See if I try to be nice to you again."

o O O O o

Easter supper happened early in the afternoon, with grandparents, aunts and uncles, and some cousins joining them. Vegetable casseroles and creamy salads surrounded Mom's roast lamb on the table, and everyone served themselves buffet style. Calvin filled his plate like all the others, but stared at it for a long time. His stomach rumbled. His mouth watered. His mind argued that the food would taste delicious and make him happy, but his heart wouldn't let him take more than a few bites.

Was Stacey doing the same? Is this what she felt when she sat down to a meal? Perched on the front steps with his plate on his knees, Calvin tried to analyze the reasons for his lack of appetite. It was just feeling sad and worried, right? He'd yet to hear anyone mention Michael's name, but his absence created a gaping hole. Added to that, the problem with Stacey kept tugging at his thoughts, no matter what he did. And the sight of Peyton with her fiancé—who somehow was excluded from the "family only" regulation — acting as if nothing had happened last night set Calvin's anger on a low simmer. It was enough stuff to kill anyone's appetite.

What was Stacey upset about? What wasn't she telling him?

Yeah, secrets. That's what I needed to be thinking about right now.

He made himself finish the food on his plate, so he wouldn't offend any of the chefs. Aunt Sally, who'd brought her "famous" butternut squash casserole, would take it quite personally if she didn't go home tonight with a bowl scraped clean of every last bit of baked-on cheese.

Inside the house, the kids were crashing or cranky from too much Easter basket candy, and the adults were settling down in every available chair with loosened belts and half-lidded eyes. Calvin disposed of his plastic plate and drink cup and headed toward the stairs. Maybe he could disappear into his room and no one would notice.

A seven-year-old cousin foiled his plan. Her blonde hair a wild halo about her head, Morgan ran up and attached herself to Calvin's leg. "Take me for a ride on your bike, pleeeeese!"

He clasped her little hands to gently peel her off. "Sorry, baby girl. Bike's busted."

A much larger hand clamped down on his shoulder. "Yeah, let's go out to the workshop and talk about that, buddy."

No escape. Calvin ruffled the little girl's hair and dragged himself outside behind his father.

In the workshop, Dad fiddled with a wrench as he rested his backside against the worktable and began the parental interrogation. "Kinda concerned about you, bud. Everything okay?"

Calvin shoved his hands into his pockets and stared at the tarp-covered Mustang. "Yeah."

"School? Doin' any better?"

Not up to his "full potential." He'd heard the speech before. Last fall he'd signed up for the toughest classes of his life but botched the first semester because he had to deal with a funeral. Things hadn't improved much since then.

"I'll get through it," he said.

"I know ... it's tough. But you gotta find a way to make it work. If you want to get into college—"

"I know, Dad."

Dad hummed and made fleshy tapping noises with the wrench in his hands. "What else is going on?"

Calvin turned sideways, taking in his bike sitting near the wall. The Yamaha looked tired. Lonely, dull, like a stray dog hiding in the shadows, remembering the days when someone loved him. Its chrome didn't pick up any reflection from the daylight just a few feet away.

Calvin swallowed. He grabbed at his ready excuse. "I gotta find another throttle cable."

"I hear ya. Mike had trouble finding parts for his car too. But that ol' bike ... Don't know you can find too many parts for it anymore. Might have to let it go, I'm afraid."

Calvin snapped his head up to look at his father. "I'll get one. Somehow."

Dad's expression—not quite scowling, but almost—told Calvin he didn't call him into the workshop to talk about Michael's classic car or a broken-down motorcycle. "Cal, what happened last night?"

"Nothing."

"Son—"

"I couldn't sleep, so I came down to use the computer. Peyton thought she saw something, but she didn't. And she wouldn't believe me when I told her it was nothing."

Because he'd panicked and clicked away from everything, like any guilty person would.

"What did she see?"

"Ah ... I don't know." He reached up toward his hair then dropped his hand and slapped his thigh. Just like a guilty person would. "A popup ad. A woman in a bathing suit. I can't control stuff that pops up. I was looking for motorcycle parts."

Dad drew a slow breath through his mouth then blew it out. "Motorcycle parts. Yeah, they got some raunchy stuff on some of them sites."

"Yes, they do. But Peyton wouldn't believe me, and she started screeching and woke you up."

"She can be a little high-strung."

Calvin thrust two index fingers toward his father. "Exactly."

"Why couldn't you sleep? Something bugging you?"

"The bike! Tyler and Flannery want to go riding this week."

"Hmm. Your mama said Stacey got sick yesterday."

Calvin jiggled his head. Switch gears. He'd spent more time that morning thinking about how to defend himself than what he could say about the truth.

"I-I don't know. She's just ... sick lately. She almost passed out at school Thursday."

Dad's eyes narrowed and he tilted his head. Suspicious questions were coming. "She pregnant?"

Calvin gulped and choked on air tainted with motor-oil stink. "Dad—no. No. That's not even possible. Besides, she's losing weight, not—"

Female problems? Passing out, throwing up—not possible. No way. Not unless she had some other guy ... No. Not possible.

"You can tell me the truth, son."

This can't be happening.

"I am!" He took a step toward the bike, turned back, wished he could feel the throttle in his hand and the wind in his face. Anything but standing here telling his father he was being honest when he couldn't be fully honest because ... because he just didn't know. That was the truth. He didn't know for sure what was wrong with

Stacey. Maybe she had cancer or something. Could he talk about that before he knew for sure?

"Dad, we're not having sex, and I'm not looking at pornography. I promise. Yeah, I'm still having a hard time with stuff because of Michael. But that's it! All I want to do is fix my bike and go riding."

Dad narrowed his eyes and moved his jaw like he was rolling tobacco around his mouth, a habit he'd given up years ago. "Hmm. All right. I believe you."

Okay, just breathe now. "Thanks."

"Think Dave Moore will be able to get you a cable?"

"Hope so. He found me some brake pads on eBay last time." He turned toward the bike and allowed himself to tug on his hair. Stupid habit. "I just want one more season with the bike. You know?"

Dad's hand settled on his shoulder again. "I hear you. Listen, son ... sorry 'bout this, but I need you to work the fields for me this week. Joe at the shop has taken sick and he might need surgery. That means I can't take time off to do the planting."

Rainbow colors shimmered and swirled behind Calvin's closed eyelids. Roast lamb and butternut squash casserole felt too heavy in his gut.

"I know it's your break from school," Dad went on, "But I don't know when Joe's going to be good to come back to work, and that cotton needs to get put in the ground. Now, I figure you can take one day off, maybe two if you push it."

"Stacey ..." Calvin muttered.

"You can see her in the evenings. Your girl has got to understand, we work this farm as a family."

We? This year, apparently, it'd be all Calvin. He'd eat up his whole spring break working alone. Just him and the rumbling tractor and the squawking crows.

Kill me just a little bit more, Dad.

Chapter 8

Tyler laughed about something. From her location in the back-seat, Stacey couldn't tell if Calvin responded. With the throb-bing bass of Tyler's rear speakers and the muscle-car roar of the Camaro's engine, whatever the guys said didn't reach Stacey's ears. Maybe they'd forgotten about her.

They cruised through downtown Bentley, past the hundred-year-old storefronts, the police station, and the country café with its collection of teapots in the windows and rocking chairs out front. Some of the doors were open, inviting in the fresh air and bright sunlight of a perfect spring day.

Perfect for motorcycle riding, as a herd of noisy bikes going the other way demonstrated. Maybe that explained why Calvin wasn't saying much. He'd rather be on his motorcycle than watching other people ride theirs. But that didn't justify his absolute silence about what happened Saturday. He hadn't responded to her email either — the one that had kept her awake all Saturday night and fidgeting through the day on Sunday, unable to concentrate on the sermon at the church Mom found in Clarksville, unable to touch the dried-up turkey breast she made for dinner.

Calvin's silence screamed in Stacey's heart. She'd told him to trust her, to not press for explanations. She didn't mean that he shouldn't talk to her at all! Finally, this morning, he called and simply invited her to hang out with him and Tyler. Like nothing had happened. Just an ordinary day off school.

Anxiety fluttered through her like a wild thing caged in her chest. Her arms ached to reach around the leather bucket seat and shake him.

A poorly maintained set of railroad tracks sent a violent rattle up Stacey's tailbone and made her head flop around.

"Ty-y-ler! I'm back here, you know." She pushed hair out of her face.

"Sorry." He turned his eyes toward her in the rearview mirror. "Those tracks are killer."

"Try slowing down next time."

"I did slow down. I—Whatever."

Though the music continued at the same volume, a kind of heavy silence permeated the car. Neither boy spoke or looked at her. She was an intruder into their sacred guy time and she'd dared to complain. Why did Calvin even invite her?

Stacey pulled her knees up. Holding her cell phone in the space between her thighs and stomach, Stacey typed out a text message to Zoe.

Help. I'm going crazy.

They crossed the four-lane intersection where downtown Bentley officially ended. The Camaro zoomed along country roads, and with the acceleration came wind whipping through the open front windows that tossed Stacey's hair into her face again. She barely heard Zoe's text coming back.

Sup?

Stacey scrunched herself into a ball as her thumbs flew over the letters.

*I'm trapped in a metal cage with two gorgeous guys and
neither one is paying attention to me.*

Zoe's answer came back quickly.

Kinky why dint u nvite me?

Stacey pressed the back of her hand against her smile. Zoe was
always good for a laugh. Before Stacey could answer, another text
came through.

Wat guys?

Calvin and Tyler

The CD ended, and in silence Zoe's answer came back. At the
chirping message alert, Tyler's eyes flicked to the rearview mirror
again. Stacey stared back at him, wanting to stick out her tongue.

tyler dorset is hot!!! dont u dare tell hm

Stacey snorted. Oh, evil! "Someone thinks you're hot, Tyler."
That had his eyes dancing back and forth. "Who?"
"It's a secret. I can't tell you."
His big white teeth appeared in the mirror. Thousands of dollars
in orthodontics had gone into that amazing smile.
Stacey's phone chirped again.

Hes 2 preppy tho

Tyler muttered something to Calvin, the words lost to the wind.
Calvin snapped off his seat belt and twisted around, making a grab
for her phone. Stacey squealed and jerked away. The cell phone
fell to the floorboards, and they both scrambled to get it. Stacey's
hand found the phone first, but Calvin's fingers changed course and
found her ribs.

"No-no—Ah!" She fought against the giggles and Calvin's
tickling.

He overpowered her, snatched the phone away, and flopped back into his seat. Stacey tried to reach around him, but her seat belt restrained her, giving Calvin the time he needed to check out the phone.

"Zoe," he announced.

Tyler groaned.

Calvin reached over his shoulder to pass the phone back. Stacey snatched it from him then looked out the window at a tractor rumbling through an open field. The game wasn't fun anymore.

Tyler made a left turn while Stacey typed another message.

Calvin hasn't said a word about my email.

Jerk

Stop it. He's not a jerk. Maybe he didn't get it.

Or maybe he was making a point of giving her just what she'd asked for, punishing her for telling him not to bother her.

Talk about a plan backfiring.

Tyler turned onto a driveway between two concrete eagle statues. In the center of the wide front lawn, large rocks bordered a circular garden filled with daffodils and decorative birdhouses on stakes. Winter pansies still bloomed in twin planters on either side of the beveled-glass door of the ranch-style house. The homey country feel stopped at the carport, where at least three motorcycles shared the space with a massive clutter of parts and equipment. Another metal carport in the side yard sheltered an RV.

Flannery Moore's house. Lovely.

Stacey sent Zoe a final text:

We've breached enemy territory. TTYL.

She glanced at Zoe's response as she followed Tyler and Calvin up the driveway.

show no mercy luv u

The filthy stench of gasoline and motor oil in the carport made Stacey wrinkle her nose and look away. Didn't that smell drift into the house?

Flannery came out the side door, barefoot and wearing short-shorts. Her sleeveless top rode up her torso as she slung her arms over Tyler's shoulders for a quick hug. She didn't pull the blouse down before turning to Calvin.

Temptress. Tease. Polite words weren't strong enough.

Smile. Don't cause trouble.

Flannery glanced at Stacey then gave Calvin a tamer sideways hug. Would the girl jump on Calvin too if his girlfriend weren't there? Stacey forced a smile and waved.

Flannery waved back. "How's it going, Stace?"

Fine. Good. If I could be anywhere but here. Stacey merely nodded.

"How's the bike running?" Tyler gestured toward a yellow moto-cross bike near the brick wall of the house.

"Great. Y'all bring your gear? No extra bikes right now, but we can take turns on mine."

"In the trunk," Tyler said.

They were going riding? Calvin had failed to mention that detail. Stacey crossed her arms and pivoted toward the front yard.

"Stace?" His voice was near her shoulder.

"Yes, my love," she sang.

"I brought the extra helmet for you. Want to try again?"

She raised one shoulder. "I'm not dressed for riding. Besides, I can't ride the ..." She swung a hand toward the carport. "... the motocross bike. I can't even sit on it."

She could sit on Calvin's old Yamaha, but the seats of the newer bikes were ridiculously high. How did any of them — except for lanky Tyler — hold those bikes upright? Calvin had explained about necessary ground clearance and such, but didn't they have to put their feet down sometimes?

"Dave's got an ATV you can drive. I'll show you how."

She nudged a weed in the still-brown lawn with her toe.

"Stace? Is that okay?" he asked.

"Whatever. I just didn't know we were going riding."

He put an arm around her shoulders. "We don't have to. We always bring the gear to Flannery's, just in case."

She met his placating smile with one of her own.

"Last time we came over, Dave had an '09 Street Bob he picked up at an auction. It was for the shop, but he let us take it up and down the street."

"A what?"

"Harley." Calvin grinned. "I think Tyler fell in love that day."

Stacey laughed appropriately. She took a long breath of untainted air then turned back to the carport. Tyler and Flannery stood near another motorcycle that looked to be half the size of her car. White metalflake with as much chrome as paint.

A woman in tight jeans and a T-shirt with the words *Riding for the Son* printed on the front appeared in the carport. A faded tattoo peeked above the neck of the shirt. Easy to envision Flannery's mother in black leather with her long red hair braided and a bandana wrapped around her head, straddling a loud motorcycle. Today, however, she had a dishtowel in her hands.

"Y'all hungry? I bought some watermelon this morning. You can eat it on the table out back"

None for me, thanks. The words stood ready to spring from Stacey's lips before her brain surged into action. Watermelon: only thirty-seven calories in a serving. It was a guilt-free food, as long as she didn't pig out—which she would have gleefully done a year ago.

Stacey went to the backyard and sat down at a picnic table on the patio. Flannery sat *on* the table, like a guy, beside Tyler, who'd straddled the bench. How could she be so pretty yet so clueless? Or was she making a point by sitting with her back turned toward Stacey?

Mrs. Moore brought out a whole watermelon cut into four pieces. Apparently that was her definition of cut up. She handed Stacey a spoon. "Here you go, baby doll."

Baby doll? After a second of staring, Stacey took the spoon. "Thank you, Mrs. Moore."

"No need to be formal here, honey. You can call me Patty."

No, she couldn't.

The woman left spoons and paper towels and a salt shaker for anyone who wanted it, and went back into the house. Flannery shifted sideways to eat, but apparently saw nothing wrong with having her butt on the table at the same time. Stacey's appetite for the watermelon sagged.

Calvin scooped up a huge chunk and shoveled it into his mouth. "So, Flan, can we go see your dad today? I want to ask him if he could rig up a throttle cable for me."

"You busted your throttle cable?" Flannery held a piece of watermelon halfway between the table and her mouth.

"Yeah ..."

So Calvin hadn't spilled his troubles out to Flannery over the weekend. Good. Stacey carved out a sliver of melon that nestled perfectly in the bowl of her spoon. Maybe Flannery could take notes.

"Sure, we can go." Flannery chomped then dug in for another bite. But she dropped her spoon back, and juice splashed onto the picnic table. "Oh, hey! I meant to tell you. There's a bike at the shop you've *got* to see. Would be just right for you."

Calvin groaned softly. "I can't afford a new bike."

"Talk to your parents. Maybe they'd let you make payments. Or maybe they'll be really sweet and buy it for you for your birthday."

Calvin huffed. "Yeah, right."

Was the girl completely clueless? She had to know that Calvin's family didn't have a lot of money. Maybe Stacey had misjudged the depth of their friendship.

Calvin's misery killed Stacey's moment of triumph. She slipped her hand around him, cupped the gentle outward curve of his waist.

"How do you know unless you ask?" Flannery pressed.

Calvin winced. Stacey caressed his side and leaned her cheek toward his shoulder. At the same time she angled her face to lock eyes with Flannery. *Shut up, girl.*

Flannery tilted her head. "What?"

"Leave him alone."

"Huh? What's wrong with me talking to him about a bike?"

"Open your eyes. Can't you see he's upset about the one he's got?"

Flannery threw her hands out, and her eyes flashed. "Hey, I'm trying to help him feel better."

"Stop it." Calvin surged to his feet but wobbled between the table and the bench.

Stacey tried to reclaim her hold on him. "Calvin—"

"Just forget it, okay? I'll be right back." He stepped over the bench and crossed the concrete patio to the back of the house. He eased open the sliding glass as if he was trying not to make any noise. Deliberate movements. Maybe so he wouldn't slam it.

"Nice. Good job, y'all," Tyler muttered.

Stacey turned in time to see Flannery wilt. Yet the glare didn't leave the girl's eyes.

Though her fingers trembled, Stacey picked up her spoon and watermelon, which she could only stare at.

Flannery straightened her back, which meant that long spine and the sliver of flesh above her jeans was all Stacey could see. "We talk about bikes all the time. Why is that suddenly wrong?"

Tyler sighed and turned his gaze in the direction of the RV. "It isn't. Picking a fight is."

"I didn't pick a fight. She basically told me to shut up."

She. Like she wasn't sitting there looking at that girl's back. Like her opinion didn't matter. Like she didn't belong with them at all. Her presence alone had caused conflict.

Tyler's voice murmured in Stacey's brain, but she couldn't grasp it. She mustered all her will into moving gracefully as she stood and negotiated the bench. "Maybe I should go home."

"Stace, come on. Don't be like that," Tyler said.

She raised a palm toward him. "It's okay. Y'all are here to talk about motorcycles, and I don't even ride one."

"You're here because Calvin wants you here. Don't—" Tyler bounded up and came around the table. He caught her by the shoulders. "Don't make it any worse, okay?"

Stacey trembled beneath the pressure of his hands. "Why is this my fault? Why am I the odd person out?"

"You're not, and it isn't. It's just ..." His eyes shifted from her face, almost like the words he wanted were printed in the air behind her. "I don't even know what this argument is about. It, like, came out of nowhere."

She tilted her chin up. "Calvin's upset because he doesn't know how he's going to get parts for his bike. And his family doesn't have the money to buy him a new one."

"That's not ... quite the whole story, but—" Tyler sighed. "Look, why can't we all just have a good time today. No stress. Okay?"

"Calvin asked to go to the shop," Flannery cut in. "So I thought we were talking about bikes. She's the one—"

"Shut up!" Tyler snagged a napkin from the table, wadded it, and tossed it at Flannery's face. It bounced onto her plate.

Stacey crossed her arms and turned toward the house.

"Come on." Tyler touched Stacey's shoulder again. "Let's sit back down and pretend none of this happened. Just be cool, okay?"

Stacey settled back on the bench and stared at a crack in the concrete. As they waited silently for Calvin to come back outside, video clips of the argument replayed in Stacey's mind. Flannery had to know Calvin's parents couldn't buy him a new bike. Yet what did Tyler say? That it wasn't the entire reason? Did Tyler know something that neither Flannery nor Stacey knew? Had something happened over the weekend that Calvin was keeping from her?

Bro-friend before girlfriend.

She blinked at tears, forcing them back just as she heard the patio door slide open behind her. She swung off her seat and went to his side to take his hand. "I'm sorry, babe. I didn't mean to upset you."

He shrugged. "I'm not upset. I had to go to the bathroom."

"Oh." *Pretend nothing happened ... That's what Tyler said.*

"Hey, I just want to eat this watermelon, go to the cycle shop, and have some fun with my girlfriend and two best friends on my one and only day off this week. Is that okay?"

She licked her lips. A little sweetness from her two bites of watermelon lingered there. She forced a smile, pretended nothing was wrong.

"'Kay."

○ ○ ○ ○ ○

"Dude, check it out." Flannery slung her leg over the narrow seat of a bright blue motocross bike. "A 2012 Yamaha YZ250, practically brand new. Soon as I saw it, I thought, that's Calvin's bike. No doubt."

Stacey walked with Calvin up the aisle of the motorcycle shop. The moment the bike was in front of them, Calvin's grip on her hand slackened, and he brushed his fingers along one of the silver levers on the handlebars. Stacey looked down at the aggressive-looking lines of the front fender and the square treads of the tire, then up at the smile spreading on Calvin's lips. Maybe Flannery was right; motorcycles were Calvin's cure.

Which meant Stacey had guessed wrong. The thought stabbed her as Calvin squeezed the lever against the grip.

Flannery got off the bike. "Have a seat."

He released the lever like it had sprung back on him. "Thanks, but, uh ... no. I'll fall in love with it and be depressed because I can't ride it."

Flannery's shoulders slumped.

"Maybe later. I'm just going ..." Calvin took a step back and pointed toward the sales counter. "I need to talk to your dad about my throttle cable."

He tugged Stacey along. Another customer stood at the counter, so Stacey wrapped both her hands around Calvin's one and brought him to a stop. "It's okay. You can sit on the bike if you want."

"I can't afford it."

Something like inspiration flickered through her mind. She smiled. "Do you feel you're betraying your old motorcycle by looking at a new one?"

Calvin's eyes widened. "Huh?"

She gave a coy shrug. "It's kind of sweet. Being loyal to your first bike."

He laughed. Much better!

Calvin pulled his hand from her grip and draped his arm across her shoulders. "Actually, it's like I have to choose between going to college or riding motocross or becoming a farm boy."

Too much to process in a rush. "What do you mean?"

He took a deep breath. "The farm and Dad's auto repair place don't bring in enough money for anything extra, including college. That's why Michael joined the service. And that's probably where I'm heading too, unless I want to stay on the farm *and* work with Dad in the shop— which I don't. I mean, it's okay for a summer job, maybe, but ..."

So *that* was what Tyler was hinting at.

"When I told my father I was worried about getting my bike

fixed, he was like, 'Oh well. It's an old bike.' Like it's just over and I should move on with my life. So what if the Yamaha only cost two hundred bucks at somebody's yard sale. It was mine. I got it running again and it was mine. You'd think he'd get that, you know? The way he loves cars and stuff."

"Ouch."

"He and Michael used to go to scrap yards all over the place, looking for parts for the Mustang." Calvin shook his head. "I mean, I know he cares and feels bad, but ..."

Stacey wrapped her arms around him and pressed her cheek to his shoulder. *I get it*, her thoughts cried. *I hear you. Maybe I don't ride motorcycles, but I know exactly how you feel. It's like you want something so bad and then your father shoots it dead with his personal version of reality. I totally get it.*

"Hey there, Cal! Stacey." Dave Moore, Flannery's father, grinned at them across the sales counter. "Ah!" he cried, holding up a finger. He ducked down and then reappeared, flashing a book in the air. "Picked this up off eBay, just for you. Figured you're in here so often looking for parts for that old bike, I ought to have it handy."

Calvin let go of Stacey and moved to the counter. He took the book in his hands. "Yamaha 250DT service manual. Sweet! Thanks, Dave."

"You owe me ten bucks."

Calvin's smile dropped. "Oh ..."

"Nah, don't sweat it, boy. You and Ty are practically family. I ain't worried about it." Mr. Moore winked and nodded his head toward the showroom area. "Hey, Ty! We gonna get you on a street machine today?"

Tyler, sitting astride a gleaming red and chrome motorcycle, flinched as if he'd been caught dipping his fingers in birthday cake icing. "Oh, ah, no. Just ... nice. Nice ride."

"Bring your pa around, I'll make you a deal."

"I'd have to sell my car."

"Is there a question in there somewhere?"

Stacey laughed a little at the joke, although she thought it was possible for Tyler to do just what Mr. Moore suggested, to come in with his father and leave with a new motorcycle, without having to give up a thing.

Calvin leaned his elbows on the parts counter. "I need a new throttle cable. Any chance of finding one?"

"Well, let's see." Mr. Moore made a show of touching his finger to his tongue and flipping the pages in a Yamaha service manual one by one. "Throttle cable, throttle cable. Here it is. Hmm." His face turned serious as he studied a page in the book. Muttering a part number, he turned to a computer. His thick fingers thundered on the keyboard.

Flannery joined them and leaned on the counter with her upper arm pressed against Calvin's. Like she'd forgotten Stacey was there. "Tyler really wants that Street Bob," she muttered.

Calvin turned the service manual around on the counter to look at the page Mr. Moore had left open. "Of course he wants it. It's cool and fast and gorgeous."

Flannery turned to lean her back against the counter. Words passed between the two of them, almost like whispers. Stacey toyed with some bells hanging from a cardboard display. Guardian ride bells. She wondered what they were for while her nerves screamed at the distraction.

Calvin straightened suddenly. "What did you say?"

"Nothing."

"Nuh-uh! I heard y—"

"Shut up, shut up!" Flannery pressed her hand against Calvin's mouth, but he mumbled behind it and his eyes danced with amusement as he tried to back away.

They tussled together, and Mr. Moore jokingly told them children had to behave in his store.

Forgotten and dejected, Stacey wandered away from the counter.

Motorcycles, helmets, clothing, tires and oil, and a wall of gleaming accessories crowded the small shop. The rich scent of leather drew Stacey to a rack of jackets and vests. She found a black fringed vest, too skimpy to be anything more than a sexy showpiece. Would Calvin keep his eyes on her if she wore a vest like that? She looked at the size, at the price tag. Too small and ridiculously expensive.

Tears stung her eyes as she ran leather fringe through her fingers. So not her style, anyway. Nothing here was. And despite her earlier revelation, she could only pretend to understand Calvin's world. What was she doing in this place? How could she hope to fit in?

Calvin came up behind her. "Dave's going to try and find a throttle cable online. He says we might be able to use a 400DT cable. We can clamp it if it's a little long."

Whatever that meant.

Stacey sniffed and blinked at the fluorescent lights overhead. She forced a smile, grabbed the fringed vest off the rack, and held it against her body as she spun around to face Calvin. "Think this would look good on me?"

Calvin's eyebrows shot upward. "Whoa."

She twisted side to side so the fringe swayed. "It could be your birthday present."

Calvin chuckled, and his cheeks reddened. She grabbed his hand, but he laughed and swiveled away. He practically ran from her and then acted like he was interested in riding gloves.

What was up with that? She'd flustered him, for sure, but why couldn't he play along? Maybe because Flannery was so close by?

Dizziness washed over Stacey. Trembling, she hung the vest back on the rack. She wove between the motorcycles, hands at her sides like a tightrope walker, heading for the wide windowsill at the front of the shop where she could sit down until the three motocross soul mates thought to look for her again.

Chapter 9

"I need the phone, Calvin," Lizzie told him for the tenth or twentieth time. She plopped onto a chair at the dining room table and gave him the stare of death.

Hopeless. Calvin rolled his shoulder against the frame of the back door and gazed out at the dark woods beyond the yard. Lightning flickered on the horizon.

"I have to go," he told Stacey for the fifth or sixth time. Maybe more. Calvin was afraid to hang up, but he'd explode if he couldn't get away and catch a breath of air.

Tension had revved between Stacey and Flannery all day long. The drama really came to a head at Oliver's Burgers, where they'd stopped for ice cream. Stacey had nothing. When Flannery said something about it, both girls bared their claws. Then Tyler got into it, and everyone went home angry.

Stacey had called twice during dinner. Mom told her she'd have to wait until seven o'clock—no sooner, no later—when they'd finished eating and the dishes were done. When the phone call finally happened, Stacey spent the entire time in tears. She still wasn't done.

She sniffed. "Forgive me?"

"Yes. I told you. Don't worry about it. Okay?"

"Promise?"

He stifled a groan. "I promise."

What else could he say? Nothing made sense anymore. He either had to forgive her or dump her. The thought of dumping her made him feel like he was having an asthma attack or something.

"Calvin!" Lizzie wailed. "You've had the phone for an hour."

He thumped his fist against the door frame and whirled toward her. "I have not! Give me one more minute, okay? Dang!"

"Ouch! You yelled in my ear," Stacey said.

"Sorry. Look, I gotta go before Lizzie blows a gasket. I'll see you tomorrow, okay? Just you and me."

She sighed. "I love you, Calvin."

"Love you too."

"I couldn't love you more if you stood inside a rainbow."

"Huh?"

"What would that feel like? Standing inside a rainbow?"

"Uh ... wet maybe?" He sensed a drawing coming. Or a poem. "I have to go."

She said I love you again, and finally good-bye. Calvin blew out his breath and let his hand holding the phone fall to his side. Lizzie stood next to him now, palm out, waiting. Calvin set the phone in its cradle on the computer desk just to spite her. He ignored her furious yapping and strode through the living room and out the front door. A rain-scented breeze ruffled his T-shirt across his chest. The porch steps where he liked to sit were soaked, so Calvin slumped into one of Mom's rocking chairs, his knees locked so it wouldn't rock.

Girlfriends were supposed to be fun. Stacey had started out that way. Her quirky way of looking at the world sometimes — *standing inside a rainbow?* — amused him. She couldn't ride a motorcycle, but he could fix that. More importantly, she listened to every word of grief, anger, or misery after Michael was killed, and never judged him even when he cried like a baby. They could sit together and not say a word, if that's what he needed, and he never felt the awkwardness of a person saying they were sorry just because they didn't know what else to say. Stacey always knew the right word and the right thing to do.

Had she suddenly changed and he didn't notice? The weight thing ... he'd just accepted her dietary quirks like all the other unusual things she did. She had all kinds of rules about food, but she'd convinced him there were legitimate reasons for them. Food allergies, too many calories or carbohydrates, studies showing cancer in lab rats—he'd bought it all. But today she'd taken tiny bites of watermelon like she was playing a game rather than eating. Calvin didn't know much about dieting, but he did know watermelon was mostly water, and that meant it wouldn't hurt her to eat it. She didn't make any excuses this time; she just left it sitting on her plate. And he didn't say anything because he just wanted to have fun, not fight. He let it go.

Staring at the black line of the road shining with the rain, Calvin sucked in a breath and held it.

All those boney women in the anorexia videos didn't *suddenly* look that way. They probably started out normal, like Stacey, and over time they managed to get away with eating less and less. They probably made excuses that other people believed, but then got weirder and weirder ... over time.

He didn't want to believe it. What was he supposed to do with an anorexic girlfriend?

Calvin stared toward the sky and said as loudly as he dared, "I just want my happy girlfriend back."

Headlights glistened on the road in front of the house. They approached and slowed, and a car pulled over to park on the grassy shoulder in front of his house. Mrs. Moore's car, which meant the slender silhouette in the driver's seat had to be Flannery.

"More bad news," Calvin muttered.

Hoodie pulled up over her head, Flannery jogged across the yard and vaulted up the steps, then stopped when she saw him in the rocker. She crossed her arms in front of her and gave him a feeble half smile. "Mad at me?"

"Yes."

She raised one shoulder until it almost touched her ear. "I'm sorry. Things got kind of crazy today."

Calvin slumped forward, his hands limp between his knees. "Yeah, tell me about it."

Her sneakers left prints on the porch as she walked over to squat in front of him. "I don't know what happened. She just got on my nerves, I guess."

"Why? What did she do that was so bad?"

He knew the answer. It wasn't one thing Stacey did or didn't do, it was an atmosphere she carried with her. Everything had to be a certain way. Changes to the plan—whatever they might be—upset her. That day the tension had started the moment he and Tyler picked Stacey up at her house in the Camaro, and Calvin flipped the passenger seat forward so she could get into the back. She'd raised her eyebrows at him and heaved a loud sigh as she crawled in. What was he supposed to do? Sit in the back and make out with her while Tyler drove? She couldn't deal with the situation for fifteen minutes while they drove to Flannery's house?

"She doesn't like me," Flannery said. "I can see it every time she looks at me or I say anything to you."

"Funny. She says the same thing about you."

"What have I ever done to her?"

He shook his head. "I don't know."

"What should I do, Cal? Seems like I can't say two words around her without saying something wrong."

"Hey, I'm caught in the middle here. She's my girlfriend; you're my friend. Y'all have to find a way to get along because I am *not* going to choose between you."

Flannery eased down to sit cross-legged on the porch and was quiet for a long time. Calvin relaxed. Even with the day's tension between them, sitting with Flannery was comfortable, like it would be with Tyler. Flannery didn't expect anything from him. And the answers they both wanted had to come from Stacey.

"She loves you," Flannery said.

Calvin sighed. "Yeah ... guess so."

"What? You doubt it?"

He smirked. "No. I know she does. Just seems sort of arrogant to say so, you know?"

She reached out to backhand his shin. "Want to know how I know?"

"Sure."

Flannery uncrossed her legs and effortlessly got to her feet. She tugged something out of her jeans pocket. A tightly folded piece of paper. She handed it to him without opening it. "Read it and weep. I did."

Calvin winced. "Weep? You don't cry over anything. Even when you busted your ribs last year, you didn't cry."

She rolled her eyes and looked away. "This made me teary. A little."

He unfolded the paper. The porch light glanced off numerous creases, making it hard for him to read. Calvin got up and walked closer to the front door.

The fancy writing was unmistakably Stacey's. She'd written another poem. The lines didn't rhyme and didn't have the meter or iambic-whatever he'd learned about in freshman English class. She called the style freeform.

"'Forever tumultuous, my heart. Gushing, spilling over. A violent wave of need crashing inside me.' Flannery, where did you get this?"

"She threw it at you last Thursday. Remember? And you ran off and left it. I saved it for you."

He remembered the wad of paper rebounding off his foot, but he didn't think she'd thrown anything important.

"Read the rest of it," Flannery said.

"'A violent wave of need never quenching the heat that lingers where your fingertips ...'" He slowly inhaled. *This* ... this was what he loved about Stacey. Her depth. The beauty that came out when she created something. The emotion she brought to everything. The way she loved him. And he'd dared to think, for one second, that his life might be better without her?

Calvin swallowed that guilt. "Why did it make you cry?"

Flannery didn't answer. Lightning lit up the yard, turning her into a flickering shadow.

"I should probably head home," she said.

"Wait." He went to stand in front of her. "Why did the poem make you cry?"

"Because. I wish someone loved me like that."

Calvin licked his lips then plunged into a suspicion. "Tyler?"

She flinched. "Not gonna happen, so don't change the subject. Did you look at that poem?"

"I just read it."

"No, I mean the shape. Stacey doesn't do anything unintentionally. I know that much about her. She made the words look like a woman."

Calvin looked again. "Oh! That's so cool!"

"No, it isn't. Open your eyes. That's a *fat* woman. And what does she need so much? This 'violent wave' or whatever she called it. That's not exactly love language."

"But you just said—"

"I know what I said. Listen to me now. There's something going on with Stacey. Something she's trying to say without saying it outright. And I'll bet you anything it has to do with the way she diets all the time." Flannery jabbed her finger at the paper.

Calvin edged back from her. "Maybe she's just thinking of, like, water and heat ..."

"I'm looking at more than just the poem, Cal. I'm looking at how emotional she is all the time. I mean, what would make her think there's something going on between you and me?"

He chuckled, although he felt anything but humor. "Wow, thanks. Now I know where I rank with you."

"Oh, stop it. You know what I mean. When we were at Oliver's, I just commented that she didn't order anything, and she totally flipped out. And she was running her hands all up and down your arm like she was showing me you belonged to her. Calvin, something's going on."

He pressed his lips in a firm line to stop the quivering he felt inside. Flannery wasn't telling him anything new, but he didn't want to face it. In his gut, he knew it would be a battle. He'd already lost the first skirmishes.

He dragged air into his lungs but couldn't ease the tension in his shoulders. "Flan ... I don't know what to do."

Flannery twisted her mouth to the side and looked away. Rain fell a bit harder on the metal roof above their heads. He shouldn't keep her there, forcing her to drive home in a thunderstorm. Yet Calvin wanted to grab Flannery's arm and ask her for help. She was a girl. She would know things. She could help him figure all this out.

"What should I do?" he asked weakly.

She shrugged. "You've got to talk to her. Find out what's going on."

"I've tried."

"Try harder. If you care about her, do whatever you have to."

Whatever he had to do. What did that mean? Calvin stared at the rain hitting the porch rail. A chill intensified the trembling inside him until it erupted in a violent shudder.

"What are you thinking?" Flannery asked.

He forced himself to move, to shove his hands into his pockets and lift his head higher. "That I need to be like Michael now. Really strong. I gotta do what I gotta do. Because ... because I'm not going to lose her. I can't lose another person in my life."

Chapter 10

"He's been so sweet lately," Stacey said. "Well, you know, he's always sweet! But the last few days he's been especially ... sweet. He came over every night, even though he was tired. We just sat and talked for hours—"

"Ugh, don't tell me anymore!" Zoe jiggled her head and shook her hands as if throwing off the clinging germs of something disgusting. Her purse slipped off her shoulder as a result. She yanked it back up and stepped toward the window of a women's clothing store.

"Hey, *you* asked me how things were going." Stacey followed her, but faced Zoe rather than the mannequins in the window display. Sunlight bouncing off the windshield of a car in the parking lot blinded her for a moment. She raised a hand to shield her eyes.

"Yeah, I did. Just don't give me a play-by-play. What is it with this place? All the dresses look like they should be worn by geriatric church ladies."

Stacey pivoted to study the clothing on display. Longer hemlines and boring print fabrics. Her mother might like this store, but anyone under the age of forty would cringe and look for an escape route. "That's Stiles County for you."

Zoe moved away. Smart girl. "Tell me about it. I can't wait to graduate and get outta here. Have you thought about that outfit you're going to make?"

"You changed the subject."

"Yep."

Stacey rolled her eyes and wandered farther along the strip mall sidewalk with her friend. Though Zoe had showed obvious disdain for talking about Calvin, Stacey's thoughts could not stray far from him. Nothing in this little shopping center held her interest. A dry cleaners and an insurance office? Seriously? She and Zoe were walking just to be walking. Burning calories. Killing time.

It was tough, having a best friend who didn't like her boyfriend, because Stacey needed to talk about Calvin. She could say that they'd reached an agreement, that he'd settled into an attitude of acceptance and understanding. That Calvin's words and smiles and kisses made her heart leap with joy. But somehow none of those statements felt true. And she couldn't figure out why. She wanted to blurt out her scattered thoughts to Zoe so together they could assemble them into something that made sense.

The evenings she'd spent with Calvin this week, driving in her car or hanging out at his place or at hers, wandering along a path by the Tar River or sitting on a swing at the park in Clarksville, were so uncomplicated and nice. They didn't talk about anything negative.

It all just felt dishonest. A pretense.

Zoe swung around a metal signpost and pointed up. "Sign says stop."

"Uh, yes, it does."

"So, I gotta ask you something."

Stacey scrunched up her face. "O-kay ..."

"Have you changed your mind about the sex thing?"

"Say what?"

"The sex thing. You said you and the farm boy weren't doing it."

Stacey blinked. Like she really wanted to talk about this stuff with Zoe. There was only so much of the girl's critical judgment Stacey could take. "Nooo ... we're not."

"Just checking." Zoe look both ways then stepped into an alley between the two rows of stores.

Stacey caught up to her midway. "Okay, that was pretty random. Why did you ask?"

"Because teenage guys don't say they love you unless they're trying to get sex. If you and Calvin are all lovey-dovey and stuff, then he's trying to get into your jeans."

"That is *so* not true!"

"Whatever. Just giving you fair warning. Oh, look!" Zoe quickened her step toward the door of the first store. The place looked empty, but the door stood propped open.

Stacey huffed. "Girl, you're giving me whiplash."

"No one inside. Come on." Zoe reached back and grabbed Stacey's arm. "Let's go in."

"What? You can't just—Zoe!"

The air inside smelled like paint, cut wood, and glue. Beyond a small lobby area a hallway led to what looked like offices. Zoe walked straight to the first door.

Her heart thumping in her chest, Stacey hung back in the lobby. "We shouldn't be in here. What are you doing?"

"I knew it! They're putting in a dance studio."

"Great! Let's go."

"Don't be such a scaredy-cat. Come on. The floor isn't finished, but they've got the bar up." Zoe disappeared into the room.

Stacey looked toward the parking lot. There were no cars parked in front of the store, but someone must have been in here and left the door open. Which told her they'd be right back.

"Zoe, we should get out of here."

She moved farther inside to peer into the room where Zoe had gone. The girl stood next to a bar that stretched the length of one wall. A full mirror reflected Zoe's form as she raised one arm and leaned backward. Her feet pointed outward, and she hung onto the bar for balance.

"I didn't know you could dance ballet," Stacey said.

"I never said I could. Come on. Try it."

"I don't ... I can't. My body won't bend that way."

Zoe straightened then swung her leg up until the side of her foot slapped the bar. She grunted as she tried again and managed to hook her heel over the bar. The awkwardness of the movement proved the girl wasn't a ballerina at all.

Stacey laughed and came over to the mirrored wall. "I'm not going to feel sorry for you when you get stuck that way."

"I'm not gonna get stuck." She leaned forward and tried to touch her foot with her free hand. "Oh, snap, that hurts!"

"You're insane."

"Try it. Good exercise."

Stacey rolled her eyes into the back of her head. "Mommy says I'm not supposed to exert myself too much." Still, she gently clasped the bar with her left hand.

"Your mother" — grunt — "thinks you're made of glass."

Good observation. The problems Stacey had as a child were history, but Mom still fussed at her about not putting too much strain on her heart. It was stupid.

With her heels pressed together, Stacey turned her feet out as far as they would go. Not very far. Even so, she squeezed the bar hard to keep her balance. She bent backward the way Zoe had. Again, not too far. But when she bent forward, she was able not only to touch her toes, but sweep her free hand along the unfinished plywood floor.

"Oh, wow!" she said, though the pressure on her lungs made it hard to speak. "Zoe, look at this."

"What? You're bending over?"

"I can almost kiss my own knee. I could never do this before."

"See there? You're getting there, girl. I keep telling you. Maybe now you'll believe me."

Blood rushed to Stacey's head, causing an instant headache. She straightened slowly, but right away the room began to spin. She grabbed the bar with her other hand to keep herself from falling. "Whoa."

"You okay?"

Pinpoints of light stabbed Stacey's eyes as the rest of the world darkened. She clung to consciousness like she clung to the bar. "Yeah. I'm ... I'm okay."

As the world came back into focus, Stacey peered at the pinched face of her friend. *Oh no. Oh no. Don't you start freaking out over me too.* She forced a smile. "I hate it when that happens, don't you? You stand up too fast and the blood rushes from your head?"

"Is that what happened last week at school?"

"S-something like that."

"May I help you?" The male voice boomed in the open space.

Zoe grabbed Stacey's wrist and turned toward the speaker, a man who was shorter than his voice suggested, wearing a paint-spattered, mismatched sweat suit. He stood in the doorway with a big white bucket in his hand, weighing his arm and shoulder down. A slender woman pressed into the doorway behind him.

Defiance rather than fear flashed in Zoe's glance at Stacey, then the girl launched into an act. She stepped toward the man, offering a limp-wristed hand. "We heard you were opening a studio here in town. I can't tell you how pleased I am to meet you! My name is Shay Depardieu."

The man set the paint bucket down and shook Zoe's hand, though his head was tilted slightly like he wasn't quite sure about this girl.

"Perhaps you've heard of me?" Zoe said. "I danced with the New York Ballet and toured Europe with Baryshnikov in his Nutcracker show. I had to move home to take care of my ailing mother, but I would love the opportunity to dance with your company while I'm here."

Stacey's mouth dropped open at Zoe's audacity, but she snapped it shut and pulled her chin up with a little shake of her head.

"*You* ... danced with Baryshnikov," the man said, a smirk playing with his lips.

"Oh, yes. He's absolutely brilliant."

"I see. Well, I'm afraid we can't offer anything to someone with such an impressive résumé. We're opening a school for young dancers. But if you'd like to audition for placement in our teen classes ..."

"Is that so? Oh, what a pity. Well, I see that we've come at a bad time. We'll leave you to your preparations."

Unbelievable. Holding her head high and her shoulders down, her eyes half lidded, Stacey followed Zoe toward the exit.

"Yes, that would be ... good of you," the man said as they passed.

Heart fluttering in her chest, Stacey fought the urge to run. Instead, as she faced the woman in the hallway, she raised her hand as if offering it to be kissed. *"Enchanté, mademoiselle."*

The woman's head flopped to the side sarcastically, spilling a loose lock of thin hair over the bridge of her nose. She raised a hand of her own, offering only the way to the front door. *Go, now.*

Zoe kept up the act, walking with her head elevated and her feet pointed slightly outward until they reached the sidewalk in front of the next store. Then she looped her arm through Stacey's and, giggling, hurried farther along the way.

"You *are* insane," Stacey said, pressing a hand over her racing heart.

"That was *brilliant, darling!* I got us out of there, didn't I? Did you see that woman? She was so thin! Maybe we *should* take up dancing."

The brief moment of humor fled. An image flashed through Stacey's memory, herself at age five, wearing a ridiculous pink tutu. Her fat knees and lumpy thighs rubbing together to shred the nylon tights they were squeezed into. She'd taken lessons for less than a year until her mother pulled her out because she couldn't keep up with the other tiny ballerinas. Nothing since then. No girl scouts or cheerleading. Her health was too fragile, Mom said. And there was too much competition, too much opportunity for ridicule from mean girls.

Too bad she didn't have to attend a dance class or go hiking to encounter ridicule. She found it in her classroom at school, and in her own home.

As the adrenaline of their escape wore off, Stacey's headache intensified. Feeling nauseous, she handed her car keys to Zoe. "Let's go back to my house. My parents are both at work, so they won't bother us."

Zoe took the keys, but peered squint-eyed at Stacey. "Are you sure you're okay?"

"Headache. Drive me home, okay?" She covered her eyes with her hand.

Hanging on to Stacey's arm as if she'd suddenly gone blind, Zoe guided her to the car in the parking lot. She even opened the door for her. Stacey slid into the passenger seat and pressed both hands over her face. *Don't cry. Be strong. Stay in control.*

The driver's side door creaked as Zoe closed it. Stacey winced as the sound seemed to bounce around the inner walls of her skull.

Zoe didn't start the car. "Stace, are you sure you're okay? This is twice in about a week."

More than that, but no way she'd confess it. "Don't say anything. Calvin's been asking. Just ... I'm fine. I stood up too fast."

"Are you taking those herbals? Maybe you've got some deficiency going on."

"Can we just go home, please?"

Zoe let out a loud sigh and put the key in the ignition.

Keeping her eyes closed intensified the pain and made her feel carsick. Stacey laid her head back against the headrest and opened the window beside her. The wind on her face helped the nausea, though the sound of it rushing through the window pounded against her eardrums.

Maybe she should take all the vitamins and supplements Zoe had suggested for her. Some of them looked like horse pills though. And they made her stomach churn. And didn't they have calories? Maybe not, since Zoe was so much in favor of them. Ugh, she didn't want to think about it. She needed only some water and to lie on the couch for a while, and she'd be fine.

○ ○ ◯ ○ ○

Strength. Being in control of her own life. That's what it was all about. No one was going to push her around. Not even Zoe, with her websites full of information and her list of so-called beneficial herbs and vitamins.

A line of vitamins, arranged from small to large so she could get most of them down before gagging, lay on the kitchen counter in front of Stacey. She didn't need them. Most other people didn't swallow all these nasty-tasting things. She got enough nutrients from the food she ate, even eating less than everyone else. Stacey swept the pills into her hand and dumped them into the little trash bin under the sink. She was tempted to throw all the bottles away too, but they'd take up a lot of room and Mom would notice them. So she put them back into the cabinet, then scrubbed her hands at the sink, and placed the paper towel she'd used to dry them over the pills in the trash bin in case Mom decided to look close.

Be in control.

She chugged a glass of cold water to fill her rumbling stomach, then walked to the laundry room. Her mother stood at the ironing board, humming along to the music on the radio she kept in the room where she spent so much time. Steam erupted from the iron, filling the air with the smell of hot cotton.

"I'm going to fix supper tonight," Stacey said.

Assertive. Good. Don't ask if it's okay, just take control. The only way to cut the calories from suppertime was for Stacey to fix the meal herself. She could oversee everything that went into it, cut whatever loaded on the calories, and keep what was safe to eat.

Mom set the steam iron carefully in the wire rack at the end of the board before she spoke. "That would be fine. What are you going to fix?"

"Do we have chicken breasts?" Less fat, easy to cut into specific portions. Less than a hundred calories for a whole breast, depending on how she cooked it. Fish would be good too, if they had any in the house.

"There's some in the freezer. You'll have to defrost it in the microwave. Take it out of the Styrofoam tray first and set the microwave for the exact weight."

"Yes, Mom."

"Stacey, are you all right? You look tired."

Stop . . . judging me! Everyone was judging her. Even Zoe, who'd gone so far yesterday as to suggest that Stacey wasn't "doing it right" if she was getting dizzy all the time. Calvin hadn't said anything in a week, but Stacey wasn't so dumb as to think he'd stop watching her so easily. She couldn't afford for her parents to start taking notice of anything and start snooping into her life.

Stacey waved her hand as she fled the suffocating room. "I'm fine."

While the microwave zapped the meat, Stacey rummaged through the baker's rack where her mother kept her cookbooks. She found international recipes, holiday menus, recipes for cookies and cakes, clippings from epicurean magazines, grocery-store recipe cards, quick-fix meals, books for poultry, beef, pasta, and fondues, everything fancy and nothing—*nothing*—that would keep the fat from growing on her body. No wonder she'd been a blimp for so many years.

Just bake the chicken. How hard could it be? She could throw a few potatoes in the microwave, and Renee and the parents could load them up with whatever junk they wanted. Some steamed broccoli would make the meal enough for anybody.

She arranged the chicken in a baking dish and sprinkled it with lemon juice and pepper. No butter. No salt. Just water to keep it moist.

This was good. This would work. She could even invite Calvin over Saturday night, and he'd see that there was nothing for him to worry about.

While supper cooked, Stacey brought her computer to the dining room table and searched the Internet for low-calorie recipes. She bookmarked websites and sent page after page to their wireless printer, so she could start a binder of recipes. Later she could do a drawing for the cover—herself holding a tray with steaming plates of food. "Stacey's Favorite Blimp-free Recipes."

She left her computer and stuck little red potatoes in the microwave. Broccoli went in a pot with some water. As everything cooked, she polished the dining room table and set it with their nicest casual dinnerware.

Daddy dragged himself home before she was ready. After working a double shift, he was sure to grumble like a bear for his supper, practically inhale the meal, then fall into his chair to watch television and be comatose in ten minutes. All good.

Stacey quickly dressed each plate with a sprig of parsley and lit the tall centerpiece candles. She brought the veggies to the table in bowls, the chicken on a platter, still steaming in her pale lemon-pepper sauce.

Scowling, Daddy settled at the head of the table. "What's this?"

"Stacey cooked dinner." Mom adjusted her silverware as she sat. "Isn't that nice?"

"Are we all on a diet now?"

"Hush, Stan. It looks delicious."

They passed the food around. Stacey watched Daddy cut his chicken and shove a bite into his mouth. Mom got up to fetch sour cream and butter from the fridge. And a jar of bacon bits. They loaded junk onto her carefully prepared feast.

Renee complained that the chicken was tasteless.

Mom sprinkled salt on everything. She made suggestions on how Stacey could enhance the flavor next time. Cream-of-whatever soup, fruit sauces, Italian, Mexican, blah, blah, blah.

Stacey forced down half of her four-ounce piece of chicken along with two broccoli florets. She made the rest look like crumbs on her plate. Maybe one hundred calories? Not counting the lemon juice ... She couldn't calculate because it was impossible to tell exactly how much was on her chicken. Fish next time. Or no meat at all. Except that Calvin would want meat.

"Is there anything for dessert?" Daddy asked. "Some sugar-free Jell-O, maybe?"

Mom's breath hissed sharply through her nose. "Stan."

"What? There's always room for Jell-O."

"It wouldn't hurt you to lose a few pounds," Mom grumbled.

Stacey wadded up her napkin in her lap. She couldn't look at anyone at the table. This wouldn't be as easy as she thought.

"I'll make a run for ice cream if you'll pay," Renee said.

Daddy laughed without humor. "That ain't gonna work, little girl. You're on car restriction, remember?"

The voices of her family members clawed at Stacey's skull. She got up and collected the plates. No way would she bring Calvin into this mess of a family. Although maybe he'd understand her better if he saw what she'd had to put up with for so long.

Stacey rinsed the plates and set them in the dishwasher, then cleaned the kitchen so nothing remained of the fiasco meal.

And no one thanked her.

Chapter 11

All his life Calvin had seen these trenches in the field, defining the contours of the land toward a borderline of trees three-quarters of a mile away. As familiar as the lines of his own hands. This year, though, they were all his doing.

Calvin hooked his thumbs into his pockets and pushed his shoulders back to stretch. "I wouldn't have had time for much riding anyway."

Stacey slipped her hand around his forearm and tugged him away from the tractor that had been his "ride" for all of spring break. "Come over here," she said.

"What?" Calvin took two steps then planted his feet.

Stacey gave up trying to make him move. "I'm sorry, that machine makes me nervous."

"It's not even running."

"I know. It's just—" She shook her hands and flinched like she'd seen a bug. "It's big, and it smells . . . dirty."

Calvin snorted. "It's a tractor! And I still need to hose it off before supper." All his muscles hurt a little more at the thought. "At least I'm done. I can rest tomorrow after church." He grinned at her. "Want to help me clean the tractor?"

Her glossy pink lips parted in shock. She didn't have to answer.

Her textured sweater looked like it would unravel at the smallest snag, her jeans were creased, and her stark white sneakers with glittery laces were already dangerously close to a mud puddle. "Um, I suppose you can't leave it that way."

"Nope. Tell you what. Go wait for me on the porch—this won't take long."

Calvin watched Stacey walk away, her steps delicate as she crossed the gravel driveway, as if she might get dirty along the way. He wiped his brow with his forearm and turned to find the hose.

What is she doing with me, anyway?

Could his appearance be any different from hers? Could his life be any different?

His hands still felt the vibration from hours gripping the steering wheel of the tractor. Heat rose from his chest, and sweat stained his T-shirt. A layer of dust covered his work boots. While Stacey couldn't stand to get a tiny stain on her sneakers.

He was too tired to be thinking about anything deep. He'd work himself into a dark mood again, and not be able to keep up the happy game he'd been playing this week whenever he saw Stacey.

Calvin uncoiled the heavy-duty hose attached to the spigot next to the workshop. He dragged it to the tractor, then went back to turn the water on.

Love her through it, the websites said. *Gently encourage, don't argue.*

It felt like lying. And he couldn't do much more of it before he cracked.

Too tired, too tired. Stop thinking about it.

Calvin hosed the tractor from the top down, focusing the spray behind the wheels and in the tire treads and all around the seed hoppers where dirt from the field got trapped and would turn to rock-hard clay if left alone. He huffed and sighed with the work, but his mind sought to rest with the simplicity of the task. Still the problem kept sneaking back, like a recurring dream, each time he closed his eyes for more than a blink. How was he supposed to keep doing this? He wasn't even certain Stacey was anorexic, but how could he even ask the question if he was supposed to treat her like glass?

He was soaked when he finally coiled up the hose and stowed it in a plastic bin next to the workshop. His clothing clung to him, and water dripped from his hair. Without so much as shaking his head, he snuck around the far side of the house and peeked onto the front porch. Stacey sat in a rocker, her phone in her hand and earbuds tucked into her ears. Her back was angled toward him.

Calvin grabbed the porch railing, eased himself up the side, and swung his feet carefully to the porch. Stacey continued gently rocking, waving a finger in the air to the beat of whatever song played on her smartphone. Oblivious. Four steps, and he stood beside the rocker. He leaned slightly forward, then rattled his head like a dog coming in from the rain.

Stacey squealed and rocketed out of the chair. She spun to face him, weaved toward the railing, then looked down with disgust at her clothing. "Calvin!"

"It's just water." He laughed, but the glazed look she gave him robbed him of the humor.

Stacey brushed droplets off her sweater, but her hand trembled with each swipe, as if she couldn't quite see where the water had fallen. She pulled the earbuds out and tucked her phone into her purse. It was like watching an old lady perform the simple task.

Calvin took a step closer to her, reached out to touch her shoulder. "Are you okay?"

"I'm wet! Are-are you sure that was just w-w-water?"

"Yeah. Well, maybe a bit a sweat mixed in."

Her head snapped up. "Eww!"

He caught her hand and held it gently. "Come on. It's just water from the hose splashing."

"And dirt from the tractor with it, I'm sure."

"I don't see any dirt. Stace, come on. It was just a little prank."

She sighed and turned to look toward the street. "It's okay." She slanted a wicked glance at him. "I'll get you back sometime."

Calvin forced a grin. "Go for it. But I'll be watching and ready."

Stacey leaned into the railing, and the sunlight caught in her white hair, lighting up tiny wayward strands like fiber optics. The pretty contours of her face glowed. Her jade-colored eyes reflected both the sun and the patchy green grass in the front yard. Like a painting. Like a model in a magazine photograph. Something caught in Calvin's chest, warming and choking him at the same time. He set his hand on the railing and inched it forward until his fingertips touched and entwined with hers. They stood like that for a while.

"It's quiet here," Stacey said. "All the time we've been standing here, not one car has passed by. All I can hear are the people moving around inside."

Calvin grunted softly in agreement. "Pretty loud inside, though. Bet that's pretty different for you, from where you used to live."

"We were in a subdivision. It wasn't too bad. Lawn mowers and neighbors coming and going."

"I thought your dad moved you outta there because of the crime."

He sensed her stiffening. "My dad's a cop. He could deal with any sort of crime Rocky Mount could dish out. But he wanted a place away from, like ... prying neighbors and stuff."

Prying neighbors? She'd moved to a small town where everyone was in everyone else's business. There was something more to this story. Calvin tried to remember all that Stacey had told him about living in Rocky Mount. It wasn't a huge city, like Raleigh or Charlotte. Calvin had been there plenty of times, for school field trips and helping his mother sell her baked and canned goods at the farmer's market. He hadn't gone into the neighborhoods, though. Hadn't driven the streets himself. He had no clue what it would be like to live there. Though what he'd seen didn't strike him as dangerous.

Did Stacey find Stiles County dull, like her best friend Zoe did? Was that one of the things that drew the two girls together, despite how different they were in so many other ways?

"Calvin, supper's on," Peyton called from somewhere inside the house.

Peyton, another person who was itching to get out of Stiles County. She was using her wedding as a stepping stone to do it.

Calvin shrugged off that thought and took Stacey's hand to go in. "Wait for me in the dining room. I'm going upstairs to dry off and change clothes."

She tilted her head in a smug way. "Yes, please."

○ ○ ○ ○ ○

A soft chorus of amens echoed Dad's suppertime prayer. Hands reached for bowls of vegetables and the platter of fried catfish on the table. Older family members loaded the plates of the younger ones, keeping Calvin busy. Zachary fussed that he was old enough to have Pepsi to drink with his meal rather than milk. Emily blew noisy spit bubbles and pounded the tray of her highchair.

Wearing fresh clothes but with his hair still damp, Calvin sat crowded between Peyton and Stacey. Under the table, he pressed his knee against Stacey's. She glanced sideways at him, and her perfectly shaped lips tightened in a smile just for him.

Calvin smiled back, though his heart wanted to plead with her. *Prove to me there's nothing I need to worry about!*

Peyton passed a salad bowl to Calvin. Using the tongs, he took his portion, then handed the bowl and tongs to Stacey and watched her deftly sift through the radishes, onions, croutons, and carrots. Only lettuce landed on her plate.

She took the smallest piece of fish from the platter and some asparagus. No fried potatoes. No dressing for her salad. She cut her food into little pieces and followed each tiny portion she ate by wiping her napkin across her lips. So precise. So weird. So ... not right.

Smile. Pretend to listen to conversation. Calvin shoveled food into his mouth.

"What's the hurry, Calvin? You're eating like you need to catch a train," Mom said.

"Hungry." True. Although the idea of catching a train to get out of this awkward nightmare sounded good. He nudged Stacey's knee again. *Please. Please eat.*

Mom waved a fork at him. "Slow down. It's better for the digestion."

"She's right," Stacey said, and followed the statement by gracefully raising a single piece of asparagus to her mouth.

Why am I suddenly grossed out by that?

Too tired. All this thinking ... He should just say good night and go up to bed. Escape this mess.

A warm, furry body bumped Calvin's leg. Someone had forgotten to put Scamp outside before supper, and the dog had wormed his way under the table. And then, within minutes, the nice part of their family dinner disappeared. Jacob complained that he was finished eating and wanted to watch cartoons. Zach argued that the TV tonight was his and Dad's for the rest of baseball season. Emily managed to get the top off her sippy cup and splashed her apple juice onto Peyton's jeans. Peyton's protest—since she was going to see Ryan tonight—set the baby to wailing.

Stacey nudged Calvin's knee. "Want to go somewhere after supper? Maybe watch the stars come out?"

He'd probably fall asleep in her car.

Scamp bumped Calvin's legs again.

"Dog, what—?" Calvin leaned back to look under the table.

Scamp chewed something twice and swallowed. The dog's eyes

widened, and he dashed away as Dad and Mom both hollered for him to get out. Zachary jumped up from the table to open the back door for the dog.

Calvin straightened and locked gazes with Stacey. She blinked and lowered her eyes, unable to pull off innocence. Her plate was nearly empty. Calvin guessed most of it had gone into the dog's stomach.

Be cool. Don't argue. Love her through it.

He stared down at his own empty plate. The food churned in his gut, stirred up by the realization of what Stacey had done.

Chapter 12

Stacey stroked a charcoal stick across the newsprint paper attached to her drawing board. Pleased with the line, she smudged it with her pinky finger, softening the edges to make a shadow. The muscles in her forearm burned from holding her arm up, and her hand trembled against the paper. She lowered her arm to let the blood flow back and used the time to study the model seated on a stool in the middle of the studio.

The male model was shirtless, but wore a sheet draped over one shoulder, belted with a drapery cord so it looked like a toga. His biceps were impressive, but his bushy chest hair grossed Stacey out. Some old farmer. And though he was supposed to be sitting still, his mouth and jaw kept moving like he was chewing something. Stacey envisioned a Styrofoam cup filled with tobacco spit sitting on the bench seat of the man's battered pickup truck. Yuck.

"What . . . are you doing?" the teacher barked behind her.

Stacey jumped and dropped her charcoal stick. It broke at her feet.

Mrs. Chandler touched her shoulder. "I'm sorry, Stacey. I wasn't talking to you." The teacher swung around and confronted Noah Dickerson, whose easel stood to Stacey's right. "This is a figure drawing class, not drawing for comic books."

Resisting the urge to peek at Noah's drawing, Stacey squatted to pick up the shards of her charcoal stick.

"I'm a comic book artist. This is what I do." A dark-haired, angel-faced troublemaker, Noah could charm most any girl right out of her sneakers. Except, maybe, Mrs. Chandler.

"You are not a comic book artist." The teacher's voice reflected neither anger nor amusement. She sounded bored. "You are a high school student in a figure drawing class. Take advantage of the model, Noah. You don't get opportunities to study the human form every day."

"He's a geezer in a sheet. No offense, but that's not very inspiring."

"You're wasting your time and talent."

Her concentration ruined and her charcoal in intolerable tiny pieces, Stacey gave up and stole a glance at Noah's drawing. He had deftly sketched the outline of a warrior, sitting in the same position as the model. He'd added a dragon-crested helm and a two-handed sword in a scabbard at the man's hip. Creative, if slightly out of proportion; Noah's drawing was way more exciting than Stacey's.

"I'm wasting my time and talent if I don't follow my heart." Noah made anarchy sound so noble.

Mrs. Chandler drew a long, audible breath. "I'm not going to argue with you. If you cannot follow simple procedure—"

"Procedure? Aren't we free to express ourselves in art?"

A long silence followed. Students in the circle around the model slowed their sketching motions to stare. Zoe moved away from her easel to crowd Stacey's left side and gawk.

"Noah, I am going to make a recommendation to your guidance counselor that you should not be allowed to take an arts elective next year."

"What? *What?*" Noah's confident demeanor crashed like a skateboard stunt gone bad. His mouth hung open as the teacher strode away.

"That's time," Mrs. Chandler called to the class. "Three-minute break, then one more quick pose."

The model stretched his limbs and shot Noah a scathing glance.

Stacey unclipped her sketchpad from her board and turned to a new page. Her fingertips left smudges on the clean paper. Why did such a beautiful medium have to be so messy?

Zoe leaned in close. "Unbelievable," she whispered.

At the sound of paper ripping, Stacey looked at Noah. Shaking his long hair away from his face, he ripped his drawing a second time. And a third.

"Ooh, too bad," Stacey said. "I liked it."

He stopped moving. "You did?"

"It was good. If you go for that whole Marvel, DC, Dark Horse kind of thing."

Noah blinked. "You're into comics?"

Stacey could feel Zoe's breath on the side of her face.

"I like manga."

"But you draw ..." He gestured toward her easel.

Stacey grinned. "Just following procedures." She moved a little closer to him so she could lower her voice. "Don't let Mrs. Chandler get to you. Believe me, I know how it feels to be beat down for your art. My father is always on me, like I should be doing something *sensible* with my life. But like you said, you gotta follow your heart."

Noah's lush eyebrows puckered, but he nodded. "Yeah, that's right." His expression softened. "Pretty cool. This whole year, I didn't know you were into comics."

Because the whole year he'd never said two words to her. Cute guy talking to the fat chick? So not Noah's style. Unless he was like, like ...

No, don't think about it.

She turned away, busied herself with her sketchpad. In the center of the classroom, the model got ready for another pose.

"Can I see some of your manga work?" Noah asked.

Zoe let out a squeak. Stacey's cheeks warmed. She hadn't meant for the conversation to go the direction Zoe obviously thought it was going. Noah had a reputation for finding and dropping girlfriends practically every week.

"They're in a sketchbook at home. I-I could bring it in one day, maybe."

Points of light from Mrs. Chandler's spotlights glistened in Noah's bluish-gray eyes. His full lips curled into a smile. Kissable lips and long black lashes, and not a hint of a pimple anywhere on his face. Artsy, angst-filled appeal. No wonder girls fell for him.

Calvin, think of Calvin.

"Cool," he said.

Would her heart have trembled more if he'd said, "I love you"? Stacey blinked and dragged her gaze away. Crazy thinking. Noah Dickerson was trouble. Period.

The model sat on the stool with one knee hitched up, his back turned toward Stacey. Probably to spite Noah. The guy had a full crop of hair on his shoulders. Eww.

"Ten minutes for this one," Mrs. Chandler said, strolling behind the circle of easels. "Use this time to capture the general shapes of the form and the perspective of his limbs. Those of you facing him, pay attention to the foreshortening of his leg. Don't make it too long, and I don't want to see any stumps."

"And those of us on this side can stare at a flat, hairy back," Stacey muttered.

Noah snorted. Stacey glanced at him and was rewarded with a white-toothed smile. Her cheeks warmed again.

"Like your hair, by the way," he said. "Awesome colors."

She mumbled thanks. To her left, Zoe's hand sat motionless against her sketchpad.

Stacey felt like her clothes had suddenly gotten heavier, like the air of the art studio, smelling of linseed oil and eraser crumbles, pressed in on her. She didn't want to draw the man with the hairy back. Something trembled in her chest, and she imagined the pressure against her body was Noah's stare.

Calvin!

She stared at the model, searching for some challenging detail she could sketch. There was a tricky space between his jawline and shoulder, but drawing it meant staring at the man-fur glowing in Mrs. Chandler's floodlights.

She skittered broken charcoal across her paper, making tiny marks. Was Noah watching her draw? Her lines were off, hopelessly distorted. Black dust had coated her fingers and collected under her nails. Ugly. Filthy.

"Time," Mrs. Chandler said. "And we're done. Thank you for posing for us today, Mr. Stanley. Students, for your next independent project, you'll be choosing another person in this classroom to work with, and each of you will be doing a portrait of your partner. The portraits can be full figure or partial — *with clothes on!* — and the finished piece should give us a sense of the personality of your sketch buddy."

"Who's going to be your *sketch buddy*?" Noah asked, grinning.

Stacey almost dropped her charcoal again. "Zoe. Probably. Yours?"

Noah's smile twisted. He smoothed his swoop of hair across his forehead. The movement reminded Stacey of Calvin's nervous hair-tugging habit. "Uh, I don't know. Can't really go with Katie, since we broke up over spring break."

Nice way to tell her he was *available*!

"Stacey can be your partner." Zoe lunged into the conversation and practically jumped between them. "I don't mind, Stace. Really."

Stacey gathered her charcoal, kneaded eraser, and chamois cloth from the easel tray and placed them in the decorated tackle box she used to store her supplies.

"Do you want to work together?" Noah asked.

Sketching that beautiful face. Spending time with the most alluring bad boy of South Stiles High School. Was this really happening?

"I've got a boyfriend already."

Noah winced. "Huh? I was just asking—"

Her face burning, Stacey snatched her drawing board off the easel and hurried to the storage closet. At the studio sink she scrubbed her hands and dug the charcoal out from underneath her nails. When she returned to her easel to get her tackle box and purse, Noah was gone, summoned to Mrs. Chandler's desk for a lecture. Stacey grabbed her things and fled.

Zoe met her outside the door and paced alongside her in the hallway, huffing as if they were on a jogging track. "Why did you turn him down? I can't believe you did that. He was just asking you to do a project with him. What's the matter with you?"

Stacey refused to look at her. "I have a boyfriend, remember?"

"Oh, right. Why spend time with Noah Dickerson when you waste it with a dumpy, dull farm boy who doesn't know the first thing about art."

Stacey whirled. "Stop it. Calvin's my boyfriend, okay? He was my boyfriend before I met you, and he'll be my boyfriend after—whenever. Deal with it." Her knees felt rubbery, and her pulse hammered in her throat. "If you think Noah's so special, why don't you be his sketch buddy?"

"Stacey ..." Zoe rolled her eyes. "He's into you, not me. And there's nothing wrong with working on a class project with him."

"Calvin wouldn't—I'm—Zoe, I love Calvin. It wouldn't be right."

"Oh, sure. But it's okay for the farm boy to hang out with that biker chick."

Stacey's defense crashed into Zoe's logic. What was the difference? There had to be a good reason. Because ... because ...

"I'm not interested in becoming Noah's next ex-girlfriend." There. That made sense.

But Zoe moved in closer. "Stacey, I know you've been with Calvin a long time, but it's not like you're going to marry him and become a farmer's wife or something. I mean, I'm sorry, but you can do better."

And maybe she could do with a better best friend too. Stacey blinked and glanced toward the art studio. Noah came out of the classroom, his swagger diminished. The angry pout touching his perfect lips tugged at Stacey's heart.

Stop it!

She had to find Calvin. She needed to touch him and remind herself why she was devoted to him. Hearing his mellow voice would drive out all these crazy impulses. She hitched her purse strap higher on her shoulder. "I gotta go."

Zoe flipped her hair. "Whatever."

Okay, whatever. Stacey left Zoe to sulk and rushed toward the new wing of the building. If she hurried, she might catch Calvin at his locker. She bumped someone with her supply box, swung in a circle to apologize, then kept going. Her feet flew, just shy of running. The lines on the walls and tile floor made her dizzy. Her pulse thumped in her temples, and her breath came in gasps.

Danger. Slow down.

And then she saw him. Her art supply box slipped from her fingers and clattered on the floor. Calvin turned to look, wide-eyed. Stacey jumped and threw her arms around his shoulders, and pressed her face against his soft cotton shirt. It smelled like fabric softener. The hint of aftershave at his neck sent a welcome thrill through her.

"Hey, hey, what's wrong?" Gripping her shoulders, Calvin tried to ease her back.

Stacey dug up an excuse. "Can't I just miss you?"

His fingers traced the contours of her shoulders. "Are you feeling okay?"

Stacey eased away and pushed her hair behind her ears. "I'm okay. Uh, Zoe and I had an argument. Sometimes she's just ... you know."

He grunted. "Well, I'm glad you're here. I, um ... I have something for you." He reached into his back pocket and pulled out a folded piece of paper.

"A note?" She took it from his hands. How sweet was he! How did he know something like this would be just what she'd need to —

"I looked up some stuff last night." Calvin touched her face, lifting it to get her to look at him. "Stace, you're so pretty. I mean it. And I want to help you. So this" — he pointed to the folded paper in her hand — "is some information I hope you'll think about."

Not a love note? What kind of information?

He pulled a book from his locker and closed the door, then glanced around and leaned toward her to kiss her cheek. "Give me a ride home from school? We'll talk then."

Talk? His softened voice sounded like he was consoling her for the death of her favorite cousin or something.

"Oh — okay."

Stacey looked around for her tackle box. Stupid to throw it down. She'd probably broken all her charcoal sticks and Conté crayons. Calvin picked it up for her then walked with her, touching her elbow as if to make sure she wouldn't stumble.

"I have to get to class," he said. "See you later by the parking lot?"

Stacey nodded then watched him move down the hall. Her next period was lunch. She dragged her feet toward the cafeteria, but stepped into a bathroom and locked herself in a stall. With her tackle box on the floor by her feet, Stacey unfolded Calvin's two-page note.

Her fingers trembled. The note was typed, carefully prepared. She held her breath with the opening words.

> *Stacey, I love you, but I'm really worried about you. I'm scared you might be anorexic. I looked it up on the Internet, and so much of what I read seems to fit the things that are happening with you. Here's some of what I found.*
>
> *Anorexia nervosa is an obsessive-addictive behavioral disorder in which a person engages in deliberate self-starvation. Causes for the disorder stem from biological, sociological, and psychological triggers. Effects of anorexia nervosa include: anemia; malnutrition; kidney dysfunction and failure ...*

What? She didn't have any of those things. Yeah, she used some of the diet tips Zoe found on those pro-ana websites, and maybe she took it a little too far sometimes, but she didn't have some kind of ... *disorder.* How could Calvin say these things about her?

The note shook in her hands. She skimmed past the cold information, looking for something personal. Something real. Her eyes stopped at a bit of bold type.

Scripture — 1 Corinthians 6:19 – 20, to be exact.

Not satisfied with science, Calvin threw God at her, like not only was she afflicted with a *disorder,* but she wasn't being very Christian about it as well. Just because she didn't go to church every single Sunday like he did ...

At the bottom of this travesty of a letter, he'd typed, "Love, Calvin." He couldn't even sign his own name.

How could he even think these things about her? *Obsessive-addictive* ... like she was crazy, on drugs, whatever. How could he?

And that Bible verse, like God was on Calvin's side. If she found a Bible, she was sure she could find verses that said people shouldn't be gluttons and shouldn't judge. How would Calvin feel if she shoved those in his face?

Every muscle in her limbs ached, and her chest felt like a watermelon thumped there instead of a heart. A flood of tears would release the tension, but she wouldn't reward Calvin's note by crying over it. Stacey tore the pages into tiny pieces and let them fall into the toilet. She flushed and watched the paper bits swirl and disappear. Finally she snatched up her tackle box, wiped off the bottom, and scrubbed her hands with super-hot water at the sink.

She strode to the cafeteria. Today she would have a salad. And a burger. That would show Calvin she wasn't starving herself.

Except he wouldn't see it. He'd be sitting in his computer class thinking he'd done something good. He was fixing her, like he'd fix his motorcycle. Study the causes, get the parts, use the right tools, make it all the way it was supposed to be. The way *Calvin* thought it was supposed to be.

At Stacey's table at the corner of the cafeteria, where she ate and studied and no one paid attention to her, she removed the burger from the bun, scraped off the ketchup, and nibbled the meat down to half. No sense turning into a blimp just to prove she wasn't anorexic.

Calvin would not win this battle over her will. No way. No one could make her turn into Chubbikins again.

Stacey's hands trembled and her heart fluttered as she turned the pages of a textbook. Stupid tears blurred the words. Cold, hard words. Like Calvin's note. She slammed the book closed and covered her face with her hands.

I'm wasting my time if I don't follow my heart.

Noah's words, and they were true. But what if her heart was torn between loving someone and her need to shed the ugly, bloated, painful past? To break free of the things that still oppressed her? To be in charge of her own life?

Noah Dickerson would understand those desires, for sure.

Chapter 13

Standing on the sidewalk by the school parking lot, Calvin pulled a deep breath of cool, rain-scented air into his lungs and looked again at his watch. The buses would be rolling out of the bus lot on the other side of the building in less than a minute. Only a track star could run to catch one now.

None of the faces emerging from the building belonged to Stacey. None of the voices were hers.

He tugged his hair. Had his note been too much? Had he put in enough I love yous to soften the harsh reality?

Would she really make him walk home when those clouds threatened rain?

Calvin scanned the lot for her car. Any one of those pickup trucks or SUVs could hide the little blue Honda.

"Hey!" Arms wrapped around his shoulders, and someone's weight on his back pulled him off balance. Strong, slender legs kicked past his knees. Skater shoes with no socks. Calvin teetered and shuffled to keep from falling. He turned and found Flannery giggling.

He breathed out a laugh. "Warn a guy, would ya?"

"What fun is that?" she said. "What are you doing here?"

Calvin rolled his shoulders to straighten his shirt. "Waiting for Stacey. She's supposed to give me a ride home."

"I'm riding with Tyler." She grinned and rocked on her toes. "Riding with Tyler" had greater implications now than it had just a few days ago. "Is everything okay?" She tilted her head, but her giddy grin didn't entirely disappear.

"Uh ... I'll find out soon enough, I guess."

"What do you mean?"

Calvin sighed and stepped closer to her. "I did some research, and I wrote her a note with some of the stuff I found—"

"You didn't. Calvin! A *note*?"

"How else was I supposed to tell her—"

Flannery groaned and whirled around. "Dude, I can't believe you. You wrote her ... what, like a research paper? You're supposed to talk to her. Hold her hand. Hug her."

Heat rushed to Calvin's head, dimming his vision, tightening his gut. "Okay, I've done that. I've been real nice and tried to drop hints and ... whatever. It isn't working. She doesn't eat. The other day at my house she gave her entire meal to the dog. What else am I supposed to do?"

Flannery's brows puckered. "She's got to be eating something. Calvin, are you sure?"

"Positive." Wanting to punch something, Calvin turned away from his friend and stared at the building.

Light flashed on a glass door as it swung open. Tyler held the door for Stacey, who frowned and said nothing as she walked through. Calvin stood straighter and pushed a smile to his face.

Stacey's pace slowed as she met his gaze. Her face seemed the same color as the sidewalk and almost as inflexible.

Keep smiling. "Hey. How's it going?"

Her eyes shifted to Flannery, then she turned her head as Tyler strode past her.

"You okay?" Calvin asked.

"I'm fine."

She looked anything but fine. Calvin swallowed against the worry that swirled in his gut and threatened to come up again. His armpits felt swampy. "What's wrong?"

"Didn't I just say I'm fine? Do you have to jump to conclusions all the time?"

Calvin jerked his head back as if dodging a slap. "Whoa. Excuse me for caring. You just look pale. Thought you might have a headache or something."

She sighed. "No, I don't. But I need to talk to you. *Alone*, please?"

Flannery grabbed Tyler by the arm. "Let's go." She shot a dark look at Stacey as she dragged Tyler down the sidewalk to the asphalt.

Calvin tugged his hair and half wished he could go with them rather than stay and endure Stacey's emotional critique of his stupid note. "Guess you're going to tell me I messed up."

Stacey pressed the heel of her hand to her forehead. Her eyes drifted anywhere but toward him. "I'm not anorexic, Calvin. How could you even think that?"

Calvin blew out his breath. Should he argue with her?

"Anorexics starve themselves, okay?" Words spilled out of her. "I eat plenty. Just because I don't want to eat burgers or catfish fried in ... bacon grease or whatever doesn't mean I'm starving myself. But you just don't get it. You don't know what it's like to be called names because you're fat, or to have people think you're not worth getting to know or—or assuming you won't amount to anything."

"Yeah? That's what you think? Well, I was fat once. Until I started riding my bike and getting more exercise. So I do know what it feels like. But you know what? Anyone who thinks someone is less valuable as a person because they're overweight isn't worth listening to."

"Even if it's your own father?" she blurted.

"What?"

Tears shimmered in her already red eyes. No makeup. That's

why she looked so pale. Probably wasn't the first time she'd cried that day.

Calvin's gut clenched, and his anger teetered. He'd hurt her.

Stacey lowered her head, allowing her hair to fall forward like a curtain over her face. She mumbled something. Calvin lifted his hand but lost the will to touch her halfway toward her arm.

"I didn't hear ..." he said.

She sniffed and lifted her head, looking at the school building rather than at him. "I never told you this before. I didn't want you to worry about me and treat me like ... like I'm fragile or something. My mother does that, and I *hate* it."

She stopped, and he waited. Two students walked behind her, staring at him like it was any of their business. He narrowed his eyes at them. The pair went on to the parking lot, leaving Stacey and Calvin alone.

Stacey raised her hand to her eyes as if to rub them, but her fingers trembled at her forehead, hiding her expression from him. "We moved here because ... because ..."

"Because of your sister. Because she was getting in trouble and things were getting bad in the area where you lived." The words coming out of Calvin's mouth felt false, although that was exactly what Stacey had told him before. Yet he knew. There was something more serious, and it had to do with Stacey. Otherwise she wouldn't be crying now.

"My uncle. Mom's brother. He ... did things. Said things to me."

Calvin's heart stopped beating. At least it felt that way. "Did what? What did he do to you, Stacey?" His voice was too loud.

"I'm still a virgin, if that's what you're thinking." Shoulders hunched, Stacey looked around, but no one was close enough to hear.

Okay, okay. Silence the panic. Don't run for Dad's shotgun yet. "What happened?"

"It's really hard to talk about. Like, it's my family, you know? But he's ... not right. Messed up in the head. He drinks too much. Daddy wanted to arrest him, but Mom begged him and, I guess, to keep our family together, Daddy transferred to Stiles County."

Blinking, Calvin tried to process this information. "But what did he do to *you*?"

"He told me ... he told me, that he liked ... chubby girls. And if I ever wanted to ... you know. And he stared at me. All the time."

"Your dad should have arrested him." Calvin could barely break his teeth apart to talk.

"He didn't actually do anything illegal. Just ... looked at me and said things."

"And your parents were *okay* with that?"

"Calvin, he's the only family my mom has left. She tried to help him with his drinking and stuff, but Daddy just got mad and—" A violent tremor ran through her, bringing forth a whimper. "We had to leave. We thought it would be better here. And ... there's more. But I can't tell you right now, Calvin. I can't. You just have to trust me. I know what I'm doing."

Was that it? "So your uncle made a pass at you, and that's why you don't eat properly?"

"Calvin!"

"What? I'm trying to understand this."

"No. Enough. Look, I was fifteen, and they yanked me away from everything I knew. They said, 'we're going,' and we left. Renee didn't want to, and neither did I. They wanted to lock us away where nothing bad would ever happen to us. But guess what? No one controls me anymore, Calvin. No one. Including you."

He winced and shook his head. "I'm not trying to control you."

"You are! Why can't you just believe me when I say I'm okay? Why can't you trust me?"

Calvin exhaled and looked at his shoes. "Okay, the note was a dumb idea. I'm sorry. But some of the stuff I read online—"

"You think I'm lying to you?"

"No."

"You think I'm crazy? Is that it?"

"No." Calvin ground his teeth on the word.

"Then what?"

"Prove me wrong, Stacey. Please."

"How am I supposed to do that? Stuff my face and turn into a chunky bunny again? So only drunk old men are attracted to me?"

"Huh? No. No! But Stace, I don't understand—"

She swiped her hand across one wet cheek. "Well, why don't you look it up on the Internet. And by the way, maybe you should catch up with Tyler or you'll be walking home."

Calvin's jaw dropped. Stacey hugged her purse beneath her crossed arms and tilted her chin upward.

He swallowed. "Seriously?"

Stacey's face stayed hard even as another tear rolled down the side of her nose. She'd meant it.

Calvin groaned and rocked his head back to look at the sky.

"Better run. I see the Camaro, right over there."

He jerked his head around. The bright red car slid between the parked vehicles, heading for the main driveway out. When he looked back, Stacey was already walking back toward the building.

"Fine! Whatever. See ya." Calvin whirled and ran along the curb, his backpack hammering his shoulder blades. He put two fingers in his mouth and whistled as Tyler turned toward the exit. "Ty! Wait!"

The Camaro's tires skidded on the damp asphalt. Flannery opened the side door and stood. Calvin kept his eyes down, avoiding whatever scowl or look of shock she might be wearing as he crawled into the backseat.

"I don't want to talk about it," he said before either of his friends could voice a question.

○ ○ ◯ ○ ○

Was it a breakup? Had he ruined everything? Had she confessed what happened in Rocky Mount only to show him what a jerk he was to say anything about the way she ate?

Calvin played with the straw in his Coke, studied the crisscross indentations in his forearm made by the metal mesh table at Oliver's, and only half listened to the conversation going on between Flannery and Tyler. They should have just dropped him off at home.

After the fifth or sixth time, Flannery stopped asking him what had happened in the school parking lot. Instead, she gave him disapproving looks across the table, as if she blamed him. *A note? Really, Calvin?* And anyway, she probably wanted to be alone with Tyler so she could flirt with him.

Tyler made lame, forced jokes and sucked down his chocolate shake, like he was trying to make things normal, to break the literal ice between them.

Calvin stared at the few vehicles parked diagonally next to menu boards. A mom accepted food from a roller-skating waitress while three little kids bounced around in the back of her van. A man sat alone behind the wheel of a pickup with a magnetic sign on the doors. *General Jake's Greenscapes.* General of what? A couple of jocks from school turned up the thumping music in their car, probably so they couldn't hear the "oldies" crackling through the drive-in's ancient ceiling speakers.

Calvin imagined a blue Honda Civic flying into the parking lot and screeching to a stop next to Tyler's Camaro, Stacey jumping out without closing the door and flinging herself into his arms. Tears and kisses, promises that everything would be okay.

He blinked, and the parking space was empty, shining with moisture from the earlier rain, a purple-and-blue oil slick in the middle.

Flannery's cell phone chirped. She pulled it out of her pocket and read a text. "Well, here's some good news for you, Calvin. My dad found your throttle cable. Says he should get it by the end of the week."

Calvin closed his eyes. "Thank you, God."

Empty prayer. Just something to say. He could be happy later.

"So, you'll be able to fix your bike," Flannery said without smiling. "Think you can keep it running until summer?"

"Flan," Tyler muttered.

"Okay, sorry. But seriously. My parents are talking about going camping and fishing soon as school lets out. They were looking at some places, and we found one about four hours from here that has riding trails too. Badin Lake."

Tyler slurped the last of his chocolate shake. "I've heard of that place," he said, setting the cup down. "ATV and dirt bike trails. Some are supposed to be super hard."

Flannery brightened. "Right! So I was thinking, maybe y'all could come with us. We could take the bikes and do some serious riding."

"I'd rather do the motocross track than trails," Tyler said. "We could go back to that MX track with the little cabins."

"We can do that too! Go MX riding for a weekend, and go trail riding for like, a whole week."

Calvin ground his fingertips into his eyes. Did they really expect him to think about summertime when he was on the brink of breaking up with his girlfriend?

"Cal? What do you think?" Flannery asked.

He dropped his hands to the table. "Dad probably wants me to work in the garage with him this summer."

"You worked practically all spring break! He's got to give you some time off this summer."

"I guess."

"You guess? I'm trying to cheer you up, dude."

He sniffed. "Yeah. Thanks."

"Ugh! I hate it when you're like this."

"Flannery." Tyler groaned, throwing his head back. "Can we not do this again, please?"

Calvin rattled the ice in his cup then thumped it on the table. "Right. Are y'all finished? I've got homework."

"Cal ..." Tyler got up when Calvin did.

"I'm bummed about Stacey, okay? Flan? Tell your dad thanks for finding the cable. And ... I'm sorry."

Flannery's thumbs danced on the tiny cell phone keyboard. "Calvin ... says ... he's ... sorry ..."

"What? No! I didn't mean—"

"I'm joking!" She sent whatever her real message was and rose from the metal bench. The phone went back into the pocket of her shorts. "Look, I know you're upset. Just don't take it out on everyone else. Okay?"

Calvin rolled his eyes. So he had to apologize, but Flannery didn't? No doubt he'd have to go through the same routine with Stacey.

If she even wanted to speak to him again.

Chapter 14

*L*et *hm w8*, Zoe had said in her text message. *Let hm suffr til he begs u 2 4giv hm. DO NOT call hm 1st.*

Zoe could say that. After hearing about Calvin's note, she hated him.

But text messaging aside, Zoe wasn't here in Stacey's bedroom. She wasn't here to boost her morale with anger and colorful language. Stacey suffered alone, her nerves like a static machine and her eyes making pillow puddles every time the digits on her alarm clock rolled over another five, ten, fifteen minutes and Calvin didn't call.

Eight fifteen. His family would have finished with dinner long ago. The dishes would be washed and put away, and his mother trying to wrangle the little kids into bed. Calvin and Lizzie might be settling down to do their homework on the dining room table.

Stacey's stomach was an empty cavern. Who could eat under this kind of stress? She'd made excuses and hidden her uneaten food in her room. Now, sitting with only a tiny pink vanity lamp to light the room, Stacey's sobs sent a burning echo into the dark abyss of her belly and a warbling distress call to her heart. *Flutter. Flutter.* The stress murmur she'd had all her life kicked in worse than she'd ever felt before.

Why did she have to tell Calvin about Uncle Murray? Why?

She didn't want him to feel sorry for her. Didn't want to remember what happened and all the fights before they moved. It was just ... if Calvin knew ... it wasn't just bullies at school ...

Stacey yanked three tissues from a box on her bedside table. She blew the junk from her nose, grabbed two more tissues to wipe her eyes, then an antiseptic wipe to kill the germs. She'd fill her little trash bin with tissues before morning.

Did Calvin have any clue what he was doing to her?

Eight thirty. Fully dark outside. Calvin's mother would light one of her homemade scented candles on the table for her busy students.

Stacey's breath rattled past her lips as she flipped open her chemistry textbook. The letters blurred, became meaningless.

She'd forgive him for everything if he would just *call*.

Her cell phone lay on the bed next to her wrist, the little screen black. Betraying her.

What would Calvin say was the Christian thing to do? Forgive seven times, or whatever it was Jesus said?

Her fingers caressed the outline of her phone. She nudged it, touched the first digit of Calvin's number. Two. The number showed white on the screen.

She could hear Zoe's groan and cry. *You're pathetic!*

Eight thirty-five.

Outside her window, frogs in the long, wet grass by the street chirped their nightly song. The world turned. Life went on.

Was Calvin done with her? Too much drama. Maybe they'd hung on to each other too long anyway. After Michael's death, he *needed* her, and she'd loved that feeling. She was important to him. But now, in his mind, she was broken, something he had to fix or throw away.

I don't need to be fixed.

This was stupid. Waiting around for him to call, agonizing over it, unable to do anything else. Stacey pushed herself up. She had to get this thing resolved.

Zoe would hate her for it. Too bad, so sad.

Stacey punched two more numbers on her phone.

No, not good enough. Calvin would refuse to speak to her or hang up.

Stacey rocketed off the bed and yanked on a pair of jeans and her pink hoodie. She grabbed her phone, purse, and keys and flew downstairs.

Her father's voice stopped her before she reached the front door. "Where are you going?

She turned toward the living room, where Daddy sat in his recliner with the newspaper in his lap. If she'd thought to grab a textbook, she could have used it as an excuse. "Uh, I'm going to Calvin's house."

"What for? It's almost nine o'clock."

State-mandated driving curfew. Of course her father would hold her to the law even though almost no one she knew paid much attention to those regulations.

"I—we need to talk about school."

A subtle downward tilt of Daddy's head and the narrowing of one eye told her he wasn't buying it. "Call him. That's what your phone is for."

"I-I know, but . . ." She should have lied, said she was going for a short walk or even to sit on the front porch to have some fresh air.

Mom got up from her usual perch on the couch. She straightened her blouse and glided around the furniture. "Sweetheart, do you really think you should be going out?" She touched the back of her hand to Stacey's cheek. "Your face is hot. Are you feeling okay?"

"I'm not sick." She fought the urge to slap her mother's hand away. Instead, she moved her face to the side. "Calvin's having a problem at home, and I just want to go see him for a few minutes."

Drawing on Mom's sympathy for Calvin's "loss" always worked. Yet Mom copied the exact questioning tilt of Daddy's head. "You can't sort out all his problems for him, sweetheart. I know you care, but he really should be drawing close to his family at times like this."

Change the subject, quick. "It isn't about Michael. Calvin's problem *is* his family." *Yeah. Familiar story.* "He's really upset. I'm just going over to give him a hug and talk for a few minutes. I won't be late."

She stepped back, caught her father's glare. He started to get out of his recliner. Stacey bolted for the door.

Her sister's scantily clad figure leaned against the rail on the front porch. Cigarette smoke swirled through the air. Stacey rushed past Renee without making eye contact, focused on how quickly her feet could navigate the stairs. Hopefully Renee's smoking would be the greater offense when her father came out, giving Stacey a chance to escape. She unlocked her car door and fell into the driver's seat without looking to see what happened on the porch.

Her pulse fluttered in her throat as she drove, her hands moved on the steering wheel with each beat. Stacey's determination wavered, going back and forth like a caged animal unable to find any means of escape. What if Calvin was so angry that he wouldn't talk to her? There'd be an ugly scene at the front door. Maybe they'd break up forever. But what if he was so devastated that he'd locked himself in his room and only her voice could bring him out?

Yeah, right. Maybe in some cheesy romance novel. She wasn't worth that kind of despair from anyone.

She made the sharp turn onto Victory Church Road. One more mile.

A scream wanted to break out of her. It scratched at her insides, pushing, tearing. Maybe she was having one of Mom's anxiety attacks. Little pills always sat in the medicine cabinet ... so easy to steal one later.

Stacey gave her head a violent shake. Was she really thinking about taking drugs?

Someone was on the front porch of Calvin's farmhouse. His

mother, lighting citronella candles on the porch rail. Would Mrs. Greenlee tell her she should go home? Protect Calvin from his crazed girlfriend?

Had Calvin told anyone in his family why she'd puked in their bathroom? Or that she'd given the dog the fried catfish?

Stacey drove past the house, her eyes fixed on the road. *Don't look at me!* Her heart felt like it would explode in her chest and kill her. Why was this happening to her? To them?

She hit her brakes hard at the entrance to the old church that gave the road its name, and swerved right into the parking lot. Then she made a big loop around the empty lot until she faced the way she'd come. A quarter mile away, Calvin's house was almost invisible in the dark. Only a dark shadow with a few rectangles of warm light in the midst.

Breathe. Breathe. Figure it out. She was sitting like a stalker looking at her boyfriend's house. How sad. What a sorry wreck she was. She should've just called him. She could still do it.

Stacey pulled her phone from her purse and dialed Calvin's number. Peyton answered and yelled for him to come to the phone. Stacey wiped a fresh flood of tears from her face, waiting for his voice to come through her cell.

"It's Stacey," Peyton yelled.

Then nothing. The pause was too long. Any instant now she'd hear a loud click as he hung up on her.

"Hey." His deep voice and the single monotone syllable sent a shockwave through her.

What could she say? She'd left her sanity at home. "Hi."

I'm sorry. Please forgive me. I need you to understand. The words wouldn't come to her lips. *Say something!* "Are you okay?"

He hummed.

"Calvin?"

"Not really."

"I'm sorry. I should have given you a ride home."

A hiss on the line was his deep intake of breath. "I don't think that's what's really important right now."

Stacey pressed her hand over her eyes, leaning her elbow against the steering wheel for support. "Well … I know. But. We need to talk."

"You basically told me to go away. I've been thinking we broke up or something."

"I'm trying to keep us from breaking up. Calvin—" A sob broke through. "I love you! I-I'm sorry. I didn't say anything right this afternoon. I was upset and I got it all wrong. I'm just trying to get you to understand."

"Understand what? That your uncle is a pervert who deserves to be strangled? I get that. What I don't get is how I'm supposed to stand around and let you starve yourself."

"I'm not … I'm not …"

The world darkened. Pressure built in her head, like she'd been dunked underwater and every cell in her brain screamed for oxygen.

"I can't do that, Stace. I can't watch you kill yourself to be skinny. Besides, you're not fat. Since I've known you, you've never been fat. I loved the way you looked when I met you, and I love you now."

"Calvin …" She sobbed again, but choked out more words. "You're the best thing that ever happened to me. Please. I can't lose you."

His breath whispered through the phone. "I'm not going anywhere," he finally said, his voice strained. "I just don't know what to do."

His inflection yanked another sob out of her. So what could they do? Compromise? Stacey stroked her thumb and forefinger along her eyebrows, rubbing away an assault of vertigo.

Calvin would never understand. He'd make himself an expert in anorexia, and then one day, despite any promises they made tonight, he'd throw all that information at her again and they'd argue. Maybe even worse than today. How could she live with that inevitability looming all the time?

Stacey shifted the phone to her other ear. "I love you."

"I love you too." Too fast, too easy. Did he mean it or just say it automatically after her?

"What do you want me to do?" she asked.

"Eat like a normal person. I mean, people go on diets and lose weight all the time, but they still eat. You can do that. You don't need to ... stuff your face and turn into a chunky bunny."

She winced. He'd thrown back the words she'd used against him that afternoon. Obviously, he wasn't done being angry.

"I do eat." She caught her breath and forced her bitterness down. "Please ... Do we have to go through this again? I know it looks bad. Passing out and stuff. But I promise there's a good explanation for it."

"Maybe you just need a doctor to give you a diet that's safe. You know, because of that heart problem you had when you were little."

Now she wished she hadn't told him about her surgeries. He'd use that against her too. She could see him already fussing over her, playing the hero in her life. Bossing her around like her parents. The silent scream inside her rose up again, grabbed her by the windpipe, and sent a cold tremor down the rest of her body. "Calvin, I had surgery to *fix* those problems. Forget about that. I'm fine."

His groan sounded distant, like he'd moved the phone away from his face so she wouldn't hear it. "You keep saying that. You're fine."

"I am!"

Except for right this moment. Was the temperature dropping outside?

In the distance, the farmhouse looked almost creepy. Somewhere inside Calvin paced the floor, tugged his hair, and devised ways to get her to confess everything he thought she was doing. The battle she waged wasn't over the phone. It was inside Calvin's head. She had to convince him. Their relationship was at stake. Because she couldn't live with his suspicions, and today's confession had failed.

Start with a promise. Buy some time. She'd try harder and make it work.

"Calvin, I promise, if I get sick again I'll have my mom take me to the doctor."

"Okay." His tone went up with the last syllable, making it a question.

"And if I don't pass out or anything, you have to promise you'll trust me. I know how to take care of myself."

"Sure. If you're healthy, then I don't have anything to worry about."

"So we're agreed?"

He sighed, took too long to answer, but finally said, "Yeah, I guess so."

She closed her eyes and rested her forehead against the steering wheel.

How could she keep herself from getting dizzy again? Stacey didn't even know what had caused it the first time. Vitamin deficiency? Maybe she should swallow some of those pills. She'd have to do some research of her own to figure it out.

"It'll be okay, Calvin. Really. I promise."

"'Kay."

"Want me to pick you up in the morning?"

"Sure, that'd be great."

"I'm really sorry. I treated you horribly, and I know you're just concerned for my health. I was just so — I don't know ... That note. It was ..."

"Yeah ... I'm sorry about that. It was stupid. I'm not like you. I'm, like ..." He paused for a second. "Ah ain't too good with wrahtin', y'know whut ah mean?"

She giggled at his comedically thickened drawl. A tiny shaft of warmth seeped through her, easing the chaos a little. "Promise me something else?"

"What?"

"You'll never talk about breaking up again."

"Ever? That mean we gon' git hee-itched?"

She imagined his sweet lips widening, creasing his cherubic cheeks. That smile could rival the angelic expression in any Renaissance painting.

"Ma-a-ay-be," she cooed.

"Oh, Lord, save me."

"Hey!"

"I'm joking."

At the sound of Calvin's soft chuckle, Stacey gazed at the house. In a few seconds, she could be there. She could hold him, press her ear against his broad chest and hear his heartbeat, feel his strong arms around her. Maybe he'd agree to go for a drive with her. In some quiet corner of the county, they could be together for a little while—

Headlights dimmed her view of the house. A car slid past, a light rack on top, Stiles County Police painted on the side. Stacey's desire choked. Had Daddy summoned his friends at the police department to look for her?

"Still there?" Calvin asked.

"Um, yeah. Calvin, I have to go. M-my father is calling me."

"Oh, okay. I'll see you tomorrow morning then."

She twisted in her seat to watch the taillights of the squad car diminish in the distance then disappear around a curve in the road.

"Stace?"

"I'm here. Yes, tomorrow morning. I love you, Calvin."

"Love you too. G'night."

She hung up and stared at the dark road behind her. If Daddy had sent the police after her, they would have recognized her car sitting alone in the church parking lot. Just coincidence that they'd passed by.

Stacey sat up straight and drew several deep breaths to calm her racing heart. Would she ever be free of Daddy's controlling rules? Sometimes the urge to leave was so strong. Take the car, drive to California or New York, get a job with a fashion designer fetching coffee or whatever they'd let her do. Start a real life.

Maybe Calvin would go with her.

A light clicked on in the dormer windows of his house. His attic bedroom. She'd never been up there; it wasn't allowed. More rules. A shadow passed over one window. She imagined him there, sitting on his bed, kicking off his shoes, opening a book. Oh, how sweet it would be to snuggle in his arms as they studied together. Even if they could just sit on the porch ...

In fifteen seconds, she could be there.

Blue lights flashed in Stacey's rearview mirror. Gasping, she jumped in her seat and grabbed the steering wheel. Her car was still running. Her right hand leapt to the gearshift lever, pulled on it.

Stacey closed her eyes. She could never outrun a cop cruiser in her little Honda.

She put the car in park again. Her heart thudding in her throat, she lowered her window. A man in a khaki uniform filled her view.

"Did my daddy send you? I'm not doing anything wrong."

"Driver's license, miss."

She fished it out of her purse and handed it over.

"Varnell?" he said. "You're Officer Varnell's daughter?"

Like he didn't already know.

"You can call my father and tell him I'm on my way home."

"Miss Varnell, may I ask why you're sitting here in the church lot?"

"Just thinking about some stuff."

Would those blue lights flash against Calvin's window? If he looked out, would he recognize her car? Stalker Stacey. Her heart froze at the thought. She had to get out of there.

The cop leaned down to look at her, practically sticking his face in her window. What? Sniffing for drugs or something? Was he going to haul her out and frisk her? Search her car? Call in a K–9 unit? Teach her a lesson for defying Daddy?

"You all alone in there?"

"Yes. I had a fight with my boyfriend today. I'm ... I'm just upset." She pressed the heel of one hand against her forehead. It'd be nice if she could raise some more tears.

His hand came through the window, her license between the fingers. "Think you'd better head on home, Miss Varnell."

She blinked and grabbed her license back. "You're letting me go?"

"Any reason why I shouldn't?"

"Uh—no. No reason. Are you going to call my father?"

"I'm giving you a break because you're Stan Varnell's daughter. I suggest you take advantage of it."

"Yes, sir. Yes, sir. I'll go home. Right now."

Stacey put her car in gear and rolled slowly to the entrance of the parking lot. The blue lights stopped flashing, but the squad car followed her. There'd be talk in the station house tomorrow, for sure.

As she drove past Calvin's house, she rolled her eyes toward the dormer windows. No silhouette darkened the rectangles of soft light.

What was he doing up there?

Her heart fluttered. If there wasn't a police car just behind her, she could stop, get Calvin, run away with him. Leave this nightmare behind.

Chapter 15

Calvin paced the floor between his bed and Michael's. Angry, ugly words assaulted the synapses in his brain and breached his will until they spilled out of his mouth. He punched the air with each phrase. "Freakin' idiot. Moron. She did it to me again."

He'd caved. Apologized for everything and let Stacey off. Because her crying had ripped him apart. Tyler was right; Stacey ruled him.

Calvin buried both hands in his hair and pulled. "Argh! I'm such a wuss!"

But what options did he have? If he fought with her, they'd only break up and he wouldn't be able to stop her from becoming one of those skeleton girls he'd seen online.

He slid down onto the floor and put his head between his knees.

According to Flannery, he was supposed to be nice and loving to Stacey. Too bad it felt false, like he was manipulating her until he could figure out how to get her to see a doctor.

What was a guy supposed to do when someone he cared about was anorexic? According to what he'd read, anorexia nervosa was like an obsessive-compulsive disorder. People who had it convinced themselves they were fat even if everyone else saw them as skinny. He'd watched a video showing a chubby girl looking into a mirror, then the camera panned back and showed her as she really was, with bones sticking out everywhere.

Calvin pulled his hair until scalp pain drove the image away.

He had to stop this thing, this disorder. Before he had to see Stacey as a skeleton girl.

But he had to go carefully, so he wouldn't drive her away. He had to stick with her, while at the same time making sure she didn't distract him from what he needed to do.

"How much am I supposed to take?" he said to his knees. "This is crazy."

Other guys would walk away. What was wrong with wanting a normal girlfriend?

He sniffed and raised his head. Across from him, Michael's bed was neatly made up with pillows and a comforter topped by his red, black, and white NC State fleece throw. All arranged as if nothing had happened. Like Michael would come walking up the stairs at any moment, snatch a foam football off a shelf, and launch it at Calvin's face. "*Think fast, lump!*"

Calvin drew in a sharp breath at the memory of Michael's favorite nickname for him. Yeah, like Stacey was the only one who'd *ever* been called a name because of her weight. Thing was, Michael never meant it to hurt. What Calvin wouldn't give now just to hear that teasing name again, to throw something back at his brother, to wrestle on and between the beds until Mom came upstairs to tell them they were keeping the little kids awake with their racket.

But Michael's bed was empty, and the silence in the room echoed in Calvin's heart.

He turned his eyes to the ceiling, where a thousand times he'd directed questions asking God why his brother had to die. He'd figured out the only answer anyone could have: Michael was dead because guys died in wars. That was it. Nothing profound. All the causes and slogans and reasons didn't change the simple fact that

Michael had left home to fight for something he believed in, and he died because someone else in a dusty desert country had buried a bomb along the road.

Leaving a gaping hole in Calvin's world.

He couldn't lose Stacey, couldn't make that hole even bigger.

Calvin's hands fisted painfully against the floor. His throat closed up just as tightly.

And that man, that uncle of hers. Names filtered through Calvin's brain that a good Christian boy should never utter. He had to think God would forgive him for it. Maybe. The guy deserved to be in jail. But if he never touched Stacey, how could what he said affect her so much that she would just stop eating?

Too many questions. He'd go crazy trying to figure everything out. Still, there had to be something online that would tell him how he was supposed to watch her body dwindle away day by day without going crazy himself.

Calvin lurched to his feet, pulling his own comforter halfway onto the floor. He left it there and padded softly down the stairs and past the rooms where his brothers and baby sister were sleeping, past the door with light seeping through the crack where Lizzie — and hopefully Peyton — would be reading or polishing their nails or whatever girls did before bed. He slipped past the living room where his father was watching television, and into the dining room, where the computer waited for him, still on, the screen saver shifting pictures. Calvin claimed the chair, and his fingers flew over the keyboard, typing words into the search engine: *my girlfriend is anorexic.* He banged the enter key.

Calvin scanned the websites his search had found. Lots of message boards with guys in his exact predicament, all looking for the same answers. He clicked on the first promising link and squinted at small print against a pale blue background. At least this time anyone snooping around would think he was studying.

He read questions and answers on website after website. All voicing the same worries he had, the same questions he had, and the same answers he'd feared. "My girlfriend is anorexic. What should I do?" was answered with "You can't fix her" and "This is going to be hard" and "Don't argue with her, it'll only make things worse."

Were these people real? The concerns of guys Calvin would never meet swallowed his sense of himself. He was floating, living their thoughts and fears, sucked up by the same questions. Yet there were no faces or names. Each person told Calvin's story over and over, with slight variations that warned him of what was to come.

The only definitive thing he learned was that things would only get worse.

The behavior, the symptoms, the damage. Anorexia was a "relationship killer," one person said. And a problem far beyond counting calories; it was not really about losing weight, but about being in control. Seeing something completely different in the mirror and hating the way it looked, even if other people said it was beautiful. It all meant that Stacey was at the beginning of a terrible ride that could ruin her, even kill her. And Calvin was buckled in beside her. If he chose to stay.

"She needs counseling," was the only answer that made sense.

How was he supposed to get her to go to counseling? She didn't even realize she had a problem!

He cussed, and that single spoken word broke the illusion, brought him back to the reality that he was sitting in a chair inside a farmhouse in North Carolina. Air infused with the warm scent of the roast beef they'd had for supper filled his lungs. Dark paneling and cross-stitched decorations surrounded him. The television mumbled in the background. Calvin blinked and sniffed, found tears on his face.

He glanced over his shoulder. His dad snored softly in his chair. A tiny glow through the front window told him Mom was outside still, rocking and praying or just finding some quiet to end her day. No sound filtered down from the girls' room upstairs. Each person had retreated to their own little sphere of existence. Not a one of them would have the answers Calvin needed even if he tried to talk to them. He doubted even Michael would have any clue.

He turned around and stared at the computer screen. All those guys with anorexic girlfriends had gone to the Internet for answers rather than their own parents or friends. And what did it get them? Did anyone have *the* answer for them? Calvin couldn't tell. Because the stories were never finished. No additional posts saying, "She's cured!" or even "She's dead."

Love her through it. But how?

Chapter 16

The pink tulip petals turned to yellow at their delicate edges without transitioning through orange. They felt like fine silk beneath Stacey's fingertips. Calvin had clipped the flower from his mother's garden and had given it to Stacey as he slid into her car, a gift-bearing Romeo chasing away the nervous tremors that had robbed her of sleep and plagued her as she drove to his house.

It wasn't his only gift, though. He'd also brought her one of Mrs. Greenlee's big, soft blueberry muffins. The aroma filled her car and eroded her resistance. She had to eat it, couldn't stop at just a few nibbles. Calvin watched too closely. Now the thing sat like a giant lump in her gut. She could imagine the muffin breaking apart, the calories dancing through her bloodstream like ecstatic parasites, attaching themselves to her stomach, thighs, butt, arms, and face.

Maybe she could use the stench of simmering chemicals as an excuse to go empty her stomach. All around the lab area of the classroom, students were lighting up Bunsen burners and collecting the chemicals they would need for today's experiment. Stacey's partner, Kenny, had gone to fetch a beaker of hydrochloric acid and some strips of magnesium.

"What's that?" Zoe flopped her hands down on the lab counter next to the tulip.

Stacey tilted her chin down and stared at her friend.

Zoe rolled her eyes. "Okay, I know it's a flower. Does this mean everything is nice-nice with the farm boy again?"

"Yes, we made up. We love each other again."

"Eww." Zoe's eyes narrowed to slits.

Stacey shoulder-bumped her friend. "Come on. Why can't you be happy for me?"

Zoe sighed and looked off somewhere in the classroom. "I guess I'm just worried that you'll end up pregnant and then married, and you'll give up all your plans for college. Maybe you'll have twenty-seven kids and end up on a reality show."

"Oh, you're just so sure I'm going to get pregnant and give everything up."

"He's a farm boy. Isn't that what they do? Marry young, have a gazillion babies, inherit the farm, get excited about things like John Deere tractors and NASCAR?"

"Oh, please. Zoe, stop it. Aren't you supposed to be at your table working with Ashley?"

"Miss Straight-As likes it when I stay out of her way. Besides, Stace, what's old Calvin gonna do next year when we're ready to leave for design school? Cry? 'Oh, don't go, baby. I l-l-love yo-oo-oou.'" Zoe deepened her voice and tugged on her hair.

Stacey turned her eyes toward the ceiling. "Zoe, it hurts me when you say bad things about him. Can't you *try* to be nice?"

Zoe's breath hissed through the air between them. "Fine. Be with the farm boy. I don't care." Yet she pouted, and something like real pain puckered her eyelids.

"I do care," Stacey said. "Just tell me straight. Please?"

Zoe groaned. "Okay, I don't *hate* him. He's a *nice* guy. But boring. I think you can find someone better."

Stacey brought Calvin's flower to her nose, inhaling its sweetness. "You don't know him the way I do."

Zoe pushed her body away from the counter, looking down at the floor. "I'll never let any guy tie me down. Ever. They act like they own you, take everything you've got to offer, then cry like a wounded puppy when you try to leave."

Stacey studied her friend. Was she speaking from experience? She'd never mentioned a boyfriend before, and all her talk about this hot guy or that hot guy lasted only a moment.

"Zoe, did you — I mean — did some guy hurt you?"

Her eyes hardened. "No. I learned enough watching my mother get hurt over and over. So no guy is getting close enough to me to hold me back. I'll get what *I* want, then I'm done."

Stacey gasped as understanding dawned. "I see. So that's why — you think Calvin is going to hold me back."

"Not think. Know."

Movement beyond Zoe's shoulders slammed the conversation shut. Kenny had returned, bearing gifts in beakers and vials. Zoe snatched up Stacey's tulip. "Can I borrow this? Thank you." She circled behind Stacey. "Ken, darling — "

"What the — that's mine!" Stacey whirled and grabbed Zoe's wrist. She pried Zoe's fingers away from the stem of the flower.

Zoe backed up, giggling, but lanky Kenny didn't get out of her way fast enough. He lifted the glass beaker up to avoid Zoe's body, but the liquid inside sloshed over the brim. It made a high, dribbling arch and splashed across Stacey's arm.

Stacey's gasp seemed trapped between her ears. The acid immediately turned the pristine ecru of her linen sleeve a pee-yellow color. She felt the heat on her arm. She stared at it, her arm petrified in the position it had been when the acid rained upon her. The tulip slipped from her trembling fingers.

"Sink! Now!" Kenny shoved the remaining chemicals onto their table and grabbed Stacey's shoulders.

Germs! Acid! Burning, burning, eating away at her shirt and her skin! Grunting sounds blurted from Stacey's throat with each crazed step as her lab partner pushed her to the stainless steel basin at the back of the room. Dizziness wrapped clammy tentacles around Stacey's face and rushed down to her stomach. She tasted bile and pushed it back. Darkness danced at the edge of her vision as her brain fought the urge to purge.

Kenny turned on the water, grabbed Stacey's arm, and shoved it under the gushing flow.

A distant part of her brain told her she wasn't going to die. Yet that rational thought couldn't stand against the onslaught of her phobia, and her body would have its way. Her arm still under the faucet, Stacey pitched forward and dumped blueberry muffin into the sink.

A chorus of yells and groans erupted in the classroom. Heat flooded Stacey's face in a double portion of sickness and humiliation. Somewhere Mr. Emerson tried to take control of the situation, barking orders at the students. Kenny, the hero of the moment, tried to tell Stacey it was okay, just keep her arm under the water. She crooked her other arm on the edge of the sink and used it to pillow her forehead as sobs took the place of retching.

And that distant, rational part of her brain told her that this time, at least, she had a whole classroom full of witnesses who could provide a very good reason for her purging.

∘ ◯ ◯ ◯ ∘

Calvin's promise to trust her lasted barely a week. What was he thinking? First the blueberry muffin — the memory of which made Stacey's stomach queasy all over again — and then another note. At least this one, creased and wrinkled from having been forced through the vents of her locker, was in Calvin's own handwriting.

I love you. Please eat. I want you to be healthy.

Totally clueless. *I love you, but let me boss you around and think that I know so much better than you about your own body.* He'd never get it.

Stacey sat in a corner of the library, a stack of research books untouched. Starting her report for history class on nurses in Vietnam was the furthest thing from her mind.

Beside the books, Calvin's tulip wilted, in spite of its rescue from the puddle of hydrochloric acid in the chemistry lab and the wet paper towels she'd wrapped around the stem. Wilting ... like his promises.

A tear ran down Stacey's cheek. She didn't care if anyone saw it. What could she do? If she ate the way Calvin wanted her to, stuffing herself on blueberry muffins and cheeseburgers and barbecue, all the weight she'd worked so hard to lose over a year would come back. Then she'd have no choice but to marry him and have babies and become a fat farmer's wife like ... like his mother. But if she didn't do what he wanted, he might get frustrated and dump her.

She knew what Zoe's solution would be. But she couldn't dump Calvin first. She just couldn't. Where would she find another boyfriend who would even put up with her?

Skinny Stacey inside her clenched her fist in defiance, while Sad Stacey on the outside lay her head down on her folded arms.

"Are you okay?" someone asked.

Go away.

The girl behind her murmured to another person, and they both went away.

What if she showed Calvin the pictures in the family photo albums? All the snapshots of Mommy's roly-poly sweetheart. The class pictures where she was the fat kid sitting at the very end of the row wearing a stupid fake smile, hurting inside from all the taunts on the playground. The image of a sad fourteen-year-old whose boobs were already too big, whose parents thought her pout was only some kind of emo phase that would soon pass.

Did Calvin really want her to go back to that? She'd die if she did. Forget it; if Calvin truly loved her, he'd accept her choices and embrace the model-slim Stacey she wanted to be.

Banging, shuffling, and voices surrounded her. Did the period bell ring?

Stacey lifted her head. Black eye makeup had stained her rolled-up sleeve. Her face burned, and that meant there'd be ugly red blotches. She couldn't go to art class looking like a mess. And the thought of food, of chicken nuggets and greasy burgers and dried-up salad after that — Ugh! Stacey put her head down again and sucked in air from the tiny space between her face and the table.

"Stacey? What's wrong?"

Go away.

This time it didn't work. "Stacey, why are you crying?"

"Go away. Whoever you are."

"Hey ..." The chair scraped the floor as someone brazenly took a seat. Definitely not going away. The person nudged Stacey's elbow to make sure she was paying attention.

Really?

Stacey lifted her head and sniffed. Her eyelids fluttered and her vision focused.

Flannery.

Stacey's heart skittered. She snagged and crumpled Calvin's note before Flannery could see it. "Oh, uh, I'm not feeling well."

Flannery blinked her huge green eyes. Almost no makeup. She didn't need it. "You and Calvin okay? I know y'all had a fight. Stace, I'd like to help, if I can."

Oh yeah, like she was *so* going to talk to Flannery Moore about

Calvin. Might as well give the girl written permission to ruin her life.

"No—I mean, we did, but it's okay now. See?" She lifted the tulip. Its head drooped pathetically, like her lie. "It's just, I'm having a really bad day and I'm ... hurting. My period." Stacey put on a trembling smile. "I get cramps really bad sometimes."

"Gotcha. Can I get you a cold drink? I have a package of crackers in my locker if you wan—"

Stacey jumped off her stool. "Are you trying to stuff me with food too? I eat! Okay? I eat all the time. Did Calvin send you to—" *What am I doing?* "Forget it. I'll eat during lunch. Thanks for checking on me, though. I'm fine. I have to go to class now." She grabbed her things. "This happens every month. It'll pass."

She hurried out of the library and found a bathroom mirror where she could make herself look acceptable again.

Flannery would tell Calvin.

Heat flooded Stacey's skin again.

Cramps. That was her excuse after her face-plant on the floor. Same excuse today. Calvin would put those pieces together real quick. Fifteen days wasn't enough time to repeat the lie. A hundred and six days had passed since the excuse could have been true. What would Calvin say if he got wind of *that* fact?

Scared Stacey in the mirror lifted an eyeliner pencil and drew a wobbly black line beneath her eye.

Chapter 17

"Man, I can't wait. I *so* need to ride." Calvin squatted beside his Yamaha and applied a wrench to the nut connecting his old throttle cable to the carburetor. His fuel tank and seat lay off to the side.

Flannery stood beside him in the workshop, running her fingers along the length of the new cable. "I hear you. I'd go crazy without my bike for so long."

Sure, Flannery heard his words, but she didn't hear his heart screaming for relief from the juggling act his life had become in the last week. Seemed the more attention he gave Stacey, the more she needed. Until Flannery showed up at the front door with the new throttle cable in her hands, Calvin rarely had a moment when he thought about something other than how to make sure Stacey felt beautiful and loved. It left him exhausted each night.

Calvin tugged the wrench and grunted. The nut didn't budge. "Rusted solid."

"Need some WD-40?" Flannery asked.

"Or a stick of dynamite."

Flannery chuckled. "Where's the spray?"

Calvin tried again, and the wrench bit into the flesh of his palm. "Cabinet next to the tool chest. Thanks." He laid one hand on the motorcycle frame for balance and tried his weight against the wrench.

Flannery rattled bottles and cans around in the cluttered metal cabinet. "Um, I wanted to ask you a question."

"Whh-at?" Calvin said through another grunt.

"Does Tyler ever talk about me?"

"Sure he does." He settled back on his heels and looked over his shoulder. "Find it?"

She handed him the narrow canister. "Really? He does?"

"Yeah — Oh. Wait. You mean like — "

"Like he might like me. More than just friends."

Calvin didn't want to have this conversation. Did she make the special trip with his throttle cable just so she could quiz him about Tyler? The only truthful answer he could give — that Tyler had never talked about the possibility of dating Flannery — would hurt her.

Again, he had to hold back his real thoughts to avoid hurting someone's precious feelings. Calvin held his breath while he doused the throttle nut with WD-40.

"I know I'm asking you to, like, betray some best-friend code," Flannery said. "I just don't know what to do or say to him. Maybe if I knew whether it's even worth my time ..."

Calvin set the canister on the concrete floor a little harder than he'd intended. He stood, slipping his hands into his pockets. "Have to let that soak in a bit."

"I shouldn't ask. I'm just frustrated."

"If Tyler wants to ask you out, he will when he's ready."

"He sees me as just a friend. I know he does."

Calvin blew out his breath. He took the new cable from Flannery and examined the carburetor end.

"I don't know how to act around him anymore." Flannery's voice sounded soft, not like her at all.

Calvin's chest tightened. He wanted to turn away, fix his bike, fly through the woods, and leave everything behind. He could smell the exhaust, taste the fresh air, hear his bike's two-stroke song ringing in his ears.

"I'm sorry," Flannery said. "I shouldn't be burdening you with this right now. You've got enough on your mind with Stacey."

"The thing is I don't really know what to say." Calvin knelt down beside his bike, set the new cable on the floor, and picked up the wrench again. "Do you want me to ask him?"

"Yes—no. Yes. I don't know."

Calvin grinned. Kinda funny that Flannery was just now trying to figure out how to be a girl. He applied the wrench to the nut again. This time it moved, but the wrench couldn't grip the slick metal, and Calvin's hand slammed down against the cylinder block. He cussed, dropped the wrench, and stuck his knuckles into his mouth.

"Ooh!" Flannery bent over the seat of the bike to look. "Are you okay?"

Calvin whirled away from her and paced to the back of the workshop, shaking his stinging hand at his side. "Why can't *anything* be easy?"

Flannery followed him. "Are you hurt? Let me see."

"Just scraped the snot outta my knuckles." He held his hand out, palm down, for her to inspect. Blood collected in a bunch of tiny scratches. Soon the knuckles of his index and middle fingers would be covered in a deep purple bruise.

"Knuckles don't have snot," Flannery said, holding his hand in both of hers. "And these aren't even bleeding much. Can you flex your fingers?"

He did it for her. The pain was on the surface, not deep. *Shake it off. Come on.*

She smiled at him. "I think you'll live."

Her humor didn't make a dent. Calvin tugged his hair with his other hand. His eyes stung. *Forget this. Forget everything. Just walk away.*

"Calvin?"

"I'm fine."

"Cal ..."

He raised his eyes to meet hers and lost it. The tears flooded out. "I can't—My bike's a wreck, my life is a wreck. I don't know what else I can do."

Though the glow of the fluorescent shop light was behind her, Flannery's eyes glistened. "Maybe we should stop right now and pray."

Pray. Okay. Yeah. He sometimes forgot Flannery's family was so religious. Calvin swallowed against the knot in his throat and nodded.

Flannery inched closer and put one hand on his shoulder as she closed her eyes and lowered her head. "Lord, please help Calvin. He's hurting, and I know he's really worried about Stacey. At least make it easier for him to fix his bike so he can get a break and go for a ride. And help him with Stacey. I don't understand what she's doing to herself or why. Maybe Calvin can't even help her, but she's got to find a way to get some help from somebody."

Calvin sniffed and squeezed his eyes shut hard. Maybe God would hear Flannery's prayer—he sure didn't seem to be listening to Calvin's lately.

"Seems she doesn't want to listen to anyone, no matter how nice they try to be or ... you know. And I see Calvin pouring out everything he's got for her every day. So help her. Help her to see the truth of what she's doing to herself, and help all of us know what we need to do for her."

Calvin pressed his thumb and index finger into his burning eyes and muttered the only words he could get past his clamped-shut throat. "Yes, God. Please."

"Amen."

"Amen." With his fingers still against his eyes, Calvin breathed in and out, waiting for the tension in his throat to ease up.

"Oh crud," Flannery muttered.

What? Amen and oh crud? Calvin looked up.

Stacey stood in the workshop doorway, silhouetted against the afternoon sunshine. "Praying for me? Seriously?" She gripped the doorframe as if to hold herself up.

"Of course we're praying for you," Flannery said. "We're worried about you."

Oh no. No, no. Calvin closed his eyes against the coming train wreck. He grabbed two handfuls of hair and tugged hard. A wail passed through his clenched teeth. "God!"

No train wreck. No crashing, yelling, beating, or scratching. Just silence in the workshop and intense scalp pain. Calvin let go and looked up. Both girls stood where he'd last seen them, and both were staring at him. Stacey's glare captured him.

"Uh, I should go." Flannery's voice sounded far away. "See you Monday, Cal." She navigated the space between the motorcycle and Michael's car and mumbled something to Stacey as she left the workshop.

Calvin spread his arms wide. "Yes, we were praying for you. If that's wrong, I'm sorry. Well, I'm not sorry for praying, but—"

Stacey pointed toward the driveway, where Flannery had gone. "So, you *told* her?"

The answer stalled in his throat, came out as a pathetic squeak.

"What about Tyler? Did you tell him too?"

He inhaled and forced out the truth. "Yes."

"Does the whole school know?"

"No! Stacey . . ." He walked toward her. "You talk to Zoe about stuff. I needed someone to talk to, to try and figure out what to do to help you."

"I don't need any help! Except with studying for my history quiz, which is why I came over here. Like we agreed. Or did you forget?"

He stopped next to his motorcycle, his tools, throttle cable, and the can of WD-40 at his feet. Yes, he'd forgotten. Flannery showed up with the cable and everything else went out of his head. Calvin let his chin drop to his chest. "Flannery brought my new throttle cable over. We were out here putting it on the bike."

"And talking about me."

No sense in arguing it. Calvin spread his arms again. "Fine. Guilty." He stepped over the bike parts. "I won't talk about our problems with anyone else ever again. I'm sorry."

Stacey looked down, and her hair fell limply forward. She held her backpack at her knees. Her slender hands stuck out of the sleeves of a pretty green and blue top he remembered from last fall because it made her eyes look like jewels. Now the blouse hung on her like it was many sizes too big. And why was she wearing long sleeves in seventy-six degree weather anyway?

"Are we going to be apologizing to each other forever, Calvin?"

He rushed to her and wrapped his arms around her narrow shoulders. "I don't want to," he said into her hair. "Please, Stace, tell me what I need to do."

She dropped her backpack on the floor and grabbed him. Her hands moved against his back and the neck of his T-shirt tightened against his throat as she tugged the fabric. "I just want you to love me," she said against his shoulder. "Can't we be like we were before?"

"That's what I want too. That's all I want."

He squeezed her for a long moment, then took her hand and tugged her away from the workshop. They crossed the backyard to the gazebo his father had built for his mother years ago. The white paint on the posts and railings was chipping, but still caught the sunlight and dazzled his eyes. Calvin led Stacey up the steps and into the shade beneath the gazebo's roof. They were far enough from the house that only the faint breeze rustling the leaves of the oak tree broke the quiet. Azaleas bordering the nearby woods bloomed in shades of pink, tulips still stood proud in the beds around the gazebo, and Mom had already hung fern plants from the hooks in the ceiling. A tiny paradise. Here they could pretend everything was okay. For a little while.

Calvin guided Stacey onto the bench. He sat close to her and started to put his arms around her.

She rested a hand against his chest and eased away. "Calvin, what do you want?"

"Wha? I want to spend a little time with you."

"No, that's not what I mean. What do you want with us? Where do you see us going?"

"Do we have to talk about it now?"

Stacey wrapped her arms about her ribs. "All the arguments lately ... I don't want to lose you. I'm scared. I mean, next year, when I go off to study fashion design somewhere, what's going to happen to us?"

Calvin leaned back against the wooden railing and trained his eyes on the knobby trunk of an oak tree in the middle of the yard. Why was she worried about next year? What about next week? "All I want is to have a normal relationship with a girl who really likes me and who I really like back. That's all."

"In other words, I'm just too much drama for you."

"I didn't say that. I don't know what's going to happen in the future. I don't even know where I'll be going to college yet. What I mean is, I want to be happy now. I want you to be healthy and for everything to be okay with us. If we can get that working, then we'll be able to deal with whatever comes later."

Stacey lowered her hands, clasped them in her lap. "I don't know what I'm doing anymore. I thought I knew. I had it all figured out, what I was going to do start to finish. Lose weight, go to college, be successful, get out of this place. I guess I thought it would be you and me, somehow. But everything seems to be falling apart. Calvin, I'm ruining things." She sniffed and looked away. "I'm making things hard for you, and you haven't done anything wrong."

Calvin sucked in his lips. He had no answer for what she'd said.

"I don't deserve you."

"Stace, I'm right where I want to be." He slipped his hands around her waist, and she let him. "I just want to be with you."

A breath shuddered past her lips. Stacey opened her arms, let him in, and ran her fingers up his back. She hung on, her fingers like hooks over the tops of his shoulders. Stacey's need wrapped around Calvin, swallowing him, until the rest of the world lost its meaning. Moment by moment as they kissed, Calvin's thoughts and impulses hurdled further away from innocence.

Giving up his virginity would be worth it if he could take away all her doubts about how she looked and how he felt about her. Wasn't that what she worried about? She wanted to be beautiful. He could prove it to her.

But not on the bench in the backyard gazebo, completely exposed to little brothers or a spying sister. Maybe they could go somewhere in her car—

What am I thinking?

Calvin straightened, laughed a little, and knocked his unscraped knuckles on the narrow bench. "Not very comfortable."

Stacey smoothed her blouse and hummed agreement.

"But, man. That was intense."

"Sweet," she said over his assessment. She slipped her hand around his neck as if to pull him back. "With all my breath, I love you. With all my heart, I see you. With all my being, I need you, for all my life."

Something inside Calvin quivered, fed by both confusion and

amazement. He blinked, said, "Wow," then blinked again. "Wait ...
did you just make that up, just now?"

Stacey tilted her head as if the question didn't make sense.

"That's poetry," he said. "It's a gift. You've got a gift, Stacey."

Her smile trembled. "Calvin, this is one thing I totally love about
you. You *see* me. Most people don't. That's why I didn't just make
up words to be saying something romantic. I really do *need* you."

The quivering sensation intensified and identified itself as fear.
She needed him? Emotional connection, physical longing, sure. He
got all that. But need? Her emphasis of the word eroded the passion
he'd felt moments before.

She looked down and toyed with her impossibly clean fingernails. "And that's why it hurts me so much when we argue. You're the
only person I can really talk to—well, there's Zoe. But you know
Zoe. She's ..." Stacey giggled and her whole body seemed to tighten.

"Yeah, I know," Calvin said just to get past that part of the
conversation.

"It hurts me that I can't get you to understand about my weight.
I feel like you're judging me and suddenly you're not really seeing me
anymore. All you're seeing is this ... thing ..."

Shoot the romantic impulses dead. Bang. Calvin sighed. But wasn't
this the conversation he'd wanted to have with her?

"I understand you want to be pretty, and that you had a really
hard time in the past. I don't even care if you want to stay away from
junk food so you can stay thin. That's cool. I'm just worried that
you're going about it the wrong way. I'm scared you'll get really sick."

Maybe even die. But he couldn't say that much.

She sniffed. "I don't want to get sick either. I feel like my life is
out of control. You know?"

Calvin didn't dare move or speak. Even breathing might disrupt
the course of what Stacey was saying.

"Everyone expects me to behave a certain way, do certain things, say 'yes, sir' and 'no, ma'am,' and be this perfect little girl with no mind of her own. Ever since I was little, that's the way it was."

His shoulders relaxed. She wasn't about to confess her eating disorder after all.

"But you've never been like that. You let me be me, and you get excited when I draw pictures for you, and you tell me I'm beautiful. I *love* you for that. But, the last few weeks ..."

His throat tightening again, Calvin swung his head to look away.

She slipped her hand over one of his, calling his eyes back to her. "Just love me, Calvin. Like you always have. If I lose your love, I'll lose everything else too."

The quivering fear turned into a rotating ball in his gut, like a gyroscopic sphere, rolling and rolling but going nowhere unless he could scream and let it out.

What exactly *was* she confessing to him?

○ ○ ◯ ○ ○

Although Tyler's guitar wasn't plugged into his amplifier, Calvin could discern the soft notes and see his friend's fingers fly over the fret board. The guy was getting good. His uncle, a former traveling musician, was teaching him. Even though Tyler wasn't into the country music his uncle played, clearly he was getting a lot out of the mentoring.

Flannery sat on the floor near Tyler's knee, glancing at him a little too often for her attention not to be obvious. The television in Tyler's "media room" competed with his plinking guitar, but no one was that interested in the afternoon entertainment news program anyway.

Also sitting on the floor, Calvin stretched his legs out and leaned back on his elbows. He liked this room. Tyler's mom had decorated it with a movie-time theme to go along with the big-screen TV. Framed posters for action/mystery films hung on the walls. The massive leather couch had its own drink holders. The windows of the room were covered with heavy drapes for optimal viewing. There was even a miniature theater popcorn popper in a corner.

The wide coffee table was covered with textbooks and class notes, but the studying hadn't gone far.

"June tenth," Flannery said. "It's a Sunday. We figure the campground won't be too busy on weekdays."

Calvin stared at the television screen and held out his hand until the reporter's head appeared to be between his thumb and forefinger. He squeezed. "I still have to ask my parents."

"Better ask," Tyler said. "My parents won't let me go if you aren't going too."

Flannery grumbled and pulled her knees up to plant her chin on them. "Obviously I want both of you to come, but I don't see why you can't sleep on the couch in the RV if Calvin can't make it. It's not like you and I are going to be alone. My whole family will be about six feet away from wherever we stand."

"I know, right?" Tyler made a circular gesture with his hand holding the guitar pick. "But I know they're going to feel better if Calvin's there too."

"So all this is on me?" Calvin said. "If I don't go, the whole deal is off?"

"Would your parents let you go if I wasn't going?" Tyler asked.

Flannery threw her hands out and let them flop to the carpet beside her. "This is so stupid! If neither of you go, then I can't go riding. I'll have to, like, hang out with my little brother the whole entire time. There won't even be any reason to go all the way to Badin Lake. My dad can go fishing a thousand other places."

Tyler set his guitar lengthwise on the sofa and leaned toward the coffee table. "Let's see what this place looks like, anyway." He extracted his tablet computer from the books and papers and swiped his finger across the screen. Flannery scooted closer to him until her face nearly pressed against his arm. Calvin stayed where he was until Tyler announced that he'd found the website for Badin Lake.

"Dude, check this out. They got a map showing all the trails." Tyler turned the computer so Calvin could see it, handing it to him as if it were a book.

Calvin's eyes chased the red and blue sketched lines of miles of trails weaving through a large section of woods, crisscrossing each other, squiggling all around the terrain. Each trail had a name and a ranking, from easy to extremely difficult, and little symbols marking their purpose. Bicycle and horseback riding, and hiking. The red lines were for motorized vehicles only. This place put Calvin's little cleared-out trail by his house to shame.

"Oh, yeah. I'm there, dude. This is sick."

"So you're gonna ask you parents, right?" Flannery slapped the coffee table in front of him. "Your dad has to give you *some* vacation time."

"Yep." Although as Calvin handed the tablet computer back to Tyler, it wasn't getting his parent's permission he was worried about. Stacey was *not* going to like this.

"Call them. Ask your dad so we can start planning this thing," Flannery said.

Calvin scrunched his face up. "Impatient much?"

"No. But it's like the first weekend after school lets out. The place might be booked up if we wait too long."

Tyler simply pulled his cell phone from his pocket and passed it over to Calvin. Yeah, he knew better than to push against the force that was Flannery Moore when she got some idea stuck in her head.

Calvin took the phone and got to his feet. "I'll be right back," he sang.

Tyler's house was as familiar as his own, and Calvin did not need permission to go anywhere on the property. The Victorian-era stairs creaked beneath his weight, in spite of their careful restoration. He passed through rooms where newer furniture mixed with antiques, and the paint colors and decorations were chosen with authenticity in mind. Tyler's house always smelled like warm candles.

Calvin's shoes waited for him next to the front door. He slipped them on without retying the laces, and went outside to the porch. A streetlight cast a gentle glow on the white railings and painted floor boards. He leaned against the carved post by the steps and negotiated the maze of options on Tyler's smartphone.

The conversation with Mom took all of two minutes. Sure he could go camping with Tyler and Flannery's family. Of course Dad wouldn't mind if he waited a few days before going to help in the garage this summer. When and where were just formalities. Flannery's parents were known and trusted, and it was all good.

The tough stuff would come with his second phone call. Calvin dialed Stacey's number. He smiled at the sound of her voice, his heart doing a little happy skip even after so many months of dating, and in spite of his worry over what she'd say about the camping trip.

"Whatcha doing?" she asked. "You're using Tyler's phone."

"Yep. Came over to study and watch television. Um, Flannery is here too. I thought about inviting you, but it's getting a little late . . ." Why should he have to apologize for this stuff?

"That's okay. I've been studying too. Got a quiz in French tomorrow."

"Uh-huh-huh, *oui oui*, I see, my *cherie*."

She giggled. "You're silly."

"Yeah. Listen, I called you because we're, um, I wanted to tell you about . . ." Yeah, make it seem like he was asking her permission. "Did you, like, have any plans for this summer, right after school lets out?"

"Mmm, no. Not really. I want to go to the beach sometime, but I haven't made specific plans. Why?"

"Well, we're trying to set up this camping trip. We're going to Badin Lake, Uwharrie National Forest. Me, Tyler, and Flannery's family. They've got these awesome trails where we can take the bikes. Now that I've got the Yamaha running again ... It's gonna be awesome."

"Oh. Wh—where's U-war—that place? Badin Lake?"

"West of here, past Raleigh. I'm not sure how far."

"Camping?"

"Yeah. For a few days. I don't think Dave can be away from his shop for too long."

"With Flannery."

"With her whole family. They've got that RV, but I think Tyler and I will use my tent. We're just starting to plan the trip."

This was ridiculous. In the two second pause while Calvin waited for Stacey's response, he thumped his fist against the porch post. Why was he asking permission? He should just be able to say, "This is where I'm going. See you when I get back."

"Stace? Look, I really want to go. I just wanted to tell you about it, so you'll know we're making plans for it." *Lame.*

"So, I'm supposed to find something else to do while you're gone?"

"Come on, Stace. It's just a few days. I didn't think you'd want to come because—"

"Because I can't ride a motorcycle, right?"

"Well, yeah. You'd probably just be bored. I mean, unless you like fishing, and I don't think I've ever heard you say you like fishing."

She sighed. "I don't. Actually, I've never been fishing. But I'm not really comfortable thinking about you going off somewhere with another girl. I mean, I know you're just friends, but it's ... not right, somehow."

"Her whole family is going. Dave, Patty, and Flan's goofy little brother. And Tyler will be there. We're just going riding, Stacey. It's no big deal."

"I-I know, but ..." Was she crying? Already? "The thing is, Calvin, it isn't so much that I'm jealous of Flannery, it's that I feel like, like, she has so much more in common with you than I do. Like, maybe she would be a better girlfriend for you than—"

Calvin thrust his index finger out, as if she were standing in front of him and could see it. "Stop right there. That's not true. If I wanted to be with Flannery, I'd be with her. But I don't. I'm with you. Because you're the one I want to be with. And you need to get that straight."

She whimpered. Definitely crying now. "I'm sorry, Calvin. It's just ... you deserve someone better—"

"No, I don't. Shoot, Stacey, I didn't even think I deserved *you* before we started dating. You're so beautiful and amazing, and I don't get why you put yourself down so much."

"It's because—"

"Because people teased you before. Because your uncle was a ... major ... scumbag. Because your dad put you down. I know all that. But here's the thing, Stacey. *I love you!* I love you just the way you are, and it doesn't matter to me that you can't ride a motorcycle. I'd still love you if you weighed three hundred pounds—"

"No you wouldn't! You wouldn't even talk to me if I was fat. No one would."

"You really think I'm that shallow?"

"It's not about being shallow. People are just like that. They make judgments based on what people look like before they know anything else about them. It's simple psychology, Calvin."

"Whatever. Even if that's true, it doesn't change the fact that my feelings for you are based on who you are, the person I know inside.

You need to get past this insecurity about yourself and about me. I'm not interested in anyone but you."

He loved her, but anger tightened his spine and made him practically yell into the phone. Weird. He had to get out of this conversation and regain his sanity. "Look, if my going camping with Flannery is going to make you crazy, I won't go. Okay? I just won't go. It's cool. I can ride at home, or go to the MX track with Tyler. I don't have to go camping."

Her only response was a wet-sounding sniffle.

"I'll make that sacrifice for you, because I love you."

"Don't ... don't decide right now."

"I have to tell Flannery something." Ugh. The girl would freak.

"It's okay, Calvin. Tell her you'll go. You're right, I have to get control of these insecurities. I'm sorry."

Calvin sighed and grabbed a hunk of hair. "You're sure?"

She huffed a sad laugh. "No. Can I think about it?"

She'd hang up with him and immediately dial Zoe. Whatever.

"Sure. Go ahead. I gotta go back inside." And figure out what lie he could tell his best friends so they wouldn't think he was a total wimp.

Chapter 18

Finally able to pull off US 264 after a rather scary ride from Raleigh, Stacey rolled into a Waffle House parking lot, eased the Honda into a space, and leaned back in her seat. She placed her hand over her chest and released a long breath. "Thank God that's over!"

"I thought we were going to get squashed by that one truck." Zoe yanked her hands from her eye sockets as if the near-accident had just happened.

One truck? Try six or seven before they were able to get off the Interstates. Daddy would kill her if he knew what she and Zoe had done — she wouldn't need an eighteen-wheeler to do the job. But they were at last back in Bentley, a couple of miles from Zoe's house where they were *supposed* to be having a sleepover. The trip was so worth it, though. Zoe's antics in the malls drowned out all her guilt about Calvin for a while.

"So, what are we doing here?" Stacey asked. "This is definitely not a low-cal eatery."

"Don't worry, I got it covered. Bring your sketchbook." Zoe jumped out of the Honda — escaping the nightmare — and started toward the door of the narrow yellow building.

Stacey grabbed her big purse, with her sketchbook inside, and hurried after her friend. A warm blast of bacon-scented air swept over her as she stepped inside the building. The contrast to the cool night sent a shudder chasing down her spine. She clenched her arms against her body. Late April; why was it still so cold? Zoe had lunged into spring with flip-flops and layered tank tops, while Stacey fought the urge to bring her Uggs back out of the closet.

The sight of someone in a police uniform standing at the counter jolted her. She swayed, caught Zoe's shoulder to regain her balance. City cop, not county.

The cop sent a scowling glance at them as he turned away from the cash register, but he walked past and out the door. Stacey let herself breathe again.

Three men sat at the counter, empty stools between them. A couple at a booth shoveled food into their mouths. Seemingly unfazed by the departing cop, Zoe strutted to an empty booth by the windows. Showing off her makeover for the truck drivers. Head down, Stacey followed.

Those makeup consultants sure knew how to push a sale. *Let me show you how to make your eyes look big without that heavy eyeliner. Look in the mirror! See how beautiful you are? You'll be breaking hearts for sure. Buy this mascara, this foundation, this color, and look gorgeous every day.*

And spend three times what similar stuff cost at Kerr Drugs.

Stacey caught her reflection in the window beside her. She smiled at the new Stacey staring back. Maybe if she turned up the sex appeal a little she could turn Calvin's thoughts away from Flannery, and away from how much she did or didn't eat. Maybe he'd even get a clue about what she was trying to achieve and give her a break.

Not likely.

"Just order water," Zoe whispered as the waitress approached their table.

"Y'all ready or you need a couple minutes?" The smiling, pony-tailed waitress held her pen and pad ready to scribble down their order.

Zoe sat up straight. "We're ready. Scrambled eggs, but use egg substitute. And tell the cook no butter. Two slices of turkey bacon, again no butter. Or grease. And a salad. No cheese."

The waitress wrote. "Dressin'?"

"Just some lemon slices."

"Toast? Grits?"

"No, thanks." Zoe turned her face toward the window, showing she'd finished her order.

"What you want, honey?" the waitress asked.

"Oh. Uh, I'm not hungry. Just water, please."

A quick scowl creased the woman's forehead. She shrugged and turned away.

Zoe reached over and squeezed one of Stacey's hands. "Size five! You're doin' it, girl!"

Stacey gave Zoe a grin she didn't feel. She'd hoped for size three. And the little skirt she'd bought to go with Zoe's lace top made her backside look bigger than a size five.

"When the food comes, we'll share it. That way we cut the calories in half. Okay, inspiration time." Zoe slapped her sketchbook open. "When I say go, start drawing the first design that comes to your mind."

Stacey dug a pencil out of her purse and opened her book. "Ready."

"Go."

They'd seen so many amazing and beautiful things in the high-priced stores, ranging from soft and flowing contemporary designs to glittering retro glam. Why not a combination? Stacey lightly sketched geometric shapes and lines to create a humanlike form. She glanced at Zoe's paper; Zoe worked the opposite way, drawing clothes first. Stacey rushed her sketch, taking the blocked forms to a feminine shape in a few strokes.

Sleeveless, strapless, tight. Little dots and lines forming stars to hint at sequins.

"Wow, y'all are so talented." The waitress set their drinks on the table.

Stacey smiled and said thanks. Zoe kept drawing.

Bodice finished, Stacey moved to the skirt. Light material flowing in the wind, long in the back, short in the front. Leggings ending in lace just below the knees. Tiny high-heeled shoes on the model's feet.

Pausing to sip her water, Stacey considered the head. She couldn't leave it blank. Hair was so much a part of the total look. She sketched an oval face with a tiny nose and mouth and one large eye. Sweeping, layered hair, blowing in her imaginary wind, concealed the other eye.

The waitress carefully set their food on the table.

"Done," Zoe said.

Stacey held up a finger and finished her drawing with wristbands, adding a bit of the sparkle treatment. "Okay."

"Switch. Let me see yours."

They exchanged books. Zoe's drawing was less stylized and detailed. Her model wore a sleeveless hoodie with a long, diamond-shaped cutout over the chest. The top fit snugly over the hips, then flared in bunched fabric that looked like a ballet tutu. Tight leggings with diagonal slashes, and stiletto boots. Trashy chic.

"I like this a lot," Stacey said.

"Yours is amazing. So, you ready to make it?"

"We're actually going to make these?"

"Yep. That's the challenge. You gotta make it. In one week. Then we'll go again. By the end of summer we'll both have new clothes that no one else is wearing. We'll rule that school!"

"One week?" Stacey took her sketchbook back. "I don't have money for fabric. I spent too much on makeup and that skirt." She'd be doing a whole lot of begging and babysitting this summer to keep up with Zoe's project.

"Dang, that's really good!"

Stacey jumped and whirled toward the person who'd spoken over her shoulder. For an instant Noah Dickerson's brilliant smile dominated her vision. Stacey blinked, and two other guys she didn't know materialized behind him. They glanced at her sketchpad without comment and moved on down the aisle to another booth.

Noah stayed, leaning on the back of Stacey's seat. "So, what are y'all doing?"

"Designing new clothes," Zoe blurted.

Noah stretched to glance at Zoe's drawing. "That's cool." He gestured to Stacey's paper. "Looks like manga."

Stacey pursed her lips. Her drawing did look like Japanese comic art. She'd have to break that habit to do fashion design.

Noah sat beside her. His musky boy-smell sent a thrill through her. Stacey held her breath and scooted over to make room for him. "Uh, aren't your friends going to miss you?"

Zoe kicked Stacey's foot under the table.

"Nah. Let me see the rest of your book." He took the sketchbook and flipped to the front.

Everything from doodles to fully rendered manga panels to serious drawings interspersed with awful to adequate poetry covered the pages. Noah studied a half-finished portrait of Calvin.

Zoe jiggled in her seat, her eyes never leaving Noah. The plate of eggs and turkey bacon, and the little bowl of salad, sat untouched on the table. Every nerve in Stacey's body rattled like dry grass blown by the wind. She sipped her water but couldn't think about eating.

Noah's knee touched hers. The sensation seemed to stick there after he'd moved.

"You're really good," he said. "I mean it."

"Really?"

He handed the sketchbook back. "It's awesome. I didn't know you write poetry too."

"Thanks." She hugged the book to her chest.

"So, what are y'all doing tonight? Other than drawing pictures at Waffle House. Wanna hang with me and my friends?"

Stacey glanced at the other boys, who'd claimed the booth near the elderly couple and had them looking nervous. Scruffy gamer/skater types. Not the kind of boys Stacey would want to "hang" with even if she wasn't dating Calvin.

Across the table from her, Zoe wiggled in her seat like she had to pee.

Something like frigid air grabbed hold of Stacey's intestines. "Oh, um ... Noah? I already have a boyfriend. That—that was his picture you were looking at."

Zoe slapped the table with both hands. "Sta-cey!"

Eyes wide, Stacey leaned toward her friend. "Zo-ee!"

Noah was grinning when she looked back at him. "My bad luck. You know, if I had a girl drawing me pictures like that, no way she'd be sitting at Waffle House with another girl on a Saturday night."

"We—I—uh, we were out last night."

"Last night, huh?" He plucked her pencil from the table, took her sketchbook out of her hands, and scribbled something on the last page. "There's my number in case ... you know." He flipped his black hair to the side and slid out of the booth. Her pencil rolled slowly off his fingertips, as if reluctant to part from him.

"See ya," he crooned. He glided past Zoe down the aisle to join his friends. Tight pants, like Calvin would never—could never—wear.

Zoe slowly turned in her seat to face Stacey. Her gawk turned to a glare, clearly saying without words, *Are you out of your freaking mind?*

Stacey sighed. "Zoe, I keep telling you. I love Calvin. I don't want anyone else."

"Calvin," Zoe said through clenched teeth. Then she slumped back against the booth. "Even though he wants to go camping with that other girl—Okay, whatever. It's your life."

The waitress went to the booth where Noah and his friends sat. Noah flashed that charming smile when he ordered. As the waitress turned away, her cheeks pinked and she nibbled on her lower lip. Amazing. Noah could make a forty-something-year-old woman blush.

Stacey stared down at her sketchpad. There on the clean page, Noah Dickerson's phone number. The first three digits were the same as Zoe's, suggesting he lived near her. Noah's handwriting reminded her of script, the straight lines on the five, nine, and sevens elongated.

Was it possible Noah Dickerson really wanted to go out with her?

Stacey dragged her gaze from the book and looked at Zoe. A hiccup-like gasp shook her. She smacked a hand across her grin.

Zoe turned her eyes toward the ceiling. "Better not let *Cal-vin* find that number."

Calvin wouldn't question her about a phone number with no name beside it. Maybe. But having it there on the page—she would think of Noah each time she opened the book to draw.

Stacey creased the page to make careful rips around the number, then slipped the torn paper into the pocket of her hoodie. She sipped her water, but couldn't eat. Her flip-flopping stomach wouldn't accept it.

Noah Dickerson. Another artist. Never happen, but tempting to think about. Noah was more like her than Zoe, even. And certainly he had more in common with her than Calvin.

Just like Flannery had more in common with Calvin . . .

Okay, kill those thoughts right now.

Chapter 19

Calvin stood at Stacey's front door, holding a bouquet of white, pink, and purple flowers he'd bought at the grocery store. Around him, a profusion of flowering potted plants decorated the porch along with pristine white wicker furniture. Petunias and freshly mown grass scented the air. And the silk flowers on the door wreath looked better than the bunch Calvin held in his hand.

Pretty lame. Should've bought the expensive ones.

He cleared his throat and rang the doorbell.

Show love and provide gentle encouragement. Don't argue, because that only makes the person defensive. That's what he'd read online. Stacey had already proven that little slights could lead to big fights. Lack of proper nutrients, emotional denial, and an innate sense of wrongdoing battling her desire to be in control of her body and her diet made her sensitive to the slightest hint of judgment. At least that's what the websites said.

He was going to have to work past all those things and tread very carefully if he would convince her it was okay for him to go on that camping trip. And if he could keep their relationship from falling apart until he could convince her to go to a doctor for help.

Renee answered the door and let him in the house. She yelled up the stairs, "Stacey, your *boyfriend* is here," then disappeared into the kitchen.

"Be right down!" Walls and doors muffled Stacey's answer.

The carpet beneath Calvin's feet had fresh vacuum tracks. The plump cushions on the beige leather furniture in the living room looked like no one ever sat on them. A huge cabinet with carved accents and built-in lights covered the open wall leading into the dining room. Not a china cabinet, but a three-thousand-dollar computer desk.

"Hello, Calvin, dear." Mrs. Varnell glided into the room from upstairs, wearing a silky top and pressed khaki pants, her hair and face made up like she was going somewhere. She always looked that way, like at any moment someone would take her picture. Stacey said her mother ironed every stitch of her clothing, even her pajamas. She swept toward Calvin, touched her fingertips to his arm, and brushed a kiss against his cheek. "How are you doing, sweetheart?"

Everything about her felt fresh, like a crisp head of lettuce just plucked from the bin at the grocery store. Cool and lightly fragrant.

"I'm fine, ma'am."

"And your mama? How is she doing?" Six months after the funeral, Mrs. Varnell still looked at Calvin as if he were standing beside his brother's casket, her head slightly tilted, her eyebrows pinched upward on her forehead.

"We're doing fine, thank you."

"Oh, that's good to hear. Stacey tells me the two of you have a special day planned today, but she didn't tell me where you're going."

"Um, it's a surprise."

"How sweet. Y'all aren't going too far, are you? I worry about you kids driving on the highways. Is that truck running well?"

Calvin rubbed his hand across the back of his neck, where embarrassment burned. He glanced out the front window at his father's ancient, two-toned pickup truck in the driveway. "It doesn't look like much, but Dad keeps it going."

Mrs. Varnell kept smiling. "Won't you sit down? I believe Stacey's fixing her makeup. She might be a few moments."

Calvin stepped toward the leather couch, but the rattle of the patio door beyond the dining room drew his eyes that way. Officer Varnell, dressed like an ordinary person in grass-stained sneakers, jeans, and a baseball cap, strode into the room. The combined scent of grass clippings and gasoline preceded him. Stacey's father nodded at Calvin in greeting. "Cal."

"Sir." He reached out his right hand.

"Stan!" Mrs. Varnell's gasping outburst froze both of them. "You're tracking grass and dirt onto the carpet."

Officer Varnell glanced down at the floor, where bits of green and dusty gray were pressed into footprints through the vacuum tracks. "Cost of a manicured lawn." He smirked and winked at Calvin.

Stacey's mother scuttled away as Officer Varnell claimed his recliner.

Calvin wavered at the arm of the sofa. Despite the man's macho joke, Calvin balked at the idea of getting chummy with him, anticipating a lecture the moment he relaxed.

"No motorcycle today?" Officer Varnell asked.

"Uh, no, sir." It had been so tempting to grab his helmet and ride, but today had to be all about Stacey. Everything he did had to be with her happiness and security in mind, so she would know he loved her, that she didn't have to change anything about herself to be attractive to him.

The vacuum cleaner roared. Mrs. Varnell maneuvered the machine over the mess her husband had created. Calvin watched as she, seemingly not content with *clean*, pushed the vacuum in straight lines to match the other lines from her previous cleaning. She even vacuumed her own footprints.

Yeah. Easy to see where Stacey got her super-neat habits.

"Hello!" Stacey called over the noise of the vacuum.

Calvin turned and stared.

She wore a lace top showing a sliver of flesh below the hem. A heart-shaped cutout in front revealed cleavage he had only imagined before. Her short black skirt hugged her hips. Her legs — Calvin had no idea she was *that* thin. Had he ever seen her bare legs before? He jerked his gaze to her face.

She'd stopped wearing the Zoe-inspired gaudy makeup colors a week ago, but whatever else she'd done today was ... he didn't know how to describe it. Beautiful. And her hair swirled about her face in big, soft waves. She could be a dancer in a music video or a model on a runway. Was she taller? He glanced down at her high-heeled sandals. She'd painted her toenails dark red. Calvin couldn't remember seeing her toenails before. In any color.

A sharp squeak and thump of the recliner signaled her father's reaction. "What ... are you wearing?"

"Oh, sweetheart, you look beautiful!" Her mother left the vacuum cleaner to rush over. She brushed Stacey's hair off one shoulder. "But isn't this just a camisole? Shouldn't you have a jacket in case you get chilled? What about that pretty dusty-green jacket you made? Though that might be a little too country to go with this look. I have a black cardigan that should fit you."

Stacey eased her mother's hand away and edged toward Calvin. "It's fine, Mom. We have to go."

"No, no. It'll just take a moment to go and fetch it. Renee, dear," she called toward the steps. "Would you run to my closet and get my black sweater for Stacey? The one with the little pearls and the three-quarter sleeves."

Renee appeared at the top of the stairs, her arms crossed. "That outfit rocks. Let her go."

Calvin took a step backward. The thoughts in his head stalled, unable to go one way or another in the debate. Taking a stand against Stacey's parents would be *bad*. But he'd never seen Stacey look like this. All the puffy sweaters and handmade flowing blouses, topped with jeans and sneakers or boots—all of that stuff was gone.

It tickled—the tantalizing thought that this was *his* girl. Farm boy with a fashion model. Amazing. He dumbly held out his flowers.

Stacey clasped his forearm and urged him away, as if she didn't see the gift. "Let's go."

People moved around him. Voices talked over each other. Stacey fled out the front door.

"Uh, I gotta go." Calvin pointed his thumb at the door.

With Stacey gone, her father turned a hard gaze toward Calvin. "Your driver's license still provisional, boy?"

"Oh. Uh, I—"

"Have her home by eight thirty. So you'll be legal driving home."

"Yes, sir." Calvin kept his arguments to himself and backed toward the door.

Stacey had already climbed into the truck and sat waiting for him. Aware that eyes might be watching them through the front windows, Calvin handed his flowers over to her with only a smile. She accepted them with less.

∘ ○ ○ ○ ∘

Keep smiling. Calvin crossed his arms on the table and held his breath as he voiced a most-dangerous question. "Aren't you hungry?"

Stacey turned her head to look at him. She'd been peering all around the Arby's restaurant since the moment they'd walked in, her shoulders hunched and her hands clasped in her lap. "Oh! Are you finished already? You must have been starving."

A roast beef sandwich and curly fries didn't take long to eat.

Stacey nudged the stuff in her salad bowl with her plastic fork. She'd scavenged all the lettuce out of the bowl, then cut the rest into little pieces and shoved it up against the sides so the middle of her bowl was empty. He'd watched her do it.

How could her parents, with all their rules and interfering, not notice how Stacey ate her food? How had Calvin missed it for so long? Maybe it took knowing the truth before anyone could see her clever deceptions.

"Are you ready to go?" she asked.

"No hurry."

She pressed her fingers to her shoulders and gazed around again. "It's freezing in here. Are you cold?"

"Uh-uh."

She rubbed her arms. "This top is a little skimpy. Maybe I should have worn my jacket. Not Mom's cardigan, though. That would have been ... wrong. Just wrong."

With her arms crossed that way, Calvin noticed that at least she hadn't lost much weight in her—He cleared his throat and turned his attention to her salad bowl. "What is that, chicken?"

"Yes. You want some?"

"No. It just looks good."

Stacey picked up her fork again and speared a tiny chunk of meat. She wiggled her eyebrows at him and slipped the bite into her mouth. As she chewed, her red lips pressed and relaxed. Calvin wondered if the taste would linger there. She touched a napkin to her mouth then wadded it up.

She'd done the same thing the last time she had supper at his house, and somehow the dog under the table got a treat.

"Excuse me. I need more napkins." Stacey slid out of her seat and went to the condiment table.

As soon as her back was turned, Calvin glanced at the floor under the table. Clean.

Stacey returned with a small pile of napkins in her hand. She could have carried a baseball in the gap between her knees.

Calvin buried a hand in his hair and slouched in his seat. "Uh, bike's running pretty good now. And I was thinking ... about that camping trip."

"Oh." Stacey pushed a dainty bite of salad between her lips and looked out the window.

Stupid, stupid. Too soon to bring it up. But now the subject was out there, and Stacey waited for him to say more.

"Dad says I can work in the auto shop this summer. He'll pay me to do tune-ups and oil changes. But he said I could have some time off before I start."

She nodded and dabbed. Wadded the napkin and squeezed it together with the first. Had she always done that?

"You'll be working full time, then?" Another bite, another dab.

Calvin stared at the growing ball of napkins on the table. Something pink soaked through the thin paper. Not lipstick; a bit of tomato. She was spitting each tiny bite into the napkins.

Calvin's sandwich felt like a lump of lead in his stomach. He toyed with the box that had held his fries.

"Calvin?"

"Huh?"

"I asked if you're going to be working full time."

"Oh. Yeah. I mean, as long as there's enough work. Dad's not going to pay me to stand around if there aren't any jobs I can do."

How was it possible to feel so much desire and disgust at the same time? None of the websites mentioned what to do in this situation.

Calvin looked out the window. His father's rusty pickup was the only vehicle in the parking lot that didn't shine in the sun.

"Zoe showed me a brochure from a fashion design school in California," Stacey said, filling the awkward silence with a change of subject. "She *so* wants to get out of here, but California? That's too far. And besides . . ." She reached across the table and stroked the backs of his fingers. "I wouldn't want to be that far away from you."

Oh, super. Make him feel guilty just when he was talking about going somewhere without her. He scowled. "I don't get why Zoe thinks y'all have to go to the same college."

Stacey withdrew her hand. "Well, we're both going for fashion design, and it'd be nice to know someone already when we get there."

"Yeah, I get that. But all the way to California? Why does she have to dictate your life? That's what I wanna know." Warning. Danger. He'd dropped the everything-is-wonderful act.

She pulled her hands beneath the table, staring downward. "She doesn't. She's my friend, Calvin. She doesn't judge me."

"Judge you? What—?"

"I don't want to talk about it, okay? Can we talk about something else?"

Calvin sighed. "Sorry. I guess I don't quite get the whole BFF thing with girls."

"It's the same with you and Tyler." She toyed with her salad, pushing the bits around.

"Tyler doesn't care where I go to college. I mean, yeah, it'd be cool if we went to the same place, but if we don't, that doesn't mean we'll stop being friends."

Stacey raised her shoulder in a half shrug. "Maybe that's because you've known him so long. I don't have any lifelong friends like that. I don't have anyone who really knows me and would even think about me a year from now if I left."

He wanted to protest, to point at himself and ask if he didn't count. *Don't argue. Be encouraging.* He slid his open hand across the table. "Stace, come on. You're pretty, talented, and smart. And funny. You make people laugh. Everyone I know likes you."

She didn't take the hand he offered.

"Know what? The other day when you wore that sorta tight purple shirt, Tyler said you looked pretty hot."

Her eyes widened. "Tyler Dorset said that about *me*? Half the girls in school would *die* if he even said hello to them."

And Tyler would probably die of embarrassment if he'd heard Stacey say that.

Her smile grew until her eyes sparkled. The dimples he loved weren't completely gone. "Tell him I said thank you." In a flurry of movement, she swept the wadded-up napkins onto their food tray, tossed her salad bowl on top, and grabbed his sandwich wrapper and fry cup. "Where to next?"

Calvin couldn't move. Stacey could have been holding him pinned down in the booth instead of rushing to the trash bin and depositing their tray on the stack. Yeah, he'd encouraged her all right. Saying she looked good made her dump the remainder of her salad in the trash. He'd encouraged her to keep doing the thing he wanted her to quit.

Way to go, idiot.

But if she wanted to be beautiful, how was he supposed to let her know she already was if he couldn't compliment her?

She walked back to the table swinging her hips. Or swaying on those spiky heels. The reason didn't matter. He'd rather have her waddle like a penguin than starve herself to be thin. Well, maybe not waddle.

"What's wrong?" she asked.

Calvin pulled himself across the booth seat. "Nothing. Let's go."

Chapter 20

The graphite image, depicting an old man with a lined face sitting in front of a building with weathered siding, didn't look like anything created by something as simple as a pencil. Stacey stared. The beautiful drawing confronted her. If she had that much talent, could make something look so perfect ...

"That's pencil?" Calvin leaned in closer.

Stacey pulled on his arm. "Stand back and look at it."

He backed up. "It looks like a picture, I mean, a photograph."

The artist had rendered the texture of the old man's coat, individual broken threads along the tattered lapel. Amazing. And the eyes looked alive, like they would follow Stacey when she moved away.

Calvin slipped his hand behind her back and guided her to another frame filled with confidence-crushing perfection.

"Know what?" he said. "I'll bet your drawings will hang here someday."

How sweet was he? "Oh, come on." She pressed her shoulder into the space beneath his arm and brushed her hand across his chest.

"Why not?"

Why not? Because Daddy would call it foolish. Mom would sweetly point out every little flaw. Even if Stacey worked alone, their voices would haunt her. What if she failed? What if all the people from her past had told the truth and she'd never amount to anything?

Besides, showing her work in a local art gallery meant she'd still be … here. Still in Stiles County or maybe living in an apartment in Rocky Mount. Her drawings weren't good enough for New York galleries. Or Raleigh. Or even Rocky Mount.

Stacey sighed. "To be that good I'd have to study fine art, not fashion design."

"Would that be so bad?" He gestured toward the next drawing. "You could do this."

Stacey took the drawing in, though the gentle image clawed at her heart. An old woman this time, her gnarled hands knitting an afghan. She could envision the woman's slow movements, stitch by stitch, and imagine the clicking of her needles. She could feel the soft yarn warming her lap.

A desire crept into Stacey's heart, a longing to feel a pencil in her hand and the textured surface of a clean sheet of Canson paper beneath her fingertips. To fill the empty space with something meaningful, something worthy of Calvin's awe.

She swallowed. "Daddy says artists don't make much money."

A soft grunt showed what he thought of this. "They should. How long did it take this artist to draw that?"

"Hours and hours. Days."

"My dad charges seventy-five dollars an hour for labor. 'Course, that pays for the building and utilities and all that other stuff too. Not just what he makes."

"No one would pay me even twenty dollars."

"I would." He swung her around to face him. "More than that."

She wanted to cry. He was so sweet. Although he'd gotten angry with her at the restaurant — she could tell from the way he pulled his hair at the table and his silence in the truck — bringing her to the Imperial Arts Center in Rocky Mount was an act of love. When she first met him, Calvin didn't know a thing about art. He was learning just for her.

She toyed with a button of his shirt. "You're biased."

"Hey, I'm serious. I think you're incredibly talented. Too good for fashion school."

Stacey edged closer to him. His smile widened and his eyes took on an almost sleepy expression. Like he wasn't just saying those things to be nice. Like she was special to him. Like he wanted her. His fingers caressed her lower back, brushed the line of bare skin.

He laughed and turned away. Flustered again. Too cute.

Calvin guided her toward the other end of the large, brick-walled gallery and gestured toward a sprawling metal sculpture.

"Now this ... I could make this. A few exhaust pipes, some old bike spokes—"

Stacey lightly smacked his stomach. "It's abstract."

"Ya think?"

She wanted him to look at her again, with his eyes all sultry and his fingers moving in little circles, the silky lining of her top sliding against her skin. Instead he was making jokes.

She pressed her cheek against his shoulder. His cologne was faint, not enough to cover up the earthy smell of him she'd grown accustomed to. The two scents enticed her to breathe in. She did and then gently blew against his neck.

Calvin flinched. "Stop that. It tickles."

She grinned and tilted her head. "You like it."

"*Hee*-yeah! A little too much." He pulled away but took her hand. "What's in this room?"

Exasperating.

Calvin walked, dragging her behind him, their arms fully extended. She whimpered, but it didn't help. Mr. Proper Behavior was putting up a fight. Yet she'd put a crack in his defenses. The way he'd looked at her—she'd see that look again before the day was done. She wouldn't go home without it. She'd put all thoughts of Flannery and that stupid camping trip right out of his head.

○ ○ ○ ○ ○

Stacey refused popcorn at the theater, and Calvin didn't say anything. At least he understood she couldn't eat junk food while on a diet. All she needed was a large cup of ice water to keep her stomach feeling full during the movie.

He held her hand as they walked through the lobby, cradling his popcorn in the crook of his arm and clutching his drink cup in that hand. The buttery smell multiplied inside the darkened theater. She inhaled it, and her mouth watered. It smelled heavenly. Could she be satisfied with just the aroma? The old Stacey craved satisfaction. She willed her stomach not to gurgle in desire as Calvin led her to a seat halfway back. As he got settled, she plopped down and sucked water through her straw.

Be strong. Be beautiful. Power is resistance. Giving in to food is weakness.

She was seeing the rewards of all her work in the way Calvin looked at her.

He laughed through the idiotic comedy. His hands stayed busy with the popcorn, his eyes and mind on the screen. Did he notice she didn't laugh as much? Was the theater so dark that it hid her struggle from his view?

Someone behind her rattled plastic wrap, opening a box of candy. She could hear people chewing their snacks. A voice in the back of her mind screamed for control. *Don't give in! Fight!*

Stacey held her breath so she wouldn't smell the calories; soon points of light burst in her peripheral vision. She shouldn't have agreed to come to this stupid movie. Blowing out the stale air from her lungs, she gave up. Just one handful of popcorn would end the private abuse.

She eased her hand over Calvin's lap and probed into the bag. He'd eaten most of it so she had to reach deep. Calvin turned his head to look at her then tipped the bag toward her. Light from the screen glowed on his face, his smile.

"It smells so good," she whispered.

"Take it. Finish it."

"No. I just want a taste."

Warning!

There wasn't much left. Stacey dipped her hand into the container and touched the puffed morsels. One handful. Just one. She munched it slowly and licked the salty butter from her fingers, then leaned her cheek against Calvin's shoulder. She'd lost the plot of the movie but didn't care what was going on. The lingering taste in her mouth had opened a floodgate of evil desires. Her stomach churned, both rebelling and needful, and the single handful of popcorn seemed to expand like a Mylar balloon.

"I'll be right back," she whispered.

She lumbered over Calvin's knees and tried to keep her posture straight as she walked down the aisle to the exit.

Calvin would figure out what she was about to do. All his sweetness would turn to anger and their date would be ruined. Why? Why did all this have to be so hard?

Stacey studied her reflection in the bathroom mirror. Calvin had gazed at her with longing. Tyler supposedly said she looked hot. Was it true? She breathed in, and the lace top squeezed her bust and torso. Her stomach begged for freedom from the popcorn, from the creamy dressing on her salad and the bits of chicken she'd eaten. All congealed together like a lava lamp rolling, dripping. *Glub, glub.*

Heat rose to Stacey's face. She ducked into a stall and stuck her fingers down her throat.

○ ○ ◯ ○ ○

Out of money and time, they headed home. Stacey held Calvin's hand as he drove his father's rattling old pickup truck. She tickled her lips with wilted flower petals that still smelled sweet.

Calvin let go of her hand to turn the steering wheel, heading north on Turner Creek Road. They'd be at her house in just a minute. The clouds were painted peach on the horizon, which meant they had fifteen minutes or so before it would be dark. And soon after that Officer Varnell and his peers would be on the lookout for teens with provisional licenses cruising around and getting into trouble on a Saturday night.

Stacey gasped. Daddy was working. He wouldn't be home.

"What? You okay?" Calvin asked.

She turned and gave him a sly smile. "We don't have to go home yet."

"We don't? But your dad said —"

"I know, but he has a shift tonight. So, can we stop somewhere for a while? Just to talk?"

"Uh, like where?"

"Pull over here and we'll decide."

Ingersol Produce Company. The parking lot was empty, the building a hulking gray cube against the vermillion sky. Calvin swerved off the road, shoved the shift lever up into park, and left the engine running.

Stacey played with her lower lip. "No, um, drive around back. If my dad is on patrol and he sees us parked here, he'll come banging on the windshield."

"*Chuh*, yeah! And slap me in handcuffs for messing around with his daughter."

"Calvin Greenlee, are you telling me you're afraid of my father?"

"Afraid? No. I've been in back of this building, though. It's a stinkin' loading dock. You'd hate it." A crooked grin slid onto his face. "I know where we can go."

She narrowed her eyes playfully. "What are you thinking?"

Calvin pulled the shift lever back into drive. "You'll see." He drove the truck back onto Turner Creek Road, going the other way.

Stacey couldn't keep her eyes on the road or the landscape outside the truck. Calvin sat on his side of the bench seat, wearing that quirky grin on his face. His fingers tapped on the steering wheel and sometimes drifted up to tug his hair. Nervous?

Stacey trembled inside. Calvin wouldn't try anything. Maybe he'd take her somewhere they could watch the sunset together.

Guys never say they love you unless they want sex.

Zoe's words came back to her. Isn't this what the day had been leading up to? Hadn't she started it with her sexy outfit, so he'd look at her and forget about Flannery or any other girl? He'd never tried anything with her. Ever. *Why not?*

He drove past the high school and turned onto Victory Church Road. Stacey sighed and settled back in her seat. He was taking her to his house, where they could sit inside the backyard gazebo. Sweet. Safe.

Maybe he didn't really want her.

"I can't be too late," she said. "My mother will tell my dad."

Calvin ran his tongue over his lips. "I can turn around."

"No! It's okay. I'll just call her and say I'm at your house for a little while."

"We're not going to my house." He shifted in his seat as if he couldn't get comfortable. "No privacy there."

He turned left, and the truck rattled down an uneven dirt path.

In the dimming light, Stacey wasn't sure where they were. The cotton field by his house? Yes. In the distance, maybe a quarter mile away, was the silhouette of his house with tiny rectangles of light at a few windows.

Stacey rocked side to side as the truck bounced along the path. Dark woods loomed ahead. No sunset watching. It was nearly gone.

"Calvin?"

He tugged his hair and looked at her. "Just for a few minutes."

She couldn't read his expression, couldn't tell if he still smiled. He turned the headlights off as the road curved toward the house. No one would see them there.

Was this really happening? Stacey quivered inside, pressed her knees tight together, and smoothed out her skirt and the lace top.

Calvin stopped the truck beside the woods, put it in park, and turned off the engine. He was a shadow behind the wheel now, but she heard him take a deep breath. He unsnapped his seatbelt, the click loud enough to make her wince.

"Come here," he said.

She undid her seatbelt too and scooted to the middle of the bench seat. Calvin wrapped his arms around her and pulled her the rest of the way to his side. He kissed her so deeply that her back slid against the vinyl seat, pushing her off balance. His fingers brushed the skin at her waist then slipped beneath the blouse. She gasped, and a giddy thought entered her mind: the blouse wasn't so tight that his hand wouldn't fit.

"You're so beautiful." His breath warmed her cheek. "So beautiful. I love you, Stacey."

Beautiful! Say it again.

His curls at the back of his head were soft and lush in her fingers. "I love you too."

Stacey shifted to get more comfortable but instead slipped farther down the seat. Calvin caught himself before his body could squash her, but his new position left Stacey's knees bent at an extreme angle, both feet still touching the floor. Suddenly, all the musty smells of the old truck were stronger. Motor oil and gasoline, cracked vinyl and dirt.

Germs. Not here. Surely he won't—

She could barely see Calvin's face above her in the dying light.

This whole thing was crazy. Calvin said they'd only be a few minutes. They'd laugh about it later. *Remember when we were in the truck and we tried . . .? Were we stupid or what?*

But he continued kissing her deeply, and her stomach convulsed. His dark form covering her, he could be Uncle Murray, fondling, telling her he liked a little extra flesh on a woman.

No, no. This so wasn't happening. This was Calvin, and Calvin was safe.

He moved, trying to maneuver around the steering wheel, and the truck's shocks squeaked. No way. Not here. Not anywhere.

Stacey closed her hand on the fabric of his shirt. Her fist pushed weakly against his chest. She wiggled her other arm beneath him then pushed his shoulders upward with both hands. "Calvin, I don't think we should."

"It's okay. I promise I won't do anything you don't want me to. I love you, Stace."

His fingertips brushed her ribs, probing higher. He gasped the same moment she did.

"No. Calvin—" The icy sensation in her veins reverted to hot, for a different reason. Was he paying any attention to what she said? Had she just become a sexy body for him to do with as he pleased? She pushed harder.

He made a strangled sound and lurched away, slumped behind the steering wheel. Some part of him thumped the driver's door. He grunted like he'd been punched.

Stacey crab-crawled back to the passenger side. "I'm sorry. You just, kinda, forced yourself on me."

"Force—No, I didn't! Ouch." He massaged his left elbow.

She finger-combed her hair. "I don't mean forced, exactly. It was too much too fast."

He breathed out and shifted to a normal position on the seat. "Yeah, my bad. I thought you wanted to park somewhere."

"To talk. And make out a little. But not to have sex. Calvin, where did that come from? You've never been like that before."

Calvin wrapped his arms over the steering wheel and rested his forehead against them. "I just thought ... I don't know what I was thinking. The way you're dressed, I got carried away."

"So it's my fault?"

"I didn't say that."

"You were about to." She flipped her hair away from her face. "What happened to waiting for marriage, huh? One outfit drove all that talk out of your head?"

"Hey!" He jerked upward, shot a look at her that was probably a glare. "I stopped, didn't I? I didn't force you to do anything. I'm just trying to show you that, that—never mind. My mistake. I shouldn't have brought you here."

Stacey tugged her clothes into place and peered at the cotton field. The plants looked like spindly weeds in the dark. Not a field she'd want to walk through if she had to leave the truck.

Calvin cranked the engine and yanked the gearshift lever into drive. The truck lurched forward, and Stacey bounced and fumbled with the seat belt until she got it latched. The headlights illuminated a dusty trail. They flew past trees that seemed to lean and branch out over the path.

"You can slow down, you know."

"I have to get you home." His voice was flat.

"So, what, you're mad at me now?"

"No. Kind of."

"What did I do?"

"Just ... nothing. It's a lot of stuff."

"Which is it? A lot of stuff or nothing?"

He made a right turn on the dirt track, the truck skidding.

Stacey planted her hands against the dashboard. "Please slow down."

"I know where I'm going."

Sure he did. Because they were in the field his family owned. But did that mean he could get away with driving crazy? A big piece of farm equipment rose up out of the darkness, scaring Stacey. She held her breath as Calvin drove up a rise. At the road the front tires left the ground then slammed back, the shocks creaking and bouncing. Stacey's hands flew up and her hair whipped around her face. And then the nightmare ride was over. Victory Church Road lay before them, a nice, smooth path.

Stacey pulled a strand of hair out of her mouth. "Calvin, don't be mad at me."

He shifted in his seat, pulled his seat belt over his lap. He just now put it on?

"I don't get it," he said.

"Get what? I wanted to look nice for you."

He looked at her, and the dashboard lights glinted in his eyes. "You always look nice. I tell you all the time. I tell you I love you, but you keep starving yourself. So today I wanted to prove to you that you don't need to do that. That you're sexy enough and ..."

So now he had all these noble motives for trying to put his hand up her shirt? Yeah, right.

Calvin sighed. "Stacey, I'm not sure I can keep up with you. I'm trying. Really trying. But this anorexia—"

"Calvin Greenlee, I am not anorexic."

He snorted. Like a laugh. "Okay, look, forget everything that happened tonight. I got carried away, okay? Blame me if you want. I don't care. I don't want to fight anymore."

With one wrist draped over the steering wheel, his hand clenching then unclenching, Calvin drove past the high school. Stacey focused on the dark landscape sweeping past Calvin's head. It felt alien somehow. Unwelcoming. Because the guilt that invaded Stacey's mind made her feel removed, a self-conscious spirit exposed, ashamed of her flesh. Ashamed that she'd let Zoe talk her into wearing this horrible lace top that turned her nice boyfriend into a drooling fool.

"You're right. I get confused sometimes. Zoe gave me this blouse. I knew I shouldn't have worn it, I knew it was too skimpy and tight. I just wanted you to think I'm pretty and sexy. That's all. I didn't even think about, you know, going beyond kissing."

His heavy exhale announced his frustration. He made no other answer.

Stacey collapsed in her seat and hugged herself. Tears burned in her eyes and stayed there while he navigated back toward her house. Would the day end in angry silence like this?

For the second time, he turned onto Turner Creek Road.

"I'm confused too, Stace. There's some stuff we really need to talk about. I've been trying to, but it seems we never get a chance."

Something wedged in her throat, like a giant bug had flown into the pickup and got sucked into her mouth. Or like the scratchy feeling when she rammed her nails down her throat. She knew what "stuff" he wanted to talk about.

"When do you want ...?" her voice croaked.

"I'll call you tomorrow."

No. No. She had to put it out of his head tonight. "What if I don't want to talk about it?"

Had she really said that? A shriek of agony ripped through Stacey's brain.

The pickup jolted into her driveway so hard that the seat belt probably bruised her hips. Calvin jammed on the brakes. The only sound was the chugging of the truck engine taking a break after the crazy ride. Calvin stared forward. Stacey shivered in her seat.

"I'm just trying to help you." His voice was a low rumble. "I love you. I want to know that you'll be okay."

"I love you too," she mumbled. "Kiss good night?"

Calvin sighed and rolled toward her. His hand touched her shoulder and his lips pressed against hers for only a second. He pulled away. "I'll call you tomorrow."

She made her hand move to the door handle. Forced her shoulder to push open the creaking door. Put her feet on the hard surface of her driveway. Pushed the truck door shut, tried not to wobble when her legs carried her back a step.

Calvin backed out to the street. The pickup's transmission groaned and clunked into gear, and she stared as the rattling vehicle moved down the street, turned a corner, and was gone.

The force of will holding Stacey up slowly released her. She sank down in the grass, weak and gasping.

Chapter 21

He couldn't sing.

Peyton pushed the open hymnal closer to Calvin, and he felt the scrutiny of her glance. He stared down at the words on the page while voices swelled around him. He opened his mouth, but the words stalled, wouldn't even form in his brain.

He couldn't pretend to sing praises to God when his heart felt like a football in his chest. The guilt of that, and of sitting through a sermon he'd already forgotten, added to the weighty shroud he'd worn since last night.

Calvin's eyes burned from little sleep. He dared not close them for more than the instant it took to blink, because the dark images would return. Stacey's face, a landscape of shadows and what he thought was desire, against the cracked vinyl upholstery of his father's pickup truck. If she'd protested, he couldn't remember. The argument that followed was a blur. Shock had bashed aside all other sensations and emotions and overlaid a nightmare image upon her face.

Bones.

The hymn ended and Calvin closed his mouth.

Girls were supposed to be soft. But his fingers had passed over bones so pronounced he could have counted them by touch.

How could she hide that so well? How long had this been going on and he hadn't seen it? Her parents — why didn't they do something about it? Stacey's mother, constantly wanting to know what, when, and where, had to have noticed. Her father, a cop — wasn't he trained to look for details? Why was Calvin the first person to figure out what was going on?

Mom touched his sleeve. "Excuse me, hon. I have to fetch the kids."

Calvin's gaze snapped to hers. Her tone might not be so sweet if she had any clue what went on in the pickup last night.

No, he couldn't think about that. He would have stopped before he and Stacey went too far. Maybe. But it didn't matter. It definitely wouldn't happen again because ... those bones. They just freaked him out.

A wailing built in the back of his mind, like echoes in a canyon. *How did this happen?*

"Calvin?" Mom said. "Move, please."

He found his voice and made his limbs obey. "Yeah. Sorry."

In the aisle he bumped elbows with other people, made his way out of the sanctuary and into the lobby, and waited there while his parents went to collect his younger siblings.

Peyton stepped around to face him and leaned close. "Are you okay? You look like something's really bothering you."

In her pale blue eyes, he saw compassion. She wasn't trying to get into his business. She cared. Lizzie joined them, forming a tight circle. No sympathy in her expression, though. She wanted to be in the know.

Girls. Either one of them might have something to say that would help him. But neither one was beyond taking his confessions to their parents.

Even Michael would have judged him. *A real man knows how to control his desires and respect a woman.*

Crash and burn.

Calvin tugged his hair. "Just, uh, had a fight with Stacey last night."

Lizzie looked at the floor, or at her glittery sandals, Calvin wasn't sure which.

Peyton clasped Calvin's shoulder. "It'll be all right. You'll kiss and make up soon. If ever I saw two people meant for each other, it's you and Stacey."

Calvin snorted. "Yeah, right."

"I'm serious. What did y'all fight about?"

For one second his brain stalled, sending panic racing down his spine. "Um, like ... college, and ... stuff."

Peyton raised one eyebrow. "College? That's another year away."

"Yeah, but she wants to go to fashion design school, and I don't even know what I want to do yet. So, like, that kind of guarantees we'll break up, doesn't it?"

"Not necessarily," Peyton said.

"Maybe," Lizzie said. "But you've still got a year to have fun together."

His gaze moved from one girl to the other. He couldn't keep up this conversation, making up concerns as he went along.

Peyton rubbed his arm in a parting gesture, making it easy for him. "It'll be okay. You'll see."

Mom came out dragging Jacob by the hand and carrying crying Emily on her hip. Dad followed with Zachary, who danced at his side, yammering about something. Lizzie led the way out of the church lobby, bounding down the stairs as if leaving school for the start of summer vacation. Calvin paused at the top step to take Jacob's hand from his mother, easing her burden.

"I can go by myself," Jacob protested, pulling away.

Whatever. Calvin dropped to the back of the pack and plodded along the sidewalk to the parking lot. Dad had parked the family van in the last row, near the neighboring feed store, in almost the last available slot. Calvin shoved his hands into his pockets and tried to think about lunch. An early heat wave radiated off the asphalt and robbed his breath away. How could Stacey possibly have thought it was cold?

"Hi," a soft voice said.

He stopped. Stacey stood beside the van. She'd pulled her hair back and wore a flowery dress that draped loosely past her knees. Cowgirl boots covered the rest of her legs. All covered up and conservative, with her hands folded in front of her and her chin tilted downward.

Calvin blinked. "Hey."

That was how she did it! She covered everything up so it was impossible for anyone to see how skinny she was. All the thick sweaters and denim she'd worn all winter ... But if she wanted to be thin, why would she hide her success?

He and Stacey stared at each other while his family loaded into the van. She smiled a little, but not enough to hide the apology or embarrassment plastered all over her face and shifting stance. Maybe he looked the same way.

He moved close enough to kiss her, but didn't. The memories crashed back, and heat rose up the back of his neck.

Stacey sucked her lips in and lowered her head even more. "I was stupid yesterday. I'm really sorry. Forgive me?"

Something trembled in Calvin's chest. His hand jerked toward hers but he retracted it. Not ready yet. "Yes. I'm sorry too. I acted like a jerk."

She shook her head and sniffed. "You didn't do anything wrong. I'm just a ... slut."

He sucked air through clenched teeth. Had anyone in his family heard that remark? He glanced past Stacey's shoulder. Mom backed away from the middle row of the van, where she'd strapped Emily into her car seat. Dad was already behind the wheel.

Calvin bumped his shoulder against Stacey's, clasped her elbow, and spoke in a soft growl. "Don't say that about yourself. Don't *ever* say that. Is that what your uncle told you?"

Stacey pressed a finger joint to the puffy flesh beneath one of her eyes. "Please, let's not—I feel horrible. You were so angry when you left last night."

He sighed. "I wasn't angry. Just really frustrated." He glanced at the van again to see how much time he had left. Not much; Lizzie was the last person crawling in through the side door. "Look, I don't understand everything that's happening, but we have to find a way to fix this thing. We have to talk and be completely honest with each other."

She stroked fingertips down his tie. "You look good, all dressed up."

He fought down the exasperation churning again in his chest.

"Okay. You're right," she said. "Things are a little crazy and ... maybe I haven't been eating as much as I should. I want to do better, Calvin. I want to be healthy and—I promise you, I'm okay. I'm stressed out and trying to get over the stuff I didn't want to tell you about."

"Yeah, I know all about trying to get over stuff that hurts. But you're only hurting yourself more by what you're doing. You're hurting *us*."

She tossed her head and looked away. Her hair was held back in a clip, so none of the pink hair showed. Fashion model one day, school librarian the next. Weird.

"It's not all my fault, Calvin. Please don't. Don't ... go there."

Calvin blew out his breath and folded his fingers around hers. "I'm sorry. I shouldn't have said that. Let's go somewhere now and talk."

"Don't you have to spend the day with your family?"

"Ugh. Okay, wait here just a minute." Leaving Stacey, he went to the driver's side of the van and leaned against the window his father had already opened. "Dad, is it okay if Stacey gives me a ride home in a while?" His eyes flicked toward Peyton, who sat crowded between Lizzie and Emily's car seat in the second row of the nine passenger van.

"We're meeting Pastor at the Bentley Café today. Stacey can come with us," Mom said. She turned to shout an order back at the two boys in the rear seat, then flopped back into her seat and exhaled loudly.

"Follow us to the café," Dad said. "Y'all can talk in her car."

Stacey wouldn't go. No way. All that heavy country cooking and a room full of people going up for second and third helpings? Wouldn't happen.

"Please?"

Peyton leaned forward to stick her head between the two front seats. "They had an argument," she said softly. "They need some private time. Let him go."

Thank you, Peyton!

"Mo-om! Zach won't stop kicking me," Jacob wailed from the back.

"He's putting his foot on my side of the seat," Zachary protested.

Mom groaned. "All right, let Calvin go with Stacey. Just—let's get these kids some lunch so they'll settle down."

"Fine." Dad pointed a finger at Calvin. "Don't go in the house with her when no one else is home. Got it, sport?"

"Dad, I know the rules." Calvin backed away from the van.

His father yanked the gearshift lever into reverse and pulled away. Calvin watched the silver van maneuver through the lot and onto the road. He could feel Stacey's presence behind him as a pressure, like waves of heat off the pavement. He suspected his afternoon would've been easier if he'd gone with his family.

Calvin pivoted slowly toward Stacey. "So ... where do you want to go? I'm hungry." It just popped out, like what any guy would say to a *normal* girlfriend at the start of a Sunday afternoon together.

Stacey twisted her fingers together in front of her stomach. "I ate be—"

"Before you came. Right. I got it." He tugged his hair. Messing up already, letting his anger and frustration surface. "Sorry ..."

She tilted her head up and blinked in the sunlight. So pale. "I can't stay out long. I still have some homework to do. Can I just drive you home?"

That would take all of five minutes, including getting into the car and strapping on their seat belts. She was trying to dodge the issue again. Arguing about why she couldn't give him more time meant they wouldn't talk about what was really important. Calvin shrugged. "Sure."

They walked to her Honda without holding hands or speaking. Stacey got in the car first then pushed a button to unlock the passenger door. Calvin plopped into his seat and buckled up.

Country pop blared from Stacey's CD player, a crooning song with a sad message.

It don't matter to me what all my friends say.
You're killing me slowly, but I love you anyway.

Is that what she'd been listening to on the way to see him at church?

Stacey snapped it off. She sniffed, and her hands flew over the car's controls, shifting, turning, accelerating, while she stared ahead and said nothing.

It'd be up to him to start the conversation, and he didn't have much time.

"Stace, I don't know what to do or say anymore. Seems everything I do is wrong. It's driving me crazy." He waited for a reaction, but static tension filled the silence. He plunged onward. "I know you don't want to hear this, but I'm really worried about you. I'm afraid I'm going to lose you—like, *really* lose you."

Her brow pinched, she glanced at him. "What do you mean?"

"Like, if I don't do everything right, you might ... die."

"What? You think I'm suicidal or something?"

"No. You're not, are you? No, I mean, I'm trying to understand why you're doing what you're doing and what I can do to help you."

Her tight grip on the steering wheel looked painful, especially her knuckles poking upward against pale skin. Sick. Not normal. Calvin forced himself to look out the side window. They drove over a narrow concrete bridge crossing Flowers Creek. That little slip of water snaked through the woods for a quarter mile before it marked the southern property line of his family's farm. They'd reach his driveway in about a minute.

"Calvin, do you honestly think I'm so stupid that I'll kill myself?"

No time for subtleties. He stared at her, his eyes narrowed. "You are killing yourself day by day. You're starving yourself right before my eyes."

She drove on without responding, but her chin quivered and the car slowed, as if she couldn't maintain firm pressure on the gas pedal. Before the car reached his driveway, it was crawling along Victory Church Road. A tear traced down Stacey's cheek and she sniffed.

Calvin looked away. Her tears would destroy him. "Why?" he said aloud without meaning to.

"Why what?" Her voice was thick, choked.

"Why is this happening?"

Gravel popped beneath the tires as she rolled into the driveway. Sights Calvin had known his entire life pressed in on him, no longer safe and secure, instead telling him he had no time. If he got out of the car, she would leave — he was certain — and then he'd be alone with a hurting heart and no answers.

He took a deep breath and forced out what had to be said. "It's got to stop, Stacey. You have to see a doctor. I'm not going to watch you starve yourself to death."

"What are you saying? If I don't do what you want, you'll break up with me?"

He squeezed an answer through his tightened throat. "Yes."

"Calvin!"

He clamped his eyes shut. "Yes. I don't want to break up with you, but I can't do this anymore. I can't pretend I don't see the truth." One hot tear leaked onto the bridge of his nose on the wrong side, where she couldn't see it.

"Please, no," she whimpered. "Calvin, I know things are really weird right now, and that's why I *need* you. My life ... my life is like ... spinning out of control. I don't have control over *anything*. I need you to ... to ... be my hero. To be here for me when everything's crazy."

"So you can control me?" he muttered.

"No! I need something that's constant and someone who loves me. You said ... you said you loved me."

The tightness in his throat spread to his chest, his gut, and threatened to crush him from within. If only she could see how he was drowning in his love and his fears. He gasped, as if coming up for air from the bottom of a deep pool. The crushing sensation eased in his chest but moved at once to his sinuses. "I can't ..."

"I need you to love me," Stacey squeaked.

"I do! That's why this is killing me." He sniffed, cracked open his eyes, and turned his face to her. "What am I supposed to do?"

Though her cheeks were soaked with tears, she reached up to

touch his. "You're the only good thing in my life. Don't—" She choked. "Don't leave me."

"Then please, go to the doctor. Please. Do it for me."

Stacey lowered her head, and a tear fell onto the gearshift lever. She nodded. She *nodded*! A shuddering sigh escaped Calvin, and he clasped her head in both his hands. As he lifted her face to kiss her, she whispered, "I'll try."

He kissed her anyway, though those two simple words dug a trench through his brain. She'd try. What did that mean? All she had to do was make an appointment, get in the car, and drive there. Easy. The choice was either doing or not doing. What was there to "try"?

Stacey flung her arms around him, and her soft lips moved against his, caressing away his dark thoughts. Calvin's fingers jammed against the plastic clip in her hair. He tugged it free and let it fall so he could tangle the locks in his hands. He kissed her as if it were the last time.

The bizarre thought tightened his chest again. He came up for air and rolled into his seat.

They held hands, staring at each other. Calvin couldn't smile, and Stacey didn't either. Her promise to "try" hung between them like smoke from a blown-out candle, seen and smelled but without substance he could hold on to. It forced an unspoken promise of his own, that he would wait, taking no further action, until she fulfilled her part or walked away from it.

In the end, Stacey was in control.

The tightness in his chest sent tension down his limbs. He clenched his jaw, not really seeing Stacey's face anymore. Sticking with her didn't make him a hero, it made him a slave.

"Ouch. Calvin, you're squeezing too tight."

He let go of her hand and reached for the door handle. "I've got homework too. Probably just as well I didn't go with my family. The house will be quiet for a while."

"I love you," she said as he opened the door.

Calvin hesitated, exhaled, and said, "Love you too, Stace."

You're killing me slowly, but I love you anyway.

He propelled himself out of the car and swung the door shut, stepping back off the gravel as Stacey put the car into reverse. Calvin stared at his scuffed brown dress shoes until he could no longer hear the sound of the Honda's engine.

... but I love you anyway ...

No way he'd be able to study. The quiet of the house would only make the pathetic song that had invaded his thoughts echo louder. He had to do something to drive all the worries and anger away, if only for a few moments. He had to find *himself* again.

Calvin ran up the front steps of the house and found a key beneath a decorative planter filled with dirt and nothing else. He let himself in, allowing the screen door to slap behind him. He had his tie off before he reached the steps leading to the bedrooms, and tugged his dress shirt out of his pants as he thundered up to his room. *You're killing me slowly, killing me slowly ...* Calvin stripped out of his church clothes and pulled on a T-shirt and thick jeans. He yanked on the hiking boots he used for riding, then took the stairs back down two at a time.

The *ring-ding* song of the Yamaha's engine drove the annoying tune out of Calvin's head soon enough. He followed the service road around the cotton field, then cut into the woods, passing the place where he'd busted his throttle cable what seemed like months ago.

No memories. No worries or anger or remembrances of Stacey's kiss in the night. He wanted to feel nothing but the rumble and surge of the motorcycle beneath him and the cool, woodsy air battering his face.

The uneven trail was a challenging ride. Calvin poured himself into it, let the rocks and the short, steep ridges beat his body and push his endurance. Like an old friend, the bike would not betray him or demand its own way. Their goals were the same. He followed the trail to the border of the Greenlee property, splashed through shallow Flowers Creek, and headed into government-owned land bordering the Tar River. Here the trail was crowded with bushes and vines. Calvin slowed down, carefully picking his way through. He had a destination: a small clearing at the side of the river that was sheltered, quiet, and secluded. He and Tyler had discovered it and had camped there last summer. The mosquitoes had been unbearable.

But nobody would find him there.

Calvin found a relatively flat spot and cut the Yamaha's engine. He set the kickstand and swung his leg over the seat. The sound of rippling water and a breeze in the leaves gently drowned out the ringing in Calvin's ears and the echoes of a song he now hated. He sat cross-legged at the top of a ridge that fell down to the river's edge, and pinched a chunk of papery bark off a birch tree. Sunlight sparkling on the water dazzled his eyes. He mindlessly toyed with the bark while his heart reached for some kind of peace ... but couldn't find it.

He was supposed to pray at times like this. Pain clamped down on his heart again.

"God ..." Desperate, hurting, frightened, confused, angry. What could he say? "Please. I don't know what to do. Show me what to do."

Taking deep, desperate breaths to ease the pain in his chest, Calvin looked at the sky and grimaced — the prayer felt meaningless, like all the words he'd used trying to save Stacey from herself.

Chapter 22

Calvin's Facebook message dimmed as Stacey's computer shifted to sleep mode. Cradling the laptop in a nest made of her quilt and her crossed legs, she flicked her finger across the touchpad to make the screen go bright again.

Weary from a third day battling the flu, Stacey tugged at her lower lip and jiggled her foot to keep herself from falling into sleep mode again.

Though she'd read Calvin's message nine times, she was no closer to giving him an answer. It didn't seem like he really wanted one. Stacey stretched out her cramped legs. When her computer settled into the new position, she read the message one more time.

> Hey, Stace. Hope you're feeling better. I'm at Tyler's house right now. Can you believe there's only three weeks left of school? Anyway, we were talking about our camping trip. Here's a link to a website that has pictures of Badin Lake. It's going to be so cool. You're coming back to school tomorrow, right? I'll see you there. Love you. Cal.

She wanted to cry, but there didn't seem to be a rational reason why she should.

With her first reading, she'd been stunned. Weren't they going to talk about that trip? He hadn't mentioned it in a long time, and she'd forgotten about it.

With her second reading, anger darkened her vision. Nothing in his message suggested that he really cared what she thought about him going away and leaving her behind, about him going away with another girl.

With the third reading, fear crept in. Other than his closing declaration of love—which could have been obligatory or just a habit—the message could have been written to anyone, a friend, family member, or someone he knew casually at school.

With successive readings, a feeling of loneliness had settled over Stacey like Calvin was already gone.

Maybe he was. Maybe the camping trip was actually irrelevant.

For days after Calvin's ultimatum it seemed they were together but just existing in the same space. If they looked at each other in the eyes for more than a second, hurt surfaced, and they turned away. Their private moments had become awkward and their kisses rare.

He didn't press her to answer any of his questions, didn't beg her again to see a doctor or ask if she'd eaten anything. Rather than feeling relief, she knew the peace wouldn't last. The conflict between them had fallen back, and meaninglessness had moved into that vacant battleground. The conflict would lie hidden, like a patient predator, waiting for the smallest cue to roar into action again.

Stacey leaned back against her pillow and let her eyes rest, gazing at the gentle movement of her curtains over the air conditioning vent. A lavender-scented candle flickered on her bedside table. Her body settled into her mattress, calling her back to sleep.

Not yet. She needed to respond to Calvin's message with something that would matter. She had to pull him back. Maybe a poem.

Stacey forced her lethargic muscles to move. She sat up, settled the laptop in a workable position again, and opened a new document. Then she breathed, waiting for inspiration. Should she pour out her heart to him in hopes that he would understand? Or tell him how much she loved him, so he might forgive and forget? What could she say that would reverse time and take them back to the place where their lives danced together?

Dancing. Maybe something with dancing as a metaphor.

Pas de duex *is a dance of two, but my heart dances alone.*

Not right. They weren't really alone. They were just ... not moving. Stuck. Paralyzed.

Pas de duex, *a dance of two, a maiden and her prince.*

Erg. Not happening. The lines were as meaningless as the time they'd spent together over the weekend, watching television and hardly speaking to each other.

A fog settled over Stacey's mind, while parts of her body twitched involuntarily. A muscle in her leg. A twinge in her back. Her fingers, jumping off the computer keys for no reason at all. She gave in and closed her eyes.

In what seemed like a second later, the door of her room opened. Stacey's body jumped at the sound. She shut her laptop before anyone else could see the screen.

Her mother came in with a tray. "Here's your supper, sweetheart." She first slid the tray onto Stacey's dresser so she could set up a TV table beside the bed. "Have you taken your temperature again?"

Stacey nodded. "Normal. I think I can go back to school tomorrow."

"Ah, good. I made you some soup. Hopefully you'll be able to keep this down."

As her mother moved the tray down onto the TV table, tomato broth rolled up the side of the bowl and left a liquid red stain on the white stoneware. Too thick to ebb back into the bowl, which meant there was something fatty in the soup. Stacey pulled her pajama sleeve down to cover her knuckles, then placed the back of her hand against her mouth.

"I added cauliflower and garlic to tomato soup," Mom said. "I read in a magazine that certain veggies are especially good to boost a person's immune system."

That's all she needed, medical advice from a supermarket tabloid. "Mom, you know I hate cauliflower."

"Don't worry. I cut it up small and added a touch of brown sugar to sweeten it. You'll hardly taste it. Try to eat it all, sweetie. You can't get better without food in your stomach."

Stacey fell back against her pillow. "I'm tired. Can I eat it later, please?"

Mom arranged a napkin and the silverware on the tray. "Eat it now, then you can go back to sleep." She then lifted one side of Stacey's rumpled quilt off the floor and smoothed the whole thing across her bed. "You don't need to be missing any more school. I'm sure to be hearing from the principal's office soon."

And then she reached for Stacey's laptop.

"No! Mom, please. Leave it there."

"But you're going to sleep after you eat. You don't want to risk kicking it off the bed."

"I've got the flu, not a broken leg. I can move it when I'm ready."

Her mother tilted her head in disapproval at Stacey's tone then pointed at the tray. "Eat that soup. I want to see the bowl empty when I come back."

"Yes, Mom."

No big deal. A little while after her mother left, she could sneak into the bathroom and dump the stinky soup in the toilet. Even the small mountain of crackers next to the bowl would go down easy if they were crunched up. The veggies by themselves didn't have a lot of calories, but Mom had to add all kinds of junk to the soup to make it taste better. Brown sugar? Really?

Yet the woman wouldn't be so easily dismissed. She stood there at the foot of Stacey's bed, her arms crossed, as if she would supervise the eating of the miracle soup. Stacey groaned and pushed herself up. She swung her legs over the side of her bed. Cool air hit her skin laid bare by her bunched-up pajama pants. Somebody had turned the air-conditioning up full blast, and when Stacey complained Mom just said her chills were because she was fevered. With her fever gone, so was the excuse. Stacey rubbed her legs. The movement brought her nose too close to the soup, and the smell of cauliflower made her stomach lurch.

"Ugh, why did it have to be cauliflower?"

"Stacey ..."

"What? I'm sorry. I'll eat it." She picked up the spoon. "See? I'm eating."

Mom came around the side of the bed, her eyes wide and her brow pinched. "Stacey, baby ..."

"What?"

"Your legs! Your ... your feet!"

She looked down, then jerked her legs back under the quilt. She bumped the TV table in the process, and soup sloshed out of the bowl and into the plate beneath it. "They're cold, Momma, just cold."

"They're blue! And so thin."

Mom reached for the quilt to pull it back, but Stacey fought her, tugging the quilt tight over her body. "I told you, I'm cold. Can you please turn the air-conditioning down? Please? Or at least close the vents in this room?"

Mom straightened, but her face was flushed. She raised trembling fingers to her face. "I'll talk to your father. Just ... eat that soup. I'll be back."

She left. As soon as the door closed behind her, Stacey flung off the quilt and dove down to the floor to look for her slippers under the bed. Better yet, she could put on those thick wool socks Grandma Jenny knitted for her for Christmas. She planted her arm on top of the bed to brace herself, but as soon as she pushed upward, the familiar dizziness attacked her and rocked her backward. She fell onto her butt, and the impact rattled up her spine to her skull.

Stacey lay on the floor while the room spun. Tears flooded down the sides of her face and pooled in her ears. Her heart jumped around inside her ribcage. She'd fallen too hard. She needed to still the panic. Breathe in, breathe out, slowly, deeply. It was okay. The pain eased some, and Stacey rolled to her side. Gripping her bedpost, she carefully pulled herself up, then settled on her bed by the TV tray and breathed to still the swaying in her brain.

The floor creaked in the hallway outside her room. Stacey tugged her quilt over her legs and filled her spoon with soup. She raised it up toward her mouth just as her doorknob turned.

Daddy entered the room before Mom. His scrutinizing eye passed over her. "What's going on in here?"

Stacey blinked. "I'm eating my soup." She lifted the spoon, a whitish lump sitting in the pool of red, as irrefutable proof. With Daddy watching, she daintily sucked the tomato portion into her mouth and swallowed it.

Behind her father, Stacey's mother held on to the door frame as if for support. Her eyes were red rimmed. "It's all those fashion magazines she reads," she said softly.

Daddy's lips pursed for a moment. "Your mother says you're not eating enough, and you're getting too thin. Is that true?"

"What do you mean? I'm sick. I've been throwing up, so I haven't had much of an appetite. But it's coming back. See?" She took another bite to prove it.

"You've been dieting a long time. Don't you think you've lost enough weight? You're probably sick because you don't have enough energy to fight things off."

Stacey looked down at the tray and gently slid the spoon into her soup. Daddy wouldn't buy denial. Maybe another tactic, just to satisfy him. "Maybe that's true. But Daddy, everything Mom cooks is, like, really fattening. Sorry, Mom, but I just have to say it. Can't we try to eat healthier? I'm so afraid I'll get fat again."

Mom eased farther into the room until she stood beside Daddy. Unity. This was going to be bad. "Sweetie, you're not one of those girls who refuse to eat, are you? Like, what's her name? That singer. Karen Carpenter?"

Stacey winced. "Who?"

"Anorexia," Daddy said. "That's what the disease is called. Back in Rocky Mount, I got called to a house where a young woman died from it. That better not be what's going on here."

The tears sprang out of Stacey's eyes again. "It's not, Daddy. I promise. I'll start eating more. Please believe me."

Daddy puffed a long breath out of his nose. He nodded toward the bedside table. "Get rid of those magazines," he told Mom.

"But I use those so I can learn about fashion design. Please don't — "

Daddy held up his hand to silence her. "For a while. When I'm convinced that you're eating properly, you can have them again."

Mom bent to collect everything that was in the cubby of Stacey's nightstand, including her sketchbook. She shuffled the magazines into a pile in her arms and turned to leave the room without a word of apology. Daddy remained where he was. He stared, and his lower lip quivered before he spoke again. "Eat your dinner. When you're feeling better, we're going to sit down and talk about this."

"Yes, Daddy." Beneath the TV table, Stacey clasped her hands together to stop their shaking and squeezed until it hurt.

He glared down at her for another long, agonizing moment, then finally turned to go. He left the door hanging open.

Worst thing ever. She didn't care about the magazines. She wasn't afraid of what her parents would find in her sketchbook. But now they were watching her. Like Calvin had been watching her. Nowhere was safe anymore. Her privacy had been invaded, and if she knew her father, it wouldn't end with the magazines.

Stacey tried to spoon soup into her mouth, but her hand shook too badly. How could she eat anything when she stood on the verge of a total collapse of everything that mattered to her?

What if Daddy confiscated her laptop and read Zoe's emails?

Or Calvin's?

Stacey pulled her laptop under her pillow, then forced herself to eat the soup. It was worse than she'd thought. She managed to down half of it. By the time Mom came back to collect the tray, she'd curled up under her blankets and pretended to be asleep. As soon as Mom blew out the candle, turned off the light, and shut the door, Stacey rolled onto her stomach and pulled out the computer.

She kicked her heels up and down, up and down, burning off soup calories while she went from one program to another on her computer, deleting all the evidence.

Chapter 23

The scents of a May morning ride, of dew and fresh grass and honeysuckle in the woods, lingered on Calvin's clothes. They wouldn't last, though. Soon the closed-in atmosphere of the school building, with its noise and schedules and the heavy smell of floor polish in the hallways, would demolish all the sensations from his five-minute ride. Especially the sense of freedom.

He leaned against the wall opposite the administrative offices, his jean jacket still on and his helmet dangling from its strap in his fingers. More and more students passed in front of him on their way to morning classes as Calvin watched through the office windows, waiting for Stacey to reappear. The secretary behind the high partition scuttled back and forth, handing out passes and forms and answering questions for other students and a couple of parents. Stacey had hoped she could simply hand in the note from her parents explaining why she'd been out for three days. Instead, the assistant principal had taken her past the partition and into the inner sanctum of the administrative offices.

This couldn't be anything but bad.

The large clock suspended on a bracket above the office door reminded Calvin he had only three minutes until class. He still had to go to his locker. He pushed away from the wall and paced four steps one way, five steps back. Stacey would understand if he left. But he just couldn't, not until he knew she was okay.

With a minute and a half to go, Stacey finally emerged. She walked with her head down, her books held tightly to her chest, and a white business-sized envelope clutched in her hand. She wove her way through the remaining people by the front desk then turned left in the hallway as if she didn't see him.

Calvin caught up with her. "Hey. What happened?"

She jumped at the sound of his voice. "Oh! I didn't think you'd still be here." Her face was wet with tears, and she backed away from him as if she didn't want him to know.

"What happened, Stace. What did Mrs. Farley say to you?"

She sniffed and looked at the envelope. "If I miss any more days of school, I'll have to do summer school, maybe even repeat my junior year."

Calvin's jaw dropped, and he was barely able to make it move to speak. "But—but you're an honor student. How can they do that?"

Stacey sniffed again, and a renewed flood of tears gushed from her eyes. Still hugging her books, she leaned into Calvin to cry on his jacket. He could only hold on to her with one arm and wait for her to get control of her sobbing. Around them, the hallway cleared out, and the clock over the office ticked down toward the first bell.

"I hate this place." Stacey's voice was muffled by his chest. "I wish we never moved."

The sting of that remark lasted only a second. She was upset and didn't mean she wished she'd never met him. Calvin cupped her cheek in his hand and lifted her head up. "It'll be okay. We've only got three weeks left. You can make it."

"Calvin, you're the only good thing in my life. I don't know what I'd do without you."

He forced a smile. "I don't know about that. But let me help you,

Stace. I know you had the flu, but I think if you ate more healthy food, you might not get sick so often."

She tried to shake her head, but he hooked his thumb under her chin to stop her.

"Listen, okay? Please? I'm not trying to make you gain weight or anything. A healthy diet. You need vitamins and stuff that you get from food. So let's get together, either at my house or yours, and we'll look up some good diets online. We'll do it together, okay? I'll even eat the same stuff as you."

She lifted a shoulder coyly. "No more bacon cheeseburgers?"

"*Blee-yuck.* No. They're history."

The little smile she gave him disappeared. "How can we even do that, Calvin? Both our moms are in love with butter and potatoes and stuff. I've tried to cook for my family, and all they do is complain."

He took a deep breath and plunged. "We'll talk to them."

She shook her head and pulled away from him. He had to catch up to her again as she started down the hallway.

"I appreciate the offer. It's sweet. But this is my problem, Calvin. I have to deal with it."

"I want to help you!"

"I have a pass, but you don't. You're going to be late for class if you don't run."

She was right about that. "Okay, look," he said, "we'll talk about this later, after school. I'll meet you in the parking lot, okay?"

Stacey blew him a kiss. "Run. You don't need to be in trouble too."

Nothing more he could do or say. He took off, walking fast and running when he thought he could get away with it. He skidded into his physics class before the teacher had closed the door, but his classmates were all in their seats and every eye was on him, his helmet still in his hand, and a big wet mark on the front of his jean jacket.

"Thank you for joining us, Mr. Greenlee," Mr. Atkinson said. "We were thinking we wouldn't be able to start without you."

A few of the students chuckled as Calvin swung into his desk along the wall, two seats back from the front. His helmet clunked as he set it by his feet and then rolled into the middle of the aisle, prompting more awkward laughter. At least the teacher hadn't busted him. Mr. Atkinson resumed his opening statements for the class while Calvin rescued his helmet and dug into his backpack, trying not to make any more noise.

He breathed out, made an effort to rearrange the synapses in his brain to focus on school, not Stacey. But he couldn't escape one thought: she'd shut him down again. No matter how understanding he was, how nice he acted, or how much he tried to "love her through it," Stacey was the one with the power to say no. Now she was in trouble with the school. She might think herself fat or unworthy or unloved, but the one thing she prided herself on was her academic achievements. With those in jeopardy, maybe she'd wake up and change.

Somehow he doubted it.

o ○ ◯ ◯ o

Kneeling in front of a chair in the dining room, Calvin touched a wet cloth to Jacob's bloody knee. "Okay, this isn't bad. You can handle this little scrape, right, big guy?"

Jacob's mouth trembled into a smile. "I caught the ball. Did you see me?"

"I did! That was awesome. But Dad's got the smoker going, and there's a lot of people out there, so maybe y'all shouldn't be throwing the football in the driveway right now."

A pout replaced the smile. "It was Zach's fault. He don't throw good." Jacob waved his uninjured leg, his heel thumping the rung of the wooden chair. "Michael said he was gonna teach me to play football."

The comment stopped Calvin's hand as he reached for a Band-Aid on the table. Jacob still didn't quite understand that Michael was gone. On this Memorial Day, when the family was gathered to honor their fallen soldier, could Jacob have misunderstood and thought his big brother was finally going to come home?

Calvin forced his hand to retrieve the bandage. Without lifting his eyes, he tore open the paper sleeve. "Hold still." He stretched the Band-Aid across Jacob's knee. "Done."

Jacob slid off the chair and ran back outside.

Calvin didn't want to follow him. He wished Mom hadn't set this whole thing up. It gave her something to do, a way to focus everyone's thoughts on Michael, because, she said, he deserved it. But would Michael even know, sitting up in heaven? Calvin wasn't sure about the theology of that question, and he really didn't care. He'd woke up that morning, with the sun already beating down on the roof of the house, baking the air inside his attic bedroom, and pulled his sheet over his head anyway. Wuss. Coward. He didn't have the emotional strength to face the day. Whatever he might have had, dealing with Stacey had sucked it right out of him.

Calvin pushed himself to his feet and forced them to carry him outside. Bright sunlight blinded him, and he squinted to pick his way down the two concrete steps to the backyard. Southern gospel music blared from the speakers in the open workshop. Jacob chased Zachary and two cousins toward a soccer net at the back of the yard. Beneath the old oak tree, Grandma Elizabeth fanned herself, over-flowing a webbed lawn chair, while Emily toddled over to show off a yellow dandelion. Lizzie lay sunbathing with their cousin Bailey, their beach towels spread across the weedy grass. And all around aunts, uncles, and cousins clustered in every available patch of shade.

Kids Calvin didn't bother to count chased each other around the yard, shouting and laughing as if there was nothing different about the day.

It all felt wrong.

Calvin sighed and leaned against the corner of the workshop. Michael wouldn't want him to mope around like this. He would've been running around with the little kids, acting like a goofball, or cutting up with the uncles talking about NASCAR. He'd make it his mission to cause at least one aunt to blush.

But Michael wasn't there. And Michael didn't have an anorexic girlfriend who'd promised she would be there by ten a.m. to help him get through the day.

It was almost noon.

The warm breeze shifted, bringing smoke thick with the aroma of barbecue across Calvin's face. Standing next to the big metal smoker, Dad pulled meat off a side of pork that had been roasting since before dawn.

Calvin wandered to the top of the driveway and peered toward the street. No blue Honda; she wasn't coming. All the food had scared her away. How sad—how wrong—that her need to avoid food, even after all her promises, could overrule his need to have her there with him.

Almost choking on the thought, he wandered toward two long folding tables draped with mismatched tablecloths, where Mom and Aunt Sally were arranging the food. Wide mixing bowls and big casserole dishes contained potato salad, slaw, baked beans, macaroni and cheese, and Jell-O salad. Sliced watermelon, peach cobbler, and pie—at least three different kinds. Calvin filled a red plastic cup with lemonade.

His little cousin Morgan, looking so cute in her blonde pigtails and pink overall shorts, reached up to clasp his hand. "Is your bike fixed now, Calvin?"

"Uh, yeah, but I think we're going to eat soon. Tell you what, though. I bet Lizzie will watch VeggieTales with you."

"Really?"

"Yep. Go ask her. She's right over there."

He pointed, and Morgan scurried off toward Lizzie. Calvin swigged more of his lemonade and ducked around the side of the house before his sister could launch a counter assault. He sat on the front porch steps, where the squealing of playing kids and the chatter of adults who could somehow be happy didn't surround him. He stared at the street, until gulp by gulp, his drink cup was drained.

Still no Stacey.

He could go inside and call her, but what was the point? She'd just make an excuse, and he'd feel even worse. Calvin certainly didn't know everything there was to know about love, but he'd learned it involved sacrifice. He'd sacrificed a lot for Stacey. It seemed a long time since she'd sacrificed anything for him. All the drawings and poems and the deep conversations about Michael, the things that made him love her so much and made him feel that she loved him, he hadn't seen any of it for weeks. Things had got tough for them, and it seemed she was withdrawing—even pushing him away—more each day.

"You said you needed me," he muttered to the air. "Actually seems like I love you more than you love me. This hurts, Stace. It hurts bad."

In the backyard, Mom yelled, "Y'all come on. We're ready to eat."

Calvin lumbered off the steps and shuffled toward the backyard. There, Dad carried a huge platter of pulled pork to the table and set it in the spot Aunt Sally had cleared for him. People gathered in and formed a circle around the tables. One by one the voices fell to whispers and stilled.

"Let's pray." Dad's voice was barely loud enough to be heard.

Twenty-six family members clasped hands. Calvin set his empty plastic cup on the ground between his feet then took hold of Zachary's hand to his right, Bailey's to his left. He swallowed and looked down. *Get this over with.*

"Father God . . ." Dad said.

The breeze whispered in the oak tree and birds chirped. Calvin opened his eyes enough to see his father with his head lowered to his chest.

Don't. Don't start crying now.

"We're gathered here on this day . . . to honor our brave men and women in uniform for their service to our country. Yet our hearts are burdened as we think of . . . a son, a grandson, a brother . . . a loved one, who gave the ultimate sacrifice and is with you now. We thank you . . ."

Dad's voice failed. Calvin squeezed his eyes tight. He couldn't look up again, couldn't bear to see the pain that would be written on his father's face, the trembling of his lips as he tried to find words. Tears burned beneath Calvin's eyelids, the pressure built until it felt like the water was behind his eyeballs too. It wouldn't take much for him to lose it.

Dad sniffed. "We just thank you for Michael, for the time we had with him. Help us to find peace in the knowledge that he's in your keeping now, healed from all wounds and happy in your presence."

Happy . . .

Water rolled down the side of Calvin's nose. A muscle in his forearm twitched, desperate to wipe the tears away.

Finish! Finish already!

"Would anyone like to add anything?" Dad said.

No. No, please. Can't we just eat?

Mom started talking. A different prayer erupted in Calvin's head. *Oh, God, please, no. I can't take this.*

"Lord, Michael was a very special young man, and we all miss him so much. He made us laugh and was always there to help out wherever he was needed. We were so proud that he wanted to serve his country—"

"Stop ..." Calvin swallowed, choked, and whimpered. "Stop, please."

Someone whispered. He was attracting attention. His mouth fell open and rasping breaths came out. *Hold on. Hold on.*

"Cal?" Zachary said softly.

"I'm okay." *No I'm not.*

"—but he left a hole in our family and in our hearts that can't be filled by—"

He broke, and his sob stopped Mom's prayer. He felt the weight of everyone staring. Calvin let go of hands and turned around without opening his eyes. He staggered and caught himself on one hand, the gravel tearing into his palm. Allowing in slits of light, he could see colors blurred by his tears as he ran toward the cotton field. Voices called after him, so he ran faster.

Michael! Michael, you went away, and I need you!

As he reached the field and moved between the rows of cotton plants, Calvin's feet bogged down in the soft soil. This was stupid. He didn't even know where he was going, and now he'd made a spectacle of himself. He slowed down, stopped, put his hands to his knees and huffed. He heard the whispering footsteps of someone coming up behind him.

"Leave me alone. I'll be fine."

"Calvin ..." Peyton's hands were on his back and shoulder before he could straighten to look at her.

"I'm sorry. Just give me a few minutes. I'll be all right."

"I don't think so. Calvin, talk to me. This is more than about Michael, isn't it?"

He coughed out a laugh. "You don't know everything."

"I know you've been really down lately. I know we don't see Stacey come around much anymore. I know you had a fight with her a few weeks ago. And I know she's not here today. So, come on. Talk to me. Let me help you if I can."

Calvin stood and looked at his sister. Sudden awareness that his face was soaked with tears and snot made him turn in a circle and mop up the mess with his sleeve. He looked back at the house, at the people milling around the tables of food, and wondered what they were saying about him. *Poor boy. Losing his big brother has been so hard on him.*

Peyton did know more than the others. And maybe — maybe — she'd let go of her judgments for a few minutes to hear him out.

He coughed, stuck his hands in his pockets, and turned to face her. "Stacey is ... she's got ... she's anorexic. And I've been trying to help her, but she's not listening to me. I'm scared ..." He sniffed and looked at the sky. "I'm scared she's gonna die," his voice squeaked.

"Anorexic? Calvin, are you sure? I mean, I know she's really thin, but that could be, uh, a thyroid problem or — "

"I'm totally sure." He looked out over the cotton field, at the rows of green plants. They were doing well. Dad was proud of him. If only the rest of his life could be so simple.

"Do her parents know?" Peyton asked.

Calvin shrugged. "I don't think so."

"But how could they not know?"

"She's good at hiding it. She's good at lying. She's got all these tricks to make it look like she's eating."

"Did she tell you she's anorexic?"

"No. I figured it out." Bones. His fingers touching them where there should have been soft, enticing girl-flesh. No way could he tell his sister how he knew for sure. "I know she is. No doubt about it. Remember that night you thought I was looking at porn on the computer?"

"Cal—"

"I wasn't, okay. I was looking up anorexia. I wanted to find out everything I could."

Peyton sighed deeply. "I'm sorry. I saw a picture and I made a mistake. I wish you had told me then what was really going on."

He squinted into the sun. "Forget it. Doesn't matter."

"Maybe you should talk to her parents."

Calvin shook his head hard. "No. No way. She'll never speak to me again if I betray her like that. Besides, they have to figure it out sometime if they haven't already. She's been sick a lot lately. She's even in trouble at school because of it."

"If they take her to a doctor, he'll be able to see something isn't right with her."

"Exactly. That's what I'm hoping. I've begged her to go to the doctor, and she promised me she would, but she didn't. Just like she promised me she would come to our barbecue today, but she didn't."

"Has she said why she's not coming?"

"No. I haven't heard from her at all. She probably doesn't want to see all the food."

"Wow. I knew there were problems, but I didn't imagine ... Wow."

"Sweet, huh? Now you know."

Peyton reached up to stroke Calvin's shoulder, but didn't say anything for several seconds. "Would you like me to talk to her?"

Calvin pushed his lips out as his sinuses burned again with fresh tears. He shook his head. "No. She's not going to want to talk to you."

"Maybe she will. I'm another girl. She might be willing to open up to me."

"You're my sister. She'll think I put you up to it. Besides, she talks to her friend, Zoe. I think Zoe actually *helps* her, covering up for her and stuff."

"That's awful. What kind of friend does that?"

"She's weird. Uh ..." Calvin looked over his shoulder at the people settling down to eat. "We should get back."

"Are you okay?"

"Yeah. It was, like ... it was too much. You know?"

She smiled a little. "You weren't the only one crying."

"That makes me feel a *whole* lot better."

"Calvin, come here." Peyton pulled him toward her and wrapped her arms around his shoulders.

He hugged her back, finding that he didn't want to let go. So good, just to have someone hold him like this, knowing a little bit about what he was going through.

"Calvin, if you're right," Peyton said, her voice soft next to his ear, "she's very sick. She needs counseling. It's more complicated than just deciding not to eat so she can be thin."

"I know that."

"Try again. Do everything you can to encourage her to see a doctor. And if it doesn't work, you're going to have to talk to her parents."

He sagged. He didn't want to think about what Officer Varnell would say to him, much less about what Stacey would do. They'd be done. She'd never speak to him again.

Would it be worth it if it saved her life?

Chapter 24

The collage would certainly push the boundaries of Mrs. Chandler's instructions for their final assignment. Except for what Stacey had initially sketched on the eighteen-by-twenty-four-inch illustration board, there wasn't any drawing at all. Rendering, yes, but no actual sketching by pencil, marker, or brush to create the image. Stacey backed away from the easel and nibbled a torn cuticle.

"Should I do some sketching on top, like, with a marker or something, so it'll still qualify as a drawing?"

"Stop worrying," Zoe said. "It's going to be awesome."

The girl sat cross-legged on a sheet spread across carpet in Stacey's room, tearing food labels into tiny pieces. She sorted them by dominant colors and shades and placed them into mason jars Stacey had provided.

Stacey knelt down opposite Zoe and sifted through the stack of canned goods labels that remained. "Keep some of these big, so the words can still be read."

"Pick out what you want, so I don't tear it up by mistake."

Canned spaghetti, vegetables loaded with salt, soups full of cream and starch. The colors were all garish and way too bright to be used to depict a human form, but that was sort of the point. It was all wrong and evil. Stacey sifted through the labels, looking for familiar brand names and icons.

"Thanks for helping me with this," she told Zoe.

Zoe paused in her tearing and looked up at the image on the board. "So amazing. I would never have thought of it."

Her knees and ankles complaining, Stacey rolled down to sit on the sheet, where she studied the image from another angle. She'd drawn inspiration from one of those horrible pictures of herself from a few years ago, all pudgy at the beach, wearing a two-piece swimsuit, of all things. She covered the illustration board with torn construction paper in beige, aqua, blue, and white, to represent the sand and the water. When all the glue was dry, she carefully sketched the outline of her figure, and recruited Zoe to help her tear up the labels she took off all the scrubbed-out cans her mother was recycling. Zoe had brought a stack of her own, along with a hilarious story of what happened at home when her mother discovered all her canned goods with the labels gone and Sharpie marker notations telling the contents of the can. Apparently Zoe's consolation that now their pantry had a unified, modern look didn't go over well.

"You going to be able to finish it in time?" Zoe asked.

"Thanks to you, I will." Stacey found enough whole labels she thought would be sufficient to make her point about the conspiracy of the food industry. She pushed herself to her feet, careful to go slowly, and moved to her dresser beside her easel. She placed the labels in the stack with all of Calvin's recent notes.

He'd made himself her psychologist. With lovely notes of encouragement and his deep, gentle voice telling her how much he loved her and wanted her to be happy and healthy, he tried to get inside her head and undermine everything she was thinking. What, did he read a book or something? Suddenly he was an expert? It was sweet in a way, but mostly it hurt like crazy.

Was it too bold to include his notes with the larger pieces of labels?

They were on white notebook paper. The blue lines with bits of his handwriting showing would be enough. She'd need a lot of white to complete the figure anyway.

Stacey separated the notes from her big labels and started to tear them into tiny pieces. As she tore through his name at the bottom of the first note, she turned her back to Zoe so her friend wouldn't see her cry.

∘ ○ ◯ ○ ∘

One week left, with no additional absences that would hold her back. She was going to make it. Too bad that one week was finals week, and she was already beyond exhausted from staying up late to finish her art project.

Grateful to be off her feet for a little while, Stacey plopped into one of the tightly packed desks in the center of her chemistry classroom, next to Zoe. The cold water she'd just swallowed at the fountain trickled through her insides to do battle with the acid burning in her belly. Her fingers trembled as she dug into her purse for one of the brand-new number-two pencils she'd sharpened for her exams. Other students bumped and chattered, milling around their seats as if reluctant to sit. She wasn't the only one with test-day nerves.

Zoe leaned across the aisle and muttered, "Were you able to study for this test?'

"Yeah. During the day." While Calvin was at church and studying for his own exams. In her heart she'd been tempted to invite him over so they could study together. But she didn't want to risk hearing another gentle lecture.

One more week. And then maybe she would have proved to him

that she was okay and he would go back to being her boyfriend instead of her self-appointed savior.

The bell rang and Mr. Emerson loudly tapped a stack of papers against his desktop to straighten them. Desks and sneakers chirped on the tile floor as people settled into their seats.

Breathe. Focus. Be strong and in control. "Ugh. I think I'm going to be sick."

"Seriously? Are you, like, really sick or is it just—" Zoe straightened as the teacher moved to the front of her row.

Mr. Emerson handed tests to the person in each front desk. Stacey accepted a stack from the guy in front of her, took one copy for herself, then swiveled to hand the remaining copies to Kenny sitting behind her. She wrote her name on the cover sheet. When the tests were all distributed, Mr. Emerson told the students to begin. Stacey flipped over the cover sheet and stared at the first question. Multiple choice. Her eyes blurred over the words and a sick headache throbbed at her temples. She drew another deep breath and bent closer to the paper.

1. *Ternary acids commonly contain which of the following elements?*

   A. *Hydrogen and oxygen*
   B. *Hydrochloric acid and hydrofluoric acid*
   C. *Hydrogen, a nonmetal, and oxygen*
   D. *Hydrogen, a metal, and oxygen*

Stacey blackened the circle for answer C and rubbed her eyes with her left hand. At that touch her headache intensified. Acid gurgled in her stomach. Was there a question on the test about the composition of stomach acid?

She grimaced and moved her pencil down to the next question, read it, and answered A.

Sick, sick … she shouldn't have stayed up so late last night. She could still smell the odor of white glue that permeated the air of her bedroom.

Question eight didn't make sense. It should make sense, but the words ran out of her head as soon as she read them.

8. *Identify the symbols of the formula used in indirect calorimetry: $q=mc\Delta T$.*

   A. *Heat, mass, and internal energy*
   B. *Energy, mass, specific heat, and temperature change*
   C. *Energy, mass, calorie intake, temperature change*
   D. *Quantity, mass, calories, temperature*

Her brain buzzed. The test paper drifted away. Her body felt distant, yet thick.

Zoe's pencil tapped out a beat beside her. The room smelled of pencil lead, chemicals, and Kenny's aftershave lotion. Stacey focused on these tangible things.

C. No, B. The answer had to be B. She blackened it in.

She needed water. And Tylenol. Ten minutes with her eyes closed would be a good thing. No way would Mr. Emerson give it to her.

Stacey pressed on and managed to get to page three. She counted the remaining pages of the exam and looked at the clock on the wall. Getting through the test on time would take a gargantuan effort.

Ten minutes with her eyes closed. She'd be golden after that.

She glanced at Mr. Emerson, who was busy at his desk with some other papers. Maybe he wouldn't notice if she rested for just a moment. Stacey folded her arm on her desk and lay her head down. She closed her eyes and listened to the sound of her breath against the desktop. Her skin felt clammy.

Something nudged her foot. She lifted her head to look at Zoe. "Hey. You okay?"

Stacey slowly straightened and nodded. She puffed air through her nostrils. What energy was being expended to create the heat she felt? Maybe the heat migrated out from the churning brain cells and thumping hearts and sweaty palms of twenty-two students in the classroom.

"You look like you're about to puke," Zoe whispered.

Mr. Emerson lifted his head sharply. "Ms. Bernetti, is there a problem?"

Zoe jolted. "Stacey doesn't look good."

"Shh!" Stacey whipped her head around to glare at her friend.

"I'm sorry! But you're all sweaty and pale."

"I'm fine." She slumped in her seat as more heat rose to her face.

Mr. Emerson leaned forward, his head tilted and his left eye squinting. "Stacey, do you need a pass?"

"No, Mr. Emerson. I'm okay."

Eyes turned toward her, every student in the classroom taking a peek to see her perspiring like a slob. Maybe they thought she was on drugs.

Don't look at me!

She bent over her test. Plowed through the questions. Blackened circles, one after another. Fought the throbbing pain and the heat. Control. She needed to be in control.

At last she finished and slogged up to the teacher's desk with her exam. Mr. Emerson crooked a finger to urge her closer.

"Stacey, are you ill? You know you can arrange make-up exams."

"I didn't get enough sleep last night, that's all. May I get a drink of water, please?"

The teacher rolled his lips inward. "Perhaps you should go to the nurse's office, just to be on the safe side." He pulled a pad of hall passes out of a drawer and scribbled information on one.

Stacey didn't argue. She accepted the pass, and after gathering her books and purse she nodded to Zoe and left the classroom. No way was she going to the nurse. The woman would send her home, and that would be a disaster.

She stopped at a water fountain and drank her fill. It helped. With the hall pass visible in her hand, she walked past the administrative offices and gently pushed through one of the double doors of the media center. The librarian at the checkout desk was zoned in on a computer screen and didn't look up. Stacey snuck over to a table in the corner, putting a rack of books between her and the librarian. She quietly took a seat and folded her arms over the top of her books.

Just ten minutes with her eyes closed . . .

"Excuse me. Ex*cuse* me! Shouldn't you be in class?"

Stacey gasped and jerked her head up. The librarian, Mrs. Patterson, stood over her, one hand planted on the tabletop. Blobs of light and dark morphed into shelves, books, tables, and chairs. A clock on the wall read 10:15. No, 11:15.

Where *was* she supposed to be?

Art class. Oh no! The one class she *wanted* to go to!

"I'm late." She pulled her books back into a neat pile. "I have to go."

"I don't think so. You're going to need a pass from the office, and they're going to want to know why I caught you skipping class."

"No, no, I'm not skipping. I fell asleep. I don't feel well. Please, can I just go?"

Mrs. Patterson's face blurred, distorted, looked like someone else. Stacey pressed the heel of her palm into her right eye.

"Your teacher won't let you come to class late without a pass. Go to the office."

"Fine." Stacey loaded her books into her arms and trudged back into the halls. Her involuntary nap hadn't done any good. She swayed as she walked, and her eyes kept going out of focus. Summoning all the strength she possessed, she filled her lungs and stretched her neck, then walked through the open door to the administrative offices. She marched to the counter and looked straight at the secretary. "I need a pass to get into my class, please. I was studying in the library and lost track of time."

○ ○ ○ ○ ○

She arrived at the start of the critique session. Stacey handed Mrs. Chandler her pass, along with a mumbled apology, then pulled her art project out of her cubby in the supply room, where she'd tucked it before school that morning.

Fearing that the image wouldn't qualify as an actual drawing, much less a self-portrait, Stacey had used oil pastel to lightly render the features of her face and form. She'd made the decision last night, and the project she should have finished in two hours took six.

The teacher moved on and called everyone to gather around the first easel standing along the walls of the classroom. They were to critique the work of their fellow art student, and those pieces receiving the most favorable responses would be awarded a space in the display case outside the classroom for the start of next year.

Zoe grabbed Stacey's arm and hissed in her ear. "Where were you? I thought you were going to miss this."

"Fell asleep in the library. Can you believe it?"

Friends supported friends. And although no one said anything bad about another person's drawing, it was clear by the volume of comments the pieces received which ones would go into the display case. That is, if Mrs. Chandler didn't overrule the voting and make her own choices.

Stacey pointed at Zoe's image, her neck stretched back and hair cascading over one shoulder. Fashion model pose, of course, from a picture Zoe had taken with her cell phone. "I like how her lines fade in and out. Your mind finishes the line. And it's stylized. Graceful."

Ms. Chandler nodded. "Good assessment. Anything else?"

"Um, you can really see Zoe's personality in the drawing."

"In what way?"

In that she did the least amount of work she could to get the job done. Ohh...

"She intentionally leaves things out. She's mysterious."

"I am?" Zoe whispered.

Stacey cast a sideways glance at her and didn't answer.

Ms. Chandler hummed, like she wasn't sure she agreed. "All right, then. Let's move on. This is Stacey Varnell's work. To start us off, I must say, this is quite unlike anything I've seen you do all year, Stacey. It's much more abstract than your usual work."

"It's not really a drawing," someone said.

"It doesn't have to be realistic to still be a drawing," another person argued.

"I'm not saying it isn't good, but it's a collage, not a drawing."

"I think it rocks," Noah said. "Like, who says a drawing has to be ink or lead? Stacey used pieces of paper as her primary medium. But you can see, she placed all the colors so that they replicated the form, creating light and shadow, just like she does all the time with a pencil or charcoal. She almost didn't need the lines she drew on top of the pieces of paper, but that she put them in, that definitely makes this a drawing. But her *drawing* isn't just a self-portrait, even though you can tell it's her face in the image. She's making a statement. It has meaning. It really says something about her as a person."

Zoe touched the backs of her fingers to Stacey's arm. Stacey couldn't look away from the dark angel spreading his blessings upon her work.

"She's creative, with strong feelings about the world," Noah went on. "About what's right and wrong. She's not afraid to lay herself out there if it can make a difference."

"Oh, he's good!" Zoe muttered.

Very. Didn't matter that his assessment wasn't exactly right. He probably thought the whole exercise was bogus anyway. Still, Stacey wanted to giggle with joy at his glowing words.

Ms. Chandler's brow wrinkled in surprise. "Well done, Noah. Thank you."

He stepped back and slanted a glance at Stacey. "See, I'm not so useless," he muttered.

"I never said you were." Ms. Chandler lifted her chin. "Anyone else want to comment?"

No one did. Apparently Noah had settled the debate, or no one thought it was worth the effort to argue with him. As the students moved to the next easel, Stacey made eye contact with him and mouthed the words, "That was awesome!"

He nodded, his eyes narrowing and his lips curving into a smile. Stacey edged toward Zoe, but her hand went up to twirl her hair, and she tilted her chin down to return his smile.

"Shhhh-oooh," Zoe breathed. "Is it getting hot in here?"

Stacey smacked her friend's arm.

As they left the art studio for the final time that school year, Noah caught up to Stacey and slung his arm around her shoulders. Stacey's feet stopped working.

He chuckled. "So, how's it feel to know your work will be immortalized in the hallways of South Stiles High School next year?"

"Ha! Two weeks on display to impress the incoming freshmen. Hardly immortalization."

"Is that a word? Immortalization?"

"Immortification, maybe?"

Noah chuckled. "You don't give yourself enough credit. If anyone in this school makes it as an artist, it'll be you. And me. Of course." He pointed to his chest and grinned.

Stacey looked for Zoe and found her friend edging toward the opposite side of the hallway, gawking as if she stood in the presence of a rock star.

"So, you still seeing that other guy?"

Stacey blinked. "Oh! Uh ..."

"'Cause I'd really like to see you over the summer." Noah took a lock of her hair between his fingers and gently tugged it, moving his grip lower until he ran out of hair. His hand lingered near her body.

Stacey found her voice. "Yes, I am. We've been together all school year."

He dropped his hand down, but his arm stayed on her shoulder. "Long time."

"Yes. I ... we're ..."

Noah tilted his head and made a *tsk* sound. "Man. You got this sort of emo-fantasy look going on. I really like it. Does *he* like it?"

Had Calvin ever said so? After that day she'd arrived at school with her hair bleached and dyed, he hadn't really mentioned it, other than to say she was beautiful in a general way. And then he was trying to get her to listen while he lectured her.

She took her hair between her own fingers. The pink had faded, no longer neon but a soft pastel. Which still looked really good, she thought.

Across the hall, Zoe's gawk widened, like now she was watching a train wreck.

"Stacey?" a deep voice said.

Noah's hand on Stacey's shoulder fell away. "Whoops. Guess I'd better go."

"What?"

She blinked again. The world came crashing in on her senses, and Calvin stood in the center of the flood. *Oh ... NO!*

He froze before her like a sculpture, a curly-headed, cherub-cheeked, betrayed lover. Somehow his lips moved. "I heard you were sick. I came to check on you."

Noah had escaped down the hall. Zoe had vanished too. *Thanks a lot, y'all.*

Stacey's heart fluttered. Her fingernail scratched the side of her face rather than finding hair to push back. "I'm okay."

"Yeah, uh, what was that all about?"

"That was Noah. He was congratulating me. Ms. Chandler is going to hang my final project in the hallway."

Calvin's chest rose; he was moving after all. But his face was stiff, like he refused to show any emotion. "Really," he said flatly. "He congratulates you by touching your hair?"

"Oh. No, Calvin. He flirts with me, okay? He flirts with a lot of girls. But there's nothing going on. I promise."

"Really."

"I promise."

The muscles around his eyes pinched. "Stacey, stop—stop lying to me."

"I'm not lying!"

"Yeah, right." He turned away.

Three steps. Four. She gasped and forced her own feet to move. "Calvin, don't. Please." She reached for his arm but missed, her fingertips grazing his skin. "Listen to me. You can ask Zoe. You can ask Noah. There's nothing going on."

He spun to face her. His teeth flashed like an animal's. "I came here because I was worried about you. All I do lately is worry about you. And you keep lying to me. What am I supposed to do?"

She bounced desperately in front of him. "I'm not lying. I'm not—Maybe a little, sometimes, about the food stuff. But not now."

"I saw his arm around you! I saw him playing with your hair. Why didn't you stop him?"

"Because, I ..." Why didn't she? Because she didn't have the strength. "It just happened, Calvin. He never touched me before."

His breath came out in noisy billows. He didn't believe her. "Were you going to stop him?" It was an accusation.

"Yes. I told him you and I are still together."

"Still? Like, he asked you before this?"

"He—" Strength ebbed out of her limbs. If she crumbled against a locker, would he try to catch her? Would it help for him to realize how much all this upset her? "Oh ..." She folded, thumped a metal door, and slid down.

Calvin stood above her, looking down, not moving. She turned blurred eyes toward him, let tears dribble down her cheeks. "I'm not lying. I love you, Calvin." Her voice squeaked. Did he hear her pain?

Calvin sighed and reached down to her. His open hand hovered before her face. Just a hand? No gentle touch? No worried look? He started to withdraw it. She clasped it before it retreated completely and hung on as he hoisted her upward. All his strength and none of hers.

On her feet again, she tilted toward him, but he stepped back. She staggered to catch herself.

"You keep saying you're fine," he said, his voice thick. "I can't take the lying anymore, Stace. So ... call me after you see a doctor."

Stacey's gaze flicked to other faces. Staring. Intruding. *Go away, people!* "But—what about now?"

"I'll be waiting. When the doctor says you're okay, then we'll talk."

"Cal—"

His eyes glistened, but were motionless. Hard. His Adam's apple moved with a hard swallow. "Don't take too long."

She crunched her shoulders together and pushed out a sob. It didn't hold him. He forced his way through the circle of nosey students watching their breakup. Stacey slumped against the locker again and dipped her chin to her shoulder to hide her shame behind the veil of her white hair. Her face burned. Tears soaked her cheeks. She heard footsteps and whispers, but no one came to comfort her.

She was alone.

Chapter 25

Calvin's booted toe thumped a steady rhythm against Tyler's front tire. Harder, harder, to draw the pain from his chest to his foot, where it'd be easier to endure.

Not working so well.

The student parking lot had nearly emptied out. Only a few cars remained around Tyler's Camaro, including a Honda Civic parked several rows away, a blue blob beyond the teary film in Calvin's vision.

How could she? Why? What happened to "I love you"?

He kicked the Camaro's tire again.

"Noah Dickerson," Tyler said. "I can't believe that."

Calvin shook his head. "Believe it, dude. I saw him."

"But Noah is a total player."

"Tell me about it. And he's making a play for *my* girlfriend." Calvin jabbed his thumb into his chest.

Tyler folded his arms and flopped back against the car door. "Nah, man. This can't be right. Stacey's too smart to get involved with a guy like him."

"*Was*. I don't know what she's thinking anymore."

"Cal, that guy has slept with half the girls in this school." Tyler's words came to him as if through a fog. The door to the school building had opened, and Zoe came outside, followed by Stacey. They both stopped dead, hanging on to each other and staring at something. Probably his Yamaha still parked in the biker's section of the lot.

"That many?" Calvin mumbled.

"Maybe not half. You know what I mean," Tyler went on.

Stacey's head turned. Across the wide driveway and two dozen parking spaces, her gaze locked with his. What now? Did she tense up as he did? Could she sense his hurt and anger telecasting across the lot? *Why, girl? What did I do to deserve this? And on the first day of finals!*

"Uh-oh," Tyler said.

Stacey spun around and lunged toward the building. Zoe grabbed her shirt and pulled her back. They tussled and argued a moment. Then Zoe dragged Stacey off the sidewalk and onto the asphalt, giving Tyler's Camaro a wide berth. Stacey walked stiff-legged, her feet flapping on the pavement loud enough for Calvin to hear. She put a hand up to her face. Hiding from him.

"I hope you're happy, farm boy," Zoe yelled. "Look what you've done."

"Oh, real nice." Tyler practically climbed onto the roof of his car. "Hey! Who's the cheater here?"

Calvin couldn't find words or the voice to speak them. He clasped Tyler's shoulder and pulled him back to earth.

The two girls staggered to Stacey's car. They pressed together by the Honda then Stacey went to the passenger door as Zoe slid behind the steering wheel.

"Think that girl is smart enough to drive?" Tyler asked.

Calvin couldn't laugh. Zoe had won. She'd drive Stacey home, and the two of them would conspire and find ways to blame it all on him.

What did I do except love you, Stacey?

The tires screeched as Zoe drove away. Nice touch.

"What're you going to do now?" Tyler asked when they were gone. "Want to come to my house?"

"No, thanks. I think I need to be alone."

Sadness crept into Tyler's eyes, and the muscles around his jaw tensed. Calvin had seen the look before, at the funeral. Tyler didn't know what to say. It didn't matter. Nothing he could say would undo Stacey's betrayal. That he was here, slowly baking in the afternoon sun, giving Calvin that compassionate look, was enough.

Tyler sighed. "Well, keep the rubber side down, bro." He clasped Calvin's shoulder for a moment then unlocked his car. He paused with the door open. "Love stinks, man."

Calvin pulled one side of his mouth into a half smirk. "Not always. But right this second it pretty much bites."

Time blurred as Calvin plodded across the lot to his motorcycle and strapped on his helmet. The Yamaha started on the first kick, but dingy exhaust appeared in his rearview mirror when he revved the engine. *No. No trouble now. Don't you betray me too.*

He duck-walked the bike backward out of the space then screamed through the parking lot. A glance right told him the road was clear. He leaned deep into the turn. One mile south on Old Bentley, then a hard left onto Victory Church Road. The wind battered his face as always but didn't penetrate to bring that thrill he'd counted on. Exhaustion battled the urge to beat the bike and his body until he couldn't feel anything at all.

Hitting the driveway, the Yamaha's rear tire slid in the gravel. Calvin instinctively stuck out a foot to save himself from a spill and cussed as his brain told him to hit the throttle instead. He wobbled upright and slowed to crawl over the gravel. In front of the closed workshop doors he hit the kill switch then leaned forward, crossing his arms over the gas tank. His helmet clunked against the odometer. His rapid gasps fogged the chrome gas cap.

How could they go from being so close to *this*? And what was he supposed to do now? He'd told her he'd be waiting for her to go to the doctor—words spoken in anger and frustration. Maybe even smart words. But now he was faced with the wait, already feeling like each second wore away at his heart and soul like sandpaper, gritty and scratching. Like those moments after Michael's funeral when he faced the rest of his life without his brother.

What now?

Six months ago he'd felt like part of him had been buried with Michael. Then Stacey stepped up to fill that gaping hole inside him a little. Not fully, and not in the same way, but she'd brought him to a place where he could smile again.

And then ... and then ... the anorexia, like a bony finger clawing, clawing, clawing, scratched Calvin's scars, reopened the wound until he could feel the pain pouring out again.

I can't do this. I need her.

It was his fault. In front of who knows how many people at school, he'd screamed an ultimatum at her: Go to the doctor, or we're finished. He'd been pushing her, making demands of her, expecting her to change—

To save her life!

Maybe she'd turned to Noah Dickerson because a guy who made no commitments, jumping from one girl to another, wouldn't demand anything of her.

Except her virginity.

No, it didn't make sense. That night in the pickup truck she'd pushed Calvin away. After all the months of dating, of less-than-innocent flirting despite their agreement that they wanted to wait, she'd refused him.

Maybe that moment had been an unspoken ultimatum from her. Love her the way she was, or she'd move on. Maybe that sexy outfit was her way of showing him that all her dieting was worth it, so he'd stop hassling her. It didn't work. He'd only amped up his efforts.

She listened to every word about Michael, but when she needed me to listen, I blew it.

He squeezed his eyes shut and poured his guilt and grief onto the gas tank in a moan.

"Calvin?"

His shoulders jerked and his eyelids popped open.

"What's wrong?" Mom's hands were on him before he could object. She pawed his shoulders, his arm, his thigh. "Honey, are you hurt? Did you fall on your bike?"

"No." He leaned away, put his arm up to ward her off. "Don't touch me."

She planted her hands on her hips but angled her head toward him. No reprimand in her expression yet. "What happened?"

The helmet suddenly felt very heavy on his head. Awkward. He wouldn't be able to hide anything from his mother. With her focus narrowed in on him, she'd drag the truth out of him.

"Stacey," he choked out. Calvin yanked off his sunglasses, tugged at the helmet strap until it obeyed, and removed his helmet. He raised his arm to throw it but resisted.

"Oh, Calvin!" Mom's body seemed to deflate some. "I'm so sorry. You want to tell me about it?"

He didn't. Yet he did. The thought of talking through every event and all his worries over the past weeks, of revealing Stacey's betrayal at the end with the most notorious girl-hopper at South Stiles High School, weakened every joint in his body and made his brain go foggy. The one-sided advice she'd give, the parental platitudes and timeworn wisdom—could he stomach it?

"No, Mom. No. Maybe later. I just ... I'm really tired. I'd like to be alone."

She stroked his arm up and down and tilted her head. "Okay, sweetheart. Can I fix you something to eat?"

Food? He could almost laugh. "That's okay. I'm not really hungry right now."

With several glances back, Mom went inside. Calvin opened the workshop door and put his motorcycle away, placed his helmet on the shelf and closed the door again. He trudged up to his room with his backpack, dumped his books out on his unmade bed, then dropped to the floor on his knees and pressed his forehead to his mattress.

"Why, God?"

His body heated up quickly in the hot attic room, which didn't give him a good feeling about whatever the answer might be. He couldn't cry. Not yet. He was too angry. Calvin pushed himself to his feet and headed back downstairs. His social studies teacher had mentioned there would be an email containing their study guide for the final. Calvin thought consuming his brain with that stuff was as good an answer as anything else.

He made a detour to the refrigerator for a cold drink, zig-zagging around other family members surrounding Mom in the kitchen, then sat down at the computer. A new message downloaded to his email. He squinted at the sender.

XOEZOEFOX

Who was that? The address looked like a bunch of Roman numerals for a second, but then the middle letters jumped out at him. Zoe. Great. Did he really want to read whatever she'd have to say to him?

Delete it.

His eyes drifted to the preview window before his fingers could respond. Stacey's name at the bottom of the short message stopped him.

You don't control my life. I don't need anyone telling me how to live or what to do. Stay away from me. We're finished.

Stacey

Ice ran through Calvin's muscles, freezing him to the spot, while water ran in the kitchen sink, and Lizzie argued that Zachary was old enough to clean up his own stupid mess, and Mom reprimanded them both.

Over. Done.

Chapter 26

He leaned against the frame of his back door, staring out at the workshop, where his bike sat waiting for him to fix it or pour gasoline over it and light a match. Yet another betrayal. The Yamaha couldn't wait another week before it started running bad?

"Cal?"

He brought the phone back up to his cheek. "Yeah?"

"You're picking Tyler up right after church Sunday morning, right?" Flannery asked. "You're sure you'll be able to get to my place before eleven thirty? Dad'll be a pain if we don't get on the road by noon."

"Yeah, no problem. My parents already know I might have to cut out of church a little early. We'll be there."

A long pause, yet Flannery didn't say good-bye. Calvin waited for another consolation speech.

"Cal, it'll be okay. You'll see."

Really? He almost laughed. Was that all she had to say?

For the last two days of school, Stacey's moon eyes in the hallway had cut laser-straight through the bodies of other students and carried an unmistakable message: *You hurt me!* Calvin imagined his own eyes communicated the same thing. Her pained glances had intensified the ache in his chest, but there was no conversation, no making up. If Stacey's eyes didn't say that, Zoe's glare sure did. And Zoe seemed glued to Stacey's side ... while Noah Dickerson was nowhere to be seen.

He'd blown up over nothing. He'd destroyed their relationship over *nothing*.

"I don't know, Flan. Maybe y'all should go without me. I'll just be a drag."

"Forget that! No way. Cal, you need this trip. You're going, if I have to kidnap you and strap you to the truck like a deer."

He did need it. Like a drowning man needed air. To be away from all that hurt him and feel the woods permeating his whole being, the bike's engine churning beneath him. Would he be able to enjoy it for two seconds without thinking about Stacey?

"Okay, well, I'd better start packing then."

"You've got two days."

Not really. Not if he had to tear the bike apart to see why it was running like crud all of a sudden. On the ride home from school, the Yamaha's motor stuttered every time Calvin cranked the throttle. Its acceleration was more like chugging up to speed. He hoped a new set of spark plugs would be all he needed to fix the problem. He so needed at least one thing in his life to have an easy solution.

"Uh, I might see you tomorrow at the shop."

"Cool. We can skip over to Oliver's for lunch."

"Yeah. I'll let you know. See ya, Flan."

Calvin leaned inside the back door and set the phone on the dining room table. He crossed the driveway to the workshop and dug around in Dad's toolbox.

Stay active. Don't think about ...

Careful to keep his fingers away from still-hot metal parts, he removed the spark plugs from the Yamaha. As he worked, he made a mental list of all the things he had to do before the trip: Dig out his camping gear and check it for holes or anything stinking or damp.

Pack jeans, shirts, and riding gear. Flannery's parents would be providing food, but a cooler for extra drinks or snacks might be handy. Clean out Dad's pickup and find some cassettes that weren't totally lame for the old player in the truck. Old-school metal bands; Tyler would approve. Make sure the heavy-duty cargo straps—enough for three motorcycles—were in good shape. He might have to pick up some more at the shop. Gas up the truck, load the Yamaha in—

Calvin's heart sank. The electrodes of the first spark plug he'd extracted were so chalky he could rub the gunk off with his fingers. What did that mean? Calvin sat back on his haunches and stared at the spark plug dangling on its wire against the crank case.

Not fouled—that would result in dirty electrodes. No, not enough fuel. The engine was running lean. That's what caused the popping in the exhaust over the past week and a loud backfire in the school parking lot.

Great. I'm running lean. As if I needed another thing to remind me . . .

Okay, so what would cause it? Bad plugs? Timing off? He'd have to ask Dad for help on this one, and call Flannery's father at the bike shop to get some fresh plugs. Maybe extras for the trip, just in case. Another task to add to his list.

At least it would keep him occupied, so he wouldn't lapse into pointlessly staring at Stacey's pictures on her Facebook page, hoping for some status update that would give him a tiny ray of hope, or reading her past emails and poetry.

Flannery was right. He *so* needed this camping trip.

Chapter 27

The most tolerable place in Zoe's house was the screened-in patio. Frizzy hair from the humidity was preferable to Zoe's screeching little brother, her mother parading around with the angst and attitude of a teenage drama queen — without the style — and the chainsmoking stench and slobbish presence of the unemployed, live-in boyfriend. Zoe was possibly the most normal person in the family.

Stacey caught a clump of hair between her fingers and pulled it tight. Maybe that would keep it straight. Or not.

Still, it was better than being smothered at home. Summer vacation had started Saturday morning with a heaping plate of pancakes served by Mom On a Mission, and eggs and bacon with hash browns this morning. Lunch, dinner, dessert ... the house smelled like food all the time. No way could Stacey hide or discard the mountain of calories and carbohydrates with the woman hovering over her. Puking it up after each meal had taken meticulous timing and promised a long, agonizing summer break.

Stacey tossed her hair over her shoulder and tucked her legs up to her chest. The webbed chaise lounge creaked beneath her weight. She imagined the plastic strips stretching and breaking and her big butt falling through to the concrete, her legs sticking up in the air and her arms flailing. Zoe would die laughing.

Zoe rolled her head in time to the music playing through her iPod. "Don't make me say I love you," she sang, her voice thin. "Don't make me call your name in the middle of the night."

How ironic! Or pathetic. Stacey could relate to those lyrics. She'd hardly slept in a week. And since last Monday, she'd whispered and cried Calvin's name over and over in the middle of the night, and now her pillow was stained with tears. She couldn't confess this to Zoe, who now thought of Calvin as *he-whose-existence-is-an-abomination-to-all-humanity*.

"Mmm-mm-mm. My heart belongs to me." Zoe fluttered her hand over her chest and jutted her chin with each beat. "Know what, Stace? I feel good. Fabulous, in fact. I've lost four pounds this week."

"Four pounds?" Stacey hugged her knees closer.

"How about you?"

"Slowing down. Only one." The scale called to her and terrified her at the same time. Mom's meals would probably have her gaining fifty pounds in no time.

Zoe pulled her earbuds out. "Hey, you okay?"

Stacey looked at the glass of ice water on the floor next to her seat. Condensation rolled down the sides and pooled on the concrete. If she touched the glass then wiped her fingers against her face, she might cool the ache behind her eyeballs. "Um, no."

"What's wrong?"

"I can't ... I can't do this."

"Do what?"

She pressed the heel of one hand into her left eye socket. Tears flooded out anyway. "Mom's driving me crazy, and I can't stop thinking about ... Calvin."

"Oh no."

"I can't take it anymore. I need him."

Zoe sighed. "I really thought he'd call begging you to take him back by now."

Stacey whimpered and covered her other eye too.

"But he didn't. Girl, you deserve someone who's going to fall on his knees and plead for you to just look at him."

"Who does that, Zoe? Seriously. Nobody does that."

"Well, he should."

"He doesn't love me. I'm not good enough for him."

"Stop it!" Zoe's chair scraped the floor, and an instant later Stacey's chaise thumped and tilted. Zoe leaned into Stacey and wrapped her arms around her shoulders. "Shh, shh. Don't cry. Girl, you're sexy, smart, and talented, and he doesn't deserve you."

"I'm shaking. All the time. I can't sleep. My head hurts so bad."

"All right, so call him."

"You mean it?"

"Whatever. I totally don't think he's worth it, but if being away from him is making you sick, then call him."

Stacey lowered her hands from her eyes. Her friend perched on the edge of the chaise, arms crossed, looking at something on the other side of the porch.

"You're mad at me."

"So what? You're in love, so do what you have to do. I don't care."

"Zoe . . ."

She flipped her hair back. "I'm not mad. I just think you need to give yourself more time to get over him. Look, he didn't call you. He hasn't tried to apologize for yelling at you at school, accusing you of cheating in front of everybody, and forcing an ultimatum on you. He's trying to control your life. And maybe he thinks you're supposed to go crawling back to him. Stace, if it were me, he'd be history."

"You never really gave him a chance."

"It doesn't matter. Call him if you have to."

Stacey had left her purse on the table, her cell phone inside it. Her body ached to get up, leap across the patio, grab the phone, and dial Calvin's number. Endorphins flooded her veins and muscles. *Do it now.*

She touched Zoe's bare arm. "You're my best friend. I know you're just looking out for me. I wish I was stronger, but ..."

Zoe tilted her head toward Stacey and smiled crookedly. "Hmm. I can see it now. You're going to end up marrying the farm boy."

Stacey's heart fluttered at the idea. She lifted a shoulder. "Be my bridesmaid?"

"Yeah, right. Don't you dare make me wear taffeta."

A strange sound—a giggle—burst from Stacey's lips. "I'll let you design your dress."

"Deal." Zoe stood. "Guess you don't want me hanging around while you talk to him. I'll be inside."

Stacey unfolded her legs. Despite the urgency in her limbs, she could only move slowly. The world swayed as she stood, and her calves cramped when she walked—a new development. She stepped carefully to the glass-top table and opened her purse. Her cell phone waited in its assigned pocket. She clutched it hard and tapped in Calvin's phone number.

The phone rang four times.

"Hello?" Mrs. Greenlee's voice was a pleasant little melody, but it stopped Stacey's heart. What did Mrs. Greenlee think of her now?

"Hel-lo-o ...?"

Stacey shut her eyes and plunged. "Yes, Mrs. Greenlee? Hi. I-is Calvin there?"

Silence on the phone. Did she hang up? Was she checking? Then, "No, Stacey, I'm sorry. He left right after church today."

"What? He left?"

"He's gone camping. Didn't he tell you about that?"

"That's today?"

"They'll be back Wednesday afternoon."

"Um ..." She pulled her lip and pressed the phone tighter to her ear. Her thoughts ran in dizzying circles around nothing she could grasp, but she just couldn't say good-bye yet. "Did he ... say anything to you about ... about him and me?"

Another long pause. "Not since Monday after school, when he told me y'all broke up."

A sob burst out of her. "I need to talk to him. I need to know he doesn't hate me!"

"Stacey, honey, Calvin does not hate you. Now you stop thinking that way."

"But he didn't—Did he say *anything*?"

"Sweetheart, I know this is hard for you. These feelings, when you're young, are so intense, and you feel like the world is coming to an end. But it'll be okay. I pro—"

"I just need to hear his voice! I need to hear *him* say it'll be okay."

"All I can do is tell him you called. He'll get a hold of you as soon as he gets home."

Tyler; he'd have his cell phone. "Do you think it'd be okay if I called Tyler's cell?"

"Stacey, please don't do that. Calvin's really been looking forward to this trip. Don't ruin it for him. Just give him a few days, and he'll call you."

Oh, so simple. Just wait three more days, don't *ruin* his trip, and go crazy in the meantime. Did the woman have any clue what she was saying? Waiting would be torture. It meant Stacey would hang around helplessly when what she needed most was to hear Calvin's voice. Just a few words. Enough to say it'd be okay.

"P-please." She was whining like a little child. Stacey sniffed and pushed her shoulders back. "I need to know he's okay too."

"Well, I'll tell you he was in quite a state all week about the argument y'all had, and with his finals at school. Yesterday he was so busy getting ready to go that I didn't have a chance to talk to him.

He might've had a talk with Peyton, but she's over at Ryan's house visiting with his family right now."

He was hurting. She'd seen it on his face at school. They'd orchestrated an absurd standoff against each other. She loved him and he loved her—they belonged together. There had to be a way to fix this.

Mrs. Greenlee was saying something. Whole lives ahead of them, blah, blah. Stacey sniffed and waited. She glanced at Zoe's patio door and the darkness inside. She shuffled back to the chaise and sat down, wet her face with some water while her brain buzzed with options.

"Are you going to be all right?" Mrs. Greenlee asked.

"Um, yes."

"I'll tell Calvin to call you. It'll be all right, honey."

"Okay. Thank you. Good-bye."

"Be sweet. Bye-bye."

Stacey stared at the phone in her hand. Wait until Wednesday night to hear from Calvin? When it would only take a minute or two using Tyler's phone? Then he could go back to driving or camping or riding or whatever he was doing. Surely the conversation would help him too.

What time was it? Would they be at that lake yet? How far was the place?

Stacey pulled Tyler's number from her contacts and dialed. The phone rang three times then clicked.

"He—o? ... O?"

"Tyler? Tyler, can you hear me?"

"Sta—"

"Tyler! I need to talk to Calvin."

" ... breaking u—hear you."

"Please!"

" ... in the woods. I'll have to—"

The phone went silent.

Stacey's breath came out in whimpers and gasps. She redialed Tyler's number. It rang four times then went to voice mail. On her next try, the call went immediately to voice mail, which meant Tyler had turned his phone off.

Stacey dropped her cell onto the chaise and covered her damp face with her hands. Whimper, gasp, whimper, gasp. She heard the rumble of Zoe's sliding glass door.

"Uh-oh. Go bad?" Zoe asked.

Stacey dropped her hands and sniffed. "I couldn't reach him."

"How come?"

"He went camping somewhere. Badin Lake. Wherever that is. Somewhere west of here."

"Oh yeah. So ...?"

Stacey snatched up her phone and stood. "I have to leave."

"Leave? But I thought we were going to start making our outfits tonight."

"I'm sorry. I have to."

Zoe followed her to the front door. "Where are you going?"

"I'll see you later."

Stacey jogged across the front yard to her Honda parked on the shoulder of the road. She flung open the car door and tossed her purse into the passenger seat. She'd have to spend the money Mom gave her for fabric on gas instead. And a map. Daddy would have a map of North Carolina in the garage, but he'd bust a blood vessel if he had any clue what Stacey was planning.

Chapter 28

Calvin gawked, his arms held wide in question, while Tyler and Flannery wrestled over the cell phone. Flannery squealed as Tyler wrapped his arms around her, having fun at Calvin's expense. "No—Ah! No cell phones!"

Tyler caught her wrists and pulled them above her head. "Give. Me. My. Phone back!"

"I'll drop it. I'll drop it!"

"Do it, and I'll drench your bike seat in motor oil. Give it." Tyler slipped his grip higher, got his fingers around her hand and the phone.

Calvin lunged forward, reached up to grab the phone himself, but the wrestling pair skittered away from him. "Y'all, come on. I'm dying over here."

Flannery bent forward, stretching Tyler across her back. His feet slipped in the pine straw-covered ground, nearly toppling them both.

"Promise you'll turn it off," Flannery demanded, squirming but trapped.

Tyler snatched the phone away. "Relax. No good signal out here anyway."

Flannery's father came around the side of the family's twenty-one-foot camper trailer, where he'd been hooking up hoses. "You can get a signal when we make our food run."

"Da-ad! What about getting away from it all, enjoying nature, peace and quiet, and all that stuff?"

Dave barked a laugh. "Peace, quiet, and dirt bikes? 'Sides, with the ruckus y'all are making, you done scared away all God's creatures already."

With a victorious smirk, Tyler shoved his phone into his pocket.

Calvin huffed and dropped his arms to his sides. He ignored Flannery and confronted Tyler. "So? That was Stacey, right? What'd she say?"

"She asked for you, but I couldn't make out anything else. I lost the signal and then *somebody* grabbed the phone away." Tyler squatted next to the tent they had just spread on the ground before his cell phone rang. He picked up a pole and started assembling it.

Calvin tugged his hair. "I should try to call back. Might be important."

"I don't have any bars. I'm surprised she got through at all."

"No phones!" Flannery yelled from the door of the camper.

Calvin groaned. "We *heard* you the first time."

She went inside, leaving the camper door swinging. "Who was that, anyway?" she yelled.

Tyler turned back to the tent. "It was your nana. She wanted to make sure you didn't forget your jammies and pookie bear."

Sudden movement rocked the camper. An instant later, Flannery's arm appeared through the door, a stuffed bear in her hand. "Ta-da!"

"Hey!" More scrambling inside the camper. "That's mine!" her little brother Nigel cried.

Tyler fed his tent pole through the pockets of the tent. "Ah, yes. Peace and quiet."

Calvin gave up, dropped to his knees, and found another pole.

Why did Stacey wait until now to call? Did she lose her brain and forget about the camping trip? Or did she do it on purpose just to drive him crazy?

He shoved his pole through the top loop. The metal tip snagged on the nylon.

"Easy. You'll rip it." Tyler freed the fabric and straightened the pole. "You okay?"

"Yeah. Forget about it. I just need to get out on those trails."

"I hear ya, bro."

Setting up Calvin's dome tent took less than five minutes. Organizing the camper took longer, as Flannery's mother traipsed back and forth from the trailer to the SUV, carrying plastic bins filled with household stuff. Calvin and Tyler unrolled their sleeping bags and tossed their duffels and riding gear inside the tent, eager to get the important stuff taken care of. As if on cue, Flannery dropped the tailgate on the pickup truck and scrambled up with the bikes.

"Food run first." Dave waved his daughter down. "Help your mama at the store."

"I thought we were going to feast on all the humungous fish you catch."

Dave lunged for Flannery and got in a single noogie before she squirmed away. "Tomorrow. Prepare to be stunned and amazed."

Tyler opened a canvas camp chair then held his phone out toward Calvin. "You want to call Stacey back? Take the phone and go with Flannery and her mom."

Calvin looked down at the chair, at the tent behind it, at the green woods around him. No, he really didn't want to call Stacey back. This trip was supposed to be his escape from all the drama, the only chance he'd have for some fun before starting work on Thursday. Stacey had no right to ruin it for him. She could wait.

At least that's what he tried to tell his heart.

"I'll hang here with you and Dave."

"No riding while I'm gone!" Flannery called as she followed her mother toward the SUV. Her little brother rushed past her to claim the front seat.

No sooner were they gone then Dave set his tackle box on the picnic table and started sorting lures.

Calvin slouched down in the camp chair until his neck rested against the canvas. He stared at patches of blue sky poking through the tree canopy. A breeze cooled his face. His muscles relaxed, and his arms flopped over the sides of the chair. But his fingers twitched and his brain refused to switch off. It had been six days since he'd spoken to Stacey. He'd accepted the idea that it was over between them, and had hoped the camping trip and riding would be the thing to start him on the road back to normal.

Thanks a lot, Stace.

At the sound of a pull tab, he lifted his head. Tyler swigged a can of Mountain Dew.

"Where'd you get that?"

"Bought it when we stopped for gas."

"Got any more?"

Tyler held his can toward Calvin.

"No way. Not with your backwash in it."

Tyler shrugged. "*Flannery* would take it."

Calvin snorted. "No doubt."

Tyler settled into another camp chair. He leaned toward Calvin, turning the aluminum can in his hands. "What am I going to do about her?" His voice was almost a whisper.

Oh, great. "Don't ask me about relationship stuff right now."

Tyler smacked his lips and stared at the ground.

Calvin sighed and sat up. "Sorry, that was rude."

"Forget it. It's not that big a deal."

"It's a pretty big deal to her."

Tyler lifted his eyes toward Calvin. "I don't want to change anything, you know? We're friends, and, um, like, you and Stace were together for months, and now you're not even talking to each other. What if that happened with me and—" He glanced at Flannery's father, still busy with his fishing gear. "Know what I mean?"

Calvin wanted to say things didn't always end up that way. But what did he know? His one and only real relationship with a girl had taken a high-side spill into a drainage ditch. "All I can say is to be straight with her."

"Yeah. But—"

"But what?"

Tyler shook his head. "Not yet. Not while we're here."

Calvin leaned back again and stared at the sky. Conflict at camp? "Yeah, that'd be *bad.*"

His chest rose and fell as if he'd been running. His knee started bouncing. Why did Stacey call? What if she had gone to the doctor and found out she was actually sick?

She had her family and Zoe to watch out for her.

And *Noah.*

Calvin's stomach clenched. "I can't just sit here." He pushed out of his chair and strode to the pickup truck. "Let's get these bikes unloaded."

○ ○ ◯ ○ ○

Dried mud spattered his goggles. The muscles in his arms, legs, and shoulders burned with exertion as the Enduro surged up another ridge and gave him what he'd come for, a ride through open air.

Not far off Tyler's tail, Calvin skidded around one of many boulders in the trail and accelerated. Tyler must have heard him coming. Without looking back, he popped a little wheelie on his Kawasaki and tossed more dirt at Calvin's headlight.

A mud patch split the path ahead. Tyler might slow down. Might. To the right of the puddle was a narrow dry strip. Calvin took it.

There was a reason that path was the way less traveled. A thick tree limb jutted out at eye level. Calvin ducked, hugging the gas tank. Adrenaline flooded every muscle. He came off the path just ahead of Tyler but moving so fast that he struggled for control.

Calvin cranked his throttle. The engine stuttered then accelerated. That tiny hesitation made Calvin's heart jump as much as the tight space between him and the other bike. A glance in his rearview mirror showed him how close he'd come to slamming his rear end into Tyler's front tire, which would have dumped them both. He sucked in a hot breath. Part of the game. He'd apologize later.

Calvin accelerated, but the Yamaha coughed and the exhaust popped before giving him more speed. Heat radiating off the engine cooked Calvin's knees.

No problems. Not now. Please!

He powered the Enduro up another rise. His body and the bike moved in concert. Calvin felt every tree root, pebble, ridge, and trench passing beneath the tires. Though the engine struggled, the bike responded to the smallest press of his hands and shift of his weight.

A powerful four-stroke engine roared in his ears. Calvin glanced left in time to see Flannery's Suzuki 450 fly past. He hissed. Flannery was going too fast for a blind turn ahead. She hit the brakes, and her rear tire skidded. Her boot made a scrape in the dirt as she tried to save herself.

Calvin lost sight of her around the corner. He eased way off his throttle. Tyler caught up to him and did the same. They puttered around the turn together and found Flannery flat on her back, limbs splayed out, her head resting in a fern bank. The Suzuki silent six feet away.

Calvin killed his engine and jumped off, almost forgetting the kickstand.

Tyler was one step ahead of him reaching Flannery's side. "Flan, are you all right?"

The riding armor covering Flannery's chest vibrated. Her upper lip and a flash of teeth appeared above her chin guard. She was laughing. She lifted her arms toward Tyler. "My hero!"

Calvin groaned and pivoted away. No worries. Nothing to see here.

Tyler helped her to her feet. Still, Flannery rose with the grace of an old lady getting out of bed. She pointed at the bike. "I rolled over here. I was almost stopped but lost my balance."

Tyler let go of her hand and thumped the back of her helmet. "You're like a squirrel on caffeine. We need to put you on a tricycle so you won't hurt yourself."

"Ha. Beat you." Flannery slapped dirt from her riding pants as she walked to the Suzuki.

A big engine revved in the distance. Calvin looked back the way they'd come. "Four-wheeler alert. We need to fly outta here."

"Mom's probably getting supper started anyway," Flannery said. Her bike started on the first kick. Just as quickly she sped down the trail.

Tyler's helmet rocked side to side on his shoulders. "Girl's insane."

"That's Flan for ya." Calvin swung his leg over the Yamaha.

Dave had a fire going when they glided back into their campsite. Tyler won the toss for the shower, so Calvin had to be content to pound the dust from his jacket and deal with his sweat-soaked T-shirt. While he waited, he took a bristle brush over to his bike and knocked off the worst of the mud clumps. He thought about asking Dave to check his carburetor, but daylight was fading, and Patty brought burgers to the iron grate covering the fire. Tomorrow morning.

The air cooled quickly with nightfall. They gathered around the fire eating hamburgers and potato chips. In the darkness beyond the firelight, singing frogs seemed so numerous that Calvin envisioned them jumping over each other among the tree roots. Laughter from another campsite carried over, but Calvin's group settled down, happy and exhausted. Nigel burned a marshmallow and ate it anyway. Calvin sat cross-legged on the ground next to Tyler, who slouched in a camp chair, softly snoring, one hand hanging limp over the side.

Flannery snickered. "Got a bucket and some warm water? We can dip his hand into it."

Calvin grinned, imagining Tyler jumping wide-eyed from his chair and scurrying off in the dark to find the toilet. "Alas, no bucket."

Dave laughed. "Yo, Ty. Get to bed, boy," he called across the fire.

Light flashed across the tree trunks, lighting up the whole campsite. Car tires ground to a halt in the dirt. Calvin blinked at headlights and heard a car door slam.

"Calvin!" A figure danced in the light, wildly maneuvering around the parked bikes.

"Oh no," Flannery groaned.

Calvin pushed to his feet. It couldn't be. It wasn't possible.

There'd better be a real good reason.

Stacey staggered into his arms. She shook violently and sobbed against his chest. "I couldn't find you! I've been looking forever for you."

Voices and questions arose around them. Calvin tried to push her back, but she wouldn't let him go. "What are you doing here?"

"I-I thought you were staying at Badin Lake. You weren't there."

"Badin Lake is the name of the whole area, not this campground. Stacey—" He managed to pull away and look at her face. Dark streaks stained her cheeks.

"I went to Badin Lake Campground. I looked for motorcycles, but only saw big RVs. Someone told me about this place, but I got lost in-in the dark. I was so scared!"

"Stacey, what are you doing here?"

Dave appeared beside them. "What is going on?"

Calvin looked over his shoulder. Awake now, Tyler stood and pitched something into the fire. Flannery glared with her feet wide and arms crossed. Patty stood with her hand pressed to her lips. And Nigel just stared with his mouth open.

Stacey clasped Calvin's arm, her fingernails sharp on his skin. "I'm sorry. I just had to talk to you, Calvin. I *need* ... I need to talk to you."

"Oh, come on!" Flannery cried. "Couldn't it wait until we got back?"

Calvin pulled his hair. "Oh man. I so don't need this. Flan, just—"

Stacey took a step back and hugged herself as if she were cold. "I'm sorry. I didn't mean to—I won't be any trouble. I-I can ... s-sleep in my car."

"Oh, now, I don't think we'll make you do that," Dave said. "Flannery can share her bed in the camper, if necessary." He raised his hand against Flannery's complaint. "First, let's hear the story, then we'll decide what to do. Stacey-girl, do your parents know you're here?"

Stacey shrank back and didn't answer

Dave moved with her. "You tell me now. Do your parents know where you are?"

"I-I told Mom I was staying at Zoe's house."

Calvin threw out his arms. "I don't believe this." Blood pulsed in his temples, making him dizzy. How could she do this? What was wrong with her?

Stacey's wide eyes traveled over the people standing around them. She inched farther back. "Calvin, please."

"One weekend," Tyler said, his voice a soft growl. "That's all he wanted. Couldn't give him one weekend?"

"Okay, this ain't gonna happen," Dave said. "We can't harbor a runaway."

"Runaway!" Stacey blurted. "I'm not—No! I just want to talk to Calvin."

Calvin didn't know what to do or say. His friends were angry, and he couldn't blame them. Flannery's parents were discussing calling the police. How *could* she do this?

"It's okay, y'all. Let me talk to her."

"Did I hear this right?" Patty said, coming closer. "Your parents think you're staying with a friend?" She reached for Stacey's arm, but Stacey jerked away.

"P-please, don't make me drive all the way home tonight. I can't. I just can't. Please!"

"Let's all settle down, right now," Dave said. "Come have a seat and we'll discuss this. Don't want to bother everyone else in the campground. Flannery, go shut that car off."

"I'm sorry, I'm sorry. I tried to get here earlier. I got lost and, and—P-please!" Stacey stammered and shook as if she were freezing, and swayed like she was about to fall over.

Dave took hold of her elbow. "Have you been drinking?"

"No! I'm just upset." Stacey trembled, her wild eyes pleading.

Calvin pushed out his breath and tried to think. "Okay, you're here. Let's talk."

She just stood there, shaking, not responding at all. Maybe she'd expected him to fall into her arms too. Two days ago, he might have.

"Honey?" Patty was able to clasp her shoulder. "Are you sick?" She grabbed her other shoulder. "Something's not right, that's for sure. Let's get her into a chair." She guided her toward the campfire.

Flannery stomped past them, heading for the car.

Patty gave her seat to Stacey and squatted beside her, looking up at her face. Calvin slumped into Tyler's chair while Tyler paced near the tent. The headlights went out and everything got quiet except the frogs in the woods. The firelight flickered weakly on Stacey's ghostlike face.

Calvin sighed. "All right, what's going on?"

"Uh ..."

"Stacey, when's the last time you ate?" Tyler stood behind her chairs now, a barely visible specter.

"I-I don't know."

"You don't know?" Patty asked.

"S-sometime."

"Sometime?"

"She's anorexic," Tyler said.

"I ate something this morning! This isn't about that. Calvin, please make them stop."

Calvin leaned toward her. The words that came out of his mouth seemed to come from some other source. "Tell the truth, Stacey."

Her face hardened, although in the firelight her eyes looked like they were trembling. "I'm telling the truth. My mother fixed bacon and eggs this morning and I ate it. You can call her and ask."

"We should do that," Dave said. "They need to know where she is."

Stacey gasped and surged out of her chair. "No! Don't call ... ohhh ..."

Calvin caught her as she pitched sideways. He staggered dangerously close to the fire before he was able to turn Stacey around and put her back in her chair.

"Okay, something's not right with this girl," Dave said. "I think we need to call 9-1-1 instead."

"No bars. No—" Tyler dashed away, going ... somewhere.

"Is she dying?" Nigel sounded like he was about to cry.

Calvin pressed his hand to the side of Stacey's face. She was cold, but clammy. "Stace? Please. Tell me what's happening."

Tears rolled out of her eyes and her lips trembled.

"I think Tyler went to find the campground manager," Flannery said.

Something tugged the front of Calvin's shirt. Stacey's hand. He stroked her face and gazed into her watery eyes, while people came into their campsite, adding more anxious voices to the debate over what to do. Was she diabetic? Epileptic? Drunk?

Calvin licked his lips, then whispered to Stacey, "We have to tell them the truth."

She leaned forward, pressing her face to his chest. "I love you, Calvin. Please help me."

Chapter 29

Blue lights danced across the tree trunks and tents. Faces loomed over and around Stacey, strangers staring, talking about her. Police radios murmured and buzzed. Calvin sat on the ground beside her chair, holding her hand, but not saying much. The adults had taken over.

She wanted desperately to be alone with him, to explain everything to him. Five minutes. Why couldn't they give them that much?

Straining her eyes against the moving lights on top of the Jeep-like vehicle, Stacey made out that it was a park ranger truck, not a regular police car. Would a park ranger be more lenient than one of Daddy's cohorts?

"So, what we have here," one of the rangers said, "is a minor child, possibly a runaway, possibly with some health or mental condition. I want to know how she got here, and why. Did her boyfriend come with her? Was he driving the car?"

Dave Moore shook his head. "Nah. Calvin was here with us. His folks know he's here. We got in around three o'clock this afternoon, set up camp, then the boys and my daughter took their bikes out on the trails. We were just settling down for the night when she got here."

"Did Calvin know his girlfriend was going to come?"

"I really don't think so. He was shocked to see her. Hey, Cal, you didn't have any idea she was comin', did you?"

"No." Calvin's voice was flat, lifeless.

They were talking about her like she couldn't hear them, like she wasn't there at all. If she could get up without getting dizzy again, if she thought she could find her way out of this horrible place without getting lost again, she would get in her car and drive home. No one wanted to believe that she had every intention of going home in the morning. To them, there was some conspiracy going on. So what she had to say didn't matter to them at all.

Another ranger walked up to the first and handed him a cell phone. "Officer Varnell, Stiles County police. He's the girl's father."

"A cop? That's ironic." The ranger put the phone to his ear and turned away to speak. "Officer Varnell. Good evening, sir. This is Deputy Tucker, Uwharrie National Forest Service. We've found your daughter in one of our campgrounds ..." His voice was muddled in all the other conversation as he walked to the Jeep.

Dead. She was dead. Daddy would make sure of it.

Stacey's body wouldn't stop shaking. Every muscle, every joint, just shaking. She looked down at Calvin, and he turned worried eyes up to her. He looked so tired and frightened.

"Why?" he murmured. "Just tell me why."

She sniffed and her throat clenched painfully. "Because I love you," she squeaked.

Shoes crunched in the pine straw, coming toward them. Another park ranger loomed above her, but seemed to be looking at Calvin. "Are you the boyfriend? I need to talk to you a few moments."

Calvin pushed up to his feet.

Panic gripped Stacey. Squeezing the arms of the canvas chair, she tried to stand, but rocked back into the awkward seat. "He's not in trouble, is he? Calvin didn't do anything. I promise! Please don't do anything to him."

Leading Calvin away by the elbow, the ranger looked back at her. "He's not in trouble. Just a witness."

"A witness to what? I just came here to talk to him!"

The ranger didn't respond, but Calvin glanced back at her. And then they left her alone. Everyone left her alone. Their disapproving or sad glances told her she wasn't wanted here. Even people from the other campsites, who stood around, watching, didn't want her there. She'd ruined their fun time camping. She was unwelcome. Flannery's expression was flat-out hateful. And Tyler, standing with his arms crossed, pacing next to a tree, tried not to make eye contact with her. He was ashamed of her now.

Calvin stood next to the ranger's SUV, tugging his hair and talking with his head down.

Stacey lowered her own head but glanced left and right, peering into the darkness beyond the tent and the RV. Could she run and hide in those woods, and then circle back and get in her car? The keys should still be in the ignition ... if Flannery hadn't yanked them out.

Deputy Tucker came back, no longer on the phone. He stood over Stacey, his hands on his hips. "Miss Varnell, your father has asked us to take you into custody. He's on his way here, but it'll take him a few hours."

Her breath whooshed out of her lungs and wouldn't come back. "You-you're ... arresting m-me?"

"No, not arresting you. However, running away is an offense in the juvenile code."

"I didn't run away! I just wanted to talk to Calvin."

"You're two hundred miles from your home, alone, in the middle of the night. That sure looks like running away."

"I was going to go right back!" Somehow her eyes were able to produce fresh tears.

"Well, your father is on his way. We're going to take you to the station to wait for him."

"Can't I stay here? He can come here instead."

"No, I'm sorry. We're responsible for you now, and I'm sure all these people would like to get some sleep. So come on. Can you stand up?"

He held a hand out to help her, but Stacey edged away from it and managed to push herself out of the chair. She staggered toward the SUV, refusing to look at anyone else around her. But then she saw Calvin, and he turned toward her.

"Calvin," she whimpered. She ran to him, and he stepped forward to meet her. They crashed into each other and held on. His arms were so tight around her. He shook like he was sobbing.

"I'm so sorry," she said against his jacket. "I didn't mean for this to happen."

"Please, baby, please. Just . . . go see a doctor now. Please?"

"Calvin —"

"Please?"

Words she had no time to say gushed out of her. "I love you. I don't want to be apart from you. I wasn't flirting with Noah, I promise. I want to be your girlfriend again. Please, Calvin!"

His fingers tangled in her hair. "I'm right here . . ."

Stacey snaked her hand downward until it rested over Calvin's heart. "Right here."

"Always," he whispered.

Someone looped a hand around her elbow and gently pulled them apart. Deputy Tucker pressed a button on his radio, which sat on his shoulder next to Stacey's ear.

"Ten – ninety-one is a transport, one female juvenile, enroute, two-nine-seven-five-two point six. ETA forty-five minutes."

The radio returned static, then a woman's voice said, "Ten-four."

Stacey stumbled over a tree root. Only the ranger's tightened grip on her elbow kept her from falling. He opened the back door of the SUV and kept hold of her arm until she was inside. Stacey tested the door handle as soon as the ranger turned his back. Of course, it didn't work.

A metal grate separated the back seat from the front of the vehicle. The seats were vinyl and cold. Did they put criminals in this backseat? Stacey pressed her sleeve over her nose and scooted to the very front edge of the seat.

Outside, the other park ranger was talking with Calvin again, and Calvin nodded at something he'd said. Deputy Tucker opened the driver's door of the SUV, setting off door-ajar bells, and slid inside. He picked up a clipboard and wrote on it, while his partner took tentative steps toward the vehicle.

"What about my car?" Stacey slid even closer to the grate, as if the ranger couldn't hear her. "What's going to happen to my car?"

"We're deciding that now. Probably going to tow it into the station."

"Why can't I just drive home? I promise I'll go straight home. I'm not drunk or anything, so I can drive."

He looked in the rearview mirror at her. "We can't let you go, Stacey. So just sit tight. Your dad will come get you in a few hours."

"But what about my car?"

The man didn't answer. His partner reached the vehicle and opened the door. Calvin stood a short distance away, next to the motorcycles, watching her and looking so lost.

"Can I say good-bye to Calvin, please?"

"You already said good-bye to him."

"Please! I need ... I need ..." She slid over to the side window and pressed her hands against it. She shouted, so he would hear her. "I love you, Calvin!"

"Seat belt, please," the second ranger said.

How could they be so cruel? "Five more minutes? Please? I just want to talk to him."

"Sorry, we're rolling. Put your seat belt on."

She complied. She was in their control now. She'd have to comply with everything, or they might do something worse to her. Running away was a crime? Like, could they put her in jail for that? Or juvenile detention? Stacey leaned back against the seat, her sleeve pressed to her mouth to muffle her now tearless sobs. Her head pounded, and as the vehicle moved along the curving roads that had so confused her before, she was immediately carsick. At least the men in the front were nice enough to crack open the windows at her request.

o O O O o

An office with desks and papers and computers and uncomfortable chairs, and people who seemed to think she was something of a joke or a spectacle. Stacey curled up in a ball and refused to look at them. At least they didn't lock her in a cell. And it seemed she was the only person in this place who wasn't wearing a uniform. No real criminals. There were three park cops, but their phone hardly ever rang. She must have been their sole excitement for the night. Then two other people came in, wearing different uniforms, and it took only a moment for Stacey to realize they had come for her. A woman walked up to her chair and leaned forward, as if she were talking to a small child.

"Stacey? I'm Michelle, and I'm a paramedic. They called me here because they're concerned you might be sick."

Stacey kept her eyes focused on nothing. So they were sending paramedics to look her over? Maybe Calvin would get his way after all.

"Honey, can you tell me what's going on?"

"Nothing's going on. I was just really upset because my boyfriend and I broke up, and I came to talk to him, but I got lost in the woods and then I got really scared."

"They told me you're anorexic."

She twitched, fighting the impulse to look at the woman. "Who told you?"

"The officers here, and I'm assuming they got that information from one of your friends."

"I'm fine. I just want to go home."

"Have you had anything to eat today?"

"Yes."

"Recently?"

"No. I was driving here and I got lost, remember?"

"Have you had anything to drink?"

That was it! That was the reason for her headache and dizziness. She was dehydrated. She'd had a bottle of water in the car, but she only drank a few sips of it and forgot about it when she was searching for the campground.

"Can I have some water, please?"

"Yes, of course you can. Honey, I'd like to do a blood test on you, just to check your electrolytes and potassium levels. Is it okay if I do that?"

"You're going to stick me with needles? No. I hate needles."

"I'll be as gentle as I can."

"No. I'm fine. All I need is some water, and I'll wait here for my father."

And then they'll call you to pick up my dead body, because Daddy is going to murder me.

The woman stood up straight and spoke over her shoulder to someone. "Can we get her a bottle of water?"

One of the park rangers went to get the water, while Deputy Tucker came to visit. "She okay?"

"She's belligerent, but lucid. We can't force her to do a blood test if she's coherent, unless there's an obvious health issue."

Deputy Tucker waved a hand toward her, again talking about her as if she weren't sitting six feet away. "She was dizzy and falling down at the scene. We actually thought she might've been drunk, until we talked to her friends."

"Did you test her for alcohol? She's so tiny, it'd only take a little bit to affect her."

The ranger shook his head. "I couldn't smell anything on her or in her car. We can do it now, if you think it's necessary."

"I don't drink," Stacey said through clenched teeth. "And I'm right here. You can ask me questions, you know."

Deputy Tucker waved her off and went back to his desk. The female paramedic wasn't so easily offended. "We just want to make sure you're okay, that we don't need to transport you to the hospital. We're here for you, sweetheart."

"I'm not your sweetheart."

"Okay. We're still here for you."

Stacey thumped back in her chair and spread her arms wide. "I told you. I'm just upset. Can't you think back to when you were my age and you broke up with someone? It hurts! And right now I just want to get out of here and go home."

Where was this coming from? She was like a crazy person on one of those cop shows, barking at the police and making things worse. She had a sense suddenly that there were two Staceys, the smart one sitting very quiet inside her while the stupid one took over.

Shut up, stupid. Just shut up.

The woman paramedic nodded and turned to her partner, who stood several feet away. "She's not going to let us test her."

"No imminent danger, no signs of trauma, I think we're good to go."

Still, the woman, Michelle, remained there. She looked back down at Stacey, and compassion shined in her eyes. "Stacey ... Anorexia is very dangerous. It can kill you. Now, you can be as angry at me as you want to, but I'm going to tell you this and hope it sticks. Whatever caused you to believe that you're fat or that you'll get fat is a lie. The truth is you're very thin. Not emaciated yet, but getting there. And if you don't eat, you'll become deficient in all the nutrients your body needs to survive, and your organs will stop functioning."

Stupid Stacey glared at her.

"I do remember what it was like to lose a boyfriend. It hurts bad. But do you think killing yourself by starving is going to bring him back? Do you think maybe he's worried about you, scared to watch you die? If you love him, don't you want to be healthy so you can be with him?"

Leave me alone.

Michelle sighed and shook her head. "If you were my daughter ... Well, I just hope your parents are aware of what's going on and will get you some help right away."

The woman walked away, joined her partner, and left the office. Sitting partway on his desk with his arms crossed, Deputy Tucker stared at her. Another ranger brought her a cold bottle of water. Stacey accepted it, but just held it in her hand until the two men lost interest in her and went about their other business.

When no one was looking at her, Stacey cracked open the bottle cap and sipped the water. It slid down her throat and into her stomach, cooling her insides and helping her nerves to settle down. She drank more, until half the bottle was gone. And as she relaxed, exhaustion overwhelmed her. Stacey capped her bottle, cradled it against her chest, and curled up sideways on the chair in a tight ball. Stupid Stacey fell quiet and allowed her to sleep.

o O O O o

Familiar voices echoed in the room. She willed them to go away and let her sleep. Daddy bellowed her name. Stacey's eyes felt like they were sealed with glue, though she managed to force them open. Her father stood over her, his form seeming to swallow up all the light in the ranger's office.

"Before we leave here, I want answers." He wasn't yelling, but the low rumble of his voice was just as commanding, maybe worse. "Were you trying to run away with that boy?"

She rubbed some gunk from her eyes. "No, Daddy."

"Then why the Sam Hill did you drive four hours from home to find him?"

"Stan, can we discuss this after we've got her home?" Mom came around Daddy's side and clasped his arm. "Let's find a nice hotel for the night and we can all get some sleep."

"In a minute. Talk to me, young lady."

Stacey pushed herself up off the arm of the chair. Amazingly calm. Wanting only to go home.

"I'm sorry. I made a stupid mistake. I just wanted to talk to Calvin and I couldn't get him on the phone. I didn't realize how far it was to the campground, and when I got lost I freaked out. That's all that happened. Calvin didn't do anything wrong, so please don't blame him."

"Hmm, we'll see. Where are your car keys?"

"Umm, I don't know. I think . . ."

"We have them here," Deputy Tucker said. He crossed the room and handed Stacey's keys to her mother.

"No more car. My mistake was in assuming you were mature enough to handle the responsibility."

That hurt. That brought the tears again. "No, please don't take my car. I'm sorry! Please don't …"

"And her phone? Where is that?"

"No! Daddy, don't!"

"We didn't take anything out of the car, so it may be in there," Deputy Tucker said.

"Fine. Up. We're going."

Unable to stop her tears, Stacey gathered her feet under her and made them push her body up. Mom wrapped her arm about Stacey's shoulder, pulling her close against her side. Showing affection or keeping her from running? She thanked the park rangers for looking after her daughter, then guided Stacey outside.

Stacey immediately shivered in the night air. A fine mist wet her skin and shined on the asphalt. Mom briskly rubbed her arm.

Stacey's Honda was in the parking lot, but it was Daddy's police cruiser they walked to. It would have been just perfect if Daddy put her in the backseat like one of his arrestees, but he opened the front door for her instead. Which meant she'd have to sit beside him and endure his lectures all the way home. Mom walked away, and after Daddy closed the passenger door of his car, Stacey watched her mother cross the small lot to her Honda. The two spoke to each other, coordinating their destination and route, and then Daddy took the wheel of his car.

The clock on his dashboard read 2:18. Maybe he'd be too tired to talk.

With her seat belt secure, Stacey tucked her legs up, trying to curl into a ball again to ward off the cold.

"Feet off the upholstery," Daddy said.

She plunked her feet down. And stared straight ahead as they left the little town and drove along a two-lane road in the middle of nowhere. The whole world was dark for miles and miles. The mist turned to rain. The cruiser's windshield wipers slapping back and forth ticked off the moments and lured Stacey toward sleep.

But finally Daddy spoke. "I can't believe you did this. I might have expected something like this from Renee, but not from you."

She didn't bother to apologize. It wouldn't do any good.

"I'm very disappointed."

He fell silent for a long time. Was that it? No more lectures?

But then, "That boy, Calvin. You're not to see him again."

"What? Daddy, he didn't do anything wrong!"

"Maybe not. But you did. And you involved him. So we're going to remove all distractions, get to the bottom of whatever is going on with you, and fix it. Including this anorexia garbage."

Oh ... wonderful.

Chapter 30

The air inside the tent was steamy. Staring at the green nylon roof above him, Calvin dragged the heavy air into his lungs and kicked out of his sleeping bag. Tyler was gone. A female voice murmured somewhere in the campsite, and he could hear some rummaging in the distance. Calvin's throat was raw. He rubbed it and sniffed. Great. All he needed was a cold. He pulled on a pair of flip-flops then unzipped the tent flap and ducked through.

"'Bout time you got up." Flannery kept her eyes on a paperback book she held flattened against the picnic table. The only energy she seemed to expend was in jiggling one booted foot.

Answering her would probably hurt his throat. Calvin grunted. Yep. Hurt. He turned his back on Flannery and plodded down the lane to the bathroom. Grit from the moist ground got under his toes. It had rained during the night, so trails would be a mess.

If he had the heart to ride at all.

When he returned, Tyler rose from a canvas chair and gestured for him to sit. Calvin croaked thanks and plopped down, grateful for the remaining heat from the morning campfire near his feet.

Patty came out of the camper. "You missed breakfast. You were snoozing big time, so we didn't wake you. There's milk and cereal in the RV if you're hungry."

Calvin sniffed and nodded. Maybe he'd even get up in a few minutes to find something to eat. "What time is it?"

"Almost nine. Dad and Nigel have been gone since before dawn." Flannery closed her book and untangled her legs from the picnic table bench. "Get dressed. Grab an apple. Let's hit the trails before lunch."

Calvin cleared his throat. He'd tossed and turned most of the night, unable to get his mind to settle down. He blamed the thunderstorm, croaking frogs, chattering raccoons, lumps from little pebbles or bits of pine bark under his sleeping bag, and Tyler's snoring. The truth was he just couldn't stop thinking about Stacey. And now he was paying for it.

Calvin stayed slumped in the chair, staring at a flickering ember amid the ashes.

"Tell me you're not sick," Patty said.

"Stupid cold or something," he mumbled.

Flannery groaned. "That mean you're not riding? Great. Just great."

Tyler speared her with a piece of pine straw. "Dude, shut up."

So, what? They expected him to just go on with their camping trip as if nothing had happened last night? Calvin made eye contact with Flannery, but decided getting angry would take too much energy.

"I'm okay. And I *will* be riding. Just give me some time to wake up."

Patty pressed the back of her hand to his forehead. "Hmm, no fever. Tell you what, though. Let's drive in to the store and get you some of those zinc cough drops, just to be safe. Then we can call and see if Stacey made it home okay last night."

"Thanks." Calvin sniffed. At least someone understood.

Patty ran her fingers through his hair. "Come on, hon. We'll take your pickup."

∘ ◯ ◯ ◯ ∘

Calvin sniffled and cleared his throat all the way to the town of Troy. Patty parked the pickup next to a drugstore. With a good signal on Patty's cell, Calvin dialed Stacey's phone number. The call went straight to voice mail.

"The number you have reached is not available ..."

He waited for the beep and left a message. "Hey. It's me." His voice sounded like one of the frogs at the campground last night. "Just wanted to see if you got home okay. Umm, I wish things had gone different last night, but ... well, I'm happy that, like, we seemed to get a couple of things settled. Kind of. So ... Anyway, we'll be coming home on Wednesday. I'll try to call you again before then. I love you. Bye."

Calvin handed Patty's phone back to her.

She turned sad eyes to him. "That was pretty intense last night. Want to talk about it?"

He didn't. At least not with a burning throat. He stared at his feet, hoping she'd take the hint but not be insulted.

Patty sighed. "Is it true, what Tyler said? Stacey is anorexic?"

He wiggled his foot on the floorboard, bouncing slightly in his seat.

"I don't know what makes girls starve themselves like that. I saw a report on television about it. Horrible, horrible thing. Calvin, let's take a moment before we go inside to pray for her."

Calvin raised his eyebrows. Yes, prayer. They could do that. As long as he wasn't the one that had to speak.

Patty reached across the bench seat to clasp his shoulder. "Father God, we just ask you to watch over that pretty little girl, Stacey, and touch her heart with your love. I don't know everything she's dealing with, so I can only ask that you put your healing hand upon her mind and her heart and her body in whatever ways she needs it. See her through her troubles and let her know she's not alone, that she has people who love her and are pulling for her, and most of all, God, that you love her. Calvin and I are just so worried."

Calvin couldn't speak. He couldn't even get his brain to form words that made any sense. As Patty's prayer brought unexpected tears, his thoughts could only echo, *yes, God, please.*

"And Lord, I pray for Calvin. It's pretty clear to me that he's just heartbroken over this thing. I pray he'll find the right words to help Stacey, and that he is able to not only support her in the ways she needs but look after himself as well. Give him the strength to battle this cold, and help him find some peace as he goes riding. Please keep all the kids safe as they ride. And thank you, God, for your presence in our lives. Amen."

"Amen." Calvin sniffed. His bowed head and the few tears sent more gunk to the front of his sinuses.

Patty squeezed his shoulder and smiled. "Let's get you something for those sniffles."

The old truck's door hinges squealed and clunked as Patty got out. Calvin lagged behind, but as he walked into the store, a prayer burbled up from somewhere deep within him. *Lord, I don't understand all this. I read lots of stuff, and I tried everything I know how, and I still don't understand. But please let Stacey get better. Please.*

Chapter 31

Stacey lay with the hotel blankets pulled up to her jaw, pretending to be asleep. Her parents probably thought their voices wouldn't carry beyond the bathroom, where Mom was fixing her hair, but Stacey could hear every word.

"She's doing this to herself. It's a phase," Daddy said, "and it ends now."

"I don't know, Stan. Some things I read said it's a mental disorder—"

"They call everything disorders these days. Every form of bad behavior gets a name that turns the perp into a victim."

"This is our daughter we're talking about. Not some criminal you've arrested."

"It was just an example," Daddy muttered.

Stacey's stomach was hollow, but she wanted to puke. Her breakfast, provided by room service, sat on the table by the window, ready for when she rolled out of bed. No doubt Daddy would stand guard over her as she ate each bite.

"What are you doing?" Daddy asked. "Why are you cleaning the sink? They have maids to do that sort of thing."

"There was hair in it. Stan, we can't afford to ignore this. What if it damages her heart?"

Mom would stuff her head full of information that would tell her everything she needed to know about how to *fix* her daughter—Step One, Step Two, Step Three—and make everything all right again. Mom would be on the Internet when they got home, searching, analyzing, judging. Just like Calvin. Worse than Calvin.

Tears slid sideways down Stacey's face to wet the sheet. She made no effort to sniff or wipe them away. No movement; she wanted to hear more.

"We're going to have to spend more time with her," Mom said. "Make sure she eats properly. Keep telling her we love her. Maybe I'll take off work for the summer."

"We can't afford for you to do that."

"We can't afford for Stacey to be anorexic, either. What if she gets sick again?"

"That won't happen. She's going to eat properly, because we'll hold her accountable."

"How will we do that?"

"Rewards and consequences. She's not too old for it. Don't you remember when we were kids, when we did things that drove our parents nuts?" Dad paused, and someone turned the water on. The swooshy sound of teeth-brushing ensued. Daddy kept talking, which meant Mom was the one with foam in her mouth. "My father knocked some sense into me a few times, and, boy-howdy, I needed it. What we need to do now is take control of the situation and put Stacey back on the right path. She's not getting her car back until she's straightened herself up. And she's done dating that boy."

Mom spat. "It's not Calvin's fault. He's a good boy."

"She ran after him. And I'll bet he put her up to it. And then there's that girl, Zoe. She's trouble if ever I saw it coming."

Stacey pressed her fist against her mouth, stifling her squeak.

Mom muttered something Stacey couldn't hear

"Renee," Dad growled. "*She's* another matter. Girl doesn't have enough common sense to fill a paper cup. But she'll grow outta that too."

"Renee is not going through a phase! What if she ends up pregnant? She's an adult now. We can't do the consequences and rewards thing with her anymore."

"Oh, really? We'll see what happens if she gets caught drinking and spends a little time in jail. Along *with* Mr. Preston Stiles."

The water turned off, replaced by packing sounds, loud enough that Stacey envisioned Mom ramming things into her makeup case. "You're going to tough-love both girls right out of our house. Renee's halfway gone already. But Stacey is sick. She needs help."

I'm not sick.

"She's only sick because she makes herself sick."

Stop it, stop it.

"How did it get to this point? What did we do wrong?"

Nothing. Shut up. Please shut up.

"I don't know. Maybe we coddled her too much."

"So you're saying this is my fault?"

"What? I didn't say that. I said *we*."

"You know, when she was little and she was heavy, I never said anything to her like, 'Oh, you need to lose weight.' I always tried to affirm her."

Chubbikins! Chubbikins-Chubbikins-Chubbikins! Daddy said it! You thought it was cute!

They came out of the bathroom together, and Mom kept talking. "We need to find a counselor for her."

"Hush. She'll hear you. Just get her up, make her eat, and let's get out of here."

"Stan ..."

There was a long pause, and Stacey dared to open her eyes. In the mirror at the foot of her bed, she saw her parents embracing each other.

"Come on now, don't cry," Daddy murmured. "We'll get through this. We'll figure it out."

Do you feel my pain, Daddy? Do you see me crying? You never really stop to look.

○ ○ ○ ○ ○

The moment they arrived home, Mom scurried into the kitchen, promising sandwiches for an early dinner. Stacey wanted to flee to her room and lock the door, but Daddy would only find a way to open it. Maybe he'd remove the doorknob so she wouldn't be able to keep any secrets anymore. So instead, she lay down on the living room sofa, carsick and exhausted, and hoped they'd leave her alone.

No such luck. Mom called everyone to the table half an hour later, and Daddy insisted that Stacey get up.

She was met by ham sandwiches piled high with meat, cheese, lettuce, and tomato. A bribe; ham and cheese had been Stacey's favorite since the time she was able to feed herself. Mounds of chips surrounded the sandwiches. And pickles. Mom said she had an apple pie in the freezer she could bake if Stacey wanted it.

Stacey stared at the picture-perfect meal set before her. "I'm feeling nauseous from the car ride. Can I take this to my room and eat it after I've had a nap?"

Can I throw it out my window and hope a stray dog will find it?

"Eat the sandwich," Daddy said. "It'll help you feel better."

Renee dragged herself to the table, dressed in clothes that looked like she might have worn them to bed. She plopped down and rubbed her eyes, then her temples. What had Renee done last night with the house all to herself?

Eating sounds took over. Stacey stared at her plate. The food drew her and repelled her at the same time. They'd forced two meals into her already that day, not knowing that her requests to pull off into rest stops had been to get rid of the food. Mom, driving Stacey's car, wouldn't go into such places, so Stacey was free to brave the germs and do what she had to do. But now ... couldn't they let her skip one meal because she was honestly carsick?

"Stacey. Eat," Dad barked.

She jumped in her seat then touched the sandwich with her fingers.

"Where'd you go yesterday anyway?" Renee asked. "Mom said you ran away."

Stacey leaned forward, her hands gripping the edge of the table, and shouted at her sister. "I did not run away! Okay? I went to see Calvin, but I got lost, and that's the only reason anything bad happened."

"Church boy Calvin? I thought y'all broke up." Renee waggled her eyebrows like she knew some secret. "Besides, doesn't he live, like, five miles away or something? Where did y'all go together to kiss and make up?"

I hate you. "Nowhere. He was camping with friends and I went to find him."

"All right, we're not going to talk about this anymore," Daddy said. "Eat your dinner, both of you."

Renee lifted the top of her sandwich. "Needs mustard. I'm gonna sit outside, anyway." She pushed her chair back, the legs scraping on the floor, and stood.

Dad reached across the corner of the table to grab Renee's chair. "Sit back down and eat."

"No. I'm going out."

Here we go.

There'd been a time when Renee was the shining light of the family, the perfect pigtailed darling who was into Girl Scout merit badges and high school cheerleading. Stacey remembered the times she waited around with Mom while Renee attended gymnastics or cheerleading practice. Mom was the appointed chauffer and Stacey was the unwilling and bored-out-of-her-skull tagalong passenger. No one ever thought to enroll her in gymnastics. Not little Chubbikins. She wasn't strong enough. Her poor heart ... She'd just be embarrassed, like that one time they put her in dance class and she looked ridiculous next to the other little girls. *Are you sure you want to go out for the pom-pom squad, sweetie? Those girls are so competitive.*

So Stacey drew her pictures and read fantasy novels and dreamed she was someone else. Someone beautiful.

"Can I, uh, I'm going outside too. I need some fresh air."

Daddy watched her stand, one lowered eyebrow almost pinching his eye. "You'd better eat that sandwich. If I find it in the trash—"

"Stan!"

Stacey fled, leaving her parents to argue. In the backyard, Renee took over the swing, stretching her legs sideways across the slatted seat. Stacey dragged a lawn chair through the wet grass to sit next to her sister. She took a tiny bite of her sandwich. The sweet ham tickled her tongue, made her mouth water. She rolled it around in her mouth, savoring it until the taste faded and the meat got mushy.

"So, why'd you run away? You don't need to tell me the same lies you tell them. I'm not going to rat on you." Renee bobbed her feet in time to whatever song was in her head.

Stacey sighed. "I didn't lie. I honestly did not run away. But ..." She looked at her sister. An unlikely, but possible, ally. Renee would hear soon enough that she was *anorexic* and needed *counseling.* "They think I'm anorexic."

"Yeah? Ana-wannabe, maybe."

"What?"

"Come on. I've got eyes. I knew anorexic girls at college. Guys too. They were like you, except they were proud of it. The Little Ana

Club. But you, you try to hide it, but you're not that good. And you like food too much to really be anorexic."

Amazing. Did Renee sit in her room at night and make a mental list of the most hurtful words she could say? Stacey liked food too much ... which was why she was *fat*.

"Yeah? Maybe I should show you." With one glance at the house to make sure Daddy wasn't standing at the patio door spying on her, Stacey stood up and marched to the weedy field beyond the edge of their property. She carefully broke apart each piece of bread and tossed the bits into the field, spreading them far and wide so they wouldn't be easily noticed. The birds would take care of them. Broken potato chips followed. What was left on her plate looked like a picked-over meal, most of it gone.

She tried to look smug as she walked past Renee, but the girl laughed at her. "Really, Stace? You think Dad's not going to figure out what you just did? Give it up and come clean. Seriously, what you're doing isn't healthy, and you know it. Just accept who you really are. You'll be happier that way."

Stacey stopped and glared at her sister. The ugliest words she could think of bounced around inside her head, so tempting she could almost feel them on her lips. Finally she just shook her head. "You're not worth it."

She took the plate inside and left it on the kitchen counter for her parents' inspection.

Renee had raised one good point, though. How could she possibly keep this up? It was easier before to pick and choose what she ate when she said she was on a diet. Her parents allowed her to do that. And they trusted her enough that they didn't notice her deceptions. Now she couldn't count on being able to fling bad food into a field or even purge it after being forced to eat it. Mom's cooking would have her back to a size thirteen in no time.

She wandered into the living room. Her father wasn't there,

but Mom sat in her favorite chair and lifted her feet onto the otto-man. Her manicured toes wiggled as she leveled the remote at the television.

"I'm going upstairs to check my emails." Stacey pointed to the stairs.

"Wait a minute, sweetie. Come sit down."

Stacey groaned and perched on the edge of the sofa.

"You know, I understand what you're going through. How many times have I been on one diet or another? It's hard."

Yeah, you lost weight and gained it right back. And then some.

"At some point you just have to accept that you are who you are. I mean, I know we can do better with the way we eat. All of us. Maybe we should find a meal plan that's healthy, stop eating so many fatty snacks. You don't need to be rail thin, Stacey. You just need to be healthy."

What, did you and Renee read the same memo or something?

"What is it, Stacey? Why are you so unhappy with the way you look? Are kids teasing you at school again?"

"No, Mom."

"Kids can be so cruel. It makes them feel better about themselves if they can pick on someone they see as weaker."

I so don't want to hear this lecture again.

"You're a beautiful young lady," Mom said. "Don't let anyone tell you any differently."

"No one is picking on me, Mom."

"No? Then why do you eat so little? I'm so worried about you, sweetheart."

"I'm fine, Mom. I promise I'll do better and eat more. Can I go check my emails now? Please?" *Before Daddy confiscates my computer?*

"Sure. Come back down when you're done and watch a movie with me? Let's spend some time together."

"Okay. Give me a few minutes."

Mom smiled sweetly, yet a little tear glimmered in the corner of one of her eyes. Stacey's breath caught in her throat for an instant. How scared Mom must have been when that phone call from the park rangers came last night. Did she really think that Stacey was going to leave her? Really run away?

"Umm. I can do that stuff later," Stacey said. "Scoot over."

The oversized chair allowed both of them to snuggle together. While Mom flipped channels looking for a movie, Stacey leaned into her side. Soft, warm, yielding. Safe.

"Want some popcorn?" Mom said. "I can make some. Or not. We don't have to have it."

Hmm. The ally Stacey needed might be right there in the chair with her. Mom would be easy to manipulate.

Chapter 32

The tachometer needle shuddered near redline even though Calvin wasn't touching the throttle. Heat radiated off the engine and exhaust pipe, cooking his legs. Calvin pinched the bridge of his nose. His pounding sinuses made it hard to think.

His ride yesterday had been anything but fun. The Yamaha had choked out at the top of a rise, was a bear to start up again, and then limped back to camp. Calvin couldn't risk taking it out again until he fixed the problem.

Okay, engine running hot and idling way too high, but cutting out if he revved it—carburetor problem. Still running lean, even though he'd replaced the plugs and double-checked the timing—too much air getting into the cylinders. Somehow.

Flannery joined him, drying her hands on her pants legs after cleaning up the breakfast dishes. "Dude, that ain't right."

"You noticed."

"Hard not to. You're smoking up the place."

Good thing people at the nearby campsites were four-wheelers and bikers too. They'd appreciate the need to make repairs in the woods.

Calvin sighed. "Do me a favor. Hold the bike up while I check something."

Flannery took hold of the handgrips while Calvin shimmied off the back of the bike. He knelt beside the muffler. Whitish exhaust fogged his vision and breached the gunk clogging his nose, even though he held his breath. Popping sounds, but no different than yesterday. He traced the shape of the exhaust pipe, his hand an inch from the metal, searching any air movement that would indicate a crack. He rubbed his stinging palm against his thigh as Tyler walked up beside him.

"Figuring it out?"

Calvin shifted his weight to a more comfortable squatting position. "Running lean. But not bad plugs or timing. I'm wondering ..." Cylinder head, gasket ... He didn't want to voice those possibilities tugging at his thoughts. They'd be *bad*.

"What?" Tyler knelt beside him.

Would Dave have brought many tools on the trip? Flannery's bike was new, Tyler's just a year old. And it wasn't like they'd come for anything more serious than messing around in the woods. Not like a motocross race, where making repairs would be serious business.

"Flan, think your dad would have any Stick Weld?"

She leaned toward him, the bike tilting with her shifting weight. "Maybe. He had a toolbox in the back of the SUV."

A toolbox. She was probably thinking about the big tackle box where he kept all his fishing lures. Didn't matter anyway. Dave and little Nigel had headed out in the SUV again to go fishing.

The Yamaha's engine sputtered, idled down, and coughed.

Calvin snapped his gaze to Flannery. "What'd you do?"

Wide-eyed, she shook her head. "Nothing."

He stood to stretch out his knees. "Man, I totally don't need this now."

A break in the exhaust pipe might suck air back up into the cylinders. He could fix that with the Stick Weld. But if the problem was a crack in the cylinder head or a bad gasket, that would mean he was done riding. Maybe for a long time.

"Wish Dad was here."

"He should be back soon," Flannery said.

"No, I meant my dad. Whatever." Calvin pressed the heel of his hand to the middle of his forehead. "Who am I kidding? I can't fix it good enough to ride today. Cut the engine, will ya?"

She merely looked at him.

Tyler knuckled Calvin on the shoulder. "Come on, man. If anyone can fix it, you can."

"*If* it's a crack in the exhaust, and *if* I can find it, and *if* Dave has any putty. Forget it. I'm done." He stomped toward the tent. "Cut it off, Flannery!"

The campsite got quiet. Calvin plopped into a camp chair and stared into the underbrush. "Y'all go on. I'll stay here. My head hurts anyway."

Someone kicked Calvin's chair. The tilt of her head and slightly narrowed eyes suggested Flannery stood somewhere between compassion and anger. "Come on, don't give up. Maybe someone around here's got some tools."

Calvin gazed at the old bike. Tyler stood beside it, his expression pinched — trying to figure out the problem or deciding whether to shove the bike over.

Flannery slapped her thighs. "Fine. Give up. Sit there. I don't care."

Calvin scowled at her.

She scowled back. "Hey, I'm here to have fun. Not sit around and — and cry over Stacey."

"Hey!"

"I mean, I'm sorry she's sick. Really sorry. But her parents know now and they'll take care of her. And all you've done for two days is pout and snivel. No, I take that back, you were acting that way even before she showed up. She's been ruining things for you for *weeks*!"

"Flannery, what the — " Tyler jumped between them, forcing Flannery to step back from the chair. "What's the matter with you?"

Calvin groaned and tugged at his hair with both hands. "Shut up. Shut up. Shut up."

"We're here to have fun!" Flannery said. "Maybe he'd feel better if he just let himself have fun, like he used to before—"

Calvin surged up out of the chair. He lunged toward Flannery and shoved her shoulder. "I said shut up! I don't wanna hear it, okay?"

Tyler thrust his flattened hand into the middle of Calvin's chest. "Stop! I *know* you're not going to fight a girl."

Calvin stopped. His eyes flicked back and forth between his two friends, both glaring at him. *What? What did I do?*

Her full lips pouting despite the anger flaring in her eyes, Flannery turned away. "Maybe I should have gone fishing with Dad."

Her mother leaned out the camper door. "What's going on? What's with the bad vibes?"

"Nothing. We're done." Flannery squeezed past her mother into the camper.

Calvin snorted back mucus. He flopped down into his camp chair. "Y'all go riding. I'll read a book or something."

Tyler glared at him, no sympathy in his narrowed eyes. "Did you even bring a book?"

Calvin waved his hand uselessly.

"So Flannery's right. You're going to sit here and play the martyr." Tyler pointed at the Yamaha. "Why don't you go over there and *fix* that piece of junk and get out on the trails?"

Calvin crossed his arms and sank deeper into the chair. He shoved his legs out, taking the weight off his feet—so he couldn't bounce up and slug his best friend.

Tyler groaned and stepped toward the tent. "I've had enough. I'm going out. You can sit here and cry if you want."

Calvin swallowed a lump the size of a walnut. He pushed out of his chair so forcefully that the thing fell over, and stomped back to his motorcycle. He'd borrow some Stick Weld from somebody and seal up the entire engine and exhaust if it would get him back on the trails. Flannery and Tyler were right—sitting around moping would kill him.

He knelt beside the bike and stared at the engine. His breath puffed in and out, and his insides trembled. The fins of the piston casings blurred in his vision. But even if he could see perfectly, his task was impossible. A miniscule crack could be sucking just enough air into the engine to mess up the fuel/air mix. Maybe he could find it if he were in the workshop at home or at Dad's auto shop. But out here?

He heard footsteps in the pine straw on the other side of the bike. Tyler took hold of the handlebars and eased the Yamaha upright. "Want me to start it?"

Calvin sniffed, rubbed his wrist across his nose. Thank God for Tyler's loyalty. "Uh, not yet. I need to think about this."

His own meager set of tools sat in an open metal box by the rear tire. Torque wrench, a few sockets—could he tighten down the cylinder heads, maybe? Was he strong enough that it would even make a difference?

Pebbles popped under large tires, disrupting his thoughts. Calvin looked up to see the white SUV pulling into the campsite. He stood, and Tyler eased the Yamaha back onto its kickstand.

Nigel flew out of the passenger side. "Dad caught a fish, like, *this big*!" He held his hands as wide apart as they would go.

Calvin shoved his hands into his pockets. Dave's big-fish story could be a welcome diversion.

Dave got out of the SUV and circled the front. "Nigel, you left your door open." A grin played on his lips, though, as he closed the passenger door.

Nigel ran to the camper while Dave went to the back of the SUV and opened the rear hatch. His grunt, as he lifted out a big, battered cooler, sounded exaggerated.

The little boy dragged his mother out of the camper by her hand. Even Flannery followed, though she crossed her arms and refused to look at Calvin. Her father lifted something monstrous out of the cooler. Calvin gawked. Everyone in the campsite—and maybe a neighbor or two—gave exclamations of amazement. The catfish measured at least thirty inches long and its head was wider than Dave's fist.

"Eh? Eh? Pretty nice, huh?"

"Fabulous!" Patty said. "We going to cook it or mount it?"

"Eww! Tell me you're not going to put that thing on the wall!" Flannery whined. Just like a girl would. Calvin shook his head and looked back down at his bike, not ready to grin at her yet.

Patty laughed. "Not at home. In the camper, maybe."

"Oh no. Please. No. I beg you, no."

Nigel jumped up and down. "Yes! Yes! It'll be like having a pet."

"Pets are furry and cute and *alive*," Flannery said.

Calvin knelt down and grabbed his torque wrench.

"We're not leaving until tomorrow," Flannery said. "It'll stink up the SUV in that old cooler."

"No, it won't. We'll pack ice around it real good." Was Dave seriously considering mounting the thing? "Get the camera, Patty. Let's get some shots o' this sucker."

They took pictures. And Flannery stood on the other side of Calvin's bike, chatting with Tyler. Calvin sat on the ground and crossed his legs, gently tapping his torque wrench against the crankcase. Maybe eventually someone would notice him.

Selfish thinking, but he couldn't help it. They were all having fun, and he couldn't. With everything that had happened—was happening—how could anyone expect him to laugh?

"All right, we're gonna have some good eatin' tonight," Dave announced. "Start gutting this bad boy and filet it, Patty-girl."

"Ugh. I just knew you'd make me do the nasty work."

"Oh, come on now. I'll carry it in for you, then I'm going to see what's up with this young man's motorcycle that's got him all sour-pussed."

Calvin almost smiled.

∘ ○ ◯ ○ ∘

With the cylinder head tightened down and every inch of the engine and exhaust inspected by Dave's more expert eyes, the Yamaha ran a little better. Just not enough that Calvin felt confident following Tyler and Flannery on one of the trails rated "difficult." Besides, he wanted to be alone. An easy ride through the woods would clear the angry thoughts from his head.

With Tyler's cell phone secure in his back pocket, Calvin followed a rolling trail weaving southeast. Toward a cell tower, he hoped.

The Yamaha's exhaust still sputtered. He tried to think of another reason. Condensation in the gas tank? Could be something that simple. Or not. Because the work they did this morning wouldn't have changed anything.

A split-rail fence divided the trail from a gravel parking area. Calvin glided to a stop next to the fence and put the bike in neutral. It popped and coughed, but kept idling. He didn't dare turn it off. If the engine died and he couldn't start it, he'd be sorely tempted to abandon the bike rather than push it back to camp.

He removed his helmet and balanced it on a fence post, then pulled the phone from his pocket. Two bars; good enough. He dialed Stacey's cell phone. Like before, the call went straight to voice mail.

Okay, okay . . . home phone.

A tremor ran through him as he listened to the ringing. He willed Stacey to answer. Not her father.

"Hello?" a woman's voice said.

Calvin released his breath. "Mrs. Varnell. Hey. It's Calvin. May I speak to Stacey?"

"I'm afraid she's asleep, dear."

Really? "Well, um, c-could you wake her? I mean, I'm still at Badin Lake and I had to ride away from the campsite just to get a cell signal."

"Um, no, I don't think that's a good idea. She's been through a lot and she needs her rest."

"Yeah, I understand, but—"

"Calvin . . ."

There was a long pause and a sort of whooshing scrape. Then another scrape, followed by a thump. Sounded like she'd opened and closed the sliding glass door to their back deck. So someone in the house wouldn't hear?

"Calvin, I don't think it's your fault, but Stacey did run away from home to find you at that campground. Her father doesn't even want her driving far from home because she's only had her license a few months. Stacey knows that. And it's clear now that she's sick, that she's got this eating disorder."

Calvin cut into her parental speech. "So you know about it. Good."

"Yes." A short pause. "Calvin, I agree with my husband. I think it's best if you and Stacey have some distance from each other for a while. At least until we can get this problem under control. Stacey doesn't need anything upsetting her right now."

"Upsetting her? But—"

"Dear, I'm very sorry. Maybe it'll only be a little while. Right now we need to focus on her health more than anything else. I'm sure you understand."

Her words pressed down on Calvin's shoulders like thousand-pound lead weights. Suddenly the smell of the Yamaha's exhaust made him nauseous. "Yes, ma'am. I do. But, could you at least tell Stacey I called?"

"Yes, of course. I'm sure she'll appreciate that."

Appreciate it? Like he was inquiring as to the wellbeing of an elderly neighbor or something, not his girlfriend of eight months. Real sweet.

"Okay. Thanks."

"Have fun with the rest of your camping trip, dear."

"Uh, yeah. Bye." He hung up, and stared at Tyler's phone for a long time. They weren't going to let him see Stacey. He shouldn't be surprised. He still couldn't believe that Stacey had driven all that way to find him. Dumbest thing she'd ever done. Yet for a moment, ever so brief, when she looked into his eyes and touched his chest over his heart, he'd dared to think . . .

Forget it. Her parents knew everything now, and they were calling the shots.

Calvin shoved Tyler's phone into his pocket and jammed his helmet back onto his head. He grabbed some throttle and skidded the bike onto the trail. An easy trail. But he rode it hard and fast. This could be his last ride of the summer. Maybe his last ride forever if, like Dave suggested, the Yamaha really needed an engine rebuild. That alone was reason enough to be angry. Losing Stacey too . . . He might as well beat the bike as much as it could stand without falling to pieces in a mud puddle.

Chapter 33

Morning sunlight bled through Stacey's eyelids, making sleep impossible. Her vision foggy, she peered at her bedroom, met by the white furniture, her dresser top, and the shelves neatly stocked with little-girl memorabilia. A utopian illusion.

Chilled in spite of the sun, she tugged her quilt up to her face. Could she stay here? Disappear under her blankets? Would anyone miss her?

Calvin would be sitting around a fire with his friends, fixing sausage and eggs for breakfast with dented cookware and long-handled utensils. Birds would be singing. She could envision a breeze lifting the soft curls off his forehead, his chin and lip unshaved, dappled sunlight glinting in his hazel eyes. Earthy, scruffy, happy.

Snaking her hand out from under the quilt, she reached down to the cubby of her bedside table. Almost nothing there now, but by stretching her arm and fingertips she found her sketchbook, which was "safe" enough for her to keep. She teased it out until she could grasp it, then tugged it under her quilt. She pulled a pencil out of the drawer and propped the sketchbook up so that just enough light hit a fresh white page for her to write.

What word could she use as inspiration? Rugged? No, that wasn't right. Calvin's face was too soft for that. If she closed her eyes, she could see him clearly. His smile tore at her heart. Was he having fun while she lay here suffering the worst days of her life? A weight settled upon her, heavier than the quilt, seeming to press her into the mattress.

Yes, the weight of what she'd become if she did what everyone—including Calvin—was telling her to do now. Eat more, become the roly-poly princess she used to be when she lived in Rocky Mount.

Stacey threw the sketchbook and pencil away. The pages fluttered and fell to the floor somewhere near the foot of her bed. She battled the compulsion to go pick the things up and put them away properly.

Someone tapped on her door. Before Stacey could answer, Mom charged into the room. "Do you know where Renee is?"

Stacey jerked the quilt over her chest again. "How should I know? I haven't been out of bed yet."

Mom didn't even blink. "I don't think her bed's been slept in."

Oh, that's hilarious. Even now she has to be the center of attention. "Probably spent the night with *Preston*."

Mom's face hardened. "Get up and get dressed. You're not skipping breakfast, and I have to go back to work."

Good morning to you too.

Stacey folded her quilt back and swung her legs over the side of the bed. Cool air hit her, sending goose bumps across her bare arms. She smoothed out her capri-length pajama pants then ran her hands up her shins to her knees. Hard knees, no longer padded and soft. But her calves—she poked her fingers into the flabby flesh behind her shins. How could anyone think she was too skinny?

Porcelain dolls with round faces, chubby hands, and thick ankles taunted her from the bookshelf. *Aren't we cute? Aren't we precious? Come back, Chubbikins!*

"I'll never go back."

Stacey made her bed, then found the sketchbook and pencil and put them back in the drawer. She slipped into the bathroom, locked the door behind her, took off her clothes, and promptly stood on the scale. Tears blurred the digits on the scale. Half a pound heavier. Stacey staggered into the shower.

Calvin! Put me on the back of your bike and take me away from all this.

But he wasn't her hero anymore. Ultimately, he was on the same side as her parents. And running away with him would be a crime under the North Carolina juvenile code, unruly child statute, for which — Daddy had reminded her twice now — she had already received a citation.

She dressed, putting on the simple floral dress she'd worn to meet Calvin at church weeks — months? — ago. Pretty lame, but it did a good job of hiding her body from the world. She pulled on some thick black tights and found a pair of ballet flats from last year. They fit comfortably, even a little loose. Miss Frump. Sort of emo, though. Still chilled, she topped the dress with her pink zippered hoodie. Why was it so cold? In early June, the mornings should be warmer.

The smell of brewing coffee both enticed Stacey and turned her stomach hollow as she headed downstairs.

Mom's voice coming from the kitchen had a melodic edge, like a cat's threatening yowl in the night. "Maybe she isn't a child anymore, but we've got to do something to save that girl from herself."

Talking about me? Again?

Something banged to announce Daddy's response. "What? Lock her in her room and shove meals in to her? Even without a car she'll find ways to get away from the house. We can't control that boyfriend of hers."

Stacey slunk against the living room wall so they wouldn't be able to see her. She stilled her breath to listen.

"Keep your voice down. Stacey will hear."

Daddy muttered something.

"Stan, let's find a counselor."

A counselor. Someone else to take your side against me.

"No," Daddy answered.

"Why not? Why are you so dead set against getting help?"

"Because I'm not going to pay hundreds of dollars for some over-educated twerp to analyze our lives with a load of psycho-babble."

Because you have all the answers already, right, Daddy?

A cabinet slammed. "This isn't about money! This is about our daughter, our family."

Stacey couldn't stay for the insults and blaming, this confrontation of two strong-willed people with differing ideas on how to *save* her. She had to escape this place before they dragged her into some treatment program where she'd be incarcerated and reconditioned to believe that fat was okay.

Stacey's limbs trembled, and her heart fluttered. The inner Stacey cried out, *run!*

The slipper-like shoes enabled her to cross the room silently. She eased open the front door, closed it behind her just as quietly, and then let the adrenaline take over. She leaped down the steps. Her arms flailed as she ran across the front yard, but then she focused on pumping her limbs, speeding across the neighbors' lawns. Her shoes flapped around her heels, tripping her up. She kicked them off. With one shoe in each hand, Stacey ran to the end of the subdivision.

Daddy would come after her. He'd call his friends at the police department, and there'd be citations enough to lock her behind bars. She had to get out of sight and far away fast.

Several cars carrying secretaries, dock workers, or shop owners sped past her on Turner Creek Road. She bounced on the balls of her feet and hoped no one noticed her tear-soaked face.

Where could she go?

Stacey's feet slapped the asphalt as she crossed the two-lane road.

She stumbled down a gulley, caught herself on her fisted hands. Weeds snagged her tights and scratched her legs, but she plunged into the woods bordering the actual Turner Creek.

Think. Think. Breathe.

Stacey ducked behind the trunk of a large hardwood tree. She sank to the ground at its roots. With her knees to her chest, she gasped for breath.

I can't live this way. Why are they punishing me? Why doesn't anyone understand?

Stacey covered her mouth with the back of her hand. She tasted salty tears. If Daddy had his way, he'd rule over her and force her through her rebellious "phase." If Mom had her way, she'd send her to some therapist who would label her and push her into rehab. Isn't that what they did with anorexic girls? Mark them insane and send them away?

She had to get free. At least until she could think things through.

Stacey gasped and stared at the shoes in her hands. What did she think she could accomplish with just some stupid shoes in her hands? She'd left her purse at home. Her cell phone was locked away, along with her car keys. Where could she possibly go?

Not Zoe's house—first place Daddy would look. Who else could help? Who would even listen? How long before Daddy had the whole police force out looking for her?

One thing she knew for certain: She couldn't stay huddled behind a tree a quarter of a mile from her house.

Stacey thrust her feet into her shoes. She waded through the underbrush, going parallel to the road, and kept her ear tuned to the sound of car tires on the pavement. Hearing a vehicle coming, she ducked down in a patch of honeysuckle and curled her body into a ball.

Thorny vines scratched her hands and snagged her clothes as she moved on. Her breath soon came in gulps of too-thick air.

"Phone booth, phone booth."

There was an old convenience store miles down NC 19 with a rusty phone booth on the corner. Maybe the only phone booth left in the whole state. But she'd never make it. Even if she did, she didn't have any money. Not even a single quarter tucked in the pocket of her hoodie from the last time she'd worn it. Only a scrap of paper and pocket lint.

"This is crazy. I'm going insane."

The woods broke ahead at the edge of someone's field. The tobacco plants weren't tall enough yet to conceal her, though a wide truck path circled the field, just like the one around Calvin's cotton field.

Memories cast a veil over her vision. The path, the smelly truck, Calvin in her arms, kissing her, breathing against her face. Why did she have to make him stop? Would they still be together if she hadn't?

Stacey pulled her hair back from her face with both hands. She couldn't think about all that now. Not until she found a safe place to hide. She turned left to follow the dirt road. The ground beside the tobacco field was sandy and soft. Soon her legs burned with exertion, and her shoes filled with grit. Her ankle rolled against a rock, sending a hot rush of pain to her brain. She yelped and went down on her hands and knees.

She stayed there, her head hanging, blubbering. "I-I can't do this on my own. Calvin. Daddy. Please."

Something rustled in the field and snuffled near her shoulder. Stacey screamed and threw herself backward. A large black dog leaped back, legs stiff and hackles raised. They stared at each other. If she moved, would the dog attack or run away?

"Good dog. Good boy. It's okay. You just scared me."

The dog's long tail waved then lowered again. No collar. No telling if this animal was a stray or someone's pet.

Stacey clambered to her feet. The dog slunk closer, head lowered and nose quivering.

"Good dog. Please don't hurt me."

The broad, black nose almost touched her knee. The tail wagged. Stacey extended her hand toward the dog's ears. Calvin's fuzzy dog, Scamp, loved to have his ears scratched.

The dog's brown eyes tilted upward. He jumped back and barked a long "woo-woo-woo" phrase. Stacey squeaked and staggered into a tree, grabbing the trunk for support as she inched around the side of it. The dog stopped barking for a second, as if taking a breath, took a few stiff steps to the side, and started up again.

"Strider! Whatcha got, boy?" a genderless, gravelly voice called.

Stacey pressed her forehead to the tree. Dog owner. No problem.

"Whoa, hey there. It's okay, he don't mean no harm. Strider. Come 'ere, boy."

"Thank you. Thank you," Stacey puffed, her eyes closed.

"You all right, baby doll? Whatcha doin' out here?" A woman. Grizzled and sun-baked, but with dimples waiting to erupt in her round face. A wide-brimmed straw hat shaded her eyes. Stacey looked for a shotgun but saw only a walking stick.

"I'm lost. D-do you have a cell phone?"

Who would she call? Zoe. At least Zoe could get her out of there. Then they could figure out what to do.

"Lost? In my t'bacca field?"

"S-sorry. I'm sorry. Do you have a phone?"

"Not on me. You can come up t' the house and use the phone, if you want."

Could she trust the woman?

Did she have a choice?

Just some old Farmer Jane out walking her dog and checking her field, or whatever those people did in the mornings.

"I-I turned my ankle."

"Can you walk, sugar?"

Sugar. Okay. It'd be all right. Unless the woman tried to feed her.

Stacey eased away from the tree and put pressure on her right foot. It throbbed, but accepted her weight. "I think so."

"Well, c'mon then. We'll get ya fixed up." She clapped the dog on the ribs and sent him toward the field. "What's your name? I'm Miss Darcy, Darcy Meyers."

"Stacey."

"Just Stacey?" The woman's calloused hand clasped Stacey's elbow to help her along.

"Um ..."

"Hey, it's okay, darlin'. You don't have to tell me. Just not every day one sees a pretty girl wearin' a dress truckin' through the field, ya know?"

"I'm running away from ... my boyfriend. We had a fight. He's really big and—you know. I thought if I went through the woods he wouldn't be able to find me."

"Ah, one of those bully boys, think they need to be tough to prove their manhood. I hear ya. Ain't got much use for fellers like that, takin' out their aggression on a girl, like they *own* her. And such a tiny thing like you!"

Definitely not what Stacey expected to hear from the woman. Maybe she was an old hippie who decided to make her living off the land, all eco-crazy and such. But growing tobacco? The word *anomaly* popped to mind.

"Um, if I can just call a friend of mine, she'll come get me."

"Good enough. House is just 'round the bend a ways."

Strider trotted beside them, his tongue rolling out of his mouth in a doggie smile. Friends now. Mirroring his mistress's cheerfulness. Then, with a snarl, he dove between the broad-leafed tobacco plants.

Miss Darcy chuckled, her whole torso jiggling. "Found himself a mouse, pro'bly."

How quickly a tail wag turned to aggression. Stacey hoped Miss Darcy's understanding wouldn't turn to something else just as quickly. Would she want to call the police to make a report on Stacey's fake boyfriend?

All she needed was a phone for two minutes, then she'd be gone. Somehow. Zoe had to have some ideas.

Ahead was a farmhouse, an old structure like Calvin's house but with more additions cobbled on. A pickup truck and two cars were parked in front. Miss Darcy didn't live alone.

Stacey tucked her chin down and trudged along the wide path through the sandy field. She shoved her hands into the pockets of her hoodie. Her fingers curled around the slip of paper. She remembered without pulling it out—Noah Dickerson's phone number.

Chapter 34

"How was camping?" Dad grabbed the latch on the pickup's tailgate.

Calvin's sinuses throbbed. After unloading two other motorcycles at two different houses, he was ready for a nap and couldn't face a long conversation about what had really happened during his trip. With Stacey or the bike. "It was good. Good riding. I got a cold, though."

He climbed into the pickup and reached for the first hook of the heavy-duty cargo cables holding the Yamaha in place. The truck bed was a mess, covered with dried mud and pine needles, and would have to be hosed out. The Yamaha didn't look much better.

Dad grunted as he climbed up beside him. "Leave me any gas in the truck?"

"Uh ..."

"Uh-huh. That's what I thought."

"No, there might be a quarter tank. I think."

Dad loosened the cable on the other side of the bike. "Let's hurry and get this unloaded so you can clean up for church."

Wednesday night Bible study. He'd forgotten about that. "Can I stay home this time? I feel like crud."

"Better talk to your mama about that."

Calvin held the motorcycle's handlebars while Dad jumped down from the truck. Dad slid their homemade bike ramp away from the side rails and hooked it to the tailgate.

"Back her up."

Calvin eased his bike backward and Dad guided the rear wheel to the center of the ramp. They transferred the bike's weight from one to the other, and Dad eased the Yamaha down to flat ground.

Calvin jumped off the truck. Landing shook his sinuses and rattled his eyeballs. He pinched the bridge of his nose between his fingers. "Ow. That was stupid."

"Go ask your ma for medicine. I'll hose down the bike and truck. You don't need to be getting wet if you're sick. Need you healthy for work tomorrow."

"Thanks, Dad." Calvin sniffed and shuffled into the house.

Inside, the boys were arguing over a gaming controller and Lizzie was yakking on the phone. They all just glanced at him. Calvin dropped his duffle on the dining room table and pulled out the cold capsules he'd bought in Troy.

Mom rounded the corner into the room. "Take that filthy thing off the table, please. How was your trip?"

"Fine."

"What are those? Pills?"

"Got a cold." Calvin tossed the capsules to the back of his throat and swallowed. Bad move. Usually he could do it, but his sore throat closed around the pills. Ouch. He went to the kitchen and filled a glass with water.

Mom pressed her hand to his forehand, lifting his hair up. "You're not fevered."

"I feel awful."

"I'm not surprised, camping out in the rain the other night. Was it as bad there as it was here?"

How could he know how bad the rain was at home? He shrugged.

"Go upstairs and get into your pj's," Mom said. "I'll fix you some soup."

She'd concoct some kind of remedy that would either taste amazingly good or unbelievably bad. But it sounded like she would let him skip church, anyway. Calvin trudged up to his room and replaced his jeans with a pair of sweatpants. Shirtless, he flopped down on top of his bed, not bothering with his blanket. The warm room seemed to shift around him. So good to close his eyes.

Yet as he did, an early-morning conversation with Tyler replayed behind his eyelids. Their almost-argument had made for an awkward ride home.

"It stinks, man." Tyler's voice in their tent had been muted. Predawn light filtered through the mesh window, barely revealing his form sitting cross-legged on his sleeping bag. "But this isn't like working on a bike or a car. You can't fix her. Let her family take care of her."

Calvin winced. *Fix* her? Pretty cold way of looking at it. He wanted to help her, not—

"Besides," Tyler said, "you still don't know what's going on with her and Noah."

That reminder stung. "Shut up."

"Sorry. I hope I'm wrong. But there's got to be more to it than Stacey suddenly deciding she wants you back. Maybe she wasn't running away from home, but she was running away from *something*."

Calvin's eyes snapped open. Home, not the campground. Only the roof beams and God heard him cuss as he turned to face the wall.

Pretty ironic that Stacey's parents would forbid *him* from seeing Stacey. What would Deputy Varnell have to say about Noah Dickerson?

During the four-hour drive home, Calvin had let his thoughts wander over that territory. Stacey said there was nothing going on with Noah. He wanted to believe her. But what exactly did she go all that way to talk to him about? What couldn't she tell him because the park rangers came and took her away?

A now familiar tingling sensation erupted on Calvin's scalp. Cold medication doing its work. He folded his pillow around his head and welcomed the drowsiness that would come next.

He awoke to his mother's touch. Instead of a tray with soup on it, she held the phone out to him. "Mrs. Varnell wants to talk to you. She sounds upset."

Calvin lumbered upright and took the phone from Mom's hand. As he said hello, Mom stayed, touching her fingertips to her lips and staring, her forehead wrinkled with concern.

"Calvin? Is that you?" Mrs. Varnell's voice was loud in the receiver.

"Yes, ma'am."

"Have you seen Stacey? Have you heard from her? At all today?"

The walls seemed to compress around Calvin. Something bad was going on. It wasn't a medicine-induced dream.

"No, I haven't. I just got home from camping a little while ago."

"Oh. Well, all right. Your mother said you were sleeping. I'm sorry to bother you."

"What's going on?"

"I can't explain right now. We have to find Stacey."

"She came home with you. Right? From the park ranger station?"

Mom's brows pinched and she mouthed the word, "What?" Calvin gritted his teeth.

"We'll call you when we know something."

"Wait. Mrs. Varnell? Is she —"

Silence on the line robbed him of breath. He looked up at his mother and limply handed the phone back to her.

"What was that about?" she asked, staring.

"They're looking for Stacey."

"What was that about the park ranger station?"

He rubbed his eyes so he wouldn't have to look at her. When she sat on the edge of his bed, the scent of her perfume spilling over him, he knew he wouldn't get out of this conversation.

"You know we broke up. And I was like, that's it. We're done. But Sunday night, she ... drove to Badin Lake because ... she wanted to get back together."

"She did what?"

"She drove—"

"By herself? Why would she do that?"

"I don't know."

"Calvin Thomas Greenlee, you tell me the truth right now. That girl called here the other day crying, wanting to talk to you. It'd have to be something major for her to drive all that way to see you."

"She called here too?" Calvin swallowed hard. "Mom, I honestly don't know why. I've been trying to figure it out since it happened. All I know is ... she's anorexic." His joints trembled. Saying it out loud to Mom, all his barely controlled emotions threatened to break through. He squeezed his eyes shut.

"Oh ... dear ... Lord," Mom said.

He had to pour it out for her. "She's been sick a lot and now it's messing with her head. That's the only thing I can figure that makes any sense. She came to the campground and she was all freaked out. The park rangers took her, and her parents were supposed to come get her. I talked to her mom yesterday, and she said Stacey was sleeping. But now she's gone again. She ... she wouldn't go back to Badin Lake, would she? I mean, she knew we were coming home today."

Mom dropped her fingers from her mouth and thrust the phone out to him. "Call her cell phone. She probably isn't answering calls from her parents, but she'll see it's your number, and she'll answer."

Calvin blinked. That was so simple an answer, why hadn't Stacey's parents thought of it and asked him to do it? He took the phone from Mom and dialed.

Like every time before, the call went straight to voice mail. Immediately. Did that mean her phone was turned off? Well, *that* hope crashed and burned. Still, Calvin waited through the sing-song sound of a woman's voice telling him to leave a message or wait if he needed further instructions, blah, blah.

"Stacey." Too abrupt. He had to lure her. "Hey, uh, I'm home from camping. Give me a call, okay? Can't wait to hear your voice again." Too sweet? He let it stand and said good-bye.

When he handed the phone back to Mom, she was toying with the fabric of her church dress and didn't see him for a second. "How do you know she's anorexic?" Mom took the phone without looking at him, and toyed with it in her lap instead.

Calvin sighed. "We know. Everyone knows. Now her parents know. Her mother pretty much told me when I called from the campground."

"Is anyone ... doing anything for her? Girls—people like that need help, they need counseling. It's very serious."

"I know. And not yet. I wonder if, like, she ran away because her parents figured it out." The possibility seemed so right that it weighed heavy on Calvin, like a physical weight. His arms lost their ability to hold him up. He flopped down against his bunched-up pillow.

Mom inhaled sharply and straightened, giving her head a shake. "Oh, my. Poor girl. But Calvin, honey, her father is a policeman. He'll know what to do about this. He'll find her, even if she went back to the lake. He'll be notifying the police there to watch for her. So don't worry too much about it." She set the phone on the old steamer trunk that served as his bedside table. "I'll leave this with you. Try calling her again in a little while."

Calvin shook his head and swung his legs over the side of the bed. "I can't just lay here, Mom. I have to try to find her."

Mom's hands landed on his shoulders and pressed him down. She was strong, and he hadn't expected it. "*You* are going to stay right here and rest. You're sick."

"Mom. I've got a cold. Anorexia is a whole lot worse."

She leaned forward to look into his eyes. "Listen to me. If she's looking for you, she'll get that message and she'll call or come here. Right? Moreover, her father's looking for her, and he'll find her. *My* job is to take care of you. So, when we get back from church tonight, I want to find you here." She pointed at the floor, her eyes hard, like he'd already done something wrong.

Calvin's mouth dropped open. Although a plan hadn't fully formed in his head, the seeds had sprouted. Mom saw the shoots and squashed them.

"Mom, I can't just sit here if she's in trouble."

"You will, if I have to stay home to make sure you do."

"But she needs me."

"She *needs* therapy. Right now the best thing for you to do is to stay out of the way and let her parents deal with the problem. Understand? Let Stacey's parents take care of her."

Calvin's shoulders slumped, and Mom's hands slid off them. He wouldn't get anywhere arguing with her. He didn't have the energy anyway. Calvin stared at his bare feet while the floorboards creaked beneath his mother's departing footsteps.

"I'll bring your supper up in a moment."

The word "thanks" got stuck in his throat. Thanks for not understanding. Thanks for stripping him of all power to do anything.

"Stupid cold," he whispered into the quiet room.

Chapter 35

Heavy metal music screamed from the speakers on the back deck of Stuart Somebody's car, the pounding subwoofers just inches away from Stacey's ears. The air in the car smelled ashy, but not like cigarettes. A more pungent, earthy smell. Weed. Had to be.

Sitting next to Stacey, Zoe wore a smile that practically split her face in two. She flipped her hair back for about the hundredth time and pulled a compact out of her black-and-bling purse to check her makeup. How could she see anything in the shadowy car?

Stacey shuddered, freezing in the air conditioning, unable to focus for long on anything but the fear of seeing her father's cruiser pull up beside them.

In the front seat, Noah said something to his driver friend that sounded like *Nathan*. He put a cell phone to his ear. The music stayed loud while he talked.

Stacey leaned close to Zoe. "Where are we going?"

"Nathan's house, I think. Whoever Nathan is."

A highway sign flashed by. *Highway 301, 1 mile.* They were in Dawson, but on the southern side, farther than she'd ever driven.

Noah turned around and flashed a grin. "Y'all up for a party?"

"Yeah!" Zoe squeezed Stacey's hand and shook it back and forth. *Way to be obvious.*

No restrictions, motoring off to parties with beautiful people. Zoe's idea of fun. Stacey pushed her hands between her knees to keep from chewing her cuticles bloody. Her heart quivered madly in her chest, so much that it hurt.

Grounded forever, her car sold to the first taker, and all boys banned from coming within a hundred yards of her until she was thirty; that's what Daddy would do if he found out she was sitting in a weed-infused car heading to some strange person's house with Noah Dickerson. He'd even toss her in a jail cell and fling a pile of juvenile citations at her face. And that was before anything that might happen at this party.

Why did I let Zoe talk me into calling Noah?

Her entire life as she knew it was over. Going home again was out of the question. She'd have to drop out of school and find some halfway house in Raleigh—no, farther away, maybe Charlotte or Atlanta—where she could stay until she found a job waitressing or working in a factory. Bye-bye, fashion design school. Bye-bye, Calvin, forever.

Stacey looked out the side window to hide her trembling lower lip from Zoe.

Stuart Somebody pulled off the highway on Highway 301. They passed gas stations, fast food places, and a grocery store, then turned off that road into an apartment complex. Cars in the parking lot ranged from late model to old junkers, and beach towels and sports banners hung over some second-floor balcony railings. This had to be college housing. But which college? Stacey couldn't think.

Stuart parked in front of one of the buildings. Stacey's mind raced to find an excuse for staying in the car. Sick? No, Zoe wouldn't buy it. With a deep breath, she climbed out and followed the guys toward the building.

Zoe grabbed her arm and pressed close. "I'm gonna get me a hot college guy."

Sure you are ... for one whole night. This is crazy. We shouldn't be here. Stacey slowed her steps with Zoe still clinging to her arm. Her body begged her to stop.

"Don't you back out now." Zoe's whisper turned dark. "You better not be thinking about that farm boy."

Stacey jerked her arm away. "His name is Calvin."

"I know his stupid name! Come on, don't ruin this. Just be cool and have some fun. Tomorrow you can think about Calvin all you want."

Noah and Stuart led them up an outdoor stairway. Stacey's feet felt like cement bricks with each step. Stuart tapped on the door of a second-floor apartment, but opened it himself. Someone shouted a greeting. Five people sat on a garage-sale sofa and two plastic lawn chairs clustered near a blaring television. The air smelled like beer and cat litter, and Stacey wished for a hazmat suit.

A scruffy-haired, bearded college guy came out of the kitchen and grabbed Noah in a one-armed embrace, followed by a knuckle rap with Stuart. He pointed at Stacey and Zoe with his chin. "Who're your friends?"

Noah draped his arm over Stacey's shoulders. "This is Stacey, and that's Zoe. Girls, this is my brother, Nathan. And these other people are ... uh, I don't know everyone here. I know Darla, of course." He pointed to someone on the couch.

"People from class," Nathan said. "We were studying earlier."

"Y'all have to take summer school?" Zoe asked.

Way to show you're still in high school, ditz. College offers summer courses.

Still, if they were studying, maybe these people would be okay. This was the bohemian lifestyle Stacey could look forward to at fashion design school — minus the beer and cat stink. And if she wasn't grounded forever and forced to put off college completely.

Noah's musky scent washed over her, a relief from the other

smells. His velvety voice made her catch her breath, his sapphire eyes demanded that she look nowhere else. But when his fingers massaged her shoulder, laying claim to her, she inched away.

Zoe strutted into the living room. Stacey followed, moving away from Noah, and glanced at the television. ESPN logo, clips from baseball games. Stacey squeezed onto the end of the tattered plaid sofa and said hi to a girl with short brown hair.

The girl sipped from a can of beer then set it on the glass-topped coffee table. Dirty rings marked resting places of many cans before it. "Hey, I'm Darla. You're here with Noah?"

"Um, well, yeah. Kind of."

Darla laughed softly. "Kind of?"

"We're just friends."

"Really? 'Cause Noah doesn't have any *girl* friends. Just girl-friends, if you get me."

"I get you."

"I mean, he's a really sweet guy. Just scattered. Who knows? Maybe you'll be the one to help him settle down."

"Doubt it," Stacey mumbled.

"Just don't make him jealous. He can't handle it. He gets a little weird."

"I'll keep that in mind."

No one bothered to introduce the other people. Stacey wouldn't have remembered their names anyway. Finally Noah sauntered over, and Darla got up to make space on the sofa for him to slide down beside Stacey. He draped his arm on the back of the couch, his hand touching her shoulder, and took a long swig from his own can of beer. "Want one?"

Underage drinking. Forget grounding; Daddy would simply shoot her.

"I'm not thirsty."

As Noah carried on a conversation with someone else, his fingers traced Stacey's contours. He played with the collar of her hoodie, tickled the side of her neck, and drew curving shapes on her upper arm. Wanting to be subtle in the crowded room, Stacey reached up to brush back her hair while trying to push his hand aside. He misinterpreted the move, caught her fingers in his, and slanted a sexy smile at her.

Stacey shrank deeper into the sofa, wishing she could melt into the scratchy upholstery. She managed to reclaim her fingers and clasped both hands in her lap.

Where is Zoe?

Darla and Nathan leaned against a wall by the kitchen entrance, kissing and fondling. Stacey tried to watch the television but her eyes kept drifting back to the couple. Her racing heart sent a tightness to her throat she couldn't swallow down.

Zoe came out of the kitchen, laughing and flipping her hair. Just behind her was a bearded guy wearing a knit cap. At least a foot taller than her. Zoe had found her college guy, although he was anything but hot. She'd also found the beer.

A montage of baseball bloopers on TV had the others laughing. A player slid on the outfield grass and ended up in a split, which prompted a loud "Oh!" from every guy in the apartment. Stacey watched and tried to relax. Yet the beer-tainted air was too heavy to breathe.

Okay, so a few people were drinking, and one couple got a little frisky in public view. It wasn't anything terrible. Maybe she just needed some fresh air to settle her nerves.

Stacey eased off the couch and picked her way through the room to a sliding glass door. It was locked, and the latch wouldn't cooperate with her fumbling fingers. When at last she figured it out, she flung the door open harder than she'd intended.

People stopped talking and stared.

Now completely unable to breathe, Stacey shot forward. She

grabbed the balcony rail and sucked in humid air, ignoring the wood splinters poking her palms. The ground below seemed to vibrate, moving toward her then receding.

"Hey, what's wrong?" Noah asked.

She refused to look at him even when he rested a hand on her waist and tried to turn her toward him.

"I ... I'm scared."

"Of what? Your parents?"

She'd told him just enough to explain why she was away from home without her purse or car. At one statement, "My parents are driving me insane," Noah had nodded in complete understanding.

"What am I doing here? Noah, I already have a boyfriend."

"So where is he?"

"Huh?"

She glanced at him, expecting to find jealousy in his eyes. Instead a sly smile touched his perfect lips, like he was about to reveal a secret. Why did he have to be so cute?

"You called me," he said. "Why not him?"

"B-because he wasn't home."

"So you're cheating on him?"

"No. My father said he couldn't—uh ..." *Why is this happening to me?*

Stacey looked back into the living room. Zoe and that other guy had taken her spot on the couch, sitting too close for two people who'd just met.

"You called me," Noah repeated, edging closer. "I figured that meant something."

"I-I like you, Noah. But—"

The smile turned to a boyish pout. "So you used me to get away from your parents. 'Cause that other guy wasn't around."

"No. I mean—"

Noah swore softly and stepped away from her. "That's great, Stacey. What am I supposed to do?"

"Can't we just be friends?"

He leaned into the corner of the balcony railing and crossed his ankles. "Maybe I don't want to be just friends."

Stacey pressed a hand to her forehead and found it clammy. Dizziness threatened again. Her stomach was an open pit swirling with acid. *Not again. Please.*

"Noah, I'm sorry. I didn't mean to —"

"To what? Use me?"

"C-can we just sit down?" She swayed.

"Whoa, hey. You okay?" He came away from the rail and clasped her arm, steadying her.

"I need to eat. Can I have some bread or something?"

"Bread? Uh, sure. Nathan's got salsa and chips in the kitchen."

When had she last allowed anything to stay in her stomach, other than water? She couldn't remember. She needed bread, bland and dense, that would sit in her stomach and suck up all the acid. A single slice would do.

Noah led her to the kitchen and pointed to a picked-over bowl of chunky salsa and an almost-empty bag of tortilla chips. "There's that. And the beer. Anything else ... look around." He abruptly turned and left her standing there.

She couldn't blame him for being angry. It was her fault for letting Zoe talk her into calling him. Sure, Daddy wouldn't be able to find her, but now she was stuck. She glanced around the room for a phone. Nothing but dirty dishes, beer, and the salsa.

No salsa — that would burn. And who knew who had been double-dipping in the stuff? Stacey reached for the refrigerator handle. Something sticky made it hard to open — or maybe she was so weak that a stupid refrigerator door taxed her.

The door made a sucking noise as it opened, and the moment the refrigerator light spilled out, Zoe was beside Stacey.

"What are you doing?" Zoe's glare was like a storm cloud dragged into the kitchen. "What did you say to Noah?"

Stacey didn't want to discuss it.

Before her sat carryout containers, cans of soda, and lunchmeat with dried and curled edges. Beyond nasty. And no bread. Maybe they kept it in a cabinet ... which meant it was probably moldy. Stacey gagged.

"Zoe, are you still dieting?"

"Yeah. Are you cheating on yours?"

Stacey slammed the refrigerator door. "Well, stop. It'll make you sick."

"No it won't. You just have to follow the plan. But forget that. What did you do to Noah? He flew out of here spitting words I'm sure you don't want me to repeat."

"He can't handle jealousy. Can I borrow your cell phone?"

Zoe rammed her fists onto her hips. "Why?"

"To call for pizza," Stacey snapped. "There's nothing to eat here."

"You're not calling for pizza, you're fixing to call Calvin."

"So what if I do? Just because you and Noah can't handle the fact that I have a boyfriend doesn't mean I'm going to change the way I feel."

Zoe spat out her own choice words.

"Just let me use the phone. Please?"

"No. You're going to ask Calvin to come get you. Why can't you just have some fun? Why does everything have to be about stupid Calvin?"

"You can stay. I don't care. Go talk to Noah."

"You're throwing away that gorgeous guy for some dumpy farm boy. I told you before, Stacey, you stay with Calvin, you'll end up married and fat with a pack of babies hanging all over you."

Nathan came into the kitchen, his thick eyebrows raised. "Hey, what's going on?"

Stacey ignored him. "Maybe I *want* to marry Calvin and have babies with him."

"You're joking, right?"

"Maybe I don't want to go to fashion design school. Maybe I really want to draw and paint and put my artwork in museums."

"You did *not* just say that."

Nathan put both arms between them and nudged them apart. "Okay, the two of you brought way too much drama into my place. Back off, ladies."

Zoe shifted over so she could still glare at Stacey. "Fine. I'll just go tell Noah he better stay away from you."

"Go. I don't care."

"And I am *not* going to California or New York with you."

Stacey shrugged. "I didn't want to go anyway."

A vile name flew out of Zoe's mouth as she whirled away with her palms raised.

Stacey sniffed. Every part of her trembled. She realized Nathan still stood there, looking down at her.

"So, I guess you're not really my little brother's new girlfriend," he said.

That made her want to laugh. She shook her head instead.

Nathan pursed his lips for a moment. "He'll get over it. He always does."

Stacey shook her hair away from her face. "Where is he? I'll talk to him."

"Bedroom or bathroom. I saw him go into the hallway."

Two places she really didn't want to be alone with Noah Dickerson. Oh well. She'd just apologize nicely and ask him to take her home. It might not be a fun drive, and there'd be a bigger problem waiting at home, but at least she could put this night behind her.

Stacey left the kitchen and turned down a short hallway. The first door she found was closed, while the other opened to a surprisingly neat bedroom with a large bed. A cell phone sat on the nightstand, plugged into its charger. Stacey glanced over her shoulder then strode across the room to pick up the phone. She loosed it from the charger and turned it on.

"What are you doing?"

She spun to face Noah, hiding the phone behind her back. "I was looking for you."

"In here? Did you change your mind?" He stepped closer.

"Oh!" She slipped the phone into her hoodie pocket and put both hands up to ward him off. "No. I mean—"

He frowned and stopped short. "Zoe's out on the balcony cursing the birds. You're having a pretty good night, aren't you? I mean, if you planned to alienate all your friends."

"I'm sorry, Noah. I didn't mean to lead you on."

"Sure you did—that's how you get your way. That's how all girls get their way. It's cool. I get it. Maybe I should be glad you told me so soon."

"Noah—"

"Thing is, I usually get something in return. You know?"

"Don't. Please."

"Come on, Stacey. You wanted to do something tonight so you wouldn't have to deal with your parents. And you called me." He shrugged one shoulder and edged closer. "It's okay. I won't force you into anything."

"Thank you."

"One little kiss, though? Your other boyfriend will never know about it." He managed to get an arm past her barrier.

Stacey planted her hands against his shoulder and chest. "Noah, no."

He broke through her defense with little effort, and roughly pulled her next to him and covered her open mouth with his. She tasted the beer he'd been drinking. The bedroom swayed as her joints turned to mush. This wasn't romance; it wasn't even lust. If Noah's arms weren't holding her, she'd tumble to the floor.

And someone would call 9-1-1.

Stacey struggled to keep herself alert as she fought Noah off. Her teeth scraped the top of his tongue. He grunted and shoved her away.

"That hurt!" Noah pressed his hand to his mouth then pulled it away. Blood tinged his skin. "What is your problem, woman?"

She ran. Someone in the living room bellowed a protest, and she heard Zoe call her name. Stacey hit the door with both hands and found the knob. Everything looked fuzzy as she lurched toward the steps. Hands alternately clasping and flying over the stair rail, she stumbled down two flights.

A voice from above yelled something, and another person's laughter followed.

Stacey staggered into the parking lot. Woods to the left made it too dark to see any kind of path. What happened to the daylight? She collided with a dumpster. Should've smelled it coming. She pinched her nose and felt her way around the side.

Rats. There would be rats. And a billion gazillion germs.

She squealed and pushed away. Streetlamp light glinted off parked cars, giving her something to aim for. She waded through the narrow space between the bumpers and a hedge until something metal bashed her shin and pitched her forward. Stacey collapsed to the asphalt, curled up, and grabbed her lower leg. Something wet and hot oozed between her fingers.

She held her breath so she wouldn't scream.

Chapter 36

Calvin moved slowly, the cup of hot chocolate in his hands filled almost to the brim. He eased the mug down near the computer keyboard, an act that would have drawn a reprimand if his family wasn't at church. He settled into the chair, turned on the computer, and sipped while the computer booted up. The hot chocolate soothed his raw throat.

Scamp squeezed under the desk and lay down, his warm fur tickling Calvin's toes.

Desperate for anything to take his mind off Stacey, Calvin went to his Facebook page. A message and three notifications waited for him, but his eyes drifted down the page to the spot that stated "In a relationship with Stacey Varnell." He couldn't change it last week, making the breakup official for all his 216 Internet friends to see.

Single.

Calvin's throat and chest constricted around the weight of that word.

Had Stacey changed her relationship status? He went to her page, and immediately wished he hadn't. Her profile photo arrested his eyes. Taken from a downward angle before she'd put the pink streaks in her hair, her cheek pressed against his, her eyes sultry and her lips puckered, like she was about to kiss him. Which she had after the shot. A silly, happy moment in time when things were normal between them.

Beneath her picture, her relationship status still listed his name.

"Stace," he whispered. The webpage blurred as his eyes filled with tears. His heart cried out for "normal."

Where are you, Stace?

Nothing he could do. Let her parents take care of her—that's what everyone was saying. Tyler, Mom, Peyton ... But no one was telling him what to do with the worry and the pain.

Clicking away from Stacey's page ripped something out of him. He swallowed hard to open his airway then clicked on his waiting message to occupy his mind with something else.

His cousin Trevor wrote, *Where you been? Reached level eighty. Bring it on, dude!*

Hours of mind-numbing online gaming certainly work. He could melt into his character and forget everything else.

Calvin shook unwashed hair out of his eyes and clicked to the bookmarked website. A familiar logo flashed on a black screen then faded away while an alien landscape slowly appeared, revealing twin moons in a red sky along with a band of human freedom fighters marching through a ravine toward the twisted spires of a city.

He looped the headset over his head, positioned the speakers against his ears, and clicked through to the login screen. But he paused, his finger hovering above the mouse button.

Would Stacey be online? Waiting for him in her gaming guise of Shiyama Lee?

Crazy thinking. If she'd run away from home, she wouldn't be messing around on a computer. She hadn't even played in months.

"Where are you?"

A sense of smallness came over him. The world outside was so huge, and Stacey walked somewhere in it, beyond his reach. Dancing pixels on a screen could never drive that reality from his head.

Calvin flopped back in his chair, whipped off the headset and tossed it on top of the keyboard. He stared at the telephone in its cradle on the desk. The silent phone.

He grabbed it and punched in Stacey's cell number again. Same result. Calvin tugged his hair. It had been two hours since her mother had called. Would anyone remember to call him back if they found her? Gritting his teeth, he dialed the Varnells' home number. The phone rang once before someone answered.

"Hello," Stacey's father snapped.

"Uh, hi. It's Calvin."

"Calvin. Is Stacey with you?" Officer Varnell's question answered so many others.

"No. I was hoping you'd have news."

"No one knows where Zoe is either. Where would they go? Who do they hang out with?"

Zoe. Figured. Calvin tried to think. "I can call some people, but I'm not sure—"

"Do that, would you?"

"Yes, I—"

Zoe. Fashion design school. California? She wouldn't. Maybe ... go to Noah's?

Calvin stiffened. Was it possible Stacey was with Noah?

Half the girls at school might have that jerk's phone number. Calvin's free hand snapped into a fist. If Noah Dickerson was responsible for all this—

"Why didn't she call you?" Officer Varnell asked. "You're her boyfriend."

Maybe because you said we couldn't see each other anymore?

"If my wife hadn't spoken to your mother earlier—"

What? The man suspected Calvin and Stacey were running away together?

"I don't understand any of this," Officer Varnell said. "Why did

348

she drive all the way to that state park? And now this? What's going on between you two?"

Calvin unclenched his fist and clawed his head. "We had a big argument last week."

"And that's why she's acting this way?"

"I don't know. I think the anorexia is weirding her out."

"Weird is right. But we're putting a stop to that. If you hear from her or see her, make sure you let me know."

"I will. And could you call me—Uh, hello?"

Officer Varnell had hung up on him. Calvin pulled the phone away from his ear and looked at it. Scamp sat up and rested his head on Calvin's knee. Trying to comfort him. Calvin returned the phone to its cradle and tickled the dog's ears.

Who could he call? He mentally ran down the list of his friends. She wouldn't call Tyler or Flannery. No way. And she didn't really have a lot of friends at school other than Zoe. And Noah. What about friends she'd had in Rocky Mount? She hadn't told Calvin much about them.

He remembered a line from one of her poems: *My life began when our paths crossed.* He'd taken it as a kind of romantic awakening, but what if she was saying something more and he'd missed it?

Calvin paced away from the desk.

Let her family take care of her. Yeah, right.

He hung his head. "God, please keep her safe. And help me figure out a way to find her."

Calvin sniffed. His sinuses throbbed. He drew several deep breaths through his mouth then headed toward the kitchen for a paper towel.

The phone rang before he was three steps away.

Calvin lunged for it, colliding with the desk. The caller ID was unfamiliar.

"Hello?"

Static on the line and a loud snuffling sound. "Calvin?" Stacey's voice was a whimper.

"Stacey! Where are you? Are you okay?"

"Calvin." Her breathing became more ragged.

"I'm here. Can you hear me?"

"Can you come get me?"

He started looking for a pad of paper. "Where are you?"

"Dawson. My leg is bleeding."

"Your leg? Is it bad? Do you need an ambulance?"

"No. Please come get me. I ... I can't go back in there."

"In where? Who's with you?"

"Nobody. I left. Hurry, Calvin. This really hurts."

"Call 9 – 1 – 1."

"No! They'll call my parents! Running away is a capital offense!"

Calvin flinched. What? Capital offense?

Her next words were soft, almost breathy. "Can't you come? Please?"

"Stace—Yes. Okay. Where are you?"

"I can't stay here. I'm going to the store."

"What store?"

"By the street. Um. On Highway 301."

"Highway 301 is in Rocky Mount. You said you were in Dawson. Which is it?"

"Dawson. By a college. There's a-a ... Taco Bell. I'll be in the parking lot. Calvin, please hurry. I don't want anyone to find me."

Highway 301? In Dawson? That road snaked all the way into South Carolina and Georgia, but he couldn't remember if it went through Dawson. Pretty far south, if it did.

"It'll take me twenty minutes just to get to the mall in Dawson. I really think you should call nine—"

"Just come! Hurry."

The muscles in Calvin's jaw twitched. "On my way."

He took the stairs up to his room three at a time. His jeans and T-shirt lay on the floor where he'd dropped them, riding boots at the foot of the bed. He threw the clothes on then flew back downstairs.

The family had taken Mom's van to church, leaving Dad's pickup in the driveway.

But where were the keys?

He checked the usual spots: the hook by the door, a cluttered corner of the kitchen countertop, the end table in the living room, the top of the antique curio cabinet. Nothing. He flung open the door to his parents' bedroom and checked the nightstands and a pair of his father's pants draped across the end of the bed.

No keys.

Still in the ignition? Calvin flew outside and peered into the truck cab. Not there.

Probably in Dad's pocket.

Calvin swore then ran to the workshop. The camping and riding gear was stacked up where he'd left it. Calvin grabbed his filthy helmet and an older one off the shelf. Stacey wouldn't like it, but too bad. He looped a bungee cord through the second helmet strap and secured it to the Yamaha's seat.

The bike started after several kicks and backfired. His breath coming fast and hot, Calvin revved the bike to life then roared down the driveway and turned right. He'd have to get on the Interstate. Going by country roads would nearly double the time it'd take for him to get to Dawson.

The feeble light from the Yamaha's headlamp bounced on the road ahead of him, as if responding to his thudding heart. Past rush hour, so traffic on the Interstate shouldn't be heavy. He could push the bike to highway speed. Maybe. He'd only done it for short distances before. And with the engine running rough . . .

He envisioned Stacey bleeding somewhere.

Just getting to the Interstate seemed to take forever. He felt swallowed up by the dark country roads, as if he'd made a wrong turn somehow and was heading into flat, endless tobacco fields. Finally, a blue sign appeared on the side of the road. Calvin leaned hard onto the entrance ramp.

"Help me get there and not get killed on the way." The prayer seemed trapped in his helmet. The Yamaha sputtered on the ramp, but then hit its power band and accelerated. Wind battered Calvin's body and hands. He glanced at the traffic, chose his spot, and merged onto I–95. The Yamaha's engine screamed beneath him.

A refrain beat in his head along with the whine: *Keep away from the cars. Stay far, far away from trucks.* A blast of wind from a semi could toss him right off the road. The bike was way too light for this kind of riding.

An SUV flew past him doing at least eighty. Calvin held tight, bent toward his handlebars, and angled into the air blast like a surfer riding a wave. His heart hammered in his throat. He'd have a coronary and die if he didn't get run over first. He glanced down at his odometer. He'd managed to get up to sixty, though the tachometer was redlining. He couldn't go any faster or he'd blow the engine.

A car behind him swerved around. Its passenger gave him a nasty look.

Roadkill. I'm gonna be a grease spot on the pavement.

Three headlights set close together glared in his rearview mirror. A big motorcycle zoomed up behind him. Remembering rules from his driving test, Calvin slid to the right so the two bikes were staggered. He expected the other motorcycle to pass, but it stayed there, close to his rear. Roaring pipes competed with the pathetic whine of the Yamaha. Some big Harley protecting him?

"Thank you, Jesus!"

Highway 301 — that's what she said. Past the mall? Gotta be. Please let it be.

Every mile felt like ten, like he was pedaling a bicycle on the highway while the traffic flew around him. His muscles ached and his head pounded as if it were about to explode inside his helmet.

Calvin passed the Redville Road exit, the last turnoff in Stiles County. A new sound, a long beep, managed to pierce the roaring, and the other motorcycle was alongside him in a split second. The rider tried to yell something at him over the massive rumble of his pipes, then frantically waved his left arm. Universal body language for "Get off the road!" Calvin hunched his shoulders and looked away from the man. The guy might be protecting him, but he also didn't understand why this risk was so vital. A moment later the three headlights were in his mirror again.

At last he saw the first sign for Highway 301. Calvin tried to breathe normally. *Gas, food, lodging, three miles. Awesome. Blue sign with an "H." Hospital. Might need that.*

The Yamaha struggled. The power had dropped off and he'd lost ten miles per hour, though he kept the throttle cranked all the way open. Traffic flew past him on the left. A semi went by. Calvin screamed and fought to keep the bike from getting tossed by the rolling vortex behind those eighteen wheels.

Back in control and still alive. For now. Provided he didn't hyperventilate and pass out.

He swerved up the ramp heading to Highway 301. The Harley behind him continued on the Interstate.

Calvin eased off the throttle as he topped the ramp. His wrist ached. At the stoplight, he shook out his hand, but the motorcycle's engine sputtered. He grabbed the throttle and held it steady to keep the bike running. The light turned green, and even though he accelerated hard the bike slogged through the intersection as Calvin guided it toward a cluster of restaurants and motels.

A police car sat at a gas station exit. Almost no other traffic on the road to distract the cop. Calvin looked away from the squad car and cruised by. *Nothing to see here. I'm just some guy out for an evening ride.*

There, on the left, a building with red awnings and the signature bell logo. Calvin pulled into the middle turn lane and waited for a pickup truck to pass by. Was Stacey in the lot somewhere, watching him? He could see three cars parked there, but no one standing around.

The way clear, Calvin chugged across the street and into the parking lot and rolled to a stop near the building entrance. The bike in neutral idled beneath him ... barely.

He swiveled around. "Stacey?"

A woman came out of the building and walked past him, digging keys out of her purse and juggling two sacks of food.

"Excuse me? Have you seen a girl with pink hair?"

The woman did a stagger-step and looked at him. "Pink hair?" She shook her head and moved on to her car.

Sure, go ahead. Look at me like I'm crazy.

Forget the woman by her car. Forget what anyone would think. "Stacey!" he shouted.

No answer.

Exhaustion hit him like a cement wall. He leaned forward and blew out hoarse breaths against his gas tank. His hands shook and tremors ran through the muscles in his biceps, back, and inner thighs.

"You brought the bike?"

He whipped his head up. Stacey must have come from the other side of the building. Calvin squinted. Either she was swaying, or his vision was seriously messed up.

"Had to. Are you okay?"

Hugging herself, Stacey staggered toward him. "I can't ride. I'm wearing a dress."

Calvin couldn't stifle his laugh. "Thank you for coming to get me, Calvin. Thanks for riding in the dark, taking your dirt bike on the highway with all the trucks and the crazy drivers, risking your life to—"

She threw her arms around his shoulders. Her body shook with sobs. "I'm sorry, I'm sorry! Just take me away from here. I'll explain everything."

With one arm, he pulled her closer. As much as his helmet allowed, he tucked his face between her neck and shoulder, feeling like sobbing along with her. Or like breaking her.

Her embrace pushed the motorcycle off balance, so Calvin released her and put the kickstand down. He swung his leg over the seat and, keeping her near him, messed with the bungee cord that strapped her helmet down.

Could she tuck her skirt underneath her? It was loose and long-ish—Calvin's eyes went wide. Her black tights were destroyed and streaks of blood ran down her right leg, shining, fresh. She'd left drops on the sidewalk.

Calvin swallowed back bile. "Hold up! What did you do to your leg?"

"I hit something."

"Uh, ah, you need an ambulance."

Stacey took the helmet from his hands, but collapsed against him so he could do nothing but hold her.

"Just take me away. Take me somewhere where we never have to come back. I don't ever want to be apart from you again."

"That's crazy." He tried to keep his tone gentle while everything inside him screamed. "I'll take you to the hospital. You probably need stitches."

"I can't let you go!"

"Good. Get on the bike and hold on tight."

"Calvin—"

Enough. He shut his eyes and let his frustration boil. "Get on, or I'm leaving you here!"

It worked. Although Stacey moved sluggishly, she strapped on the helmet and climbed onto the bike behind him.

"Where's the hospital?" Revving the bike to keep the engine running, he had to yell.

He didn't hear her answer, if she gave one. Her thin hands slipped up to his chest and she hung on as if she was hugging him tight. Good enough.

The bike chugged and stuttered under the weight of two people. Calvin drove around the back of the restaurant, past the drive-through window, and then back down to the street. He looked left and right up the road. To the right, past the interstate, he saw very few lights. To the left, something that looked like it might be a sign for a hospital; official, not bright and garish.

"Calvin, the bike is burning my leg," Stacey whined.

"Turn your knee out, and hang on. We're going."

The motorcycle couldn't reach anywhere near the speed limit on the road. It limped along for a quarter of a mile, past the sign Calvin thought might be the hospital. It wasn't, but it was a medical building, which meant they were close. Stacey squeaked his name in his ear.

"Hold on! Almost there."

There, past another gas station, a red and white sign saying EMERGENCY.

"Thank you, Jesus!"

The Yamaha barely crawled up the driveway. It lumbered over a speed bump about as fast as if he'd got off and pushed it. Even at that low speed Stacey squealed. Her grip loosened, and Calvin put his feet out to keep them from falling.

Twenty more yards. That's all it would take. He could see light shining through a wide bank of windows, and a covered driveway where ambulances would park. Just one more tiny hill . . .

The Yamaha coughed and died. Out of fuel or just done.

"You need to get off," Calvin said over his shoulder. "I have to push it to a parking space."

Stacey nearly fell climbing off the back, staggered backward, then righted herself and smoothed her dress.

Calvin's stomach clenched again at the sight of her bloody leg. She didn't seem to be able to lift her head all the way up, as if the helmet were too heavy. This was more than a cut leg.

He pointed toward the emergency room. "Go on up there. I'll catch up."

Stacey nodded, her chin almost touching her chest. She limped to the sidewalk.

He got off his bike and leaned into the handlebars to push. Something clunked on the sidewalk. Calvin looked, and his heart jumped to his throat.

Stacey lay facedown on the ground. The noise had been her helmet smacking the concrete.

Chapter 37

He screamed her name as the bike fell from his hands and crashed to the ground. Calvin leaped over the Yamaha, tripped at the curb, and crawled the rest of the way to Stacey's side.

She didn't respond to his touch or voice, even when he rolled her onto her back and fumbled with her helmet latch. "Stacey, come on. Don't do this, please. Wake up."

He dropped the helmet. Stacey's head lolled to an awkward angle. Her eyes remained shut while her mouth hung open.

"Oh, God."

Calvin thrust his arms under her shoulders and knees then struggled to his feet. He fast-walked toward the ER doors. A shocking thought flashed through his mind—Stacey weighed about the same as one of his little brothers.

The automatic doors whooshed open.

"Help! Somebody help!"

A nurse jumped up from her station, spilling papers onto the floor.

"ER admitting area, stat," someone yelled.

A woman's face appeared in front of Calvin. "What happened?"

"Sh-she passed out. And she's bleeding bad. Her leg."

Metallic sounds approached as someone hurried over with a gurney. A man helped Calvin place Stacey on top of the white sheets;

her face almost matched the color of the linens. A dark-uniformed EMT pressed his fingers hard into Stacey's throat.

"No pulse. Code blue. Cardiac arrest. Get her inside."

Calvin felt his pulse quicken. "What? What did you say?"

Someone grabbed his arm as others pushed the gurney away. Calvin tried to shove the hand off his bicep and follow. The grip turned hard.

"They'll take care of her. But right now I need to talk to you."

Calvin jerked his arm away, but another nurse joined the first, creating a small barrier.

"Calm down. The best way to help your friend right now is to give us information so we know how to help her."

Calvin pointed at the double doors closing behind Stacey's gurney. "What's that mean, code blue, cardiac arrest?"

"It means she's in serious trouble."

"But she-she was fine. She gashed her leg open. She was walking just—" The room began closing in, trying to choke him.

"All right. Take some deep breaths. Come into the office and sit down."

Gasping, Calvin tried to make sense of what he'd heard. *Cardiac arrest.* Her heart stopped beating? It had to be a mistake.

A nurse led him toward an office cubicle, her hand looped around his elbow. "You brought her here on a motorcycle?"

"Huh?"

She gave him a small smile. "You're wearing a helmet. Sit down. Tell me what happened. Did you have an accident?"

Calvin felt the arm of a chair nudge the back of his leg. He plunked into the seat then fumbled with his helmet strap.

"Did you have a motorcycle accident?" the nurse asked again, sitting down on the other side of a desk.

"No. Sh-she was fine, like, two minutes ago. But her leg was bleeding."

"What's her name?"

"Stacey Varnell."

"How old is she?"

"Uh, sixteen."

This was crazy. Impossible. How could she walk or ride the bike if—?

"Has she been drinking or taking any drugs? The more truthful you are, the better the doctors can help her."

Calvin settled back into the chair and shook his head. "No. I-I don't think so."

"You don't think so? It's very important that you tell me. If she's overdosing on something, we need to know."

He couldn't catch his breath. Where had she been? Could she have been doing drugs or something with Zoe? "I don't know what she did today. But she doesn't take drugs or drink."

"What's your relationship with her?"

"B-boyfriend." *Ex. Doesn't matter.*

"But you don't know what she did today?"

Calvin wanted to pull his hair out. "I don't know! She called me to come get her. " He looked at the partition and flopped his hand down on top of the desk. "She's anorexic. And she hurt her leg somehow. That's all I know."

The woman clasped her hands on the desk, more frustrated than compassionate. "Anorexia can result in heart failure."

Calvin slapped the arms of the chair and bolted from his seat. He ran toward the ER doors, ignoring the people who yelled at him to stop. He hit the door with his shoulder; it rattled but wouldn't open. On the wall was a keypad. The system was designed to keep him out.

"Young man, you have to calm down! None of this is going to help her."

At least three women had their hands on him. Other people in the waiting room stared. A large man even rose from a chair and took a step toward him.

"All right! All right. I'm calm. I just need to know what's happening in there."

"Sweetie?" Another woman wearing scrubs demanded his attention. "I know this isn't easy. But if you go back and sit down, I'll try to find out what's going on."

Defeated, Calvin followed the original nurse back to the little office. He plopped down in the chair and answered all of her questions, saying "I don't know" to many of them. Around the time they were both getting frustrated again, he gave the woman Stacey's home phone number and waited while she took it to someone else. Finally, she directed him to the waiting area and promised that a nurse or doctor would talk to him soon.

Another nurse found him in the waiting room and sat beside him. Calvin sucked in his lips and bounced his knee, waiting for her news.

She let out a slight laugh. "Honey, you really need to relax. I know you're worried, but you're starting to worry *me*." Her face then turned serious. "Now, listen. She was in cardiac arrest, but she's got good doctors working with her. I'm sure she'll be okay."

"Cardiac — But she's — " He remembered something, and tugged his hair as he spoke it. "Sh-she had surgery on her heart, when she was a baby. But she's supposed to be fine now."

The nurse's eyebrows shot up briefly. "I'll go relay that to the doctor. Just you sit tight here, and someone will come talk to you when they've got more news."

She patted his knee, and Calvin nodded. Nothing else he could do.

For ten agonizing minutes he stared at a talking head on television, but ringing in his ears kept him from comprehending what was said. A commercial showed some guy riding a motorcycle, and

Calvin remembered his own bike lying in the driveway where a car could run over it. He dragged himself to the admitting desk and spoke, not caring if the person behind the desk was paying attention. "I'm going outside for a minute. I'll be right back."

Someone had picked his bike up and moved it to the curb. Calvin straddled the seat and brought his foot down on the kick-start lever. It wouldn't budge. He tried again. The lever seemed frozen in place. He'd bust it if he put all his weight on it.

"What the — ?"

Calvin popped open the gas cap and shook the bike while peering into the dark hole. Liquid sloshed inside.

Stupid. Being out of fuel wouldn't cause the kick-start lever to freeze anyway.

But the frozen lever could mean the engine had seized.

Calvin slowly replaced the gas cap, his own body and movements seeming far away. The Yamaha was dead. He'd pushed it too hard while it was running lean and he shouldn't have been riding it at all.

He looked around the parking lot, breathed in night air that smelled like diesel fuel and honeysuckle combined. Sickening. He wasn't sleeping in his bed having a cold medicine-induced dream. He was in Dawson. Awake, emotionally and physically wrecked, with a dead bike. And Stacey ...

A siren wailed, getting louder. In a moment the ambulance passed him and went under the overhang. Calvin watched, numb, as EMTs rushed around to move someone inside.

No one noticed him sitting there on his lifeless motorcycle with tears running down his face. Not that they would care even if they looked. There were more important things than a stupid old bike. People inside were fighting for their lives. People like Stacey.

∘ ○ ◯ ◯ ∘

Her parents arrived and rushed past Calvin without looking at him. Sure, the parents were sent immediately into the ER to see what was going on, but he had to wait. He was just the lowly boyfriend.

He should call his own parents. What time was it? Not that it mattered; they'd be furious no matter what. Exhaustion weighed on Calvin as he got up. He found a pay phone in a hallway around the corner.

"Where are you?" Dad growled as soon as he heard Calvin's voice. "We trusted you to stay—"

Calvin leaned into the little phone cubby and spoke softly. "I'm sorry. I'm at a hospital in Dawson."

"What?"

"I'm fine. It's Stacey. She's really sick. They said ..." He sniffed. "They said she had a heart attack."

"Calv—"

Words tumbled out, and with them more tears. "They won't let me see her. I don't know what's going on. I brought her here because she cut her leg real bad. But she fell on the sidewalk, and-and—"

"Slow down, son."

"Dad? Dad. Can you come here? I, um, I don't have any way to get home."

A crackling noise came over the line. "Calvin? What's going on?" his mother asked. She'd picked up the extension.

He ran through the whole story and was choked up again when he finished. He leaned his forehead against the wall, snuffling, the phone receiver pressed hard to his ear.

"Calvin?" Mom said. "Your father is on his way out the door. He'll be there soon. It's okay."

"No, it isn't. She could be dying. If her heart stopped—"

"Listen to me, baby. A terrible thing has happened, but you need to believe that God is in control. God is with her."

He closed his burning eyes while she went on.

"When we got home from church, I felt like the Lord was calling me to pray and pray and pray. And that's what you ought to be doing right now. While you're waiting for your father, be praying for Stacey."

"Okay," he muttered.

"Do it, Calvin."

"I will."

"Stacey's right where she needs to be, with all those doctors, because God got the two of you there. Don't you doubt that for a second."

Calvin blinked and his breath stalled. "Yes, ma'am," he heard himself say.

"You hang in there. I'm looking out the window now, and your daddy's backed the truck out to the street. He's on his way. He'll be there soon."

"Okay."

"It's going to be all right, baby."

"Yeah." He sniffed. "Okay." Calvin hung up the pay phone.

God is in control ...

Had God really arranged it so that he was able to find Stacey in time? The Harley rider on the Interstate who stayed with him—had that guy been responding to what Mom called a divine nudge?

Calvin rocked his head back and forth slowly. He didn't know. He'd never witnessed a miracle, never felt that kind of nudge. Yet if someone asked him if he believed in miracles, he'd say yes, absolutely.

What would have happened if Stacey had passed out before he found her? Or while they were still on the bike? And the Yamaha had made it to the hospital. *Just* that far.

Calvin squeezed his eyes shut, pinched the bridge of his clogged nose. *God ... I want to believe! Help me to believe. I—I can't do anything else. I'm done. I don't know what else to do.* Calvin pressed his fingers against his eyes to block the renewed flood of tears. *I have to trust you, because I don't have anything left. Nothing but this prayer.*

Calvin scrubbed his face with his hands and shuffled back to his seat in the waiting area. Several other people sat staring into space, waiting like him, not talking to each other. Dull minds focused on one thing: a hospital staff person walking into the room and calling their name. Calvin slouched way down and stretched his legs out. He closed his eyes, and despite all the worry and the grief, his body grew heavy and relaxed.

○ ◯ ◯ ◯ ○

"Hey, buddy." Someone patted his knee. Calvin jolted to alertness and his gaze darted around the room.

Dad sat next to him. "What's happening?"

Calvin pulled himself up in the chair and rubbed his eyes. "Still waiting," he muttered.

"I got here quick as I could. There are two hospitals in Dawson. I went to the other one first."

Calvin frowned. How long had he been sleeping?

A nurse came through the ER doors, carrying a clipboard. "Hildebrandt family? Varnell family?"

With a shock, Calvin realized he'd heard Stacey's last name called before, eking into his feeble thoughts and dreams. Stupid. He'd expected them to call Greenlee. He untangled his legs from themselves and got to his feet. Dad rose with him. They walked to the nurse, who directed the other family through the ER doors first, with a promise to be right with them. She touched Calvin's arm to keep him from following. "Wait. Varnell? They've moved the patient to a room in the critical care unit. You can go upstairs to the CCU waiting room, and they'll give you more information there."

Calvin looked up at his father and let out a shuddering breath. "She's alive."

Chapter 38

Tubes and needles everywhere. And Daddy standing over her. Dim light cast deep shadows in the lines of his face, especially around his frown. Stacey thought she saw a tear roll down his cheek, but she couldn't be sure. So hard to keep her eyes open.

Stuff hurt. Like a truck had slammed into her chest. Yet the pain seemed far away, as if her consciousness was somehow separated from her body. A dream danced through her memory. Was it real? She couldn't remember. The parking lot, Calvin, getting off the back of his bike. Then the pain. Had a car hit them?

She didn't want to remember, but she needed to know. "C—"

"Try not to talk, baby." Mom's voice. "Just rest. Daddy and I are here."

"C ... Ca ... win." Something in her mouth wouldn't let her make the right sounds.

"He's in the waiting room," Mom said.

Stacey couldn't see her mother, couldn't move her head toward the direction of the voice.

"He's been here all night, him and his daddy."

"Wan ... see ... h-mm."

"He was in here a little while ago, before you woke up."

A warm touch on her shoulder, stroking her arm. Mom laughed

a little. "I don't think that boy is going anywhere else for a while. He's so worried about you. But you're going to be okay, baby. You're going to be just fine."

But what happened?

She ran the images through her mind again. The wind in her face, taking her breath away as she rode with Calvin. And then he stopped the bike and she tried to walk toward the bright windows. The pain came and dragged her down, tried to keep her from reaching the light. She had to get there ... to the light brighter than any she had seen. Love was in the light, warming her and breathing life into her. A presence embraced her, flowed through her, lifted her.

A voice came with the softness of a whisper but the power of a shout. *Not yet. This is not the end for you, nor the life I want you to live.*

Machinery beeped. Tubes lay across her face and one went down her throat. She was in a bed again, and Mom spoke words she couldn't understand.

What? Take care of me? I want to go back.

It couldn't have been a dream.

She recalled something else too. People rushing about barking orders, someone bouncing on her chest. Big paddles against her skin. A jolt that lifted her from the table.

Oh, God! Oh, God! "Di ... I die?"

Daddy sniffed and looked away.

Mom renewed her stroking. "They had to resuscitate you, baby. But you're okay now. And we're going to fix it so it never happens again."

So the part with the paddles was real. Vivid pictures played out behind her eyelids. She looked down on a skinny thing lying naked on the table. Bones everywhere. That couldn't be her. Could it? How was it possible for her to see herself?

How was it possible she hadn't been able to truly see herself before?

"S-sorry."

"We love you, baby. We love you so much," Mom cooed.

"Okay."

Mom chuckled again. "Okay that we love you? Okay. I guess that's okay."

It'd have to be. She didn't have the strength for anything more.

○ ○ ◯ ○ ○

The murmured conversation outside her room was just loud enough for her to know her parents were talking to a doctor about what would happen next. One word stood out and planted itself in her mind. *Charlotte.*

Mom came back in and patted her arm. "Hey, sweetie. You're awake."

"Charlotte?"

Her mother's smile vanished. "Oh. Don't you worry about that right now. We'll talk about it when you're better. Right now, a certain curly-headed young man is here to see you."

Stacey moved her head up and down a little. *Yes, please. Now.*

More arm pats. "I'll send him in."

She turned her head as much as she could, focused her eyes toward the door, and waited. Her father leaned against the door-frame. He glanced out of the room then lowered his head as Calvin slowly came in.

Calvin's hair lay flat against his head, and his nose was red and his eyes bloodshot. Shadows Stacey had never seen before spotted the lower portions of his face. He moved to her bedside and slid his fingertips lightly across her palm, as if he were afraid to touch her.

"Hey." His voice was hoarse. "How are you feeling?"

"Heavy."

He blinked. "Heavy?"

"That's the sedatives." A nurse crossed to the other side of Stacey's bed. "We need to keep her quiet."

The woman did something with the tubes and machine, then bent over Stacey and adjusted stuff around her head. As the nurse moved about doing her job, Calvin's shoulders hunched and he tugged at his dirty hair. Daylight seeping between the slats of window blinds painted stripes across his face and wrinkled clothes.

Her bedraggled hero.

The nurse finally left. Calvin sank into a chair at Stacey's bedside. His touch stayed light against her hand. "The doctor says you'll be okay." The corners of his mouth twitched into something like a smile. Not convincing. He looked so tired. "You need to stay here and rest for a few days, get your strength back."

Maybe he knew something. She tried again. "Charlotte?"

"Hmm?"

"Charlotte." The tube in her mouth wouldn't let her make the right sounds. It came out *har-whu.*

"I don't know what you're trying to say."

Never mind.

"My dad says we need to get home soon." He chuckled. "I missed my first day of work. But it's okay. I'm pretty tight with the boss."

Humor. She grunted. All she could do under the circumstances. Or maybe a little more. She wiggled her fingers to tickle his, and was rewarded with a smile that reached his eyes.

It didn't last long enough. "I'll come see you as often as I can."

Something cold rushed through her. He was leaving. He spoke these polite words and made a joke, but he'd leave and maybe be too scared to come back.

"Don' go."

"I'll come back —"

She shook her head. The tubes pulled. "Don' 'eave me!"

"Shh! Shh." He reached up to touch her face, stop her head from moving. "It's okay, Stacey. I'm not leaving you. I promise." He took a deep breath. "I'm not going away. No matter what happens, I'll be here for you. But ..."

A tear ran down the side of her face and pooled in her ear. But what? Why was there a but?

"I need you to do something for me, baby. I need you to promise me that you'll get help." His breath trembled. "I need ... just that."

Stacey's throat convulsed. She had no moisture in her mouth to swallow. She whimpered. Fingers she barely had control of raised to touch her cracked lips.

"Here." Calvin stretched over her bed to reach a big cup on a metal tray. He dug out a chunk of ice and brought it to her mouth, rolled it gently across her lips. So cold, wet, and soothing. He moved away, dropped the leftover ice into something that made a thunk. He came back, but didn't sit down. Calvin tilted his head and stared at her through eyes so heavy and red. Like hers felt.

"Promise me, Stacey?"

She nodded and pulled air into her lungs for a big effort. "No mo' di-e-ing. I promiff."

Beneath his scruffy mustache, Calvin's lips spread into a sweet, sleepy smile.

○ ○ ◯ ○ ○

The promise was easier to speak than to keep. The thing that had stampeded like a bloated elephant into her life and relationship with Calvin hung on, fighting for its own survival, whispering she would become a blimp once again.

Stacey stood on the scale, wearing baggy pajamas from home

and a pair of thick hospital socks. Nurse Cathy pushed the counter-weights until the bar leveled out. Ninety pounds.

"That's good," Cathy said. "Getting better every day. I'll bet by the time I can push that hundred weight over, you'll be going home."

A hundred pounds? Wasn't ninety good enough?

"You can step down now."

Stacey held her breath and stared. The numbers on the bar blurred.

"Step down, hon."

"But, this ... it's ..."

Nurse Cathy came back to her side. "For your height and bone structure, this is way too thin."

"I have big bones."

Her mother had always said so. Big bones from Daddy's side of the family. She'd quickly realized it was a polite way of explaining why she was fat.

The nurse touched the small of her back. "It's okay, baby girl. I know this isn't easy. But you're getting better. And your skin is looking healthier. You got that youthful glow coming back." She chuckled and took Stacey's elbow to help her down from the platform. "Wish I still had young skin like you. You'll be knocking that boyfriend of yours off his feet again in no time. Come sit back down in your chair."

With the nurse providing a steady hand, Stacey shuffled back to her wheelchair. Although she could move about, two and a half weeks after what she called her "event," she was still weak. Dr. Bartimeus, her primary doctor, had said her heart was weakened from being deprived of adequate nutrition for so long, and when she resorted to purging everything, living only on water, her potassium ion levels dropped causing severe hypokalemia. Her starved heart couldn't continue to function. How she'd managed to hold on to

Calvin during the motorcycle ride to the hospital was a mystery. Or a miracle.

But she couldn't talk about miracles. The doctors, nurses, and her parents only wanted to talk about solutions and her "road to recovery." Step one: Treat her heart condition so she was no longer in immediate danger and could leave the hospital. That meant eating, even if they had to stuff a feeding tube down her throat. Which they had. Twice. Step two: Spend her summer vacation, minimum, at a rehab facility in Charlotte, where she'd learn to eat and to "love herself again."

Calvin had added another step — trusting in God for the strength she needed to get through all the other steps.

He called her every day and came to see her several times a week. To him, she could talk about miracles, and only with him did she share what she'd seen during those moments when the doctors struggled to bring her back to life. It excited him, and he said she should tell everyone.

Maybe someday.

Right now it was a precious thing she wanted to hold close to her heart. It gave her strength, even more than Calvin's promises to stay with her. Because if that was Jesus she'd seen, he couldn't possibly fail in *his* promise that he had a different plan for her life.

Nurse Cathy wheeled her back toward her room. Stacey watched the slowly turning tires of her wheelchair. She imagined grabbing them and pushing hard to propel herself down the hospital hallway. Freedom, if only for a moment. Being in control again, if only briefly.

Wouldn't happen. They'd catch her hammering the button at the elevator. And what kind of fashion statement would she make walking the streets of Dawson in her pink kitten jammies?

"Here we go," the nurse said, swiveling the wheelchair into Stacey's room.

Room 306, bed B. Not so home sweet home.

A person sat in the chair by the window, turning a page in Stacey's sketchbook. Zoe flipped her hair out of her face and slid the book back onto the table, then stood and crossed her arms as if she were freezing. "Hey, Stace."

Something did freeze inside Stacey. "Hey."

Nurse Cathy helped her back into her bed, clueless that the space between Stacey and Zoe trembled as if the air itself wanted to escape. "See you tomorrow, sweetie."

"Tomorrow?" Zoe said when the woman was gone.

"Daily weigh-ins and physical therapy." Stacey pulled her blanket over her shoulders. "I didn't think you were going to come see me."

"Mom grounded me. Two weeks."

Stacey nodded. Around the room were cards and flowers. A teddy bear from Tyler, who'd come to see her with Calvin and once by himself. Even Flannery had sent a get-well-soon balloon. Nothing from Zoe. Probably mortified with guilt and lying now to cover for it.

"So, what's wrong with you?" Zoe asked.

"My mom said she called and told you."

"Uh, yeah. She said you're being treated for anorexia."

Mom might have omitted the gorier details.

"My heart stopped. That night I ran out of the party, I could have died." Her tone was more accusing than she'd intended. Nothing that happened was Zoe's fault. Not really. Except for encouraging Stacey to engage in anorexic behavior and talking her into hanging out with Noah that night.

Zoe hung her head. "That's bad."

"Yes, it was. And I'm done with that stuff. I'm going to beat this eating disorder. That's what it is, Zoe. A disorder. A mental disorder. Not a diet plan." Softer words, but still blaming. And a boastful lie in their midst. Skinny Stacey inside her still wanted control.

Zoe nodded without looking up and then sniffed. "Noah brought me here."

"Noah's here?" Stacey tugged her blanket up a little higher.

"Downstairs. He wouldn't come up. He feels terrible about how he acted that night. He keeps saying nothing would have happened to you if he hadn't been such a jerk. His word. Jerk."

Yep. Right about that.

"But really it's my fault," Zoe said. "I'm the jerk. I tried to break you and Calvin up. I thought it would be you and me taking on the world, you know? But I really was thinking only about myself. I didn't even see that you were really sick."

Wow. Pretty deep and raw for Zoe.

Stacey sighed. "It isn't your fault. I did this. I thought I was in control, but the diet controlled me. It still does."

Zoe raised her head at last. "Still? But, you're getting better, aren't you?"

"Physically. Slowly. I have to go to a rehab center."

"So, how long will that take?"

"I don't know. Weeks. Months. Whatever it takes. Zoe . . ."

Could she reveal her secret? Would Zoe rationalize everything as a way of writing it off? Like Daddy and the doctors would? If it would make a difference . . .

"Have you ever heard of people having near-death experiences?"

"You mean like they see a white light and stuff?"

"Yes. That's what happened to me."

Like little flip-drawings in the corners of notebook pages, Zoe's face went through a rapid sequence of expressions. Shock, concern, doubt, defiance, indifference. She tossed her hair to finish them off. "I heard that's what happens when the brain is shutting down."

"No. It was real. And I feel like God told me this isn't the plan he has for me. I mean, why would God want a person to starve themself?"

Calvin would be proud of her little speech. Stacey held on to it, wanted it to be real, truthful. But it tasted like hypocrisy. The anorexic Stacey inside her said she was a slave now, headed toward blimpdom where no one would love her. She pushed words out that she desperately needed, even if Zoe rejected them. "To God, I *am* beautiful. Already. No matter what."

Half of Zoe's mouth turned upward and she snorted. She glanced toward the door.

"Anyway, I messed up big time. I almost died!" She pulled her arms out from under the blanket and plopped her hands into her lap. Her throat closed around the words she needed to say. "I'm just ... so grateful ... I have another chance."

Zoe chewed her lower lip. A mascara-tinged tear rolled part way down her cheek. She wiped it away. "Um, okay. Look, I'm sorry I didn't call you sooner. I was, like, scared or something. Ashamed."

Stacey slid her left hand across the bed. She lifted it and held it out until Zoe finally curled her fingers around it.

Zoe sniffed. "So, does this mean you're not angry at me?"

"I forgive you."

A smile crept across Zoe's face and stayed there while a more comfortable silence settled between them. Zoe's thumb lightly touched the massive bruise on the back of Stacey's hand. From the IVs. Zoe sniffed again. "I'll visit you while you're in this rehab place."

"It's in Charlotte."

"Ooh. Well, maybe Noah will bring me."

"So, what? You're dating Noah now?"

"No. We're just friends. He's nice, once he knows it's just friends."

Stacey wanted to laugh, but Zoe's expression turned serious.

"I think, maybe, you running out of the apartment and ending up in the hospital changed him. I know it changed me."

Stacey squeezed her hand.

Zoe lifted her head higher. "I still want to get out of Stiles County and be a fashion designer. No way I'm changing that."

"Good."

A wicked little smirk came to Zoe's lips. "Are you going to marry Calvin Greenlee now and have lots of babies?"

Stacey laughed. "I'd like to finish high school and college first, thank you very much."

"I'm joking."

Stacey gave her friend a little smirk as well. "You better be."

Epilogue

Calvin's shoulders and arms burned as he tightened the final bolt in the oil pan of Mrs. Bryant's Lincoln. He slipped the socket off the bolt and double-checked the others in the same crisscross pattern he'd used to tighten them.

He lowered his arms and mopped his face with his sleeve. His old T-shirt smelled like the garage—grease, gasoline, and sweat. The sharp scent of Gojo hand cleaner clung to his skin.

Portable fans by the open bay doors of the garage pushed around the summer heat. Country music blared from an old radio on one of the parts shelves.

Calvin replaced the socket and ratchet in his toolbox and moved a support beam next to the lift. With one foot hitched up against the beam, he lowered the powder-blue car to the floor. He opened the hood and bent over the side of the car to unscrew the oil-fill cap.

His new cell phone vibrated in his pocket, its alarm set to buzz him at the top of each hour so he could follow Stacey's specific instructions. Calvin wiped his hands on the rag he kept in his back pocket, glanced around the shop to make sure no one was spying on him, and snuck over to the shelf where he'd hidden a small manila envelope. Inside were a pile of handmade cards, each marked with a time in elaborate doodles. He opened the one marked 1:00 pm.

Things I love most about Calvin Greenlee. #11: Your hair. It's soft and curly enough that it could never, ever be cut into a mullet. Happy birthday, my sweet country love!

Calvin laughed and slipped the card to the bottom of the stack. Another laugh threatened as he fetched several quarts of oil for the Lincoln. He'd been reading Stacey's little notes since seven o'clock that morning, counting down from seventeen all the things she loved about him. Each one joined something romantic with something silly to make him smile. And each reminded him what he really loved about her. Her sweetness, creativity, and quirky sense of humor—it was all coming back.

Maybe he could find a mullet wig in a costume shop for his upcoming trip to Charlotte.

After filling the Lincoln with oil, he closed the hood and checked for greasy fingerprints.

Dad sauntered over, his hands buried in the pockets of his overalls. "Got 'er done?"

"Yep. That gasket was trashed."

"Good job. Go wash up."

"Huh?"

"Joe's got the shop covered. It's your birthday. Let's get outta here."

"Sweet."

More Gojo at the stained bathroom sink was the best he could do for washing up. He'd shower at home. Hopefully his mother would allow him enough time before she sprang whatever it was she'd cooked up for his birthday.

He and Dad arrived home to a quiet, empty house.

Dad headed for the kitchen. "Guess it's sandwiches for lunch."

"Uh, yeah. Sure." Calvin tucked in his lower lip and peered out the back door. Nothing in the yard. No crepe-paper streamers or tables with vinyl tablecloths, no smoke coming from the barbecue.

Just the weedy grass baking in the summer sun. Mom just might have spared him the huge family party this year.

He didn't trust it. "I'm going upstairs to grab a shower."

As hot water washed away the grime, Calvin thought of mullets and sang the two lines he knew of "Achy Breaky Heart." Tyler would break something over his head if he'd heard it.

Back in his room, his movements slowed and the country song faded away. Maybe not having a birthday party would be a good thing. A party would remind him of who *wasn't* there. Not just Stacey. This was his first birthday since Michael died.

His phone vibrated on his bed as he pulled on fresh jeans. He grabbed the envelope and found the official two o'clock card.

Things I love most about Calvin Greenlee. #10: The sound of your steady heartbeat when I lay my head against your chest. Wish I could be there with you now. I miss you. Happy Birthday, my love.

Sweet, but without the humor of the others. He wondered when she had found the time to do these cards. The center kept her busy with counseling sessions and classes. Maybe she had been a little stressed or homesick when she wrote this one.

The cards were something tangible he could keep. But the problem with them was that he couldn't respond. He couldn't send a text or speak to her. While Stacey was in rehab, she wasn't allowed to have a phone or access to a computer. They controlled everything in her environment. He wouldn't be able to see her again until they said it was okay. She didn't even know yet that he'd been able to get himself a cell phone.

"Miss you too, Stace," he whispered.

A female voice outside distracted him. Calvin stepped into the little alcove of one of his dormer windows. A white sedan sat at the side of the road, and two friends from school crossed the front lawn.

"I knew it!" Calvin yanked on the first clean shirt he found.

Downstairs, Mom and Aunt Sally rushed about, setting food out on the dining room table. Dad herded little kids outside.

Mom held her hands up to block Calvin. "Oh no! Not another step farther. You spoiled the surprise by coming home early. I want to keep some things a secret."

Dad turned at the back door. "You said be home at two. It's two o'clock, and we're here. What did I do wrong?"

"I meant you should leave the *garage* at two! Never mind." She waved her hands at Calvin. "Just get out. Out. Your friends are arriving."

Calvin went out the front door and joined everyone gathering on the lawn. Cousins Bailey, Matt, and Trevor arrived a few moments later.

Kendra Newell from his physics class slipped her hand under Calvin's arm. "How's Stacey doing?"

A jolt ran through him. Had rumor gotten out that Stacey was in a rehab center? Her parents had asked him not to talk about it, but if Zoe had told anyone from school—

Calvin forced a smile. "Much better, thanks." What would he say about Stacey's absence from his party? Visiting relatives, or what? Out of town? Would it be enough?

More friends and relatives arrived, and they made their way to Mom's surprise, a catered meal from Sloppy Smith's Barbecue, arranged next to several desserts from his aunts. As everyone crowded the food table, Calvin scanned the faces and found two strangely absent: Tyler and Flannery. Very suspicious.

He gorged himself on barbecue dripping with Sloppy Smith's signature sweet sauce and Aunt Sally's pecan pie, but slipped back up to his bedroom just past three o'clock.

Things I love most about Calvin Greenlee. #9: Your motorcycle. Okay, it scares me. But I love the idea that you can fly. Happy Birthday, Superman.

Didn't she remember the motorcycle was dead? They hadn't talk about the Yamaha much when she was in the hospital, but she called it his "miracle steed" that had carried him to her rescue. Maybe she thought he could fix the bike again. And maybe he could, if he could find a replacement engine. Or every single part to rebuild the old one.

He sighed. The note was still nice, and he really missed the flying part.

After the meal, Mom brought out gifts and made Calvin open them in front of everyone. Clothes from Mom, of course. Plenty of embarrassment there. Peyton and Ryan gave him a gift card to load apps onto his phone. Tyler would know exactly how it worked.

Where was he? No way would his best friend miss his party. Something was up.

Oh, yeah! He could text him. Calvin pulled out his phone. His fingers fumbled over the little keys until he'd typed his question — *where r u?* Not long after pushing send, his phone chirped the four o' clock alarm. Calvin eased over to the gazebo to read the next note.

Things I love most about Calvin Greenlee. #8: Your deep voice. It sounds like a love song, even though I know you can't sing well. But at church you raise your voice anyway, and I think that makes God smile. Happy Birthday, Mr. So-Not-American-Idol.

Leaning against a post, Calvin shook his head. "I'm definitely getting a mullet wig and learning *all* the words to 'Achy Breaky Heart' to get her back for this."

Munching even more cake and spilling crumbs, his cousin Matt squinted up at him from the gazebo steps. " 'Achy Breaky Heart'? What's that?"

"Old country song by a guy with a mullet."

"What's a mullet?"

Calvin smirked. "You need to get out more."

Sunlight glinted off a white SUV rolling up to the workshop, pulling a landscaping trailer holding something covered in a big blue tarp. Calvin stepped away from the gazebo post. Patty Moore's SUV? Bringing the ridiculously tardy Flannery, no doubt. But why did she park by the workshop instead of out front with everyone else? Pulling a trailer loaded with ... what?

Calvin launched himself across the yard toward the truck. The front passenger door opened, and Tyler stepped out.

Calvin laughed. "Dude! Where you been? You missed the piñata and party hats."

Sunglasses hid Tyler's eyes, but his cheeks creased in a broad grin. "Ah, I knew this would be a good day."

They slapped hands and held on. Flannery bounded out of the SUV and leapt onto Calvin's back, almost knocking him over. When Calvin recovered his footing, he noticed that everyone was forming a circle around the vehicle.

Calvin grabbed the back of Flannery's neck and shook her a little. "Okay, what's under the tarp?"

Her dad stood behind the trailer. "Happy birthday, Cal!" The metallic gate clanked down against the gravel driveway.

Calvin's heartbeat accelerated. Flannery and Tyler followed him to the trailer. As Dave climbed up beside the blue-covered, suspiciously motorcycle-shaped cargo, Tyler tapped a white envelope against Calvin's arm. "Got this for you."

Calvin gave Tyler a mock scowl. A card? Now? While Dave worked at removing the tarp, Calvin ripped open the flap. Several sheets of paper inside. Forms.

"What's this?"

"Maysville, next month. Cabin for the weekend, track, lessons, all paid for. And this"—Tyler touched the pages underneath—"is an application for District 29 MX membership. You'll need to fill that out and send it in for next season's racing."

"Racing? But, my Yamaha—" The words stalled in his throat

when his eyes jerked toward the tarp. A corner slipped away, and a knobby tire poked out.

"Yamaha-shamaha," Tyler said. "That bike couldn't even compete in vintage races anymore. From now on, you're riding a real machine."

"Huh? Ty? Dude. *What* did *you do?*"

Tyler tapped the papers again. "Paid for the weekend trip. Happy birthday, bro."

Calvin gestured with both arms toward the bike. "What's that? You're giving me a bike?"

"Whoa, no. I don't have that kind of cash."

"We paid for the bike," Dad said, suddenly behind him.

Calvin whirled. Both his parents stood there, grinning.

"But—"

Despite the fact that he'd rescued Stacey, his stunt with the Yamaha on the Interstate had gotten him into major trouble. If the bike hadn't died that night, his parents would have taken it away. As it was, they'd revoked his driving privileges for the summer as a consequence. His trip to Charlotte wouldn't happen if he couldn't ride with her parents.

"Mind you," Dad said, strolling to the side of the truck, "this one isn't street legal. Trails and track only. And we'll talk about the payments later."

Calvin held his breath as Dave finally yanked off the tarp. Blue fenders and gas tank, sweeping lines, high ground clearance . . .

"It's . . . it's. . . ." The 2012 Yamaha YZ250 from the shop. Practically new, Flannery had said. Just right for him. Someone had convinced his parents of it.

Something clicked next to him.

Tyler grinned at the picture he'd just taken with his cell phone. "Brilliant. Promised I'd print this and send it to Stacey."

So somehow she knew. And that explained her note about the bike. Calvin laughed and climbed into the trailer with Dave. The man tossed a strap over the rear of the bike, then reached into his shirt pocket and pulled out an envelope. "I'm supposed to give you this too."

Calvin stroked the tapered seat of the motocross bike. Shaking a little, his hands reached for the grips.

"Earth to Calvin." Dave tapped the envelope against his chest. "Read this first. I'll get the bike unloaded for you."

They were all determined to torture him.

Calvin opened the envelope. Inside was a gift certificate for Dave's shop and a note.

For your birthday . . . You saved our daughter's life, and for that we are eternally grateful. We want to give you something that could save yours, although we hope you'll never have to use it for that. This gift certificate is for a new helmet to go with your new motorcycle. Happy birthday and happy riding.

Stan and Kate Varnell

Tears stung Calvin's eyes. "Wow. Oh, wow." He blew out his breath and refolded the note. He handed the envelope over the side of the trailer to his mother then pointed at Tyler. "This new machine is gonna whup your butt, dude!"

"Yeah? We'll see about that. You got until November to be ready for the winter races. Think you'll learn to keep it upright by then?"

"Ha!" Calvin turned and dove for the final clamp at the front of the bike.

○ ○ ○ ○ ○

Things I love most about Calvin Greenlee. #1: Your heart. You loved me, even when I was at my worst. You stayed with me, even when other guys would have bailed. You knew what was right for me, even when I was blind to it myself. You rescued me, even after I'd pushed you away.

I don't deserve you, but you've chosen to love me anyway. My heart aches to hug you right now! But I know you'll be there when I'm ready to rejoin life. I love you, Calvin. Happy 17th birthday.

Lying in bed, Calvin read the note again. This one was over the top. But the core message, the poetic phrasing, the image in his mind of Stacey forming every letter perfectly like she always did — brushing her hair back behind her ears, maybe sitting cross-legged in her bed — it connected him to her.

What she claimed he did for her — he couldn't have done anything less.

Their relationship might never be easy or "normal." Between what her parents had told him and the research he'd done, he knew Stacey could battle anorexia for the rest of her life. Even after she acknowledged the dangers of eating disorders, even after she recovered to the point where she could come home and go to school, the deep mental baggage she carried could haunt her forever. Stacey's burden would be heavier than he could imagine.

Calvin closed his eyes and drew a shaky breath. The future was a big question mark for both of them. Her life would impact his as long as he tied himself to her, as a boyfriend, as something more, or just as a caring friend. Whatever happened, he would never abandon her.

He got up and tiptoed downstairs. A drawer in the kitchen was stuffed with school supplies, from crayons to calculators. Calvin extracted some notebook paper and a fresh pen, and took it back to his room. He wasn't poetic like Stacey. He couldn't write long, emotional notes. But she wouldn't expect that of him. Sitting cross-legged on his bed, Calvin wrote his feelings.

I miss you so much. I wish you could have been here for my birthday party, but it's ok. I'll tell you everything when I come to visit you. I can't wait! I'm trying to imagine if you'll look different, but it doesn't matter. I just know you'll be beautiful. You always were and always will be. It hurts that I can't see you right now and hold your hand. But soon. Soon we'll be together again. I love you . . . always, Calvin.

Acknowledgements

I'd be nowhere without the support, encouragement, and help of a whole bunch of folks. First, though, I need to acknowledge my Lord and Savior, Jesus Christ, who set me on a new path several years ago with a vision and a mission: to write books that would enlighten and entertain teens. What started as a prayer for my daughter, who was about to enter the world of twenty-first century "teendom," turned into something far greater. I am grateful and humbled by God's grace, which has been with me throughout this journey.

My critique partners have helped me more than I can articulate. I want to thank all the members of CYAW for your feedback and support. I especially want to thank Jill Williamson, who partnered with me at the very beginning and has been an awesome friend ever since, and Nicole O'Dell, who dropped everything to read the final version of this novel for me. Y'all rock!

To the extraordinary women who have been like mentors to me, Nancy Rue and Eva Marie Everson: Your wisdom and encouragement has helped me through some of the hardest times with my writing. I don't know if you know how much an encouraging word—or a walk in the woods—can mean for someone who is struggling under the weight of self-doubt. Eva, when I thought I was doing nothing but spinning my wheels, you helped me to realize that God is in control, and He gave me this task for a *reason*. Nancy, you helped to turn my darkest moment into bright sunshine! Your assistance when I was clueless and in despair was the absolute turning point for this novel and my career. Thank you both for being God's vessels in my life!

Thanks to the guys at Cycle Nation, Canton, GA — especially Shawn and Tyler — for keeping me straight with all the motorcycle scenes. I've ridden street bikes, but knew almost nothing about riding in the dirt and how to fix the machines. Thank you for reading those scenes and for not thinking I was a crazy person when I bugged you with questions.

My good friend, Debbie Jackson, you are certainly one of the most interesting people I know! You give so much of yourself to everyone around you, even total strangers. Thank you for all the fun times we've had on two wheels, and for lending your insight into the medical aspects of anorexia.

And to Lieutenant Weiland, sir ... you rock! Thanks for helping me with police procedures and the cool cop lingo!

To my husband, Brian, for your belief in me and for giving me every opportunity to write when we would have been financially better off if I had a paying job ... I love you. You are my hero.

To Sara, my beautiful dancing daughter ... every word I write is for you, sweetie. It's always been for you.

And finally, to Pastor Clint, Josh, Sara, Logan, Olivia, and all the other teens and leaders at New Life Church: You've become my family. I draw hope and inspiration from your fellowship and your faith ... and all the crazy things you do.

Discussion Questions

1. "Running lean" is an automotive term referring to the mix of too much air and too little fuel in a carburetor. This term can also be used as a metaphor for Stacey's eating disorder. How do you think the term could be applied to both Calvin and Stacey's relationships with each other, and Calvin's with his struggles? How are they "running lean"? How did this impact their actions in the story?

2. Stacey feels pulled in two different directions, caught between Calvin and Zoe. She wants to be loyal to both of them, even though they don't like each other. Have you ever felt torn between two people you care about? How did you respond to the problem? Do you think Stacey could have handled it differently? If so, how?

3. Why do you think Stacey reacted so negatively to Calvin's note about the facts of anorexia and the Bible verse he added? What might this suggest to you about how to respond to one of your friends who might be going through difficulties or dealing with an addiction?

4. Why do you think Calvin hid the truth of Stacey's eating disorder from his parents for so long? Do you think he was right or wrong to keep it a secret? Why?

5. Anorexia (Bulimia, binge eating, and other forms of eating disorders) is a dreadful and heartbreaking disorder that is not simply about being thin and looking good. Has this story given you new insight into why girls (and boys) engage in such harmful and extreme behavior? Have you ever known someone who suffered with an eating disorder? Discuss ways you might positively interact with such a person.

6. Calvin is unique, because a lot of guys might walk away from a relationship where so much drama is guaranteed. Why do you think he stayed with Stacey after he realized she was anorexic? Was he right or wrong to break up with her when he thought she was cheating on him? Do you think seeing Noah with Stacey was the only reason he broke up with her — or was it an excuse to get away from the trouble Stacey was bringing into his life? Was it reasonable for Calvin to want a "normal" girlfriend?

7. In spite of the fact that Calvin didn't know how to pray for help for himself or Stacey, and didn't take much time trying, he believed that God gave him a series of miracles — when another rider guided him along the Interstate, he was able to find Stacey before she collapsed, and his motorcycle made it all the way to the hospital before the engine seized. What does this suggest to you about faith? Did it change what you believed?

Like Moonlight at Low Tide

Sometimes the Current Is the Only Thing That Saves You

Nicole Quigley

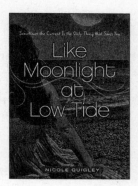

When high school junior Melissa Keiser returns to her home-town of Anna Maria Island, Florida, she has one goal: hide from the bullies who had convinced her she was the ugliest girl in school. But when she is caught sneaking into a neigh-bor's pool at night, everything changes. Something is different now that Melissa is sixteen, and the guys and popular girls who once made her life miserable have taken notice. When Melissa gets the chance to escape life in a house ruled by her mom's latest boyfriend, she must choose where her loyalties lie between a long-time crush, a new friend, and her surfer brother who makes it impossible to forget her roots. Just as Melissa seems to achieve everything she ever wanted, she loses a loved one to suicide. Melissa must not only grieve for her loss, she must find the truth about the three boys who loved her and discover that joy sometimes comes from the most unexpected place of all.

Available in stores and online!

BLINK

Doon

Carey Corp & Lorie Langdon

Veronica doesn't think she's going crazy. But why can't anyone else see the mysterious blond boy who keeps popping up wherever she goes?

When her best friend, Mackenna, invites her to spend the summer in Scotland, Veronica jumps at the opportunity to leave her complicated life behind for a few months. But the Scottish countryside holds other plans. Not only has the imaginary kilted boy followed her to Alloway, she and Mackenna uncover a strange set of rings and a very unnerving letter from Mackenna's great aunt—and when the girls test the instructions Aunt Gracie left behind, they are transported to a land that defies explanation.

Doon seems like a real-life fairy tale, complete with one prince who has eyes for Mackenna and another who looks suspiciously like the boy from Veronica's daydreams. But Doon has a dark underbelly as well. The two girls could have everything they've longed for... or they find themselves in a world that has become a nightmare.

Available in stores and online!

BLINK

Aquifer

Jonathan Friesen

Only He Can Bring What They Need to Survive.

In the year 2250, water is scarce, and those who control it control everything. Sixteen-year-old Luca has struggled with this truth, and what it means, his entire life. As the son of the Deliverer, he will one day have to descend to the underground Aquifer each year and negotiate with the reportedly ratlike miners who harvest the world's fresh water. But he has learned the true control rests with the Council aboveground, a group that has people following without hesitation, and which has forbidden all emotion and art in the name of keeping the peace. And this Council has broken his father's spirit, while also forcing Luca to hide every feeling that rules his heart.

But when Luca's father goes missing, everything shifts. Luca is forced underground, and discovers secrets, lies, and mysteries that cause him to reevaluate who he is and the world he serves. Together with his friends and a very alluring girl, Luca seeks to free his people and the Rats from the Council's control. But Luca's mission is not without struggle and loss, as his desire to uncover the truth could have greater consequences than he ever imagined.

Available in stores and online!

BLINK

Remnants: Season of Wonder

Lisa T. Bergren

In the first novel of this YA futuristic/ dystopian series by Lisa T. Bergren, gifted teens known as Remnants have been chosen and trained to act as humanity's last hope to rectify the horrors that are now part of everyday life in 2095.

The Community has trained these teens as warriors and assigned them Knights of the Last Order as protectors; together they are a force that will be difficult to bring down.

The Sons of Sheol, of course, are hell bent on doing just that.

Available in stores and online!

BLINK

Captives

Jill Williamson

One choice could destroy them all.

When eighteen-year-old Levi returned from Denver City with his latest scavenged finds, he never imagined he'd find his village of Glenrock decimated, loved ones killed, and many—including his fiancée, Jem—taken captive. Now alone, Levi is determined to rescue what remains of his people, even if it means entering the Safe Lands, a walled city that seems anything but safe.

Omar knows he betrayed his brother by sending him away, but helping the enforcers was necessary. Living off the land and clinging to an outdated religion holds his village back. The Safe Lands has protected people since the plague decimated the world generations ago ... and its rulers have promised power and wealth beyond Omar's dreams.

Meanwhile, their brother Mason has been granted a position inside the Safe Lands, and may be able to use his captivity to save not only the people of his village, but also possibly find a cure for the virus that threatens everyone within the Safe Lands' walls.

Will Mason uncover the truth hidden behind the Safe Lands' façade before it's too late?

Available in stores and online!

BLINK